The

A NOVEL

Chuck Markussen & Stephen Lance

The Reality of Chaos

Copyright © 2018 by Chuck Markussen and Stephen Lance
All rights reserved.
No part of this publication may be reproduced, distributed, or transmitted in any form or by any means (electronically or mechanically), or stored in a database or retrieval system without the prior written permission of the authors.

ISBN: 978-0-9994001-0-4 (print)
ISBN: 978-0-9994001-1-1 (e-book)

Editor: Leslie M. Carringer
Cover art: Stephen Lance
Interior Photos: Stephen Lance

Acknowledgements

Steve and Chuck would like to thank Leslie M. Carringer for reading drafts of this novel and providing feedback on everything from plot integrity and character development to grammar and spelling. Her support was extremely valuable as we worked our way through the writing and editing process.

We would also like to thank Dorothy Lance and Cathie Bishop for their patience and tolerance during the multi-staged development of this novel. Cathie's and Dorothy's support and encouragement were essential, and greatly appreciated!

The Authors

Steve Lance and Chuck Markussen have over 75 combined years of aerospace engineering experience in the areas of tactical missile development, defense electronics, and modeling and simulation. Both moved to Tucson, AZ, during the mass exodus of Hughes Missile Systems Group employees from Los Angeles in 1994, and retired from Raytheon Company in February, 2011. This is their second collaborative effort in writing fiction.

Disclaimer

This book is a work of fiction. Any references to historical events, real people, or real places are used fictitiously. Other names, characters, places, and events are products of the authors' imaginations, and any resemblance to actual events or places or persons living or dead is entirely coincidental.

Authors' Note

The *Reality of Chaos* is the sequel to *The Reality of Fiction*, first published in 2014. Many of the characters developed in *The Reality of Fiction* continue their lives in *The Reality of Chaos*, and several new characters are introduced. A list of the principal characters and their roles in these novels is provided below.

The Characters

Amhurst, Becky- Software Project Manager at Alpha Defense Electronics.
From: Birmingham, Alabama
Education: PHD Computer Science, Stanford

Andoori, Elaya- Middle East leader and sorority sister of Joy Johnson and Cathie Fletcher.
From: Bandar Abbas, Iran
Education: MBA, USC

Burdan, Frank- Lead guitar player for Logan Fletcher's Jazz band The Fourth Harmonics.
From: Denver, Colorado
Education: Culinary, Institute of Culinary NYC

Chu, Luana- CEO of a high-tech software company. Daughter of Wan Chu. Confidante and lover of Jason Stone.
From: Kapalua, Hawaii
Education: English, Computer Science & Math, Stanford

Chu, Wan- Powerful Chinese businessman with ties to the Chinese government.
From: Hong Kong, China
Education: MBA, Peking University

Colpoys, Randoff- Works for Smythe-Montgomery in security.
From: Edinburgh, Scotland
Education: Royal Military Academy Sandhurst.

Crandall, Richard- Independently wealthy computer expert.
From: Littlehampton, England
Education: PhD Math, Oxford

Deacons, Henry- Chief Engineer of Pacific-Indo-Asia Airlines.
From: Singapore, Malaysia
Education: PHD Engineering, Singapore University of Technology and Design

Eberly, Steve- Bassist for Logan Fletcher's Jazz band The Fourth Harmonics.
From: Tucson, AZ
Education: Liberal Arts, University of Arizona

Flahrety, Kevin- Ex F-15 pilot. Operation Analysis expert at Alpha Defense Electronics.
From: Marietta Ohio
Education: BS Engineering, Ohio St.

Fletcher, Cathie- Author of high-tech espionage novels. Wife of Logan Fletcher. Sorority sister of Joy Johnson and Elaya Andoori.
From: Thousand Oaks, CA
Education: PHD English Literature, USC

Fletcher, Logan- Retired aerospace engineer and married to Cathie. Longtime friend of Chuck Johnson. Leader of the jazz band The Fourth Harmonics
From: Plymouth Meeting, PA
Education: BA Music, MS Computer Science

Foster, Diana- Independently wealthy. Friend of Richard Crandall.
From: Manchester, England
Education: PhD Physics, Oxford

Johnson, Chuck- Retired Navy Seal now working for CIA as a field analyst.
Married to Joy Johnson. Longtime friend of Logan Fletcher.
From: Philadelphia, PA
Education: GC Criminal Justice, Naval Academy

Johnson, Joy- Wife of Chuck Johnson and sorority sister of Cathie Fletcher and Elaya Andoori.
From: Washington, D.C.
Education: BS Business, USC

Kamenchek, Alexander & Cassie Ada- Parents of Gail Kamenchek.
From: Holdrege, Nebraska
Education: Cassie - BS Business, Utah State; Alex - MS Agriculture, Utah State

Kamenchek, Gail- Computer software expert at Alpha Defense Electronics working for Becky Amhurst. Romantically involved with Randy O'Neil.
From: Holdrege, Nebraska
Education: MS Computer Science, UW, Madison

Kittle, Garrett- Drummer in Logan's jazz band, The Fourth Harmonics.
From: Grass Valley, CA
Education: Music Performance, Curtis Institute

Lewis, Judy- Jazz singer and friend of Logan Fletcher's family.
From: Tucson, AZ
Education: MS Music Performance, University of Arizona

Lister, Emma- Administrative Assistant to Smythe-Montgomery.
From: London, England
Education: MBA, Oxford

O'Neil, Randy- Works for the CIA under the leadership of Chuck Johnson. Romantically involved with Gail Kamenchek.
From: Booth Harbor Maine
Education: MS Security Studies, Boston Collage

Remington, Yvette- Homeless girl taken in by Richard Crandall.
From: London, England
Education: Street Smarts

Smythe-Montgomery, Conrad- Multibillionaire with global influence.
From: Cambridge, England
Education: MA Political Science, Minor History, Oxford

Stone, Jason (AKA James Kulwicki)- Ex-Army Ranger weapons expert (guns and explosives) who works as a freelance mercenary. Confidant and lover of Luana Chu.
From: San Diego, CA
Education: History, San Diego St

Walkin, Gary- Avionics expert from Alpha Defense Electronics.
From: Milwaukee, Wisconsin
Education: MS Electrical Engineering, UCLA

Zareb, Muhammad- Iran Air Force colonel, works for Elaya Andoori.
From: Tehran, Iran
Education: Pilot, Iran Air Force College

Stephen Lance / Chuck Markussen

'We are in a packing house adjacent to a stockyard—the final stop for innumerable pigs whose final destiny is to become bacon, chops, bangers, Spam.'

Prologue

'Do you know why I loathe you?' the tall Englishman asked.

It was an odd question under the circumstances. The man to whom the question was directed was kneeling on the worn vinyl tiles of a disused office in a dingy industrial building. A bizarre combination of machinery sounds and muffled animal noises filtered into the room. A heavy canvas sack, recently on the man's head, lay discarded at his side. The man had dark hair, tangled and matted from days without bathing, and an equally unkempt beard of dirty black. His arms were bound behind his back, and signs of rough handling—torn clothing, a missing shoe, a bloody elbow—were evident. His face was a collection of bruises and small cuts. A line of dried blood hung from one corner of his mouth. Peering from the thin mask of dirt, sweat, and blood, his dark eyes blazed with anger and hatred, but the large ring of white surrounding them spoke of something else: fear.

The contrast between the kneeling man and the man who had posed the question could not have been more dramatic. The Englishman stood straight as a rod in an immaculate grey suit with crisply seamed pants and a pair of handmade Italian oxfords that cost more than most houses in the Syrian village where the kneeling man had been raised. The Englishman had short, sandy hair above a high, smooth forehead. His meticulously trimmed mustache held only whispers of grey. A rather hawklike nose was set between two cold, pale blue eyes cut from glacial ice. If any emotion could be read in those dispassionate eyes, it might have been mild amusement.

The Englishman paced easily from side to side as he spoke; his words were in precise, aristocratic English, full of arrogance and disdain for the masses in general and for the man before him in particular. 'It isn't because you are filthy and have an odor of sheep feces. It isn't because you fail so dismally on the most trivial of assignments. It isn't because you've betrayed me and tried to threaten my life. And it isn't even because the attempt was so pathetically inept that you've wound up here.' He sighed. 'No, it's because you are a vapid, ignorant troglodyte with no sense of the future.'

He paused to stare at the kneeling man, who remained silent. 'The future, simply put, is empire. But is it empire at the barrel of a gun? Is it empire by strength of arms? Failures of this type of empire litter the past. The rise, the decay, the fall. It's a tired theme. But what remains when the battles are forgotten, when the armies march away, when the little kings and princelings have turned to dust?'

The Englishman continued to eye his captive as a cat would eye a mouse pinned beneath his claws. 'Apparently this question is beyond you. Apparently you are incapable of understanding. It's people, don't you see? But people, left to themselves, are quarrelsome, unruly. They must be guided, mentored, controlled. Without control, there is chaos. If kings and armies cannot control people, how can this benign state be brought about? Ahh! I believe I have the answer. And what does one achieve when one controls people? Empire!'

The Englishman smiled indulgently, but seeing no hint of understanding in the man before him, he shook his head sadly. 'Really, I might as well be speaking to a brick.' He held out a long-fingered hand, and the hilt of a sword was placed in it by one of the two guards standing at the entrance to the office. The guards were large, silent men in well-tailored suits that looked shabby compared to their employer's. They could nearly always anticipate his needs, as in this instance, and they had the other critical qualification for their job. They were essentially invisible. Though large and imposing when needed, they could miraculously blend into the scene like inanimate objects: a shrub on a lawn or a pencil on a desk.

'My God, Ahmed,' the Englishman said condescendingly, 'they say only a fool brings a knife to a gun fight. And what have you brought? A sword! Found in your dirty apartment, I'm told. To be used on me?' he asked incredulously. 'A weapon that would have been considered archaic by my grandfather!'

He hefted the sword and took a skilled swing, a hissing sound like an angry snake filling the room. 'Now a sword—a real sword—is a beautiful thing. The one my great-great-great-grandsire wore at the Battle of Canton, for instance, is a remarkable piece. Sheffield steel, of course, with a gold-inlaid guard, a knot of woven gold bullion, and a rather large stone—a ruby—in the pommel. And the balance! Oh, my dear sir, that sword was a living extension of the arm of the wielder—that is, of a skilled swordsman.' He smiled a knowing smile.

'But this'—he lifted Ahmed's sword once again—'is a mere club, more suitable for battering than for carving. A peasant's cudgel, and as filthy as you.'

'Allah willing, it would have made an end to you.'

'Ah, bravely spoken, Ahmed. But, do you know, you've actually reminded me of another reason why I loathe you.' The Englishman took a few more scything cuts through the air, missing Ahmed's head by a quarter of an inch. He frowned. 'No balance whatsoever. But to come to a point'—he swept the blade up once again in a whistling blur and halted, the tip just touching Ahmed's neck—'I also loathe you because of your faith—your blind faith. Now, faith is a wonderful thing. I have faith in many things.' He paused, considering, then shook his head with a smile. 'No, I suppose I don't. However, I do have faith in myself. It's important, don't you think, to have faith in oneself.'

Ahmed remained silent.

'Well, I see you don't disagree. But faith in religion? My dear sir, what can come of that? Disappointment. Failure. And blind faith …' The Englishman swung the sword through a sweeping arc, the blade coming to rest horizontally across Ahmed's face, cutting the bridge of his nose and stopping fractions of an inch from his now-terrified eyes. 'I think we can both agree that it would be awful to be blind.'

He withdrew the sword and stared at it with distaste, directing his words to Ahmed while he continued to look at the blade. 'Horrible balance. If you can believe it, I didn't actually intend to strike your nose. Terribly sorry, but you see what I have to work with.' He held the weapon in front of the man's face. Fresh tracks of blood were flowing down both sides of Ahmed's nose and into his mouth. His tongue darted out past his lips, and he tasted the warm, rusted-iron flavor.

The Englishman tossed the sword to the floor. Its echoing clatter filled the room for a moment and then died to silence. He looked at his watch, a diamond-studded Rolex. 'Oh dear, is that really the time? Well,

I'll say goodbye now, Ahmed. These men will see to your ... final needs.'

Gathering every last remaining ounce of defiance, Ahmed croaked out, 'Today I will be with Allah. Today I will have my reward in paradise!'

A look of perverted amusement crossed the Englishman's face.

'Now didn't we just discuss the pitfalls of blind faith? Your beliefs postulate a heaven, yes? But, don't you see, they also postulate a hell. I believe you have a grave aversion to swine? Do you know where we are?' The Englishman waited politely for a reply, but finding that none was forthcoming, he continued. 'We are in a packing house adjacent to a stockyard—the final stop for innumerable pigs whose final destiny is to become bacon, chops, bangers, Spam. But before they enter the butcher's shop below, they are fed and fattened one last time in the yard. Usually grains mixed with protein. You, my dear sir, are protein.'

Ahmed's face was a mask of horror. 'No, no, you would not!'

'Really?' the Englishman asked. 'I have no faith, let alone blind faith in the divine. As for your porcine prejudice, it's not you who will be eating the pork; it's rather the other way around. I leave it to you to sort it out with your God.'

The Englishman grasped the door handle, but looked back one last time. 'Of course, you are a bit too much to swallow, even for some of the larger swine, so these gentlemen will see to it that you are whittled down to size a bit first.' He strode over to a window in the office and drew back a curtain. The butchering facility below was empty of staff—a day off, with pay, courtesy of their generous employer. The two 'gentlemen' at the door dragged Ahmed over to the window so he could see out onto the floor. 'Normally, you see, a pig will be hoisted up by the heels, there'—he pointed to one end of an assembly line of death—'and their throats slit. It's remarkable how quickly they succumb. Being dead, they are impaled on one of those hooks, and they begin their journey down the line.'

Gleaming steel hooks ran on a track above a trough in the floor. Their first stop: a large band saw. There were other stops where large knives and meat cleavers were hung alongside, ready for use. At the end of this grisly path were divergent conveyors that carried the now-separated parts of the carcass away for further processing.

The Englishman once again glanced at his watch. 'But there's really no point in explaining further. Soon you'll be quite knowledgeable of the process—up to a point, that is. As we're a bit behind schedule,' he added, turning to the two eager men, 'what say we just skip step one. Ahmed will have a fine view from one of those hooks and, after all, this is part of a learning experience for him.'

***

Ahmed found his voice just as the door closed, so the Englishman never heard his final frantic pleading. Nor did he hear the shrieks of agony as Ahmed was impaled on a hook and sent down the line, the howls and screams growing shriller and more desperate until they suddenly ceased altogether.

Few men still alive had ever heard the deep-throated roar of a Phoenix missile's rocket motor, burning a path through the sky.

Chapter One

Unfinished Business

A brilliant flash like the birth of a new star lit the night sky over western Jordan, scattering white light and hard shadows in a beautiful, circular symmetry that stretched for a hundred miles. But though it mimicked the nuclear furnace of a celestial body, this brief interloper was one of an evil brood of man's finest creations. The initial white ignition lasted only microseconds, though an earthbound eye, unfortunate enough to look in its direction at that instant, would be melted in its socket. Luckily—though luck truly had nothing to do with it—the desert spread wide and empty for miles below the burst point. Only one man and one woman were aware that this event was about to take place, and they had manipulated luck and caused the device to detonate ten thousand feet above this empty place and not above the city of Jerusalem, its intended target. The man was near enough to see his shadow by the light of the fireball.

***

James Kulwicki was born into a lower middle class family. His father was a large, rough-and-tumble man—a Marine, a natural fighter, but gregarious and never happier than with his platoon, among his extended family. A team player in war and a team player in his domestic life, he provided a steady, though not extravagant, income for his wife and son. She was expected to manage the household and to raise James when her husband was deployed, a significant portion of James's formative years.

James's mother loved her husband well enough, but simply adored and idolized her son, encouraging and guiding him to greater and greater personal achievement. In some ways he was like his father: large and strong beyond his years, a natural athlete, unwilling to back down from a threat. This latter characteristic resulted in many a scrap at school, James usually fighting much older students and protecting his smaller and more vulnerable friends. He won most of these skirmishes, and by his senior year in high school he and his friends were treated with deference. But he never sought a fight.

In other ways, beyond his obvious physical abilities, James was much more like his mother. Though she encouraged him in sports, her emphasis was always on his own personal achievement: setting a goal for every game and urging him to exceed it. And while his father (an infrequent attendee at these events) despaired over a defeat in basketball or football, his mother would praise (or criticize) him for his own play. 'You can't be accountable for the others on your team, James, only for yourself.' His father would shake his head. For him, it was always about the team and the greater results that could be achieved by working together. James would listen to his father's clumsy attempts to explain and instill this philosophy in him, and say 'Yes, sir' at the appropriate intervals, but he was already convinced that his mother was correct.

To his father's pride, James entered the military after high school. He was smarter than most, stronger than most, and far more confident than most of his fellow recruits. He rose quickly to the rank of sergeant, and was offered special training in hand-to-hand combat, munitions and explosives, and as a sniper. He excelled in all, as they emphasized personal achievement. But his passion for personal excellence was reflected in his increasing desire for independence. He had served on active duty in Iraq, Afghanistan, Syria, and even Iran, and had grown to mistrust his superiors. In his opinion, they were far from the best and brightest. How could he reach his own personal potential taking orders from commanders so unworthy of his service? His attitude had not gone unnoticed, and serious friction developed between James and his commanding officers. Eventually, James questioned every tactical and strategic decision within the military, up to the highest levels in the Pentagon. When he realized that these men—three- and four-star generals—had allowed themselves to become subservient to an even larger group of incompetent fools—politicians—he knew it was time to make his own decisions about the missions, the campaigns, and the policies that had brought him to his final tour of duty in the Middle East.

***

The Reality of Chaos

But James Kulwicki, or more accurately, the notion of James Kulwicki, had died over five years earlier, and the man in Jordan now was known as Jason Stone.

***

The sheep had heard it first: the low, distant rumble. The shepherd, tired and eye-sore from another dusty, weary day of looking after his flock, glanced up. He didn't recognize the sound—similar to a jet aircraft, but different. There was no shame in his confusion. Few men still alive had ever heard the deep-throated roar of a Phoenix missile's rocket motor, burning a path through the sky. A moment later it was gone. This puzzled him also, and he continued to follow the path that his mind had projected for this odd noise. Half a minute passed, and he was still gazing upward—a mistake to be quite short lived—when the cursed weapon aboard the antiquated missile detonated. Radiation, delivered at the speed of light, melted his eyeballs as he would melt candle wax. Less than an instant later, his body was engulfed in vaporizing energy. The wool of his sheep was ignited and then ripped from their bodies as the shockwave hit. Nothing remained.

***

Stone had taken precautions to protect himself, sheltering behind a ridge of dusty rock, and had seen the flash only as the harsh shadow cast by the initial blast, and now softened, though of a more hellish nature, to a burnt umber that persisted for several minutes as the huge fireball twenty-five miles behind him rolled upward into the sky, sucking in oxygen and flaring persistently. Stone, injured and feverish from a firefight two days earlier, smiled at this tumbling fireball, recalling an instant when his father had lit the family barbecue on a warm July evening, thoughts of burgers and bratwurst making his mouth water in anticipation.

***

After the coals had been piled into a rough pyramid, Kulwicki senior had discovered that he had no starter fluid. But James's father was a Marine, and Marines don't postpone a barbecue to make a trip to the store, they find a solution and push forward. Oorah!

Mr. Kulwicki never hesitated, but marched off to the garage, whistling a tune. He returned with a red gas can and began to thoroughly soak the coals with the volatile fluid.

'Don't tell your mom, James,' said his father, with a wink. 'She says it makes the food taste funny, but I'll bet she never even notices.'

James's father sloshed a bit more gasoline onto the coals—there was now a small pool in the base of the grill—and then stepped back, herding James with him to what he felt was a safe distance. 'OK, now for the fun,' he said. He took a stick match from a box of 'strike anywhere' matches, and in one smooth, easy motion, rasped the match into life and released it from his grasp. To James's delight, it flew in a graceful arc and landed in the center of the grill. With a dull *whump* the gasoline fumes ignited, and heat washed over him. And though even his eyes felt hot, he couldn't draw them away, staring in fascination as a huge, spherical fireball, shrouded in brown smoke, rose above the grill like a flower unfolding, blooming, and vanishing in an instant. The fire below continued to burn for minutes afterward, sending tongues of red and orange flame into the evening sky.

When James glanced away from the fire at last, he saw his father wearing an expression of dazed surprise that transformed into a grin, which in turn vanished like the flash of the gasoline fumes as James's mother exited the house into the backyard, a grim, angry look on her face.

***

The demonic red cloud boiled into the sky, consuming all available fuel and becoming a vast black cloud, lost in the curtain of the night. Stone's eyes were haunted with the afterglow of the explosion for several minutes until, at long last, the stars began to peek out once again. He heard a low groan of pain, and was surprised to find that it came from himself. The wound he had received two nights before had become infected, and the doses of 'poppy' (a few ampules of morphine), had gone long since. How long? Stone struggled to regain a sense of time and place. Why was he here? Had he really just witnessed a nuclear explosion? Had he been the cause? And who was the Luana Chu who kept surfacing in his thoughts, driving out the other questions that troubled him? Stone tried to rise to his feet, groaned again, and collapsed in a heap, unconscious.

***

News of the horrifying nuclear detonation in western Jordan spread around the world like the shockwave of an earthquake. Accusations flew among Middle Eastern powers: Iran, Iraq, Saudi Arabia, Israel, Egypt. Every country in the region was on a full war alert. The great powers publicly called for calm while veiled threats clogged back-channel pathways. India and Pakistan rattled sabers and exchanged artillery fire across their border. North Korea threatened to punish the entire world, though on what account they were somewhat vague.

A handful of people knew what had happened, and of these, Luana Chu was completely uninterested in the outcome of world events. There would be war ... or there would not. At the moment, her only concern was for one man, Jason Stone, who she knew had been within fifty miles of the spectacular night explosion that had brought the world to the brink. Had she and Stone failed, Jerusalem would now be a radioactive heap of ash, and war would already be underway, possibly resulting in the complete annihilation of mankind. *Well*, she thought, *I suppose we did at least prevent that—for now.*

But again, this was a secondary consideration. She had not heard from Jason since the blast, and this lack of communication, of knowing, was driving her to distraction. It was a short drive.

***

Luana Chu was an extraordinarily successful businesswoman, who used her beauty and aristocratic charm like a sculptor uses a hammer and chisel. The daughter of a ruthless Chinese industrialist father and a pureblood Hawaiian mother, she had learned to envy and despise Western culture even while maneuvering and manipulating it to achieve her ends. She had received an excellent education in English communications, computer science, and mathematics (an unheard-of triple major) from Stanford and had formed a software security company, Infinity Services Group, which she had used as a platform to gain access to the military establishment and top-tier defense contractors. It had brought her wealth and notoriety, while numerous contracts had allowed her to penetrate the cyber-world that was at the core of U.S. defense. She had extracted considerable information, caused a certain amount of havoc, and left 'packages'—malicious software designed to be triggered at a later date—on the servers of many of her employers.

Throughout most of her adult life, she had been under the tutelage of her hard-spirited father, whose life ambition was to destroy U.S. hegemony in the world. But she had gone far beyond his expectations, his instruction, and, ultimately, his ability to control. They had fallen out over a flawed cyber-attack on Alpha Defense Electronics. Luana, sensing a trap, had failed to carry out her father's explicit instructions to infiltrate the facility in Tucson, Arizona, and steal critical weapon system algorithms. She had been right to suspect the trap, for Logan Fletcher, a retired aerospace engineer, and his friend and longtime CIA associate, Chuck Johnson, were aware of the plan. In the end, Fletcher and Johnson had come up empty, and no suspicion had fallen on Luana or Infinity Services Group.

For Luana, this failed attempt was responsible for two personal events of extreme importance in her life: the split with her infuriated father, who felt betrayed, and her introduction to Jason Stone, an accomplice to the plot. Luana's relationship with men had begun young, and she had used them as she had used her company and her influence to get what she wanted. Sometimes this was simple sexual gratification, but often it was more subtle: access to a new company, or an introduction to a powerful individual in industry or the military. In all cases, Luana had remained confidently in control of the situation, abandoning lovers and taking new ones when it suited her, and never committing herself in any way.

Her relationship with Stone had started the same way. Her father had acquired the services of a small group of terrorists, his own goals and theirs running parallel for a time, and Ivor Vachenko, the leader of this group, employed Jason Stone. Stone had been damaged, both physically and mentally, and his allegiance had finally turned away from the American military. Though he would never say he *worked for* Vachenko, Stone had offered his unique services—Special Forces training and an inside knowledge of U.S. tactics in the Middle East—in support of a better cause. He killed those with whom he had once served, supported the enemies of the American forces, and, through many acts of violence and betrayal, had earned Vachenko's grudging respect. Trust, to a degree, had followed. When Vachenko moved his operations to the United States, he was delighted to have a man of Stone's worth to lead his small group.

And so, Luana had begun a strictly business relationship with the tall, powerful man known as Jason Stone. Through no planning or intention, their relationship had grown, a mutual respect transforming into something far more over time. In a final act of trust, both Luana and Jason had dropped their dissimulation. Luana confessed her disillusionment with her father's goals, and her strong desire to break free of his dominance. Stone told Luana of his true mission, given to him by a nameless man while Stone (though he was still James Kulwicki at the time) was convalescing from the massive injuries he had received in an IED attack. Sharing these secrets put both at risk—possibly fatal risk. But the bond of trust, grown from the seed of respect, became extremely strong, along with something else that neither had ever expected to feel.

Stone and Luana collaborated to shape their own destinies. They had taken a dangerous path that had brought Stone to a rocky hiding place in the mountains of western Jordan to witness the culmination of their mutual efforts. Their goals had been accomplished primarily through their own unique, powerful bond, and no part of their personal secrets had ever been shared with anyone else. But they had a few unusual allies.

***

A soft moan in the background brought a smile to the face of Richard Crandall. He looked up briefly at the naked young girl lying on a large bed just opposite his seat as she shivered in pleasure. He called her Yvette, though it wasn't her real name. But something was necessary for communication, and when he found her in a dingy alley in the Whitechapel district of London—a poor, dangerous, rundown area, and hunting ground of the infamous Ripper—he had merely said, 'Yvette, it looks like you could use a shower and a hot meal. Why don't you come with me?' She had no better prospects, and many that were far worse. She had followed him.

Richard Crandall was a brilliant, aging scientist with a memory like a bank vault. He specialized in the electronics and algorithms of military hardware, particularly missile systems, and what he had learned over some forty-five years he retained, refined, and sold to some very interesting customers. He was also an unabashed pervert who enjoyed watching youngsters of either sex fulfill his fantasies. Yvette reached for another of an array of interesting toys that were near to hand. A low, humming buzz was followed a few moments later by a gasp and sigh as the willowy young girl arched her back and moved one slender hand along her body.

Crandall smiled again. Yvette was lovely, though rather thin. Her ribs still stood out from her nearly flat chest as she continued to stimulate herself, her body rocking and shifting on the bed. Her short, blond hair was now immaculately clean, and a youthful rosiness had returned to her recently dirty and hollow cheeks. Her age was something of a mystery. She hadn't said and he hadn't asked.

Though much could be said against Crandall for his bizarre perversions, he had taken Yvette from an environment that could only lead to thieving, drugs, and prostitution. In those circumstances, her likelihood of reaching the age of twenty was almost nil. But Crandall despised hypocrisy. He was no savior of London's forgotten youth. He had strong desires and he satisfied them. In return, however, he was fair enough, even generous, by his own assessment. The young men and women in his employ were well paid. But he would have never thought that fair at any amount. In the end, he was bound to tire of his chosen companions. What then? Back to the streets? It would have been horribly cruel, and he didn't believe he was cruel.

Crandall, too, had a secret beyond his own lifestyle choice. Luana had discovered it, having access to extraordinary investigative capabilities, courtesy of her father. Richard Crandall had been born into an aristocratic and wealthy English family whose roots could be traced back to the time of William the Conqueror. In his youth, Crandall's eccentric behavior had been a cause of much embarrassment. By mutual agreement, he had split with his family of ancient lineage. He had kept his word to never bring the slightest shadow of scandal down upon their honorable name. In fact, as official accounts went, he had quite suddenly died as a young man, and the family had given him an elaborate and dignified funeral. He rather enjoyed visiting his own vault on the secluded grounds of his cousin's massive estate from time to time. There was never any risk of running into a family member, and it was a quiet, green place.

The family, in return, had kept their word. And though he had never used a farthing of his annual allowance for himself (he *was* a successful scientist and engineer in his own right), he was extraordinarily wealthy through the accumulation of decades of payments. These hoarded resources solved a problem, and Crandall loved solving problems. His young companions lived in rooms—nice, though not luxurious—in a decent part of London, and were taken care of by a woman he referred to as Aunt Wilhelmina. There were never more than four, and Aunt W saw to it that they stayed out of trouble, attended school, and planned for their futures. Upon completing A levels, they received a sizeable grant that would fund a middle-class college education or a trade school.

All in all, it was one of the most bizarre symbiotic relationships known to man. Its success was still in question, but Crandall had no doubt that many of his former employees would make excellent lives for themselves, possibly more rewarding and fulfilling than his own blood relatives had achieved, though several had served in Parliament. Meanwhile, he smiled a third time as he glanced at the lovely Yvette, still consumed in pleasurable activities.

When Crandall looked back to his laptop, the smile intensified. The theocratic government of Iran had fallen and a new secular government was being formed around a charismatic leader, Elaya Andoori. The world had been on the brink of all-out war not so many days ago, caused by the eventful nuclear detonation over the Jordanian desert. The Iranians were implicated, as had been intended by the originator of the plot, a slimy Saudi would-be prince named Hasim bin Wazari. But his plans had been thwarted, and his life taken, by his less-than-loving wife, Elaya Andoori, whose own plans did not include him.

Both plans had been rewritten by Luana Chu and Jason Stone, though Andoori, ever clever and flexible, had been better at adapting than had her brainless pig of a husband. Crandall had helped Luana and her quietly imposing partner, Stone. By recoding the old Phoenix missile software, Crandall had seen to it that the weapon it carried would detonate over the empty desert, as Stone and Luana desired, and not over

Jerusalem. In the actual event, all three had been wrong. One lonely shepherd and his flock had paid the price.

Crandall didn't care for politics or political leaders. He despised them individually and as a class, offspring of aristocratic ancestors. He didn't weep for the shepherd, nor did he weep for the sheep. He didn't care that a new government—remarkably different from its predecessor—had come into being. He *did* care that his model had predicted it. *His* model. Others had scoffed. He had known better.

Numbers and symbols raced across the screen. All meant something to him. But the most significant by far was the single number: 86% probability of a dramatic change in the power structure of the Middle East, solidly within his predicted time period. Success!

The young woman on the bed let out a piercing squeal that turned into a long, low moan, and turned to face Crandall. He gave her a moment—a long moment—to come down, then gestured to her to come to him. She eased herself from the bed, wrapped herself in a bathrobe, and sat next to her employer.

He pointed eagerly to the computer display. 'You see! Here! It worked, it worked!'

Yvette knew something of Crandall's work and found it fascinating. How had he described it? Oh, yes. He had called it 'the synergistic application of chaos theory and autoregressive stochastic processes for predictive analysis of geopolitical events,' which she had shortened to 'predictive chaos.' She knew little of the algorithms involved, at first, but had been enthralled by its proposed use: to predict major world events well in advance of their occurrence. Crandall had told her the basics and had been impressed by her quick understanding. The program entered every reported event from every news medium across the globe—everything from a ballistic missile test in North Korea to a celebrity's latest love escapade—and simply connected dots. The projections were ever changing, ever in and out of balance, and were of varying degrees of magnitude. His success, with the projection of a major political shakeup in the Middle East, was right there on the screen. Yvette smiled and gave him a light peck on the cheek.

'Oh, well done, Richard!' she said, with sincerity. A very odd symbiosis indeed. 'But what's this?' She pointed to a flashing red

The Reality of Chaos

symbol in the lower right corner of the screen. He had fashioned this symbol in the shape of Lewis Carroll's Jabberwocky of *Through the Looking-Glass* fame.

Crandall was clearly surprised. 'It's a new prediction. Something of importance, happening within the year.' He turned to the young beauty at his side. 'You and I will be the first to know!'

She smiled at her employer. She truly liked it when he was like this. So much like a boy.

'What is it?'

He clicked on the icon, typed a few commands into the subsequent screen, and waited. A string of symbols and words appeared, along with a probability projection: 97%.

'Yes?' she asked, nearly as excited as he.

'It's a cataclysmic geopolitical event, within a year. It ... it ...' he faded to silence.

'Richard, are you all right?' she asked. 'Will we ... will we be OK?'

Crandall shook his head. 'Early days. We shall see.' He came back to the present. 'My dear, I intend to invite you, Carter, and Alexis to visit me next Saturday. I have a very interesting game of Simon Says in contemplation. You won't mind calling me "Simon" for one evening, will you?'

Yvette smiled.

July had been surprisingly kind in London. Jason Stone and Luana Chu walked happily, hand in hand, through St. James's Park, their favorite haunt.

Chapter Two

Happy Days

Summer, 2018

The world had stepped back from the brink, and a spring of near catastrophe had yielded to a summer of cautious hope. The Middle East had reverted to a state of muted belligerence. The great powers lowered their alert status. Around the world, people could once again find pleasure or annoyance in simple things.

In Tucson, Arizona, Cathie Clark Fletcher was shuffling through the daily mail with a profound lack of interest. 'Bills, ads, a snarky note from my publishing agent … junk. Wait … Logan, come and look at this. I think it's from the Grasshopper duo.'

Logan Fletcher looked up from the sheet music on the stand of his Steinway. He had been practicing a piece he intended to play at an informal recital organized by his long-suffering piano teacher, Gina, and was sadly frustrated at this point. 'Good. I need a break. My fingers feel about as loose and flexible as clothes pins. "Your fingers must be loose and flexible." That's what Gina always says. "They need to anticipate the music and be flowing into position before your mind is even aware." Well, my mind certainly hasn't been aware, so I guess I've got that part down.'

'Dear,' Cathie asked, with the smirking smile that was invariably followed by a stinging comment, 'what are these "clothes pins" you speak of? Perhaps before my time?'

Logan could only smile wryly. 'Well played, my dear. I *am* a number of years older than you. I believe computers were steam powered in my youth.'

'Oh, yes? And I'm certain the age difference is precisely seven years. But perhaps you do exaggerate a bit. Had steam been invented yet when you were a child?'

'You know, darling,' he said, giving her a hug and a kiss on the top of her head, 'the reason I married you is that I am an unreformed masochist. Where else could I get this kind of abuse—for free, that is?'

'Only here,' she said, leaning back and giving Logan a kiss on the lips. 'But before you get any ideas, take a look at this.' She held up a heavy, fancy envelope.

'Nice!' said Logan, feeling the texture. 'But I don't recognize the name on the return. What makes you think it's from the Grasshoppers?'

The 'Grasshopper' moniker had first been used by Chuck Johnson on his young CIA sidekick, Randy O'Neil: a reference to the '70s TV series, *Kung Fu*. Randy considered it to be an archaic reference. In fact, he had to research the program and watch several episodes before fully appreciating Chuck's fine sense of humor. And as Randy had become romantically involved with a bright software designer, Gail Kamenchek, they had adopted 'Grasshopper' as a pet name, used by each for the other. The nickname stuck, and it was now common for their friends to refer to them as 'Grasshoppers.'

'Oh, well, the last name is Ms. Gail's soon-to-be maiden name, it I don't miss my guess.' She tore open the envelope and smiled triumphantly.

'"Cassie Ada and Alexander Kamenchek request the honor of your presence at the marriage of their daughter, Gail Nicole Kamenchek, to Randolph Patrick O'Neil on Saturday, the twentieth of April, two thousand eighteen, at four in the afternoon at Church St. Djordje, Our Lady of the Rocks …" Holy shit!' Cathie interjected, spoiling the dignity of her delivery. 'Listen to this. "Our Lady of the Rocks, Bay of Kotor, Montenegro. A reception to follow in the Grand Hotel, Perast, with a second reception the following day at Restaurant Terrazza Danieli in Venice. To the dear friends of our daughter and her fiancé, as well as to our family and friends, please note that transportation and lodging will be provided." Holy double-shit! "The reception will be formal, but the gathering in Venice will be coat-and-tie casual. We would be honored to have you attend."'

'Coat-and-tie casual,' Logan remarked. 'I wonder what *that* means.'

Cathie elbowed him in the side. 'Don't be a cretin! My God, this must be costing a fortune. Who are these parents of Ms. Gail, and how could they let their loving daughter and only child marry a low-class would-be CIA operator like Grasshopper Boy?'

'Hmm,' Logan mused. 'I remember something about cornfields in Nebraska. You don't suppose the Grasshopper Girl's parents made a few bucks when tasty corn on the cob gave way to ethanol, do you?'

Cathie shrugged uncertainly.

'Cornfields and grasshoppers,' said Logan. 'It doesn't seem like a good combination. And if Randy and Gail have a number of kids, would that be a plague of locusts?'

Cathie glanced at her husband and rolled her eyes in disgust. 'Oh, for the love of God! Did I marry a perpetual high school sophomore? Because it would be an insult to them all to call your humor sophomoric!'

Logan was laughing uncontrollably at his own joke, his face turning slightly pink. 'Oh come on,' he said, 'that was good! Admit it. That was good!'

'Go away,' she said, grabbing a nearby newspaper, rolling it into a tight bundle, and swatting him. 'Go and loosen up your clothespin fingers, would you. And why in the name of all that's holy do you still get your news in this ancient format?' she added, tossing the newspaper onto the counter. 'Crap! Half the ink is on my hands now!'

'Well, I get it so that you can use it to beat the dog. Since we don't have a dog, you can use it on me. Which you did. Besides,' he said, 'there's a certain ... comfort ... in sitting down and reading a paper over a cup of coffee. It's traditional, and I kind of like it. You wouldn't want me to take away your mac and cheese, would you?'

'You just leave my mac and cheese out of this, thank you very much. And not only that, but ...'

Logan waited awhile for Cathie to finish her mocking rebuke, but when it failed to materialize, he glanced over at his wife, who was staring down at the front page. Logan moved closer and looked over her shoulder. 'And what's so interesting here?' he asked.

'What? Oh, nothing. It's just that crazy English billionaire Conrad Smythe-Montgomery has made another audacious move. Apparently he's bought controlling interest in a failing Indonesian airlines—for reasons that are unlikely to become clear. The man has more money than God. Why not just party until your liver fails?'

'Delicately put, darling. Perhaps he's trying to impress a lovely young woman.'

'Why don't you buy me an airline? Delta would be nice.'

'Oh, I know you'd never be impressed by trifling wealth,' said Logan. 'For you, the priority is to find an intelligent, mature man with astounding masculinity and stamina.' He grinned foolishly.

'Have you *seen* his picture?' Cathie asked.

Logan glanced at the paper and frowned. 'Well, umm, he doesn't seem all that mature ... buying crappy old airlines and whatnot.'

'Go back to your piano, my love, while I stare and swoon!'

Logan turned to go, a resigned look on his face, but stopped suddenly. 'This guy was born with money,' he said seriously, 'but he's making a hell of a splash in the business world.'

'So?'

'So, I don't know. He moves in a strange crowd. He does things and buys things, and it doesn't seem to make a lot of sense. Plus, he's no fan of the current administration in England. Nor the one in the U.S.'

'So?' Cathie asked again, but Logan caught a subtle difference in her tone, a hint of uncertainty.

'Oh, probably nothing. But I might just give Chuck a call. Just impose on my old friend to satisfy my curiosity.'

***

'Look, Johnson,' the Secretary of Defense began, 'I've had to change my shorts about fourteen times a day since that damn nuke went off over Jordan. You CIA guys may have cast-iron stones, but I don't. And you tell me your boy is at the epicenter of this shit quake. Now, I've got'—he glanced at his watch—'exactly seven minutes before the Defense Minister of Israel waltzes in here wanting my balls. What the fuck, over?'

Chuck Johnson gathered his thoughts. He had less time than he'd hoped and he felt exhausted already. His steadily greying hair contrasted

The Reality of Chaos

badly with his dark brown skin, and he realized—not for the first time—that he should have left this job years ago. It was a game for the young and strong. A brief smile flashed across his face as he thought of his protégé, Randy O'Neil.

'Johnson, let's hear it,' the Secretary's voice grated across his thoughts.

'Well, sir,' he began. It was just noise to fill a gap. 'I've told you before that James Kulwicki was given the assignment, by me, to locate a suitcase nuke that had gone missing after the Soviet Union fell.'

'Yep, got that,' the Secretary said.

'Kulwicki became Jason Stone. He went underground, fought for the bad guys, killed more than a few of our own people, and put himself in a position to complete his mission.'

'And you condone all this?'

'Yes, sir!' Johnson said sharply. 'Sir, that bomb could have taken a half million lives or more in a microsecond. The fallout—and I don't mean nuclear—could have taken hundreds of millions ... maybe more. He disposed of the threat and prevented those deaths. Others along the way, an unfortunate few, were collateral damage.'

The Secretary grunted and nodded once. 'Details.'

Johnson went on to explain how, in the course of trying to trap a group of cyber terrorists, he and Logan Fletcher had run afoul of the group's tactical leader: none other than Jason Stone. Missing for years and presumed dead by Johnson, Stone had reopened a back-door communication channel, and Chuck had learned that Stone was close to completing his mission—the mission Chuck had given him. In the final days of the operation, Stone had revealed his loyalty, at least to the extent of not killing Chuck, Randy, Logan, or Randy's fiancée, Gail, when it would have been far more expedient to do so.

The SecDef had listened silently, and had not even criticized the failure of the original sting operation—the use of Cathie's novels to trap the terrorists. Somehow, the terrorists had been warned or had become aware of a trap. Johnson offered no explanations or excuses regarding the failure. He ended his monologue and looked apprehensively into the Secretary's obsidian-hard eyes.

Tense silence filled the room until the Secretary finally spoke. 'I have only one question, Johnson. Where is Stone?'

***

The weeks in London had been a long, extraordinary holiday of a kind previously unknown to Stone. In fact, he had to search memories of his childhood—those magical summer vacations where entire days were squandered simply because there were so many—to find a near equivalent. Even then, he could remember his mother pushing him to stay active, practice his sports, read more, watch the news. 'Idle hands are the devil's workshop' had been her mantra. This was often followed by his father's wise advice, 'Go and have fun,' and a quick wink.

What he was experiencing now, however, was so unique that even his childhood memories could not compete. Once he had entered the military, an adult at age eighteen, there had never been a respite from the training, the combat, and the unbelievable stress. Beyond the actual fighting, a war had been raging in his head: the struggle between duty and independence, team participation and individual accomplishment, the deferral of judgment to others and his own fierce self-reliance. After leaving the military, his double role as a would-be terrorist and an undercover CIA agent would have been beyond most men—far beyond. Stone had done things that he had justified in the name of duty, but duty as he defined it, a definition that would have been incomprehensible to most. He had walked a tortuous path of his own devising. Extraordinarily, following that path had not only kept him sane, but had enabled him to move forward on the one task he had committed to completing.

And now, that mission was accomplished and he was reunited with Luana. It was a time of decompression, relaxation, and healing of a sort.

July had been surprisingly kind in London. Jason Stone and Luana Chu walked happily, hand in hand, through St. James's Park, their favorite haunt. They generally avoided the crowds on the footbridge across the lake's western end where tourists would gawk at Buckingham Palace or the London Eye. Instead, they preferred the more heavily wooded areas on the lake's southern shore where willows crowded the water's edge and ancient oaks were draped in green once again. The flower beds, always meticulously manicured, were a blaze of color under a brilliant sky, and myriads of birds fluttered nervously, chattering about the wonder of another summer.

The birds, of course, did not know how close the world had come to its final spring, with no summer ever again. Stone and Luana did. And though others might argue, they believed that their timely intervention had saved the world from a nightmare.

They didn't speak of the events that had led to the nuclear detonation over the desert of Jordan. Nor did they speak of the holocaust that would have ensued had the Phoenix missile reached its intended target of Jerusalem. And they did not speak of the madness of the individuals who had set these events in motion, where a sane person could see only death and more death. Their own gambit had been risky enough: destroy the device and kill no one. But it had succeeded. Oddly, it had also served the interests of the madmen (and women) who had been willing to risk much more to gain power.

Neither Stone nor Luana suffered from megalomania. Stone had completed his mission and fallen in love with an extraordinary woman. Luana had come to love a man who was more complex than anyone she had ever known, and she had seized her own independence from her domineering father. But summer had come. The world was moving and changing. Luana and Jason were people of action. After a well-deserved rest, it was time to talk of the future.

The two were staring across the lake towards Pelican Rock, when Jason suddenly smiled and turned to Luana. 'There really should be a parade in our honor—you know, for saving the world and all. Maybe with some of those big balloons like they use in the Macy's Parade. How about Underdog?'

'James,' Luana said (she preferred using his true name), 'what a bizarre way to begin a conversation. Yes, certainly, a parade, and possibly an annual holiday where children could set off firecrackers shaped like tiny missiles and dress as post-apocalyptic zombies.'

'And you, my dear,' said Stone, kissing Luana's cheek, 'are just a bit too grimly realistic. Perhaps it's an idea whose time hasn't come.'

'Good lad,' said Luana, with a thick British accent, as she patted his shoulder. 'Yes, that sleeping dog is best left to lie.'

'So,' he continued, 'if no parade, then what shall we do instead?'

'A rather ham-fisted segue,' said Luana, with a crooked smile, 'but timely enough. You begin. What should we do?'

Stone, having opened the subject at last, grew serious and thoughtful. 'C'mon, let's walk.' The two turned away from the island and took a path through the new grass.

'You know,' he said, 'I haven't been near the "Shirley" Facebook page since ... well, since I got back to London. I should probably check it out, even if I don't reply.'

'And might you actually reply? James, that life is past ... Isn't it?'

Stone considered and then nodded tightly. 'Yes. It's no more than tying off the loose ends. I've died several times in that world. I think that's enough.'

'Fine,' she said. 'Tie your loose ends. It makes perfect sense.'

'And you? You still have your company, ISG, and your reputation. But ...'

'Infinity Services Group was more an invention of my father's.' Though she was accurate in her statement, it was she who had nurtured the small cyber-tech company to its full potential, providing data protection, backup, and information management for major aerospace companies and the U.S. military. Of course, she had all the while been infiltrating their secure systems, leaving tiny packages designed to create havoc or vacuum out information at a critical time. All according to her father's plan. Towards the end she had grown to hate both his domineering behavior and the entire sordid business. 'I've been in contact with the board. It may be time for me to divest.'

'Hmm. I suppose I ought to start thinking about getting some kind of job,' Stone said thoughtfully.

Luana looked over at him with wide, questioning eyes, expecting a sudden laugh as though to a punchline for a rather puny joke. But she saw nothing other than serious reflection in his facial features.

'James,' she said, 'though I'm puzzled as to how, you've apparently forgotten the rather large sum of money we have at our disposal.' Stone's look remained blank, and she whispered, 'The $50 million? Remember?'

The blank look gradually melted from Stone's face, to be replaced by astonishment. 'My God, I did forget! That really worked, didn't it? It seems more like an illusion—or a dream.'

'A dream, perhaps, but true as well. We really must think this through.'

'Well, this certainly does complicate things,' he said, with a smile.

They walked on in silence for a while longer until suddenly their progress was halted by a knot of tourists and paparazzi. 'What on earth is this?' Luana asked.

'Oh, I think I read about this somewhere. Some eccentric rich man is contributing to the British Wildlife Preservation Society—contributing a *lot*—and so he gets a pavilion in the park named after him. Odd name, too. Smith & Wesson, or something.'

'Smythe-Montgomery?' Luana asked.

'Yeah, that sounds right. Know him?'

'I know *of* him. And perhaps I know a bit more about him than most. He looks like a peacock, but has the reputation of a viper. In my father's world of shady power players he was quite well known.'

Just as she finished speaking, a large man in a beautifully tailored suit approached them.

'I'm going to have to ask you to move off the path, love,' he said, addressing Luana. 'Mr. Smythe-Montgomery will be leaving the park along this route momentarily.'

'And is the park not open to the public, my good man?' asked Stone, with a hideously affected British accent.

'Just not at this moment, sir,' the man replied with a grin. 'Ma'am, if you'd be so kind.' He reached out and took Luana's elbow and began to move her off the path.

In an instant, he was on the ground with Stone's knee in the small of his back, the man's right arm twisted and pinned, and his face held firmly in the dirt of the path.

'I'll thank you to keep your hands to yourself, mate,' said Stone, as he yanked the man's coat to one side, exposing a small submachine gun slung below his arm. 'And what have we here?' He pulled the gun, and inspected it quickly. 'Uzi Pro. Impressive. I'm betting you have some friends in the IDF,' Stone added, referring to the Israeli Defense Forces, 'or maybe just a connection with the manufacturer.' He discreetly passed the gun along to Luana. 'As for me, I prefer the H&K MP5. To each his own, I guess. And speaking of guessing, I'm going to guess that possession of a piece like this is hardly legal for private security in the UK. But that's just a guess. Just to be safe, though ...' As a round of applause erupted from the nearby pavilion, he nodded to Luana. With a quick toss, the gun splashed into the water of the lake, unnoticed by the crowd focused on the nearby excitement.

'Darling,' said Luana, 'perhaps it would be best ...' The applause was dying out, and the throng appeared to be moving slowly in their direction.

Stone helped the man to his feet and dusted him off with his hands. 'Sorry for the misunderstanding.'

The man glared but said nothing.

'Shall we?' said Stone, and he took Luana's arm and walked briskly away. The two were soon lost to sight as the drifting mob engulfed the furious guard.

***

'You know, it might have been more ... prudent ... to simply leave the path,' Luana commented a few moments later. 'A bit less conspicuous.'

Stone laughed lightly. 'Do you know, Luana, if there's a word in the English language that describes us *less* accurately than "prudent," I can't think of it.'

Despite herself, she returned the smile. 'Well, how about "cautious," "subtle," or "cowardly"? Shall I go on?'

'No. No, I think not. Besides,' he continued with a boyish grin, 'You had me at "cautious."'

They walked on in silence for a while longer, both eventually slipping into thoughts of the future—a future that neither had dared to anticipate. At last, Luana sighed and glanced at her watch. 'We really will have to plan, darling, and soon. But for now ... I believe it's been several hours since you made love to me. I'm beginning to think you're losing interest.'

Stone tightened his grip on her hand and immediately steered her to the left, on a path leading directly to their hotel. 'We'll see about that,' he whispered.

The Reality of Chaos

Crandall answered the door and was not surprised to see the woman in the wheelchair staring back up at him, her grey eyes as hard as flint.

Chapter Three

Old Friends

Crandall answered the door, and was not surprised to see the woman in the wheelchair staring back up at him, her grey eyes as hard as flint. There were only a few—a very few—of Crandall's acquaintances who were allowed to call on him unannounced, and Diana Foster was one of those. He smiled a genuine smile and stepped to one side as she wheeled herself in.

Diana Foster was an enigma. The few lines on her face and the dignified streaks of grey in her dark-brown hair indicated an age between fifty and sixty. This was inaccurate. In fact, she was sixty-four. She had high cheekbones and a strong chin to complement her attractive but rather intimidating eyes—eyes that gave a mere hint at the strength of character within. She was immaculately dressed, though she made no attempt to hide the absence of her lower legs, gone below the knee. Her prosthetic legs allowed her to walk and take exercise, but she often preferred the chair for reasons she refused to discuss. But whether seated or standing, there was no doubt she was a striking woman, stunningly beautiful in her youth.

'You look lovely this morning,' Crandall said.

'Oh, please, Richard! And you look like a grubby old man from a homeless shelter. Honestly, why do you allow yourself to become so disheveled? And that beard! It makes you look decades older than your actual melancholy years.'

Crandall ran a hand over the scraggly beard, mostly a dirty-linen white now. 'I'm only a year older than you, Diana, after all.'

'Yesss, though you look fifteen at least.'

'Perhaps it's part of the clever camouflage that I present to the world,' he countered.

'Perhaps you're just lazy. And rude,' Diana added. 'Aren't you even going to offer me a cup of tea?'

'Ah. Of course.'

A few moments later Crandall was seated opposite Diana, the tea service set out in front of them on a small table. She sipped her tea thoughtfully, but her eyes clouded suddenly.

'Are you all right? Is the tea not to your liking?' he asked.

Diana reached out a slender hand and patted Crandall's arm gently. 'Quite lovely, really, Richard. It's not the tea at all. But when I let my mind stray back to that day ... well, the mind is a complex and marvelous thing! It can play me the most devilish tricks, and I swear I can still taste creosote.'

***

Crandall knew very well what she meant by 'that day.' She was young then, and so was he. They had been unlikely friends in the exclusive school they attended. They weren't romantically involved, as Crandall's inclinations were already quite different from hers. But their strong though unusual friendship had lasted beyond their school years.

She had been horribly upset when she called. Over three years had passed since their happier school times. The façade of 'Richard Crandall' had come into being, his apparent existence extinguished by his family. But he had felt it cruel to perpetrate this fiction on the one individual whom he considered a friend. He had broken his promise to his family only this once, and had confided in Diana, knowing she would carry his secret to the grave. A sad expression that had nearly come to pass on 'that day.'

She had asked to meet with Crandall in a railroad yard in a rundown industrial area; she hadn't given him any details, just saying that she was frightened and needed his help. When he arrived, he had witnessed a scene so appalling that he had bent over double and vomited until there was nothing left inside him. As soon as he was able, he had rushed to the tracks where Diana lay, her lower legs severed from the rest of her body. She was face down between the rails, biting into a railroad tie in agony— a railroad tie saturated in creosote. Though shocked and barely able to process what was happening, he had torn the sleeves off his shirt and used them as tourniquets to stop the horrific bleeding. Two frighteningly large pools had already collected at the ends of her severed legs. It was a scene from *Anna Karenina*. But Diana had somehow survived.

Crandall had yelled himself hoarse until two yard workers finally heard him. Coming towards him, one had actually tripped over one of Diana's legs, carried a dozen feet or so down the track before falling like discarded meat. That man had fallen to the ground, retching and gagging. The second turned on his heels and ran, but a few moments later, sirens were heard.

Crandall tried repeatedly to ease Diana from the tracks, but her mouth was locked on the tie. A moment later, the fragment of wood tore away from the tie and she rolled onto her back, finally seeing him. The hunk of wood and fragments of her teeth fell from her mouth and she drew a deep, ragged breath. The shriek that followed was unearthly, and seemed to go on, and on, and on.

***

'Never look so distraught, Richard,' Diana said, patting his arm once again. 'It's passed now, and I would love another cup. Perhaps one additional sugar.

'Ah, that's much better,' she said, halfway through the tea. Crandall had waited patiently, showing a touching empathy as his friend had gradually relaxed, the horrible visions of her past melting away. 'Yes, much better. So,' she said, more briskly, 'you're probably wondering why I stopped by.'

'Not at all.' Diana gave him an skeptical look. 'Which is to say, I'm very curious but happy to receive you at any time and for whatever reason. 'Good Lord,' he added, as he ran a hand through his scruffy hair, 'you do make me feel so much like an awkward, young university student. I dare say you know what I mean.'

'I do, Richard, and I'm grateful. However,' she couldn't help saying, with a wicked twinkle in her eye, 'I do rather wish you *looked* like an awkward, young university student.'

'The point is well taken. I'll do what I can, though "young" is quite beyond my reach.'

'Your latest companion ... Yvette?' Crandall nodded. 'I take it she's doing well?' Diana asked.

Crandall shrugged. Diana knew his secrets. 'She is no longer starving. And,' he continued, his face quite serious now, 'she seems extremely intelligent and curious for a young person. She's asked some rather interesting and perceptive questions regarding my predictive chaos theory.'

Diana's eyes brightened. 'Ah, she shares my intense interest in the subject. Perhaps you could collaborate with some professors at university and move your theories along more briskly.'

He shook his head. This had been a common theme from Diana—encouragement and the advice to seek additional help and support. 'No,' he said, 'it isn't ready yet. Soon.'

'Very well, Mr. Einstein. But would you care to share your latest discoveries with an old friend?'

Crandall reached for a sheaf of notes on a nearby table. 'I was hoping you'd ask. The model is making an extraordinary prediction ...'

***

Nearly forty-five minutes passed, with Crandall explaining the finer points of the forecast that had stunned him and Yvette. 'And so I tried wild variations on the input parameters, but the forecast barely budged.'

'A cataclysmic geopolitical event within the year. A 97% probability! That is astonishing,' Diana concluded. 'But surely, with such a robust forecast you must have been able to find a focal point, some large political, economic, or natural force: a head of state gone mad, a national crisis, a major pandemic, for the love of God—some cause suprême.'

Crandall gave Diana a sidelong look that contained no trifling amount of admiration, but also a hint of apprehension. 'You're quite as brilliant as Yvette. She asked precisely the same. However, I was able to deflect her question ... for now. I doubt I'll be able to manage it with you.'

Diana's smile faded as she saw his apprehension grow. 'Why, Richard, what is it? You look as though you've seen your own ghost.'

'Brilliant and phenomenally observant,' he said, with a sigh. He turned away and reached for the teapot. Cold, of course. 'Drat, my one delaying tactic exhausted.'

'Richard?' she said, a harder note of interrogation in her voice.

The Reality of Chaos

'Yes, yes,' he said peevishly. 'Well, I tried gross variations to the model: assassinations, coups, massive crop failures, weather events. Nothing, or at least hardly anything. Then ... on a lark, mind you, I tried eliminating one individual, an "industry titan,"' he said sourly. 'A man whose global reach and interests are causing comment all over the planet.'

'And?'

'Poof! No cataclysmic event. Nothing. Just a bland, mundane future beyond the model's ability to predict.'

'Who?' Diana asked, though her rigid features indicated that she already knew the answer.

Crandall nodded. 'Smythe-Montgomery.'

The two sat in silence for a long minute before Crandall rose to refill the teapot. When he returned, Diana accepted another cup. She seemed relaxed enough, though he could still sense tremendous tension.

'It would have to be him,' she said. 'He is his father's son, a peasant and a brigand with not a strand of integrity or dignity, though he puts on a good show.'

'Careful, Diana,' Crandall replied with a wry smile, 'your aristocracy is showing.'

'Yes, well, and who are you to judge?' she continued gently.

'Ah, but that's me, you know. I've been a disappointment to my family for a long time, and I've shed my aristocratic exoskeleton. You, however, still have yours, as well as your dignity ... and your pride.'

'Touché, Richard. Though I think that when it comes to judging the family of Smythe-Montgomery, I have more than ample justification.' She glanced down at her legs—her horribly truncated legs—as she spoke.

Crandall didn't reply. He knew the truth all too well.

'The thing I'm wondering now,' she said, 'is whether there might not be some way to avoid that cataclysmic geopolitical event ... by eliminating the one troublesome individual.' And though she had spoken lightly, Diana's grey eyes were cold and serious.

***

Saturday arrived, and Crandall was looking forward to his evening of entertainment, though his discussion with Diana still troubled him greatly. There had been no give in her position. Her casual suggestion that Smythe-Montgomery be eliminated for the good of humanity was a thin veneer for her desire for revenge. She had unabashedly asked for Crandall's assistance, and he had reluctantly agreed, with the weak disclaimer, 'to the extent that I am able.' He shook his head as he went to answer the door. Yvette had arrived.

'Well good evening,' Crandall said, thoughts of his conversation with Diana fading rapidly. Yvette was dressed in a very short blue dress with puffy sleeves, a white pinafore, white socks, and black patent leather shoes. Crandall smiled his approval, but Yvette gave him an astonished look.

'Richard, you've ...' She struggled for the right word.

'I've cleaned up, somewhat.'

His words were an understatement. Crandall had been barbered and shaved, and was dressed in crisply pressed pants, a silk shirt, and a quintessential British tweed jacket. Even his oxford shoes were new and dazzlingly shined. He looked a dozen years younger.

'I'm embarrassed to say that I was shamed into it by my good friend, Diana.' He shrugged. 'I barely recognize myself. But you, my dear, are stunning. And shall I be calling you Alice this evening?'

'Yes indeed ... Simon,' she replied playfully.

'Come and have a cup of tea while we wait for the others. I'll tell you more about my research.'

'Alice' entered the room and took a seat, but couldn't help one last comment on Crandall's appearance. 'I'm still overwhelmed. You know, you look almost like an English lord!'

Crandall only smiled.

The Reality of Chaos

Stephen Lance / Chuck Markussen

'Most guys are harmless drunks, like our friend there,' Becky said, pointing to the rejected man now hunched over at the bar and already halfway through a fresh beer.

Chapter Four

Getting the Band Together

The Secretary's final, pointed question was still rattling in Chuck Johnson's mind when the phone rang, offering a temporary distraction.

'Johnson,' he said, in a firm and professional tone.

'Christ,' Logan said, laughing, 'you'd think you were still at work. It's what, nearly 8:00 your time, and, uh, this is your home phone. Normal people, in which group I include you, under advisement, might answer with a cheerful hello.'

'Oh, hell, Fletcher. It's you.'

'Close,' said Logan, 'but you've still got it backwards.'

This last comment finally drew a gruff laugh from Chuck. 'Fine, fine. Hello. To what do I owe the pleasure? Oh, eff you Fletch. If I wasn't in such desperate need of a friendly voice, I might just hang up and go and cut my own throat.' Though Chuck tried his best to put a light, joking inflection to his words, there was no fooling a friend of many years.

'So seriously, what's up, man?' Logan asked with concern. 'Family's OK, I hope? Joy and Marcus are doing all right?'

'Oh, yeah. Shit yeah. This is just work BS. Man, Logan, maybe I need to pull the plug. This is just turning me into a crotchety old man ... like you,' he couldn't help adding.

'That's the spirit!' Logan replied. 'Now, why don't you remove the broken stick from your rectum and tell me whatever you can.'

'See, and that's starting to grate a bit ... The whole "I can't tell you unless I kill you first" routine is starting to wear a little thin.'

'Crotchety,' Logan said. 'C'mon, man, we've both had to eat that shit sandwich for a long time. Oh, and I think you got the ordering reversed on that last little catch phrase also.'

'Oh, up yours, Fletcher,' Chuck replied, but with no real malice. He paused a moment to consider what he might tell Logan. Years of practice in the art of highly censored communication came to his aid like an old friend helping him carry a heavy load. 'OK, so here it is. I'm sure you remember an unpleasant meeting with an old friend of mine last April. You know, the one at the air base?'

Logan knew. At that encounter, he had expected to die, first at the hands of a raggedy band of terrorists, and then at the hands of their enigmatic leader, a former American Special Forces soldier who, against all logic, seemed to be the leader of the group. This man, known to Logan only as Jason Stone, had behaved in an astonishing way, killing his own second in command, apparently trying to kill Gail, Randy O'Neil's girlfriend, and then leaving with his motley group. Unbelievably, Logan and his friends had survived, the wound to Gail superficial. It had been a bizarre sequence of events that had been further clouded when Chuck Johnson himself stepped from the shadows of the dimly lit aircraft hangar, having watched the scene unfold. It was only much later, under considerable pressure from Logan and Randy, that Chuck had explained his connection to Stone, including Stone's astonishing double character.

'Logan? You still there?' Chuck asked, after a long silent interval.

'Yeah, yeah. Just ... reminiscing. Oddly enough, I do remember that little meeting. Your friend made quite an impression.'

'Yeah,' said Chuck, rasping a hand over his stubbly chin, an invariable habit of nervousness. 'And as you know, that was pretty far down on his résumé of impressive actions.'

'Oh, yeah!' Logan agreed. After all, not many men had detonated a nuclear device, removing a massive terror threat and saving millions of lives in the bargain.

'Well,' Chuck said cautiously, 'I've got this other friend—the one with the enormous ego, the questionable judgment, and the funny name—who is interested in talking to our first friend.'

'Wow!' said Logan. 'And you always complain about having no friends. That makes two in one conversation, or even three if you include me!'

'Do you ever stop being a smartass, Fletcher?'

'Oh, hell yeah! When Cathie gets that look ... you know, the one that just precedes homicide, I get serious. With you, not so much.'

'Give it a try for just a second here, OK?'

There was just enough of an edge in Chuck's tone for Logan to realize he'd better back off and pay attention. 'Sorry. I'm listening,' he said.

Chuck grunted his assent and took a few measured breaths. 'Yeah, so that second guy really wants to locate the first guy.'

'Why, exactly?' Logan asked.

'For two pretty decent reasons. First, he'd just like to have this man back in the stable, if you know what I mean.'

'Hmph,' Logan mumbled, with a tone of contempt, 'who wouldn't? What are the odds, with a guy like that? An independent operator—an *extremely* independent operator—for years. Fat chance.'

'I agree. And the big boss agrees. It's a long shot. But the payoff would be rather nice, wouldn't you say?' Chuck knew Logan couldn't possibly argue.

'True enough,' Logan said. 'You mentioned two reasons. What's number two?'

'Ah, that would fall into the "specific threat" category. There's been some unusual buzz surrounding a certain individual. Eccentric, super-rich, with suspicious international connections. High profile in a very subtle way, meaning nothing adds up with this guy. Also, a bit of a ladies' man, or so I'm told. Personally, I can't see it.'

'Smythe-Montgomery?' Logan asked incredulously.

'Yeah, that's the guy's name. How did you—'

'That's too bizarre!' Logan exclaimed. 'I called partly to ask you if you've heard of him. Cathie and I got into a discussion about the dude. So there *is* something going on.'

'Don't jump to a conclusion just yet, brudda. But, yeah, maybe. He's on the boss's radar screen, even if he is a bit of a stealth operator.'

'Well I'll be damned,' said Logan. 'My instincts haven't turned completely to shit. And so ...'

'So, this is an open-ended assignment. Someone with no record, no history—like our first friend—might be able to get in close, get some intel, even position himself to take action, if needed. But, if our collective suspicions are correct, he'd have to be extremely capable at a variety of tasks, not the least of which would be keeping his own ass alive. There are a surprising number of dead bodies and missing persons littering Smythe-Montgomery's pathway through life. Always one or two connections removed from the man himself.'

'You can't get anything to directly connect him?'

'No. But, brudda, this guy is rotten. Maybe worse. My internal alarms are clangin' away like crazy.'

'You know, you're right,' Logan said after a short pause. Chuck listened with anticipation. 'I just don't get the whole "ladies' man" vibe.'

Chuck sighed. 'So, back to being a smartass. It was too good to last, I suppose.'

'But seriously, Chuck, I just had a brilliant thought.'

'After thirty-five years, a first!'

'No, listen. You can thank me later. It's just a thought, but it follows two well-tested adages: If you want to catch a fly, use honey. And one of my favorites: hide in plain sight.'

'I don't think that last one is a true adage. More like a principle. And the first one is like an aphorism hidden in a metaphor.'

'Now who's being a smartass?' Logan said. 'So, do you want to hear this or not?'

'OK, fine. Lay it on me.'

***

It had been a long time since Logan had met with his friends at Skybox, so he was disappointed when their reunion was derailed.

'Proposal, Logan,' Bart had said on the phone, just minutes before Logan planned to head for the restaurant. 'A last minute change in electronics volume, weight, and CG allocation. If Kevin had listened to me in the first place …'

'You can bite me, Bart,' Logan heard in the background.

'But seriously,' Bart continued, 'we will do this … probably in a couple of weeks when the dust settles. OK?'

'No sweat,' Logan replied. 'I almost feel sorry for you guys. Almost.'

'OK, Logan. We'll give you a call.'

'Deal.'

After Logan hung up, he realized that he really didn't feel like staying home. Cathie was off with friends and he was restless, wandering from room to room. He sat down at his piano and played a few chords, but even that reliable distraction didn't calm his nerves.

At last, with a grunt of frustration, he headed out the door. *Screw it,* he thought to himself, *there's a jazz ensemble at Skybox tonight, and I might as well go and listen to them as pace around here and wear a hole in the carpet.*

Logan was on his second scotch, and his inexplicably rattled nerves had calmed somewhat. The man at the piano was leading the group on stage in a bluesy, melancholy tune that suited Logan's mood, when a blur at the edge of his peripheral vision was followed by the surprising words, 'Buy me a drink, Fletcher?'

Logan turned to see Becky Amhurst, who slid noiselessly into the seat opposite him at the small table.

'Becky!' he said, in surprise. 'Wow, that was more than ninja stealth. Note to self: don't turn my back on you when you're pissed!'

'That's always good advice. But what are you doing here? Especially alone. Ah, let me guess. Abandoned by your wife, you've come to drown your sorrows and to live out your repressed sexual fantasies.'

'Nice,' said Logan, with an embarrassed smile. 'Always subtle, Becky. Sadly, however, I am still happily married—no mystery or chaos there—and I have been stiffed by my rummy friends Bart, Kevin, and Gary. Yep. Rejected in favor of some lame-ass proposal.'

'Ouch! That must sting.'

'But there are other compensations,' he said, waving abstractedly at the band, just completing their set to enthusiastic applause.

Becky gave Logan a questioning look.

'And,' he continued hurriedly, 'the company of an unexpected friend.'

'Hmm,' she grumbled. 'Not exactly a great save. But still, what's wrong with this picture?'

Logan looked at her, a puzzled expression on his face. She waved her empty hand.

'Right, right,' he said, and rapidly flagged down their waitress.

'Oh, just a glass of Chardonnay, I think,' said Becky.

When the drink arrived, she took a tentative sip. 'Ah ... better.'

'So, where's the rest of your posse?' Logan asked, after a brief silence.

Becky shrugged. 'They all begged off, like your raggedy crew. And of course Gail no longer participates in these little outings thanks to your young Cicada.'

'Grasshopper,' Logan corrected.

'Whatever. Anyway, I was wandering around home like the proverbial lost sheep. Thought I might as well come and listen to the band. Got lucky and found you instead!' she added, with a mischievous smile.

Logan couldn't help an answering smile. 'So,' he said, 'how's life at the old bomb factory?'

'Boring. You know, you and Chuck were a royal pain in the ass during that whole super-spy operation, but it was kind of fun. And work is just ... well, it's just work. I guess that's why it's not called fun.'

'Hmm,' said Logan thoughtfully. He gazed for a while at his half-empty drink, then raised his eyes and gave Becky a long, evaluating stare.

'Whoa!' she said. 'That look usually precedes an indelicate offer of a carnal nature. But coming from you, I'm not quite sure what to expect.'

'An offer, maybe,' Logan said. 'It might not be all that carnal, but ... it might be sort of fun. At least, someone with a warped sense of reality might think it was fun.'

'You have my full attention. Offer me some fun!'

Logan first flagged down the waitress. 'Two more of the same.'

'Oh, I don't really need *two* more,' Becky joked. 'At least, not at the same time.'

When the drinks arrived, Logan shifted uneasily in his chair, and then turned a serious face to his friend. 'Look,' he began, 'first of all, this may amount to very little. And it's liable to be pretty boring. But then again, if I were you, I'd say no right now before—'

'Logan, would you just spit it out? Though I must admit, you really are a pretty good tease. If you know what I mean.'

'Right. Well, I happened to be talking to my friend Chuck—you know, the pain in the ass—and believe it or not, your name came up. In fact,' he added, with a very phony, careless laugh, 'I would have been getting in touch if we hadn't run into each other in this fortuitous way.'

'Fortuitous,' Becky agreed, her voice thick with sarcasm. 'Cut the crap, Logan, and tell me something, or buy me a drink, or make me an offer I can't refuse,' she concluded, her eyebrow raised archly.

This may have been the shittiest idea of my life, thought Logan, but he pressed on. 'Have you heard of that filthy-rich English aristocrat, Smythe-Montgomery? You know, the stiff-looking guy who's always wearing an expensive Italian suit?'

'You're kidding? You mean the guy who has more money than God, whose voice melts women's hearts around the world, and who looks like Brad Pitt's slightly older, but far more handsome, brother? And as for stiff, one can only hope.'

'Yeah,' Logan said, feeling older and shabbier by the second, 'that guy. Well, he's an odd duck, for all your groupie-like admiration. Odd enough that he's raised a few red flags with Chuck Johnson's bosses. Nothing definite, just … odd.'

'Sounds like blatant jealousy to me,' Becky replied, with a roguish look.

'Be that as it may, your dream man just bought a shitty old airline … what the hell was it called? East Malaysian Deathways? Indonesian Flying Hearse? Something like that.'

'Pacific-Indo-Asia Air, you cretin. Honestly, if it weren't for your ruggedly handsome exterior, there wouldn't be much to you.'

'Hmm,' Logan said, with a crooked smile. 'Cathie says much the same. Excluding the ruggedly handsome part, of course.'

'Doubt it,' Becky whispered into her drink.

'Anyway, this guy has bought up businesses all over the Middle East and Far East. Stuff that's hardly connected in any way, from a business perspective. Much of it rundown, already in bankruptcy. Like the airline. It just seems strange. He also has some very unusual friends, such as the ousted former leadership of Iran, now vacationing in garden spots like Syria and Yemen. Plus others: Chechens, Afghan tribal leaders, disenfranchised Russian oligarchs.'

'I love it when you talk dirty, Logan, but where are you going with this?'

'It's where Chuck is going. He wants to learn more about this guy, but Smythe-Montgomery's like a human black hole. Information flows in, jack shit flows out. Chuck thinks that with the airline purchase, there may be an entrée. Especially when I told him about your past.'

'Good God, you didn't tell him *that*, did you?'

'What? I mean, no. I mean …'

Becky burst into laughter. 'You are something else! All right, seriously, what about my past?'

'Jeez, Becky, sometimes I feel like such a gullible little kid around you. Let me think.' After several serious pulls at his drink, Logan finally continued. 'You were VP of a small software company before you came to work for the bomb factory. You know, specializing in upgrading avionics software for older aircraft.'

'Yeah, I know what we did. And the title was more of a courtesy. I did everything from coding to brewing coffee at that joint. And there were only seven of us—total—in the firm. Still, we did get a few contracts, and it was good experience. That is, good experience working 16-hour days seven days a week.'

'Well, Smythe-Montgomery is in desperate need of someone to update the avionics in his shitty little private airline. Whoever does the work might get a chance to do a little … you know … nosing around. Hell, you might even get to party with the boss. So, how about it? Want to do a little moonlighting?'

'It would mean getting the band back together,' she said, after a pause. Logan gave her a puzzled look. 'Oh, I just mean reincarnating the old company, seeing if any of the old players are still available. Most of them are liable to be retired from the fray, but they knew the old systems like nobody's business. I'd have to make a few calls. And there would be the question of funding, facilities, connections, et cetera, et cetera.'

'Yeah, all good questions,' Logan said absently. 'Listen, hold the fort here while I take a short bio break. It will help improve my focus. Then we can make a list that I can get to Chuck. Let him decide if this is worthwhile.'

'I'll be here,' she replied, with a wink. 'Just don't be too long.'

It was, in fact, a very short time before Logan returned, an entertaining sight greeting him at the table. A younger man (*Shit, they all look younger to me these days*, he thought sourly) was leaning on the table with a confident attitude, eyes locked on Becky, deep in conversation. He might have been in his early forties. Logan approached slowly from behind the man. He thought he caught the flash of Becky's eyes in a quick look, amusement sparkling in them. He decided to wait and listen.

'... so I'd love to buy you a drink,' the man said. 'Hey,' he added, with a beery grin, 'I don't even know your name. How 'bout you tell me and I'll ask you all courteous and formal.'

'Ah,' said Becky, with a dazzling smile, 'here's a thought.' She leaned towards the man in a confidential way, but spoke loudly and firmly. 'Why don't you go fuck yourself? Yes, that's probably best. Why don't you take your sorry, half-drunk ass off to some quiet location, preferably in another time zone, and go fuck yourself. I may be looking for a man, but the kind I'm interested in is intelligent, accomplished, dignified, tall, and ruggedly handsome. Exactly like him,' she said, pointing towards the astonished Logan. The man turned, wobbling slightly. By this time, Logan had regained his composure and risen to his full height, a good five inches taller than the man, and had done his best to look, if not ruggedly handsome, then at least somewhat imposing.

The man glanced back at Becky and shrugged. 'Jus' tryin' to be friendly.' He smiled foolishly and staggered back towards the bar.

'Holy crap!' Logan said, as he seated himself. 'Where did you learn to do that?'

Becky laughed for a long while. 'Oh, I was a military brat. My dad was a Marine pilot. Both my older brothers were in the service. I used to hang out at the local bars like one of the boys. I got used to drunken jarheads trying to pick me up when I was thirteen. The first couple of times my dad put them on their asses, but I eventually learned to take care of myself. Most guys are harmless drunks, like our friend there,' she said, pointing to the man now hunched over at the bar and already halfway through a fresh beer.

'Shit, Becky, I never knew you were from a military family.'

'There's a lot you don't know about me. Still, always time to learn,' she added, with a crooked smile.

Logan stared back at her and nodded seriously. 'You know, in another reality …'

'Holy shit, I finally cracked the diamond-like exterior of Logan Fletcher. In another mood, I'd be happy to play you like a fish, just for the fun. But you're a good man, and you know I just enjoy teasing you. And Cathie, well, she's one lucky gal.'

'Yep,' Logan repeated, as though to himself, 'there's really a lot I don't know about you.'

'I'll tell you more some time. If you're willing to listen. For now, let's talk a little more about this offer of fun you just made and maybe come up with that list for Chuck Johnson.'

Logan continued to gaze at Becky, then smiled thinly. He looked up and waved a hand, signaling for another round of drinks. When he turned back to Becky, she leaned over and gave him a quick kiss on the cheek. 'I do love you, you know.'

***

The next day found Logan at his piano practicing a few jazz numbers with a bit more concentration (and apprehension) than usual. He had finally taken the plunge and spoken to the manager of Skybox, a restaurant and bar on Tucson's north side, and the manager had agreed to let Logan and the rest of his quartet audition. For the last year, Logan and three friends who shared his passion for jazz had been getting together and jamming. It was an eclectic group, to say the least. Even their name, the Fourth Harmonics, was a blend of music and engineering.

Steve Eberly, the bassist, was one of the cleverest men with his fingers that Logan had ever seen. His three wives might have also agreed if they had not become ex-wives over the course of time, though neither his fingering nor his bass guitar skills had been at fault. Born and raised in Tucson, Steve had gone from being a rather dissipated high school student to an even more dissipated college student, receiving, after seven long years, a BA from the University of Arizona. Drugs and low-level drug dealing had been a part of Steve's existence for all his adult life, and Logan suspected that many of his most inspired riffs had been powered by chemistry. He would have seemed a strange companion for Logan Fletcher but for their love of music.

The Reality of Chaos

Frank Burdan, the lead guitar, was another peculiar individual. His first passion was creating fine food, and he had attended the Institute of Culinary Education in New York. Working now at a high-end Italian restaurant in Tucson, he had two other distinct passions in life. One was jazz, and his chance meetings with Logan at various venues had eventually resulted in them joining forces in their unusual quartet. Through Logan, he had met Becky Amhurst, and she had become his third passion. Hardly unique among the men who had encountered Becky.

The band's drummer, Garrett Kittle, was the only one of the four to receive serious musical instruction. Having attended the Curtis Institute of Music in Philly, he had risen to some level of success, even playing a three-year stint with the Glenn Miller Orchestra. It was a puzzle, then, to find the forty-nine-year-old teaching music at a Tucson high school. Rumors of an ungovernable temper and a falling out with the Miller Orchestra's manager might have provided some explanation, though far from complete.

About two months earlier, they had played through a half dozen pieces with surprising proficiency. They had also consumed six bottles of a rather nice Cab, so their judgment might have been in question. Nevertheless, when they had finished and were busily congratulating themselves, Steve had mentioned 'local band night' at Skybox. The first Tuesday of every month, Skybox featured two local jazz bands from 7:00 to 10:00. Logan and his friends had gone to these sessions more than once. Most of the music had been good, some excellent, and it was fun to hang out with the artists and compare notes. On the fateful night of the 'surprising proficiency,' Steve had stunned the others by saying, 'Man, we're as good as at least half the bands on local band night. I say we should give Skybox a run. And I've never seen any of those musicians leaving the bar without a little companionship after a gig, if you know what I mean.' He looked pointedly at Logan as he added, 'Except for the older, stodgier types who are devoted to their spouses.'

In a musical and alcoholic euphoria, the others had agreed. And while Logan's apprehension had grown, he still agreed with Steve: they were as good as many of the bands they'd enjoyed over the last few months.

A sour note and a stumble in tempo brought Logan back to reality—and an increased sense of humility. 'Damn it! I can hardly wait to embarrass myself in front of a bunch of strangers.' This was followed by the horrified realization that if Becky found out the Fourth Harmonics were playing, she would undoubtedly attend and bring as many friends and Alpha Defense co-workers as she could muster. All in good fun, but Logan's spirits sank at the thought. 'Fuckin' Steve and his stupid ego,' he muttered. 'I hope his bass strings all snap!'

Cathie entered the room, with bunches of papers in both hands. 'Language, dear,' she said. Without any kind of transition, she began waving the pages at him. 'Did you realize there were two opium wars? One started in 1839 and one in 1856. Who knew?'

Logan sighed and shuffled through the music at his side. *I need to find a beginner's piece,* he thought grimly. What he said was, 'So this is research for your latest novel, I take it. How's it coming?'

'Bad. I'm not finding anything to easily tie in with a modern day drug cartel. I was trying to find some interesting parallels, perhaps even create some period characters, you know, to contrast with the ones I'm developing for the present day. But the entire premise seems flawed. Did you realize that in the opium wars it was arguably the most powerful country on earth, Britain, that was conspiring to force the drug on the Chinese?'

'Actually, I do know a bit about that,' Logan replied. 'The British East India Company was up to their eyeballs in it. Leaning on the Chinese to open more ports and allow access to the country's interior. They also wanted to avoid the one-way flow of silver from Britain to China. You know, the Brits bought goods from China and the Chinese didn't want anything from them. And many of the British lords owed their wealth and power to the East India Company.'

'Why, Logan Fletcher, you're a regular junior historian! Want to help me with some research? But you're still a little off. Many of the powerful aristocracy in Britain were from old money—very old money. I'm thinking the time between William the Conqueror and the rise of the Tudors.'

'That's about a 400-year span, darling,' he said.

'Well, it takes a long time to pillage and rape your way to wealth.'

'I'll take your word for it.'

'But I can't deny that Britain's empire grew vastly rich from their colonies and trade,' she said, with a shrug. 'Some of the older families—those whose wealth was based on land ownership—faded over time. And a few families rose out of nowhere to become rich and powerful. Even freshly minted lords or shiny new knights.'

Logan snorted. 'That's another thing I know about British history. The new money, the "freshly minted lords and shiny new knights" as you put it, were always considered to be just vulgar, wealthy peasants by the old aristocracy.'

'Well, right you are again, Professor History. But in these degenerate times, that distinction is rather blurred, especially since some of the old aristocracy are losing their wealth and power to some of the newcomers. And here's something I'll bet you don't know, smarty-pants. The surname of one of those vulgar peasant families who became rich and powerful during the Opium Wars was Croker. Heard about them?'

'Croker?' Logan replied cautiously. 'Can't say I have.'

'Well of course you have, darling. They don't go by Croker anymore, naturally. When the first of the Crokers was knighted, they chose a new name. Something with a little more dignity. Ever hear of Smythe-Montgomery?'

It was reported that he had been seen drinking heavily the previous afternoon in a local pub and had clumsily fallen in the Tube just as a train was entering the station stop.

Chapter Five

A is for Amhurst

Conrad Smythe-Montgomery sat behind a huge desk in the office of his top-floor suite overlooking the Thames. The two walls forming the corner behind him were sheets of glass that offered a stunning vista of central London. On this late afternoon, much of the city's typical fog had dissipated, so the view was surprisingly bright and cheerful. This ran completely contrary to Smythe-Montgomery's mood. He was irked, and he hated being irked. Everything about his facial features and body language spoke of annoyance.

The door to the office opened and his assistant stepped in, looking as though she had stepped directly off the stage at a beauty pageant. Oh, she had brains enough. Smythe-Montgomery would not tolerate an incompetent assistant. But the world was full of intelligent, competent people who could assist him. To find one with the face of an angel, the body of an Olympic swimmer, and a sheaf of golden hair like a fall harvest, now that had been the trick. The fact that she had an insatiable sexual appetite, a lively imagination, and knew which side her bread was buttered on had made her the ideal choice.

Even so, he scowled as she introduced a bookish-looking man in a rumpled business suit—the source of Smythe-Montgomery's irritation. 'Dr. Henry Deacons, chief engineer of Pacific-Indo-Asia Airlines. Your 3:20.'

The man smiled at Smythe-Montgomery in a nervous though overly familiar way that annoyed him even further. He nodded curtly, and the man entered, still bobbing and grinning like the neighborhood grocer. He was not invited to sit. The door closed silently behind him.

'Let me just say what a pleasure it is, sir ... an honor, really, to meet you in person.' Deacons stretched out a tentative hand which hung in the air. Smythe-Montgomery made no movement to rise and his scowl deepened.

'Dr. Deacons,' he said at last, 'you are my 3:20. At 3:30 I shall begin my next appointment—punctually. I have agreed to see you. Please do not waste my time.'

Deacons' hand dropped to his side, and beads of sweat began to form on his brow.

'It's about the specs, sir, for the aircraft modifications,' he began. 'You know, sir, the ones we're to use in the request for proposal we're preparing for the bidders. To upgrade the aircraft for your new airline, sir.'

'I am aware that the aircraft need modernization, particularly in their avionics hardware and software.'

'That's it, sir,' Deacons said, brightening somewhat. 'That's it exactly. Well, the lads in Finchley have been working up the specs for the RFP. They're a good, solid bunch of bright folks, sir, and generally, everything seemed to be quite clear to them.'

'Oh, that's good,' said Smythe-Montgomery, glancing at his watch. 'Well, carry on, then.'

'Oh, no sir, I'm sorry sir, but that's just it. One or two of the requirements make no sense at all, begging your pardon, sir. Encrypted communications that function only between our aircraft, for instance.'

'Commercial aviation is a very competitive business, Dr. Deacons. We do not wish for communications between our pilots regarding, say, stormy weather along a well-traveled route, to be known by all airlines.'

'But, sir, that's vital safety information.'

'And I say it is competitive information. Passengers who travel with us will have a more comfortable experience and so return to us for future travel needs. Do you have a problem with that?' he concluded sharply.

'Oh, no, sir, I mean, I suppose, sir. But, it isn't just voice data that's encrypted.'

'Automated systems, speaking between our aircraft,' Smythe-Montgomery said, with a shrug. 'So much more efficient than two people talking.'

'And sir, then there's the transponders.'

'What of them?'

'They're reprogrammable, with an unusually wide range of capability. I mean, with the specs we were provided, they could be made to look like almost any aircraft out there. It would seem to risk ... well ... confusion.'

Smythe-Montgomery stiffened slightly, and then broke into a wide smile that frightened Deacons more than the man's previous coldness.

'It is now 3:29. I'm so glad you could stop by. I do assure you that the specifications you received from my technical staff have been well thought out and are precisely correct. I'm sure your team can prepare the request for proposal and have it out in a timely manner. Are you?' he asked, with the stony note returning to his voice.

'Oh, yes, yes, sir,' Deacons replied in confusion.

'Then I'll wish you good day.'

Deacons stood frozen for a moment, then made a ghastly smile, turned, fumbled with the doorknob, and shuffled out.

'Ms. Lister, please have Mr. Colpoys step in, would you, and you may remain with him.'

A tall, sturdy-looking man in a new suit entered the room. It was the same man who had tangled with Jason Stone and whose suit (and pride) had suffered as a consequence. Ms. Lister closed the door.

'Ah, Mr. Colpoys. The gentleman who just left, Dr. Henry Deacons, is a rather clumsy and careless fellow. It seems he can hardly cross a road without risking injury. And to top it all, he is the most unlucky wight. I should not be surprised if he were to have an accident befall him. Perhaps a sadly fatal accident.'

Colpoys nodded and left the room.

'Ms. Lister, I believe that by some time tomorrow we may need to contact Dr. Deacons' team to inform them of the tragic loss of their leader. However, their sadness will be somewhat assuaged by the promotion of one of their own to chief engineer. Deacons' deputy should do. Please tell him I am as anxious as Dr. Deacons would be for them to carry on and complete the RFP on time. Stiff upper lip, and all that. Also,' he added, eyeing his assistant, whose long, shapely legs extended from a tantalizingly short white dress, 'you may tell my 3:30 that I am sadly indisposed, and that he—or she—will need to reschedule.' He continued to gaze at his assistant. 'Perhaps you might pass that on to my four o'clock as well.'

Ms. Lister smiled a predatory, hungry smile.

***

The morning news the following day ran a short story, buried in the interior folds of the newspapers and in the final TV segment before the top-of-the-hour headlines, regarding the tragic accidental death of an obscure scientist. It was reported that he had been seen drinking heavily the previous afternoon in a local pub and had clumsily fallen in the Tube just as a train was entering the station stop. The only real item of interest in the story had been that Dr. Henry Deacons had been employed at a company owned by the famous playboy philanthropist and billionaire, Sir Conrad Smythe-Montgomery.

***

Chuck had been busy greasing the skids once Becky had agreed to Logan's offer of 'fun.' And there were many, many skids to grease, since it wasn't enough for Becky's group to respond to Pacific-Indo-Asia Air's request for proposal. They needed to win. Chuck left 'getting the band back together' to Becky and Logan, and he allowed them considerable latitude in hiring. 'Look,' he'd said, 'the bosses really bought into Logan's stupid idea and for once have opened the purse strings. Get the very best people. Offer them sign-on bonuses, a 30-percent salary increase, or whatever. The agency will ensure that their old jobs are available after this little assignment. As long as the companies they work for do any business with the DoD, we have leverage. In the meantime, I'll have my cyber boys do a little corporate … well, let's just call it sleuthing. I can guarantee intel on all your competitors: technical approach, development schedule, and, naturally, price.'

'Umm, Chuck,' Becky had asked, 'I guess I don't need to know how you'll be doing your sleuthing, but isn't it … well … illegal?'

'Yeah,' Chuck replied, seeming surprised at the question. 'Of course.'

Becky shrugged. 'Just askin'.'

***

In a few short weeks, the wheels were spinning, and Logan and Becky were checking out her new offices. Becky had even insisted on stealing Gary Walkin, an old comrade of hers and Logan's, from Alpha Defense. In addition to working many programs with Logan, he had been part of her original team at ARC Avionics, the three letters taken from the last names of the co-founders. 'A' for Amhurst. Gary was used to strange projects where it was better not to ask (or know) too much. 'You mean when this gig is over, I get to go back to Alpha?'

'Yep,' said Becky. 'Scout's honor.'

'Oh, well crap,' Gary joked. 'There's always a downside, I suppose. And I'll bet you were never a Girl Scout.'

'Not true!' Becky responded. 'I was a Brownie ... for a while. We used to meet at the old Community Church in Oceanside. Got kicked out for flirting with the Cub Scouts,' she added, with a wink.

'Now that I believe,' said Gary.

'Well, I'll leave you two to get things organized in your palatial new digs,' Logan said. 'Rumor has it the draft RFP will be out in a week or two.'

'If that rumor came from Chuck, I'll bet the farm on it,' Becky replied.

'Just one last thing, if you have a minute?' Logan said, his expression suddenly much more serious. Gary leaned in, openly listening, and Logan turned to him. 'Gary, just run along and ... umm ... count the staples, would you? It wouldn't do to run out right in the middle of stapling something.'

'Bite me, Fletcher,' Gary said, as he moved off.

'Yeah, and I'm telling Kevin that you're stealing his line now. Shameless!'

Gary's final rebuttal was muted as he headed down the hallway.

'So,' Logan said, 'are you OK with all this?'

'Are you kidding?' Becky asked, startled. 'This was your idea, remember?'

'Yeah, yeah, but ...'

'Logan, don't make me beat it out of you.'

He sighed and shook his head. 'Look, this is all well and good. Super-double-secret operation, your company back in business, a proposal coming that only you can win.'

'Easy money,' Becky said impatiently. 'And fun,' she added, with a devilish smile.

'Yeah, that's the problem. Now take this suppliers' briefing in London ...'

'I plan to have a wonderful time. Chuck said to wear sexy outfits and just be myself. Sounds great!'

'Becky, I know that this was all kind of my idea, but this guy, Smythe-Montgomery, is not the type of character to fuck with.'

'Why, Logan, that was sort of the plan, wasn't it? Are you really worried for my safety or are you, against all odds, jealous?'

'I'm not joking, Becky. This guy's reputation—'

Just then, Gary Walkin came stumping back down the hallway. He poked his head into Becky's office. 'Can I borrow your stapler? Mine's empty, honest.'

Becky passed him her stapler. 'Gary,' she said firmly, 'go back to your office and don't come out until I say you can.'

'Shit,' Gary said, 'now it's exactly like Alpha Defense when I was working for Logan.'

'This job pays better,' said Logan. 'Now get out of here.' Gary's door closed behind him with a solid thud.

'You were saying?' Becky prompted.

'Yeah, I was. Becky, this guy is dangerous. People disappear when they make him unhappy.'

'I'll just have to keep him happy, I guess. Look, Logan, chances are he won't even show up at this conference. Some aged old butler-type named Jeeves will probably be the only action I'll see.' She saw Logan's persistent look of worry. 'I'll be careful, OK?'

Logan stared into Becky's eyes for a second, then nodded tightly. 'It's just, Chuck hasn't been able to contact his guy Stone yet. Now, if he was around, I wouldn't be quite so worried.'

'Not to burst your bubble, dear, but from what I've been told, he's precisely the kind of guy *to* worry about.'

'No way, Becky. If he signs on you'd be safe.' Logan thought back again to his first meeting with Stone in a hangar at Rickman Air Force Base. His recent conversation with Chuck had refreshed the vivid images of that night. At the focal point of these memories was Jason Stone, calm and in control even as he put a bullet through the head of the terrorist who had been about to assault Randy's fiancé, Gail, and then kill them all. 'Stone is nothing short of amazing.'

'Please don't worry, Logan. Maybe Chuck's guy will show up in time for the conference. But if he doesn't, well, you've seen me handle myself.' She took Logan's face gently in both hands and stared straight into his eyes. 'I *will* be fine!'

A small smile found its way onto Logan's face, and he relaxed perceptibly. 'OK. I'll leave you to it, Ms. Corporate President.'

Becky snorted derisively. 'But you know,' she said, as Logan was turning to leave, 'I almost forgot. I'll see you next Tuesday at Skybox, you jazzman you!'

'Oh, God,' Logan moaned. 'You found out. I don't suppose you'd consider doing something else that evening.'

'Not on your life, love. See,' she said brightly, 'I'm already learning my London colloquialisms. Spit spot!'

'That's Mary Poppins! Oh, hell, just promise me you'll come alone.'

'What? And deprive my numerous friends of some very fine jazz?'

'Oh, hell!' said Logan again. 'Fine. See you next Tuesday.'

'Chin up,' she said, as Logan moved down the hallway shaking his head. 'Pip pip cheerio and all that!'

***

And though it was true that Chuck had repeatedly tried to contact Stone, he had failed where another individual had not.

Logan looked at his fellow band members as they settled down to play their set.

Chapter Six

The Band Plays On

On the night of the nuclear detonation over the barren Jordan desert, Elaya Andoori had shown admirable courage and steadiness. She had played all her cards and could now only wait. Her husband, the brutish Hasim bin Wazari, a powerful Saudi sheik, was dead. She had usurped his plans and cleverly deflected his designs. With the anticipated destruction of Jerusalem, her aim had been to seize power in Tehran, displacing the ayatollahs and mullahs, and creating a secular government friendly to the West. And while it was true that the aircraft that carried the nuclear weapon was an old Iranian F-14, the plot had been hatched by a Saudi renegade group in the hopes that Israel and Iran would weaken or destroy each other, and Saudi Arabia would become the regional hegemon.

Despite her sham marriage, Elaya had been deeply attached, emotionally and politically, to Ivor Vachenko, an Iranian expatriate. The two had plotted the collapse of the theocratic government in Tehran and the return of a Shah-like regime, under their leadership. By allowing bin Wazari's plan to go forward, Elaya, Vachenko, and an Iranian Air Force colonel, Muhammad Zareb, intended to reinforce the belief that it had been an Iranian attack, but an attack perpetrated by the theocrats of Tehran. At the right instant, she and Vachenko would sue for peace, offering to take control of the Iranian government in exchange for leniency. Assuming they were successful, events would still leave the Saudis in a powerful position in the region. It would be later, the timing critical, that Colonel Zareb would expose Saudi Arabia's true involvement. It had been a risky, nearly mad plan. Much would have depended on the world's reaction and ability to restrain Israel from launching an overwhelming counterattack.

But Jason Stone's intervention had been anticipated by no one. In the hours before the event, Vachenko had been framed for stealing $50 million from bin Wazari and Wan Chu, Luana's father and the financial sponsor of the terrorists. Elaya had been too late to save Vachenko, and his head had been lopped off by bin Wazari's men. But the steel-spined Andoori had gotten vengeance on her pig of a husband, his skull shattered by a short-range gunshot that she herself delivered. After very little consideration, Elaya had decided to proceed with the attack. It was Stone's second intervention that once again upset her plans.

Zareb and Elaya had been waiting together when the news of the detonation over an uninhabited part of the desert had been confirmed. This was inconceivable. The target had been Jerusalem. But Stone and Luana had their own plans: destroy the weapon, kill no one. With the exception of a lone, anonymous shepherd, they had completely succeeded.

As the details of the premature detonation reached them, Zareb turned to Elaya. 'We've failed,' he said, his shoulders slumped, and an exhausted, fearful look on his face.

'No,' Elaya replied calmly. Her eyes were sharp and focused, as though seeing events as they were to play out in the near future. 'We *can* work with this.' She turned a hard-featured face directly towards Zareb, her eyes blazing as they burrowed into his. 'But I have this question, Colonel. Are you with me?'

***

Over three months had passed since that grim night, and much of Elaya's plan had been achieved. From a de facto Iranian government in London, to a victorious return to Tehran, to the purging and jailing of resistance throughout Iran, Elaya had risen to power. What she had failed to anticipate was the relentless resistance of the Iranian clergy. Too powerful to be expediently eliminated, these remaining clerics continued to rail against her, seeding the powerful forces of rebellion. Elaya's most loyal security forces had met with ambush and assassination. Those who remained were of dubious loyalty, bought and sold by her and her enemies at an ever-escalating price. She shared her concern with Zareb late one evening.

'Could we not bring in more loyal Saudi security personnel?' he asked.

'That would play directly into the lies being spread by the ayatollahs and mullahs. They say I am a Saudi puppet and you my treacherous ally.'

Zareb grunted and pulled thoughtfully on his beard. 'Mercenaries? Loyal only to money.'

'Yes, perhaps, but they are hardly better than the men of my current security force. A leader, a man of commitment, a man of great skill could govern such a force,' she said, with a smile.

'Surely you cannot mean …'

'Ah, Colonel, but I do. The man who came to my home in the company of Ivor. Jason Stone.'

***

It came as more than a mild shock to Stone in London. Where Chuck had failed, Elaya had succeeded. She wished to meet with him.

***

Elaya's return to London on a state visit had received mixed reviews. Supporters of her new, more liberal government had been overjoyed, waving flags and banners as her motorcade left Heathrow Airport. Others had converged on the Iranian Embassy, cheering their support. A large crowd. Unfortunately, an even larger crowd of hardline protestors demanding a return to a Muslim-dominated state, Sharia law, and the removal of the interloping infidel was also there. Events quickly got out of hand. Yelling escalated to pushing and shoving; pushing and shoving to punching and clubbing. Knives were drawn, guns appeared, and a small explosion shook the building as Elaya met with her ambassador and his staff. British security forces struggled to restore order. Over forty arrests were made. When the dust had settled, twenty-four protestors from both sides had been sent to the hospital. Three went directly to the morgue.

***

In a luxurious glass-walled office across the Thames, two men looked out at the smoke rising near the embassy. Conrad Smythe-Montgomery, seated behind his desk, swiveled his chair away from the window and gazed at the second man with a closed, unreadable expression. Smythe-Montgomery's visitor was tall and thin, dressed with impeccable British style in a dark-blue suit, white shirt, and red silk tie. Only his shoes declared his lack of full discrimination: an unflattering style of two or three years prior and of a muddy brown color that was jarring against the blue of his suit. His dark skin, heavy eyebrows, and thick beard declared him to be of Middle Eastern descent. In fact, he was Iranian.

'You see,' the tall man said, 'we do not lack for zeal. The spirit of my country's citizens—a large majority of my country's citizens—cry out for the removal of the Saudi whore and the restoration of a true government based upon the will of Allah, may he be glorified.'

'Yesss, rather,' Smythe-Montgomery replied, with a thinly veiled lack of enthusiasm. 'But you know, Ibrahim, the internal politics of your country don't really interest me, as such. However,' he continued, as the tall man scowled his disapproval, 'I have a certain ... vision ... for the future. Should our objectives align in such a way as to support that vision, then you will have all the varied resources at my disposal.'

'I am sure we can agree on many things, and I will guarantee that the restored government of the Islamic Republic of Iran will allow you great liberty in conducting your affairs within our borders.'

'Well, then, let's drink to that. I have some fine Napoleon brandy to toast our mutual commitment.'

The tall man seemed offended, and his scowl deepened. 'Oh dear,' Smythe-Montgomery said, with a smile, 'I was forgetting.' He poured his own glass and sipped it appreciatively. 'You know, it is not for me to be instructing you, but you might consider rethinking some of your rather archaic prejudices. They can lead to confusion and unnecessary disagreement. I had a small disagreement with a countryman of yours not so very long ago. Totally avoidable! Our association, I am sorry to say, ended rather ... badly.' And now there was an unmistakable hardness in his voice. Smythe-Montgomery poured out a second glass of brandy and held it out to Ibrahim.

Ibrahim's eyes widened and his scowl faded. He had heard rumors. Putting a horribly affected smile on his face, he reached out a hand and took the offered drink with a shrug. 'When in Rome ...' he said.

'Yesss.'

***

Elaya was delighted to have met with Iran's ambassador to England. At least, she said she was, and he was fool enough to believe it, though their meeting had lasted far less than the two-hour scheduled time. Elaya exited the embassy, the grounds now as quiet as an open grave. She gave her driver instructions and the small convoy of vehicles moved off to her much more important appointment with Jason Stone.

**

In the case of a state dignitary, there was no question of an anonymous meeting in the park. Yet it was imperative that Elaya meet discreetly with Stone. Luana had come up with the solution.

'Do you remember our friend, Richard Crandall?'

'The geeky old guy who likes to tinker with ancient technologies,' Stone replied. 'Sure.'

'Well, there may be a bit more to him than meets the eye—quite a bit more.'

Stone had given her a quizzical look.

Luana reached out a cool hand and stroked his face gently. 'Tales for another day, darling. For now, suffice to say that he has a lovely old home on a park-like estate near Letty Green, north of London. It has something of the quality of a museum about it. Some fine, old, unique English architecture. Something that Elaya Andoori might find interesting. I believe that Richard would be receptive to a meeting there. You could happen to be there in advance. Her men would do very well around the perimeter of the grounds.'

'Don't you mean *we* could happen to be there?'

'I'd love to be there, but perhaps we should tread carefully, at least until you know whether she still has any relationship with my father. It wouldn't do to surprise her at this point. After all, she had to pay him a second time for the jet aircraft he provided.'

Stone considered, then nodded. 'Good enough … for now.'

'I'll just contact Richard and make a few arrangements.'

**

Stone couldn't help being impressed by Crandall's 'lovely old home' near Letty Green. Though not large, it was immaculately kept, and there was some extraordinary artwork in the main entrance, living areas, and along the walls of the sweeping double stairs. The main structure sat on the crown of a hill, dense in the old growth of oak and beech, and there were several outbuildings that at one time might have been servant's quarters and stables. The tiled patio behind the home looked out over a small, formal garden. A sloping expanse of grass behind the garden wrapped neatly trimmed green arms around a lake at the hill's base. The sun shone brilliantly, and a light breeze brought a hint of coolness and the scent of roses. A table holding tea and biscuits sat under an awning, the anonymous server having already disappeared. Elaya appeared a short time later, her two most trusted guards already posted at either end of the long porch.

'Madam President,' Stone said, offering his hand.

'Mr. Stone, what a pleasure,' she replied, shaking his hand with a firm grip. 'And what a beautiful location! How on earth did you arrange it?'

'A friend of a friend,' Stone answered noncommittally. 'Some tea?'

'Oh, certainly,' she said, a trace of nervousness entering her voice, 'though I would rather have a gin and tonic.'

'By a happy coincidence,' Stone said, opening a nearby wicker basket. He removed two glasses, a bottle of Beefeater, tonic, and a small container of ice.

Elaya leaned back and took her first sip. 'As I had suspected from our brief meeting in Riyadh, you are an extraordinary and useful man to have around. I could use such a man.' Her face turned serious. 'Let me be direct. My government is under siege. Oh, not by a military force. At least'—she smiled grimly—'not yet. But you must know that there are powerful elements that wish to restore the theocracy. I have a few good, loyal men around me, but among those there is none capable of leading. I believe you are a man not only of experience and capability, but of integrity, and I would beg that you consider becoming my chief of security.'

'Wow!' said Stone, taking a drink. 'I have to say I wasn't expecting that, Madam President. I'm more than a little surprised. Surely there are others—capable, experienced, and knowledgeable—who would be a better choice.'

'None, Mr. Stone, I assure you.'

Stone considered for a long time as he watched a heron wading in the shallows of the nearby lake. 'I don't believe I can help you,' he said. 'You see, I have other commitments.'

'I understand, Mr. Stone, but please take this,' she said, passing him an envelope, 'and review the terms of my offer. I would beg you to reconsider, at least until you could train a suitable replacement. The note within explains how you may contact me if, as I hope, you choose to reconsider.'

Elaya rose and held out her hand. Stone did the same, unable to help admiring her directness and strength.

'And now, perhaps, we might walk through this lovely house. There was a painting near the staircase that can only be a Monet.'

***

'Well,' said Stone, rubbing his chin thoughtfully, 'I never saw that coming.'

Luana gazed at the sun, setting in the damp London gloom. 'Perhaps not. Yet it seems you made a very good impression with Elaya at your first meeting.'

Stone thought back to the meeting at the home of Elaya's husband at the time, Hasim bin Wazari. He had arrived with Ivor Vachenko to arrange the complicated logistics of an expensive and illegal arms deal: a cool $50 million for two MiG-29 aircraft to be supplied by Luana's father. Stone had been suspicious of Ivor, his employer at the time, and his suspicions had been confirmed when he had been attacked shortly after entering Wazari's home. He had easily dealt Wazari's guards, only damaging them slightly. It had been a test, designed by Ivor to demonstrate Stone's loyalty and capability to the suspicious Wazari. At the end of the encounter, Wazari's smiles and polite applause had confirmed to Stone what he already knew. He had passed. Elaya, always a shrewd judge of skill and loyalty, had made a mental note of his potential usefulness. He had done well. What she had not realized was that Stone had also discovered her secret relationship with Ivor. A tangled web indeed.

'You can't possibly be considering her offer,' Luana added, breaking in on his memories.

'What? No. Of course not.' But there was something unconvincing in his voice. With feline grace, Luana moved close to Stone and pressed her body tightly against his.

'Come, darling,' she purred. 'I have ways of making you talk.'

He turned towards her and wrapped her in his arms. 'I'd like to see you try.'

***

Logan continued to pace nervously. 'Are you sure this outfit is all right?' he asked Cathie. For the last hour Logan had been trying to hit the perfect studied casualness that he associated with all the coolest jazz players he had ever seen. He was now wearing a grey pullover cotton shirt with no logo and a pair of well-worn, dark-blue pants.

'Oh, for the love of God, Logan, it's fine! Besides, you and the boys will be tucked away back in the corner and you'll be on the keyboard. I doubt anyone will be able to see anything of you except your handsome face and your shoes.'

'What's wrong with my shoes?' he asked, looking down at the nondescript brown loafers he had on.

Cathie just shook her head.

'I was an idiot to let Steve talk me into this. I used to enjoy jazz. Now it's making me as anxious as if I were about to brief a four-star general and I didn't know my material. Shit, I'm stupid.'

'As I am your devoted spouse, I can only support you through sincere agreement,' Cathie teased. 'But seriously, sweetie, you'll be fine. I've heard your group. You're quite good, you know. Listen,' she continued, seeing Logan's skeptical look, 'when you were doing all those briefings and when you were nervous as hell, how did you keep yourself calm?'

Logan thought about it. 'Well,' he said, 'just knowing I was prepared was a big part, but I'd also remind myself that I was there to convey critical information and that the people attending were there to learn something from me—they really wanted to hear what I had to say.'

'There you have it, love. You *are* prepared, and the people are there to listen to what you have to say—musically. So just go and do a good job.'

Logan nodded reluctantly, but muttered under his breath, 'But what if I suck at this job?'

'Oh, you're hopeless,' Cathie said with a laugh. 'Just go!'

***

Logan looked at his fellow band members as they settled down to play their set. Garrett seemed extremely comfortable. He was, after all, a pro. Frank played through his usual chord set, tuning his guitar softly, and seemed no more nervous than if he'd been about to jam in Logan's game room. As for Steve, he was lapping it all up as though he had been Jeff Berlin, one of the greatest jazz bassists alive. Steve waved at the men he knew in the audience and smiled at all the women, contemplating the potential for a lively after-party.

When Becky and her posse arrived, Logan felt another wave of anxiety. But she had only smiled and waved in his direction, a wave that Frank had tried to intercept. Becky simply shook her head and sat down. Logan was quite surprised to see a small, dark-haired woman approach the stage. It was Gail Kamenchek. He hadn't seen her in quite a while, and it was unusual not to see her in the company of Randy O'Neil. It was doubly unusual to see her in the company of Becky and her crew. Logan and Randy had first met Gail at this restaurant. She had been a new hire at Alpha Defense and the youngest woman with Becky that evening. It was clear that Gail had been a novice to the bar scene and was more than a little embarrassed by Becky and her other friends. They had teased her throughout the evening, and had even maneuvered her into an awkward meeting with Logan's equally uncomfortable friend Randy. Oh, it had all been in good fun, but it was pretty clear that it wasn't Gail's idea of fun. However, it had worked out in the end, with a whirlwind romance between Gail and Randy culminating in their engagement and their upcoming wedding.

'Hi, Logan,' Gail said, with a smile. 'Randy's been really busy lately,' she continued, answering his unspoken question, 'and Becky kind of insisted that I come with the old group tonight. She said it would be a surprise, and it is, seeing you and your friends live on stage. I know you're about to start, but I just wanted to say hi, and also, break a leg, or whatever is good luck for musicians about to perform! I know you'll be wonderful.' She leaned over and kissed Logan's cheek, to sporadic hooting and clapping, much of it from Becky and her friends. Gail just shook her head as she returned to the rowdy group.

'Good evening, folks, and especially ladies,' Steve began. 'You know, it's a pleasure to be here. I'm Steve. We've got Garrett on drums, Frank on guitar, and Logan tickling the ivories. But you don't care about all that.' He turned to face the band. '… two, three, four,' he said softly, tapping his heel, and leading off with the bass intro to 'Moondance.'

Logan relaxed. Music had often been his escape from stress and anxiety, and it was having its usual effect now. At first he played carefully and with mechanical precision. But as he grew more comfortable, more relaxed, his music become more natural. It was positive feedback of the most pleasant kind, and the set flew by. Before he was aware, Steve was pointing to the members once again and naming them while enthusiastic applause filled the small space. It was only then that Logan noticed Cathie, standing near the end of the bar, beaming at him and applauding with the rest. He had not known she was coming—in fact, he might have been fatally nervous had he seen her earlier. Now it was perfect, and he smiled back.

'Thanks again, friends,' said Steve. 'And I have a little surprise for you all, including my mates here. If you enjoyed our set tonight, we'll be playing at the DeSalvo's Vineyards and Winery near Sonoita in about four weeks. Be there, or … you know how that goes. G'night!' The crowd clapped. Becky whistled.

The Skybox manager came over to the band and took the mike from Steve. 'Thank you, guys,' he said. 'And we sure hope you'll come back and play for us again real soon. Let's give them one more hand, folks. The Fourth Harmonics!'

As the applause faded, Logan sat there wearing an incredulous expression. *Apparently we didn't suck*, he thought.

The Reality of Chaos

'Grab a cup of coffee and come sit with me outside. I want you to look at this.' ... Cathie was staring at two envelopes that she had placed side by side on their patio table.

Chapter Seven

Unexpected Letters

'Logan,' Cathie asked, sounding dazed, 'do you believe that lightning can strike twice in the same place?'

Logan didn't reply. Since hearing that Steve had committed their band to playing yet again, he had felt compelled to practice dutifully. He had done so, two hours each day for nearly a week, and was in the middle of a difficult and provoking fingering sequence. He made a vain attempt to return to his playing.

'Logan, I'm serious,' Cathie said.

Logan sighed and let his hands and fingers relax. He wasn't really making much progress anyway. 'Well, having lightning strike twice in the same place is about as close to a zero probability as having lightning strike *once* in a particular place.'

'Darling, I'd almost want to know what that meant if I wasn't so befuddled right now. In any case, the probability of lightning striking twice in this house is one—because it just happened. Grab a cup of coffee and come sit with me outside. I want you to look at this.'

Logan rose heavily from the piano bench. *Man, he thought, I have to work in a little more gym time with this piano practice.*

Cathie was staring at two envelopes that she had placed side by side on their patio table.

'Wow,' Logan said, 'you've got mail. Amazing!'

Cathie swatted his arm with the remainder of the mail still in her hand. 'Smartass,' she growled. 'Take a look at the senders, sweetheart, and then tell me I'm not the goddess at the center of the universe.'

Both envelopes were oversized, with postage that immediately caught Logan's eye. None of it was U.S. postage, and there was a hell of a lot on both.

'Well, hell,' he said, impressed despite himself. 'This one is certainly from England. That looks like Queen Elizabeth—when she was younger. And what an ornate, formal-looking return address. "The Office of Public Relations, for the Honorable Conrad Smythe-Montgomery." Smythe-Montgomery!' Logan exclaimed. 'Jeez, darling, you've got fan mail from Smythe-Montgomery!'

'Don't be a dolt. It's not from *him*, it's from his public relations office. Hopefully it's a response—a positive response—to my request for more information regarding the rise to glory of the family Croker. I will admit, though, that I never expected to hear back at all. Still, I hope it's not a snooty, formal, very British rejection.'

'Zap!' said Logan. 'Lightning strike number one.' He turned his attention to the other letter. 'Now this letter has some bizarre postage. Middle Eastern minarets, scimitars. Hmm.' He glanced over at the return address and his jaw dropped. 'No way! No freakin' way!' It read: From the Office of the President and Supreme Leader of the Republic of Iran. He stood for a long time, speechless.

'Go on,' Cathie teased, 'say it.'

'Zap!' Logan finally managed to choke out. 'Lightning strike number two.'

Cathie laughed triumphantly. 'So, which should I open first?'

'Oh, start with the leading global industrialist, then work your way up.'

Cathie reached out and touched Logan's cheek. 'Now don't be jealous, darling. Besides, I'm sure this is a polite invitation for me to visit the local library and do my research there.' She opened the envelope and unfolded a single sheet. As she read her eyes widened. At last she set the letter down on the countertop.

'What?' Logan asked. 'I sure hope the guy wasn't rude or something.'

Cathie shook her head, but remained silent.

Logan picked up the handwritten letter and read aloud:

'Dear Catherine,
I trust you will forgive my impertinence for using your given name when we haven't yet been introduced, a situation I hope we

can rectify in the near future. When my public relations manager read your extremely polite and intriguing letter, she quite rightly brought it to my attention. I was entranced! Very few people know of my passion for the history of the British Empire. And what could be more satisfying to my ego than your interest in the role of my family in that storied history. I have done a certain amount of research along those lines myself, and have a vast collection of family documents and letters to which the public has never had access. I had planned to use this information to correct the rather prejudicial view against my ancestors that is common in what is called "popular history." Said history is sadly mistaken in their role, particularly during the time you mentioned: the Opium Wars.

So you can easily understand my excitement in learning that an author of your stature would take time from your incredibly successful fiction writing (I am a huge fan. My favorite is Address Unknown) to engage in this work of nonfiction, which is so near to my heart. Therefore, I would like to invite you to come to England at the earliest opportunity and to meet with me to discuss this project. My staff members, particularly those who maintain my private archives, have been instructed to give you the greatest possible assistance, but I do insist on the pleasure of a personal meeting to, as you Americans say, "kick things off." Contact information will be sent under a separate cover.

For now, I am deeply thrilled at the thought of our collaboration on what I am certain will be a historical masterwork.

Your most humble and obedient servant,

Conrad Smythe-Montgomery, blood relative of the family Croker.'

Logan placed Smythe-Montgomery's letter on the table in total silence. When Cathie moved to pick up the other letter, Logan reached out his hand and covered hers. 'Don't bother,' he said, astonishment overwhelming his features, 'you can't possibly top that one. Might as well just call it a day. Hell, might as well call it a career!'

Cathie freed her hand and lifted the letter. 'Don't be such a baby. Just because Conrad Smythe-Montgomery *handwrote* a very charming letter, and offered me an opportunity beyond my wildest dreams, doesn't mean you should be so over-awed. Besides,' she teased, 'it's possible my good friend from college Elaya Andoori would like me to serve on her cabinet. Ah, perhaps ambassador to America. I might consider that possibility, though I'll be sooo busy hobnobbing with the British aristocracy that it will be hard to find the time.'

Cathie tore open the envelope, and as Logan peered over her shoulder he could see another handwritten letter, this one several pages long. They both read in silence, and Logan quickly concluded that this was the most trivial and insipid correspondence he could have imagined coming from the head of a foreign government. After a while, he lost interest and backed away. He was about to return to his piano when he noticed Cathie staring at the letter, reading from the beginning once again, and muttering to herself. When she began to read for a third time, underlining certain words with a pencil, Logan couldn't decide whether to be concerned or amused.

'So, what's going on, sweetie? It looks like you're editing your old friend's letter. I've got to admit, it wasn't all that interesting the way it was. Making progress?' But when Cathie looked back at him her face was pale, and he would have sworn her hands were trembling.

'Logan, I need you to do three things. One, don't ask questions. Two, open a bottle of wine. Three, read this again, but only the underlined words.'

Logan silently poured two glasses of a heady Cabernet Sauvignon. Cathie drank half of hers in one swallow. 'Now read,' she said, shoving the papers in his direction.

Concerned, but somewhat skeptical, Logan began to read. Halfway through, he mechanically reached for his glass and drained it. He refilled it and read through the modified letter again.

Friend Cathie. Serious trouble. Government under attack from in my country. Tried to get help from a stone, declined. Can you contact appropriate agency? Need discretion but help soonest. Contact Swiss embassy.

'What the hell,' said Logan. 'Is this for real?'

The Reality of Chaos

'Real as a headache, darling.'

'So this is some sort of code?'

'We used it back in the sorority house. Posted messages for each other on the bulletin board when the sorority mother took away phone privileges. She never had a clue. Refill, darling,' she said, holding out her empty glass.

'And this "stone" she's referring to?'

'Has to be the same guy, doesn't it? He was involved in your last little adventure with Chuck.'

'Yeah, he sure was,' Logan said, thinking back. 'I'm not sure he'll ever get a Christmas card from Gail, but he did manage to keep us all alive. Oh, and Randy may still want to kill him.'

'How in the hell did Elaya get in contact with him?'

'From what Chuck has told me, there was a twisted connection between Stone, Luana Chu—aka Ms. Blue Hawaii—and a bad dude named Ivor Vachenko. It was Ivor's nephew who took the bullet to the head at the air force base. Chuck can sort this out. And maybe,' he added, 'he might just be able to finally get in touch with Stone through your friend Elaya.'

'Ah, I see. Now she's *my* friend.'

Logan ignored the sarcasm. 'Listen, sweetheart, this is what we used to call at work "deep shit and shallow water." We both need to be very careful if we get involved in this. People die when they hang out with Elaya and her friends. I've seen it.'

'I can be very careful when the need arises. Has it?'

'Let me talk to Chuck. See how he wants to play this.'

'And this?' she said, waving at Elaya's letter.

'I'll call Chuck tonight, or maybe right now. You might want to practice up on that secret code, though. You may be using it soon.'

***

'Hello,' a familiar voice answered, though not Chuck's.

'Randy, that you?' Logan asked.

'Sure is. Good to hear from you. How's the old jazz band?'

'You've heard about that. Gail, I suppose. I'll just say that it went better than I expected, right up until the point where our self-appointed manager and jackass in training decided to announce he'd already committed us to a gig at some winery.'

'Sounds kind of cool.'

'Yeah, I suppose. But he might have mentioned it to the group in advance. Turns out we're all available, but still. Oh, and we're going to have a guest singer at the winery. A gal my daughter knows, Judy Lewis. Great voice, killer looks, but I didn't say that. She kind of outclasses all of us, and I've already started working up a boatload of anxiety.'

'I'm glad, anyway. Gail invited me to town—you know I haven't been down there in a while—and I'll get to hear you guys play. Also,' he added, his voice going flat and grim, 'we're going to discuss our wedding and reception.'

'You don't sound all that thrilled.'

'Don't get me wrong. I'm looking forward to getting married, I just wish ... well, you know me. I kind of wish we were getting married by a justice of the peace with the reception to be held at the local VFW. All this fancy stuff just isn't my style.'

'Ah, the things we do for love,' Logan said.

'You've got that right, but maybe in the wrong way. I think Gail is just as uncomfortable as me—almost. But she's doing it 'cause her parents want it, which makes no sense either. They're a couple of Nebraska corn farmers, and they were married in their local church with the reception in Gail's grandmother's backyard. You think they'd appreciate "simple."'

'It may be just weird logic. You know: "We couldn't afford the luxuries in our time, but we want them for our daughter. And even though she *says* she doesn't want them, she actually does."'

'Man, that's really twisted. Why can't people just believe what others, especially their offspring, say?'

'Human nature, I suppose.'

'But hey, I'm sure you didn't call to talk to me about the psychological idiosyncrasies of my future in-laws. I'll bet you want to talk to the old man.'

'I heard that, Randy,' came faintly over the phone.

'Yeah, I do need to talk to Mr. Grumpy. But good talkin' to you. I guess I'll see you soon.'

'Too true. Hey boss,' Logan heard more faintly, 'it's Logan Fletcher.'

Chuck picked up the phone, and after a few preliminary insults Logan began explaining the reason for his call.

'Stop!' Chuck said, as Logan was giving details from Cathie's two letters. 'I'll be on the 3:50 flight to LA, and then to Tucson on whatever is available. In any case, we can have this conversation in the privacy of your backyard, with drinks, cigars, and drinks.'

'You think this is serious, don't you, brudda?'

'I think the expression "serious as a heart attack" doesn't quite do it justice. What are the odds? Two of the most dangerous people in the world and they want to talk to your wife.'

'I don't see dangerous, exactly,' Logan protested.

'You don't? C'mon, man, you must be losin' your edge. Look, Elaya is surrounded by sharp knives, and I don't just mean that figuratively. If she's in contact with our mutual friend—'

'No friend of mine,' Logan interrupted.

'Fine. Acquaintance, then. If she is, she knows how serious her situation is. And how desperate. You get involved with her, and you've de facto chosen sides in a very dangerous game: winner controls Iran, loser is dead. So in her desperation, she contacts Cathie. Some friend. The fact that it plays into our hands—sorry, my hands—is serendipity. My boss's boss is about ready to hand me my nuts for not being able to contact our acquaintance. And why's he so eager for me to contact him? Well, what do you know, it's because of that other dude who happens to be in your wife's fan club. Do you see the irony?'

'At least his letter sounded friendly.'

'Yeah, friendly like the sound of a rattlesnake to a two-year-old who thinks he's found a new toy. Logan, I say this in all seriousness, there is nothing friendly or safe about Smythe-Montgomery. Tell Cathie to tread very carefully.'

'Like she'll listen. So, steaks or burgers with the wine and cigars tonight?'

'Oh, steaks, please. A nice ribeye, no more than twenty-four ounces, medium rare. Mushrooms? Sure, mushrooms. And throw a burger on the grill for Randy. He gets to come along on this one.'

'OK, but do you think he's ready to deal with—' Logan stopped abruptly. He had almost said his name. 'Do you think he's ready to deal with the guy who shot Gail?'

'Part of the job, brudda. I see Randy as liaison with our acquaintance if we succeed in making contact.'

'No shit?'

'It's a brave new world, Logan. The Grasshopper will have to adjust.'

'Just be careful you don't adjust him right out the door.'

'Ten-four. See you soon.'

***

A full complement of steaks sizzled on Logan's grill, much to Randy's satisfaction. A medium rare ribeye sounded a lot better than a charred hunk of miscellaneous ground beef. Logan watched the steaks expertly out of the corner of one eye while refilling wine glasses. It was a glorious evening, and the sun had turned the banded clouds in the west to bars of molten gold against a pale aquamarine background. The day had been uncomfortably hot, but with the setting of the sun and a light breeze it had become balmy. The complete absence of mosquitos or flies completed the evening's perfection. To the east, a fat moon rose over the Rincons.

'This is awesome, Logan,' Randy said, lifting his glass.

'I'm sorry Gail couldn't be here,' Cathie said, with a pointed look at Chuck.

'Not a problem,' Randy said. 'This was impromptu, and she had other commitments. We'll do a little hiking tomorrow, spend a few more days in miscellaneous enjoyable occupations'—Logan grinned—'and cap off my visit enjoying the Fourth Harmonics next week. Nice name, by the way. Quite the techno-musical potpourri.'

Logan nodded. 'Steve's idea. Please don't tell him that I kind of like it. His ego is about ready to burst as it is. Though he seems a little off lately. Still manic about the band, but just ... I don't know, edgy or nervous or something. And he sure as hell didn't want to talk about it.'

'Unlike the four of us. Talking is definitely the plan,' Chuck said.

'It seems my backyard has turned into an outdoor SCIF. I really ought to charge the agency a rental fee.'

'An outdoor what?' Cathie asked. She looked towards the pool. 'A skiff? We don't even have a floating lounge chair let alone a boat.'

'Not s-k-i-f-f dear, S-C-I-F: a Sensitive Compartmented Information Facility. You know, a place to talk about highly sensitive materials.'

'Is that really legit?' she asked.

Chuck, Randy, and Logan all laughed. 'Of course not,' Chuck said. 'But I think we can keep the dialogue below the super-double-secret level. Besides, your friend Elaya didn't exactly follow protocol in contacting you as she did.'

'I wish people would stop calling her *my* friend,' Cathie grumbled.

'Well,' Chuck said, 'it may be the role you were born to play. There's a ton of opportunity for exploitation here.'

'But not before dinner,' Logan said. 'Steaks are done. Randy, just give the salad a toss and help yourself. Dear, I believe the baked potatoes were your assignment?'

Cathie stuck her tongue out at Logan and headed back to the kitchen.

***

The moon was well up, giving the desert landscaping of Cathie and Logan's backyard a ghostly appearance, punctuated with gold circles of path lighting at regular intervals. Cathie had placed a candle on the cleared patio table, and she, Logan, and Chuck were all puffing out clouds of fragrant blue smoke. Though Randy had declined a cigar, he was sipping a nice cognac from a snifter, as were the other three. A classic rock medley played on the outside speakers, Tommy James 'Crystal Blue Persuasion' casting a nostalgic glow from the '60s.

Logan blew a long, thin stream of smoke. 'Don't you wish we were just getting together for fun? For nothing more than this?'

'Amen, brudda.' Chuck replied.

'Don't tell me you're getting too old for the super-spy stuff, Chuck,' Cathie said, with a crooked smile.

Chuck rubbed the stubble of his chin as he invariably did when tired or troubled. 'Actually,' he said, with surprising seriousness, 'I'm already too old for it. It's the main reason young Grasshopper is here. This confusing bag of shit will be my last hurrah, if I have anything to say about it, and this lucky lad will inherit my dubious role when I pull the plug for good.'

Logan stared keenly at Chuck. He knew what his old friend was doing: flattering Randy, trying to set him up to take on a role that Randy might otherwise resent. It was excellent psychology, though Randy was too young and inexperienced to step into Chuck Johnson's shoes. At least, these were Logan's first thoughts. But as he continued to stare at Chuck, he realized the very substantial truth to his statement. Chuck's previous 'bag of shit' had cost him dearly. He had never completely recovered from the strain, and his health had suffered. Logan looked at him with an assessing eye. Chuck had gained a few pounds, and he looked drawn and tired.

'You're so full of shit, boss!' Randy exclaimed, breaking the mood of Logan's musing. 'You'll die with your boots on long after *I* retire.'

A hollow look on Chuck's face passed in a flash, followed by a wide grin. Logan doubted anyone else had noticed that first, almost frightened expression.

'Kiss my muscular black ass, Randy,' Chuck said. 'Let's get to work.'

Chuck glanced at Logan, and instantly knew that his best friend for decades understood the sad truth. 'May I see your highly interesting letters, Cathie?' Chuck asked after a short pause.

When both he and Randy had perused both, Chuck turned to Randy. 'OK, sidekick of mine, let's hear your analysis.'

Randy looked nervously around the patio table at the others, focused intently now on him. In his agitation, he took a gulp of the cognac as though it had been a cold brew at the local tavern. When his coughing fit subsided, Logan refilled his glass. 'You may begin,' he said, with a wink.

'Right. Great start. Well, let's take what's behind door number one, Smythe-Montgomery's letter. On the surface, it's an extraordinary opportunity to meet one of the few brilliant, flamboyant billionaire playboys still on our humble planet. That is, if we didn't know he was a cold-hearted, egomaniacal megalomaniac with homicidal tendencies.'

'You're just guessing on that last part, right?' Cathie asked.

'No,' Chuck answered. 'Oh, it's nothing that we could release to law enforcement. Surveillance, wiretaps, and … such. Not readily admissible in a court, and, to be painfully honest—which has a particular sting to it after my checkered career—not "CSI London" conclusive.'

'But there's enough circumstantial information, and some not so circumstantial, to tie him to the disappearance of a slimy Middle Eastern thug named Muhammed Farrokh al-Tikriti and to the death of a pointy-headed, pencil-necked brain named Henry Deacons,' Randy said. 'Smythe-Montgomery's dirty as hell. No doubt.'

'So?' Cathie prompted.

'Well, we're already working one angle to try to figure out this guy's play, and to nail him before he can execute it. You know, the deal with Becky Amhurst?'

Cathie nodded. 'Logan's told me a little. Not much'—she turned to Chuck—'just enough to try to scare me away from following up on the contact. By the way, I refuse to be *permanently* scared off.'

'Good for you,' Chuck said, 'because we'd like you to make that contact. Of course, Logan's absolutely right. The guy is dangerous as hell. Crocodile smile and all that.'

Cathie frowned. 'That's a bit schizophrenic. Grasshopper, please enlighten me.'

'Well, we figured that with both you and Becky on the inside, we can get a double going.'

'A double?'

'Guys like Monty are paranoid to a fault. They're always instinctively on their guard for what we're trying to do. So you overload them. No way *two* people could be after him at one time.' He shrugged. 'That's the theory. Some guys are more paranoid than others.'

'For the time being, Cathie,' Chuck said, 'a pleasant, flattering, very noncommittal response is probably best. I'll think about the next move after that. It may depend on the contact information he sends and on whether you and Logan would enjoy a not-too-luxurious trip to England, courtesy of the Company.'

'"Not too luxurious."' Cathie repeated. 'How could a girl resist?'

'Think of it as a sacrifice for the sake of the good old USA.'

'I gave at the office,' Logan commented sourly. 'OK, so that about takes care of Conrad S & M for now. What about Cathie's lovely Iranian friend?'

'Knock off the "friend," hubby of mine, or feel my wrath. We were sorority sisters in college, and that was about it.'

Chuck ignored the banter and considered briefly. 'Where to start? There's a lot of angles to this little puzzle. Just thinkin' out loud here, but you should reply to your friend—*using* that stupid code.'

'It fooled our sorority mom for years, Chuck.'

'I doubt that, but I *guarantee* that Elaya's opponents have read it, cracked it, and decided to let it go through.'

'Seriously?' Cathie asked. 'No, but wait. That doesn't make any sense, unless ... oh, shit!'

'Exactly,' said Chuck. 'They want to see if you rise to the bait. See what kind of connections you make. See if you know who 'stone' is. I doubt you guys will be surveilled directly—at least, not in Tucson. But be very careful what you say on the phone or put into an e-mail. Just assume it will all be read by people who want to hurt you.'

'Comforting thought,' said Cathie.

'A prudent thought. And you'll have a little friendly help nearby. It's an assignment that's liable to satisfy more than one objective, so to speak. Grasshopper, I want you to stay in town for the duration. Turns out, you need some private time with your betrothed. I don't know, wedding planning or some other mundane shit.'

'It's funny 'cause it's true,' Randy said, smiling at Logan.

'But still, how do I reply to this?' Cathie asked, shaking Elaya's letter in Chuck's direction.

'Ah, that could be tricky. My first inclination was to respond to the non-coded gibberish with more non-coded gibberish. Won't work. Elaya's enemies know that you know the code. You'll have to code a singularly unresponsive response. *Connections old and rusty. Not sure if can help. Will try. May be impossible.* Some shit like that.'

'Do I mention Stone?'

'No. She didn't ask for help there. Best to play dumb.'

Cathie turned to Logan with an iron stare as he spluttered into his drink. 'Don't go there, lover.'

Randy also stifled a laugh, and poured himself another drink.

'Fine. Do you intend to make contact with Elaya, and if so, how?' Cathie asked.

'Oh, I fully intend to contact her. I'll do it through Jason Stone.'

'But you haven't been able to contact *him*,' Cathie said, with irritation. 'Logan told me.'

'Yeah, but I'd be surprised if I couldn't find him now, since Elaya told me exactly where to look.'

'OK, Chuck, that was a conclusion worthy of Sherlock Holmes. But can you back it up?' Cathie challenged.

'Grasshopper?' Chuck said. 'Please explain it to the lady.'

All eyes turned to Randy once again.

Randy held up the envelope from Elaya. 'It's reasonable to assume Elaya spoke to Stone not long before this was sent. How would she do that? Not over the phone, that's for sure. It had to be a personal meeting. And would they meet in Tehran?' He paused for effect. 'Not a chance. So, when has Elaya been outside the country? Only one very brief trip. To London. She met with her ambassador and then went to visit "an old, historic English country home." Puhlease! She must have met Stone there. That gives us a date and a location down to GPS coordinates. Up until now, we didn't know what *hemisphere* Stone was in, let alone a mailing address. And, an astonishingly beautiful lady of Hawaiian and Chinese ancestry also happens to be in London. Easy-peasy!'

'Sounds that way,' Cathie said, 'but what have you got so far?'

'Actually, he's already been spotted,' said Chuck smugly. 'Only problem is how to approach him. He's got a bad habit of killing people who irritate him. So, it looks like I'll be going to London.'

The main building of DeSalvo's had the look of an old Spanish hacienda, with stonework and stucco walls, and a red-tile roof.

Chapter Eight

Concert in the Vines

'I hate to keep complaining about this, babe, but why can't we just elope?' Randy asked Gail the following day. He smiled when he said it, however. It was a pretty well-worn joke.

'We're doing it for Mom and Dad. Besides, what's so horrible about a vacation in Italy and Montenegro?'

'Oh, I know. Just don't forget, you're marrying a beer and chips kind of guy with a very iffy job as sidekick to a crazy boss.'

'Oh, it's not an iffy job at all,' Gail replied, ignoring the comment about the crazy boss. 'And Chuck implied you were his chosen successor when he leaves.'

'That's not his choice,' Randy replied seriously. 'Believe me, I don't have the necessary experience.'

'I think it was a nice compliment anyway. So, come on, dear, you're dodging. You're supposed to be helping me select the dinner menu for the reception. Do you prefer medallions of lamb with mint sauce or calamari crema for the second appetizer?'

Randy groaned. 'How about hot pretzels and mustard?'

Gail swatted his arm. 'Oh, never mind. I'll choose. Just run along and do something. We'll take a walk later and order a pizza. How's that?'

'Can I have a beer with that?'

'Yes. Yes you can.'

Randy leaned over and kissed Gail's cheek. 'Thanks, babe. You know I love you. I'll be back later.'

***

The evening before their performance at the winery, the Fourth Harmonics met at Logan's house for a final rehearsal. Logan, Garrett, and Frank set up and began their warmups and tuning. Steve finally arrived—twenty minutes late—to the collective scowls and grumbling of the other three. 'Jeez, man. Hope you can manage to be on time tomorrow,' Frank complained.

'C'mon bass man,' Logan added, 'we need to run through our set before Judy shows up.'

Steve ignored the barbs of his friends and fidgeted with his bass guitar strap, eventually giving up and turning to Logan. 'Hey, mind if I just wet my whistle?' he said, pointing to the half-empty wine glass near Logan's elbow.

Logan gave him a 'you've got to be kidding' look, and shook his head in mild disgust. 'Yeah, sure. I'll fix you up. We've got a Cab and a Chardonnay open.'

'Thanks, buddy. I'll take a bourbon, if it's not too much trouble.'

Logan hesitated. This was more than a little annoying. At last, he grudgingly motioned for Steve to follow him to the bar. Garrett and Frank exchanged disgusted looks and began practicing the transitions in a particularly troublesome piece.

Logan poured out two shots of bourbon, handed the glass to Steve, and headed back to the piano. But before he'd gotten two steps away, Steve tossed back the tumbler of whiskey and sheepishly handed the glass back for a refill. This time Logan stared at Steve before pouring out a single shot while he said softly, 'What the fuck is up with you? You show up late for practice—well, I guess that's not all that unusual—and you're bouncing off the walls like a junkie needing a fix.'

Steve started at this comment and seemed about to speak, but instead knocked back his drink. 'Look,' he finally replied, 'I'm really sorry, Logan. And I'll apologize to the boys too. I'm just a little wired, is all. I'll be fine. A couple drinks and some smooth jazz and I'll be good as new. Maybe better.' But his words did little to soften the skeptical look in Logan's eyes.

'OK,' Logan said. 'Just do your magic on the bass and charm the crowd tomorrow with your boyish demeanor and we'll be square.'

Once again Logan turned to rejoin the others, but Steve tugged gently on his sleeve. 'Just one more … for the road?' he asked, with a winning smile.

Logan shrugged. 'Help yourself, but then get your ass over there. We absolutely need to get through "Stolen Moments" and "Blues in the Night" before Judy gets here.'

Steve reached out and slapped Logan's shoulder. 'I'm there, man.'

Despite his earlier nervousness, either the alcohol or the music seemed to have a soothing effect on Steve, and he readily fell back into his role as band leader. The man had talent, Logan had to admit, and not just with the music. He could be critical or encouraging with the others and get away with it, and he guided them over the rough spots in several of their songs. Unfortunately, by the time Judy arrived, Steve had become slightly too relaxed and far too self-confident.

Judy was a thirty-one-year-old blonde with a delightfully curvy body, long legs, and a brilliant smile. And though she had dressed in jeans and a tank top, she was stunning. As a longtime acquaintance of the family, she gave Logan a friendly hug that was coveted by the other three. In his too-relaxed state, Steve walked up to her, grinning, and, taking her shoulders in a very familiar way, situated her in front of the quartet, fussing with her exact positioning. Judy gave Logan a questioning look, which he answered with an eye roll and a sharp comment of, 'Yeah, that's fine, Steve. C'mon, let's get this done.'

The practice went reasonably well after that, though Logan had to twice more redirect Steve's attention from the young woman's breasts and back to the music. At the end of the practice, Logan motioned for Judy to remain, while he took Steve by the elbow and escorted him to the door. 'Dude,' he whispered, 'behave yourself. I have friends who would enjoy breaking a few of your fingers if I just asked them. The lady is a friend of my *daughter's*, and a friend of mine, and therefore is off limits to you. Understand?'

'Oh, man, Logan, I was just being friendly,' Steve said.

'Save it,' Logan said. 'Just ...' No better word came to his mind, so he repeated, 'Behave. And if you're late tomorrow, don't bother showing up at all.'

Steve smiled his innocent smile and moved off, his ego and confidence barely bruised.

'Jackass,' mumbled Logan, as he returned to his music room. 'I am sorry about him,' he told Judy. 'He's usually not *quite* as obnoxious, though he does have an uncontrollable thing for young ladies. But I promise he'll be good from now on.'

'It's not the first time a semi-inebriated older man has made moves on me, though I don't like to brag.'

Logan laughed. 'I just hope I won't have to throttle him outright when he sees you in your performance outfit.'

***

It took a threatening stare from Logan to squelch a salacious Steve when he first saw Judy the next evening, but it hadn't required physical violence. In fact, family friend or not, Logan blushed for some unfatherly thoughts as Judy joined the group. She was in a very tight, very low-cut black dress with sparkling sequins around the neck, arms, and hem, which was just low enough for decency. Black nylons and dazzling black heels (also sequined) completed her wardrobe. Her long hair fell in waves over her shoulders, and her lips were a deep satiny red.

'Hi, guys,' she said casually. She looked around, smiling. 'What a lovely venue.'

The DeSalvo's Vineyard and Winery was located on rolling hills about five miles east of the tiny town of Sonoita, which was some fifty miles southeast of Tucson. The nearly five-thousand-foot elevation provided a surprisingly good environment for the growth of several varieties of grapes including Grenache and Merlot, and so a number of small wineries had sprung up in this unlikely area of southern Arizona. The main building of DeSalvo's had the look of an old Spanish hacienda, with stonework and stucco walls, and a red-tile roof. But the looks were deceiving. The building, only a few years old, was fitted with many 21st century amenities including huge double-pane windows looking out on its back patio, a high-ceilinged entryway, and several bar and tasting areas with granite countertops and rich wood paneling. Two wings branched off to either side at shallow angles, forming a semi-enclosed back courtyard. These branches held small, private tasting and dining areas, for DeSalvo's also served dinner Thursday through Saturday and a lavish Sunday brunch. The spacious courtyard faced west, and was now catching a golden afterglow from the sun, silhouetting the grape vines that marched in orderly rows across the lazy hills behind. Large flagstone slabs covered the courtyard and a dozen or so tables of various sizes dotted the patio. Most of the tables were occupied, as customers were doing a special tasting prior to the musical entertainment.

The band had been setting up on the stage near the end of the southwest wing.

Logan smiled. 'It really doesn't suck. The temp must be about 75, and the humidity would make the Sahara seem moist. Yeah, not too bad.'

But the concern on Logan's face prompted Judy to ask, 'You OK, Logan? Just nerves, I hope.'

There were several things troubling Logan above and beyond his usual pre-performance anxiety, but he could share only one of those with Judy. 'Oh, Steve's about as jumpy as a cockroach on a griddle, and he's drinking too much as a result. I don't know what's gotten into him lately. I mean, he's always kind of a boorish dick, but now he's just twitchy as hell.' He shrugged. 'He won't be bothering you, though.'

'Don't worry about me. He settled down just fine last night after a few cocktails. I'm sure he will again.'

Logan nodded. 'We've got about twenty minutes to show time. Think I'll say hello to a couple of folks. Don't forget, you come out—'

'At the end of "On Green Dolphin Street." And the band transitions directly into "Summertime." Steve introduces me at the end of that song, then we work the rest of the set. Relax, Logan. We're all semi-talented amateurs here.'

'Right,' he said, trying to match her level of confidence.

The second, and far more significant, item bothering Logan had been a warning from Chuck. Though in England, he had yet to make direct contact with Stone, but was carefully observing. He had also helped craft a reply to Elaya's letter to Cathie that contained many of the elements they had discussed previously—*Connections old and rusty. Not sure if can help. Will try. May be impossible*—cast into their peculiar college code. Cathie had written the letter and mailed it off several days earlier. Chuck had called Logan to remind him to be extremely careful until he was certain how Elaya's enemies would respond to this communication. When Chuck heard that Cathie would be attending Logan's next concert, he was livid. 'Now, what the hell about "be careful" did you fail to understand?' he'd asked. Logan responded rather defensively, saying he didn't realize that if they played along with Chuck she'd have to go into a witness protection program. Chuck had continued to grumble, but when he found out Randy would also be attending he'd finally agreed, provided that Cathie sit with Randy and Gail *and* that Logan keep a close eye on her as well. *Yeah,* Logan thought, *no need at all to look at my music or the other guys in the band! Shit!* But the compromise had been made, and Cathie was seated with Randy and Gail at a small table directly in front of the band. They were his first stop.

'How's it going?' he asked.

'Ooh, the star of the show deigns to speak words of greeting to his rapt audience,' Cathie said.

'Hi, Logan,' said Gail. 'It's a lovely evening. Are you ready to wow us?'

'Oh, there may be a wow or two all right. Let's just hope they won't be wows of disappointment.'

'Oh, Logan,' Cathie said, with a smile, 'relax!'

'Well, I've heard that one before—recently!'

'In the meantime,' Randy interjected, 'help a brother out.' He pointed to a neat tray of small glasses, each containing a different wine. 'I've been told this is a "vertical tasting," and I'm curious. Does that mean a tasting where I can still stand up at the end? And if so, is a horizontal tasting one where I pass out at the finish?'

Logan laughed in spite of his multi-layered anxiety. 'I'll let Cathie explain the finer points of a tasting where different *vintages* of the same wine *type* are sampled. All from one winery—in this case, DeSalvo's. It's doubtful a small winery like this would ever have a horizontal tasting. They'd run the risk that you'd like some other brand better.'

'Go away, Logan,' Cathie said. 'I see some of your work friends waving at you.'

'I hear and obey, darling,' Logan replied, rolling his eyes at Gail and Randy as he left.

Logan moved back from the stage and headed for a large table much closer to the tip of the northwest wing of the winery. 'Evening, Becky, ladies,' Logan said. 'Back again. If I didn't know better, I'd think you were becoming Fourth Harmonics groupies.'

'Don't you just wish, Logan,' Becky said, with a wink.

'And you've brought the Staple King with you. Gary, does your mom know you're out so late?'

'I think Kevin would tell you to bite him,' Gary replied. 'Just a little R&R, courtesy of the boss.'

'Sad but true,' Becky said. 'We've been burning the midnight oil as well as the 2:00 a.m. oil and the 4:30 a.m. oil, and … you get the idea. One night to decompress won't do us any harm. By the way, I meant to thank you for the insurmountable opportunity of this crazy-ass proposal.'

'Well, you wanted me to offer you fun, remember.'

'You're a sick, sadistic bastard, Logan.'

'And those are his better qualities,' Gary added. 'By the way, you need to come by the office, former boss man. There's something very weird about the preliminary specs we got from those Limey bastards—'

'Customers, Gary, they're called customers,' Becky corrected, with a frown. 'You see what I have to put up with, Logan?'

'You knew the job was dangerous when you took it!' Logan said, with a wicked grin.

'Seriously, man,' Gary said, 'you have got to see these specs. They don't make any sense unless what you're trying to do is—'

'Not here, Gary. Please?' Becky said.

But Logan caught the serious and anxious look on Gary's face. He nodded, thinking, *Another thing to worry about. Swell!* 'I'll come by soon. Promise.'

Just then the owner of the winery began to address the crowd from the mike at the stage.

'Shit. Gotta go!' Logan said.

'Break a leg!' Becky yelled at his receding back.

***

The band began with a smooth, easy piece: 'Here's that Rainy Day.' The venue was informal, so drinks and snacks were continually served, and soon there was a pleasant buzz of politely muted conversation, the band's music a relaxing background. The sky began to darken, the pale green and gold at the horizon shading to powder blue, to lake blue, to a deep sapphire at the zenith. In the east, behind the buildings, stars were beginning to peek out.

The band was finishing their final instrumental number, and a small spotlight captured Judy's entrance. She began singing during the transition and was soon deep into the throaty lyrics of 'Summertime.' Her stunning appearance and her even more stunning voice brought a hush to the crowd.

At the completion of 'Summertime,' Judy took a bow to hearty applause and a chorus of whistles. She smiled and bowed again.

Steve stepped forward. 'That, ladies and gents, was Judy Lewis. Beautiful for the eyes and the ears, isn't she?' More enthusiastic applause. 'The rest of the guys you may already know.' He briefly introduced Frank, Garrett, and Logan, commenting with a wink as he said, 'Judy is a friend of the family. We're all grateful for that, Logan! And more grateful still that she'll be joining us for the next couple of numbers, so if you gentlemen wouldn't mind jump-starting our little set ...' Logan struck a few chords and the others joined in.

The desert night had covered the local countryside with a velvety black shroud, the winery and outdoor patio glowing like a small cluster of stars in the night sky. With the crowd's attention directed to the stage, no one noticed a figure in the deep shadows near the end of the northwest wing close to Becky's table. The man moved slowly, though with a nervousness that he could hardly conceal. Slung at his side was a long, narrow shape that might have been a branch or a walking stick. It was a rifle. He assessed the crowded patio, then edged back a step or two, just around the end of the building and out of sight. There, he waited. Well into the third song of the set, he cautiously unslung the rifle. He slid around the edge of the building once again, the rifle concealed at his side. As the third song, 'Besame Mucho,' wound to its conclusion, he raised the rifle to his shoulder. A discerning observer would have noticed the slight jittering of his muscles and the rapid blinking of his eyes as he sighted his weapon, but all eyes were focused on the stage. As the song concluded, applause and whistling broke out. He fired. A whip-like CRACK filled the night air, overwhelming the sounds of the small crowd.

A brief hush was followed by chaotic action: people turning in their seats, diving to the ground, yelling and screaming. Randy leapt to his feet, his gun seemingly coaxed from thin air. Logan was off the stage, the piano bench flying out of his way with a powerful kick, and he was at the table, pulling Cathie and Gail to the ground.

Randy's eyes quickly scanned the perimeter of the venue and spotted the man, his rifle still raised, towards the back of the seating area. It would not be an easy shot. The man was at least sixty feet away in the thick shadows near the end of the building. Randy would be firing across the venue and over the heads of a dozen people. The shooter seemed to be recovering his wits, but Randy couldn't tell if he was intending to shoot again or turn to flee. Neither was acceptable. Randy aimed carefully and prayed that no one in the audience would jump up and block his line of sight. He was beginning to apply pressure to the trigger when a familiar sound rang out crisply: POP, POP. A hesitation for the count of 'one,' and then, POP. Two to the body, one to the head. One of the first techniques Randy had learned when training with a firearm. The man with the rifle collapsed bonelessly as Randy lowered his weapon and sprinted towards the back of the seating area.

When he arrived, he realized the assailant had been neatly dispatched. Two shots to the chest and one above his left eyebrow. Dead before he dropped. Randy assessed the entry wounds—small caliber, solid point ammo—then turned, and there sat Becky, her .38 revolver pointed to the ground in the classic 'rest' position, and a stunned look on her face. The rest of her party stared at her, mouths gaping, eyes wide. Gary grinned shakily and mouthed one word: *Nice*.

Randy ducked around the end of the building, looking for other threats, but could see nothing, though it was true that armed men could be hidden in the hills, with well-illuminated targets within easy range. Still, this fellow had strolled right up to the winery, and Randy was pretty sure he knew who the target was.

'Becky,' he said, returning to her table. 'Becky!' She turned dazed eyes in his direction. 'Help get everybody inside. Put away your gun, but keep it handy—just in case. C'mon, everybody inside,' he said loudly. 'Situation is handled. Please just go inside the building and wait for law enforcement.' Sirens in the distance told him the wait wouldn't be long.

Shit, he thought, *I'd better check on Cathie*. But even as he grabbed the man's rifle and hustled back towards her table, a thought nagged at him. The dead man had seemed the wrong type entirely for an assassin hired by Iranian theocratic dissidents. The quick look that Randy had gotten of the shooter in the poor light had made him think more of a scruffy, malnourished hillbilly: a thin face with sunken cheeks; scraggly, semi-beard; long, dirty hair; baggy jeans, muddy at the knees; nondescript T-shirt. *Well, the gun is deadly enough, even if this guy isn't a member of the Quds Force. Christ, I hope Cathie is OK! And Gail!*

Nearing Cathie's table, Randy felt a rush of relief as he heard Cathie grumbling to Logan. 'You haven't gained weight, have you? Come on, get off me. I'm fine, and this public display of affection is embarrassing,' she joked, but her voice trembled.

Gail flashed Randy a nervous smile. 'Just never a dull moment with you,' she said, moving to his side.

Randy quickly leaned the rifle against the table and crushed her in his arms. 'Thank God!' he said. 'Thank God! The guy must be the worst shot ever, missing with a rifle at that range.'

'Logan,' said a shaky voice. It was Frank. 'Logan, come quick. It's Steve.'

'Oh, Christ,' said Garrett, then turned away and vomited.

Logan glanced back to the stage and saw Frank on his knees, cradling Steve in his arms. A huge pool of blood was growing around both of them. It ran to the edge of the small stage and began dripping off onto the patio. Judy stood to one side taking deep, rasping breaths, her hands over her mouth, her eyes wide.

Randy knelt down beside Steve while Cathie went over to Judy, turning her away and walking her back into the building. Steve's mouth moved as though he were trying to speak, but only a few weak puffs of air emerged before his eyes glazed and he stopped moving altogether. Randy turned to Logan and shook his head. Logan collapsed heavily on the edge of the stage and stared at his dead friend. 'He was standing right behind Cathie ... right behind her. Randy, he was right behind her!'

***

It was hours before the authorities finished interviewing the patrons and coming to the same conclusions Randy had: a single shooter, a CIA agent with full authority to carry and use a firearm, and a courageous citizen with a valid concealed-carry license acting in self-defense. Net result: one dead bad guy—a murdering bad guy—who wouldn't be tying up the court system. The fact that Becky was carrying in a venue where it wasn't technically allowed seemed a minor point. Three others at the winery were also carrying. Only she had possessed the courage and skill to take down the man before more lives were lost.

The possible motive for the attack? Now that was something of a mystery, at least to the police. Randy had a pretty clear notion of what had happened. At least, he was 99 percent sure. Perhaps that had dropped to 95 percent. In the back of his mind was the nagging thought that the killer just hadn't matched the profile in Randy's mind. *A contract killer? Who the hell would hire this ass clown?* Randy thought. And to miss his intended target at that range was beyond baffling. *Down to 90 percent. Better have a long discussion with Chuck. Something isn't right.*

Chuck was alone in his Oakland office when Randy called ...

Chapter Nine

Getting the Story Straight

Chuck was alone in his Oakland office when Randy called, and within minutes was seething as he heard Randy's version of the night's events. 'Damn it,' Chuck snarled, 'I warned them. I can't be fuckin' everywhere! You had the assignment.'

Randy realized that this was the first time Chuck was disappointed in him. It was fair enough. Randy was furious with himself. He had walked the perimeter of the facility early that evening and once again when he took a head break, but everything had seemed OK. Now he recalled the battered pickup truck in the parking lot, flanked by Caddies, Lexuses, Infinitis, even a few Porsches. It had looked out of place, but Randy had dismissed it as either a utility vehicle for the winery or the dubious ride of an employee. He cursed his own lack of follow-up. The truck had belonged to the killer.

'I'm sorry, boss. I fucked up big and I apologize.'

A perfect apology. No excuses, no deflecting of responsibility. It was, Chuck had to admit, precisely what he expected of his talented protégé. After a few more moments of silence, Chuck broke the tension. 'It's OK, Randy. You couldn't have been with Cathie and walking the perimeter. The truth of it is, even with my paranoia, I never expected an outright attack. Cathie's letter was clear. She didn't commit to helping Elaya at all! It was just the ambiguous response of a concerned acquaintance. If I had been Elaya's opposition, I would have monitored the situation. They might have had a better play if they were patient—and smart.'

'Given that she survived, maybe we should assume they'll take that wise approach starting now.'

'Agreed. But something stinks about the whole thing. There was no logical motive, and the guy you describe just doesn't fit. Is there any more intel on the dude?'

'Still waiting for forensics and on the personal background data. There is one more thing I noticed about him, though.'

'Do tell, Grasshopper.'

Randy was pleased the boss was willing to let the episode slide and that he had not completely fallen from Chuck's good graces.

'Well, I checked out the body one last time before the PD hauled him off. His teeth were completely rotten, and I would have sworn there were needle tracks on his left arm.'

'Your conclusion?' Chuck asked.

'Meth head, for sure. Possibly doing some horse as well. In other words, a druggie loser with a rifle. I'll tell you, my original certainty about him being connected with Elaya Andoori's enemies isn't more than 60 percent anymore.'

'You're being generous, partner,' Chuck said. 'What about the vic'?'

'Still working the details, but this guy has a bit of a back story. Past drug involvement, as a user. A couple of misdemeanors for possession. Supposedly went clean after his third divorce. Always late, always chasing the ladies. A charming rogue, you might say. But Logan noticed nervous, erratic behavior over the last week or two. Above and beyond his apparently normal "I don't give a shit" style.'

'Are they running toxicology on him?'

'Not sure, with the cause of death being kind of obvious.'

'Run the tox. Don't take no for an answer. Your nose is right on this one.'

'Will do. By the way, how's England?'

'Cold, gloomy, and wet. But I have a feeling things are going to warm up pretty soon.'

'Got a plan to renew an old acquaintance?'

'Yeah. At last. He's got a bit of a routine that involves walking the paths of St. James's Park with a lovely lady. It complicates things. But I understand she's on a business trip for a couple of days. He was there alone today. If he is again tomorrow, we'll chat.'

'Hope the weather doesn't get too hot.'

Chuck laughed. 'I'm counting on the fact that he won't see a raggedy, old former operator as a threat. God knows I'm not!'

'I'll take care of stuff on this end, boss. Good luck!'

***

Growing up in Philly, Chuck Johnson had seen some grey, gloomy days, but the worst ones he could remember were matched by the London weather on this October morning. A light drizzle failed to wash away the persistent fog, and the blanket of dreary clouds seemed merely an extension of the fog. There was no color anywhere. Even St. James's Park's lush greens were dulled to monochrome, and the lake itself was a mirror to the dismal surroundings.

Who the hell would want to take a stroll through the park on a day like this? Chuck asked himself. *This damp could rust a battleship to powder in minutes.* He unconsciously rubbed his left shoulder, one of his many old injuries that were making a comeback in the intolerable weather. As he neared the eastern end of the lake, walking slowly, he spotted the familiar figure he'd seen here every day at the same hour for the last week. *Christ*, Chuck mused, *even taking a leisurely stroll the guy looks dangerous.*

Chuck adjusted his speed to intercept the path as Stone walked past. He was just abreast of him when he casually remarked, 'Good morning, James.'

Stone halted and turned his head to evaluate the man who had spoken. 'I'm sorry,' he said, 'you must be confusing me with someone else. My name is Aloysius Crumbford.'

At first, Chuck was taken aback. Could it be that James Kulwicki (aka Jason Stone) didn't recognize him? But a ghost of a smile had hooked the corners of Stone's mouth, and there was a glint in his eye.

'Funny,' Chuck said, walking on. Stone said nothing, but fell in at Chuck's side.

After a bit, the enigmatic man said casually, 'It's still Jason—sort of. Luana can't help calling me James sometimes, but that's for private use. Stone will do. Incidentally, I don't think I ever knew your name.'

Chuck laughed softly. 'Well, shit, I guess that's right.' He turned to Stone and offered his hand. 'Chuck Johnson. Big fan of your work.'

Stone considered, then took Chuck's hand in a firm grip. 'I'm not. A big fan of my work, that is.'

'Shit, Stone, you accomplished at least two miracles in under a month. The first, by the way, involved not killing three of my favorite people at Rickman Air Force Base. I want to thank you for that.'

Stone was unmoved. 'I've killed plenty who didn't deserve to die. I doubt I'll ever forget that.'

'But you got the mission done.'

Stone stopped and gave Chuck a venomous look. 'And that's what matters, after all? Haven't changed your tune, I see.'

Chuck had swallowed that insult from others he cared for, Logan and Randy among them. His shoulders sagged. 'I have, whether you believe me or not. It's why I started off by thanking you for that other little act of kindness.' He shrugged. 'Old dog, new trick? Who the fuck knows? I've certainly gotten older.'

Stone's attitude softened perceptibly and he began walking again. 'Still, I'm guessing you didn't come here just to thank me for not killing your friends. What do you want, Johnson?'

'Oh, I wouldn't even trouble you if the fate of the world weren't in the balance again,' he joked. But even his pathetic attempt at humor fell short, and Stone could sense his anxiety. 'It started out as one thing, but now it's two.'

'That's singularly unhelpful, Johnson, so let me smooth the path. Elaya Andoori must be a player in all this. How the fuck you know I met with her is a mystery, but that meeting and this one can't be unconnected.'

'You've nailed reason two dead on. We found you through her. Oh, don't get your panties in a bundle,' Johnson added hurriedly, sensing Stone's sudden anger, 'she only told her old college friend, Cathie Clarke Fletcher. Using, by the way, an absolutely childish code that they'd invented in college to fox the sorority mom. Everyone in Tehran opposed to Andoori must know by now. Not about you, exactly, but the name Stone did pop up in her communication. I'm connected with the Fletchers, and so got the word. My sidekick, Randy O'Neil, worked it out pretty quick.'

The Reality of Chaos

'The young man who wants to murder me and piss on my corpse?' Stone asked, with the hint of a smile.

'The same. I've explained that you miraculously saved him and his fiancée. He believed it—eventually—at an intellectual level, but I wouldn't be expecting a Christmas card this year.'

'Good for him,' said Stone. 'I like a little honest emotion.'

Chuck felt the comment was aimed at him, but refrained from a comeback. Stone was right. Chuck had a list of regrets that would match Stone's, if not in direct bloodshed, then in pure deception.

'So, having guessed number two on your hit parade, I'll take a wilder guess that number one has to do with Sir Conrad Smythe-Montgomery.'

'Are you some kind of mind reader?' Chuck asked.

'You mentioned the fate of the world, and that guy is one hell of a big fish—a barracuda, I'd say. It was just a guess.'

'A damn good one,' Chuck said.

'Then there are the people who work for him like Dr. Henry Deacons who suddenly wind up accidentally dead. That's just a bit cliché. And also,' Stone added hesitantly, 'I've had a minor personal run-in with one of his staff. That gentleman just happened to be carrying an Uzi Pro. Not the usual security guard equipment.'

'No shit. A run-in, you say?'

'He was being rude. I might have damaged his suit, and if you were to send a diver into the lake, right about there'—he pointed to a spot roughly thirty feet from shore—'you might find the Uzi. Unless he went in and got it later, which I doubt.'

'Well I'll be damned,' said Chuck. 'You know, Stone, trouble seems to find you in large doses.'

Stone smiled. 'And now you're here.'

'Yeah, I am. And I could sure use your help.'

'I'm guessing the hours are shit, the pay is lousy, and my life would be in danger. I just finished a very messy assignment for you, Chuck. Took over five years, a dozen scars, and a few pints of blood. Also, I just turned down a much better offer from the President of Iran. Why the fuck would I want any part of this?'

'It's good you turned her down. Really good. That means she can hire some incompetent boob who *will* be taken out before breakfast, and you can operate without all the scrutiny. I'm not surprised you said no.'

'Maybe you weren't listening,' Stone said, 'but I just said no to you also.'

'Actually, you didn't, which sort of surprised me. Look, James, I don't know what you have going on in your life. I honestly hope it's good. I know you're involved with a beautiful and brilliant woman. What the two of you do is no concern to me as long as U.S. interests aren't at risk, and I mean that. Maybe I know you better than you think, and you know that when I say a job is important, it sure as hell is. If you choose to help out, I'd be much more involved than on your last assignment, and my friendly sidekick—the one who wants to murder you—would be working with you. Plus, it's probably time you get to meet my best friend, Logan Fletcher, who you kindly didn't shoot. It's his wife who's the longtime college buddy of Elaya Andoori. It's possible the Quds force has already tried to kill her, but that's still a bit murky. Oh, and she has a personal invite to meet with Sir Conrad Smythe-Montgomery to discuss his ignoble ancestry.'

'Shit, Johnson, and you say trouble seems to find me! I hope you discouraged the Fletchers from any further contact with those two.'

'No. In fact, we're going to nurse both of those relationships along. The connection with Andoori is risky, but less so if you're willing to help. Cracking into the network of Smythe-Montgomery has been nearly impossible. The invitation to Cathie is one potential chink in his armor, and we're playing another angle as well.'

'Why are you even telling me this?' Stone asked. 'What if I say no?'

'You won't. But … if you did, I know this wouldn't be the kind of information you'd share.'

'You're sure?'

Chuck almost laughed. 'Yeah. I'm sure.'

'I was kind of looking forward to a quiet semi-retirement. Spend time on a small lake with some big bass in it. Possibly a little place in Colorado. Breckenridge is nice. Maybe keep an apartment in London.'

'I had a feeling that you and Ms. Chu wouldn't be anywhere in particular. You're right about this job. The pay is crap. But sometimes, when you have the right credentials and the stakes are high enough, the per diem can be pretty good. For instance, a small lake with some big bass seems reasonable enough.'

'I'm not really strapped for cash,' said Stone.

'Then save it for the grandkids.'

This comment brought a blush to Jason Stone's otherwise impassive face. It was astonishing to see.

'I'll want to talk to Luana first, naturally. And possibly to one of her friends.'

Chuck handed him a business card declaring that his name was Sherman Carlyle, an insurance agent specializing in long-term assisted-living policies. 'Call this number when you're ready. The operator will tell you how we can get in touch.'

***

'I would ask why you're even considering this, but it would be insulting to both of us,' Luana said sulkily.

'It would,' Stone replied. 'Both of us excel at what we do. It would be ridiculous for us to just think we could retire in our thirties and sit in rocking chairs for fifty or sixty years. Admittedly,' he added, with a grin, 'my line of work tends to be a bit harder on the body: broken bones, gunshot wounds, et cetera. I wouldn't mind retiring from that part.'

'It goes with the territory, my love.'

'It does. But I haven't told Chuck yes or no, just that I had to talk to you first.'

'And you think Richard and his predictive models can help you decide?'

'When you first told me about his crazy computer models, I laughed.'

'I recall.'

'Putting aside the obvious objection to anyone trying to predict the future, he did nail the whole upheaval in the Middle East. The one that you and I were involved in. I'm still plenty skeptical of his prognosticating abilities for specific details—like what we're having for dinner tonight—but his models may be good for pointing to the big stuff. The people that Chuck mentioned—Elaya Andoori and Smythe-Montgomery—are already making a big splash on the world scene. I'm just wondering if Mr. Crandall can get down to the level of potential individual players.'

Luana sighed. 'You really don't want to encourage him too much. He can go on and on about his pet models ... Very well. I'll set up a meeting if you think it will help you decide.'

The Reality of Chaos

'Richard will be along shortly, but he asked me to make you comfortable and show you any modeling results that might interest you until he arrives,' ...

Chapter Ten

Clydes

It was Yvette who met them at the door of Crandall's home. Stone was surprised. But the slender girl with the short blond hair, dressed casually in jeans shorts and a weird dragon-logo T-shirt, simply smiled and led them into a study containing several computer towers, keyboards, and monitors. She rearranged a few swivel chairs near the largest monitor.

'Please sit here,' she said. 'Richard will be along shortly, but he asked me to make you comfortable and show you any modeling results that might interest you until he arrives,' she added proudly. She sat down at a desk off to the side that held a keyboard and a smaller monitor along with scattered pages of notes, liberally dotted with Post-its.

Stone gave Luana a quick questioning look, and she smiled back, barely able to conceal her amusement.

'I'm Yvette, by the way,' said the girl, with a slight blush, as though just remembering her manners. She extended her hand, and Stone took it solemnly.

'A pleasure, Yvette,' Stone replied. 'I'm Jason Stone, and I'm certain that you already know Luana Chu.'

'Actually, I know both of you. You only by reputation, Mr. Stone. I'm pleased to meet you in person.' She swiveled back to her monitor and typed a few commands. In a short time, an icon identical to her T-shirt logo filled her screen and made an imposing appearance on the 34-inch monitor facing Stone and Luana.

'Cool!' said Stone.

'It's the Jabberwocky from *Through the Looking-Glass*,' Yvette said. 'Richard has a penchant for the dramatic, as well as for fantasy.' She flushed as she realized the obvious interpretation of her words. She quickly turned back to face her screen. 'So, what would interest you?' she asked, in a businesslike manner.

'Near-term events,' Stone replied. 'Major power shifts, political or financial disturbances, unusual alliances. And if possible, whether specific individuals—that is, those not running world powers—are predicted as players.'

'Why, Mr. Stone,' Yvette said, as her fingers typed parameters into the menu screen, 'what astute questions! Richard said you were intelligent and perceptive.'

'Did he really?' Stone asked with a laugh. 'Is that all he said?'

'No, indeed!' replied Yvette, but she failed to elaborate.

A Mercator projection of the earth appeared on the monitors, with numbers and text appearing in certain locations, along with tiny images of the Jabberwocky in various colors. A large concentration of these symbols was located in the Middle East. Others in China and North Korea. A few in England. A few in D.C., Paris, Moscow. At the bottom of the screen was a slide bar that indicated year, running from 2015 to 2025. It was currently pointed to April, 2018.

'This was the model's prediction immediately preceding the extraordinary events in the Middle East. By clicking on Clyde—'

'Clyde?' Stone asked.

'Richard let me name the Jabberwocky,' Yvette said.

'Ah,' was Stone's only reply. He was accumulating a long list of questions regarding Yvette that he intended to ask Luana in private.

'A red Clyde indicates additional political data is available.' She clicked the red Clyde in Iran. The screen zoomed in, exposing considerably more geographical detail, plus a new collection of Clydes. Apparently, there were many layers of detailed information. The country itself was displayed on the left side of the screen. On the right side were snippets of text, graphs, figures, and an assortment of numbers, each with a '%' sign. At the very top of this set of data were the words Unconventional Shift in Governmental Control, followed by 82%. She made some blurringly rapid parameter changes and Saudi Arabia appeared. Now the words Unconventional Shift in Government Control were followed by 21%. 'For the entire region,' she said, her hands flying across the keyboard, 'you get this.' Now, the entire Middle East region

The Reality of Chaos

was displayed, including Iran, Iraq, Saudi Arabia, Kuwait, Jordan, and Israel.

'The total cumulative probability for an unconventional shift in government control is 86%. As you see, the timeline is still on April, 2018. It was Richard's last full prediction prior to the remarkable events that we all witnessed. The overall probability of 86% was quite good. The specific indicator of potential countries is dominated by Iran, with the only other significant probability associated with Saudi Arabia. As it turned out, it was Iran's government that was replaced in an unconventional way.'

'If you don't mind my asking,' said Stone, thoroughly impressed, 'where do you go to school?'

Yvette turned to face him, and another smile flashed out. 'I don't mind you asking at all!'

It was an old joke, but Stone laughed appreciatively. It was clear she didn't intend to answer him.

'The interface has improved tremendously since the last time Richard gave me a demonstration,' Luana said. 'The other colored Clydes must represent different types of information.'

'Yes,' Yvette said. 'Green is for items of fiscal significance, yellow for disease, blue for commercial ... I'm only displaying the basic parameters right now. And as remarkable as the new interface is, the algorithms—Richard's true contribution to predictive chaos theory—are far more sophisticated than they were even three months ago. I've only shown you this prior prediction as an example. Obviously, you are much more interested in the future.'

After a few rapid adjustments, the full world was displayed once again. Yvette slid the timeline indicator to the right, roughly six months out from the present time. In the upper right corner of the screen, a purple Clyde flashed ominously. Adjacent to the words Cataclysmic Geopolitical Event, 97% was displayed.

'It's held pretty solid for several months now. As has this number.'

Yvette performed more dazzling keyboard gymnastics, and the number dropped to 12%.

'Quite a difference. What's the cause?' asked Stone.

'That, Mr. Stone, would be the crucial question, would it not?' Crandall said, as he made a quiet entrance into the study.

Stone looked for the speaker of those words, and was astonished to see not Richard Crandall—at least, not the aging, slovenly techno-geek of his memory—but a dignified man in his sixties, impeccably dressed and groomed. His bearing was straight and proud, with a dignity that was almost palpable. Yvette gazed from Stone to Crandall and back, an amused look lighting her face.

At last, Crandall spoke again. 'A pleasure to see you again, Mr. Stone. Let me reintroduce myself. Shocking, isn't it? I blame this young lady here,' he said, indicating Yvette, 'and another dear old friend. Perhaps you may meet her as well someday. A pleasure to see you too, Luana.'

'You might have warned me, at least, regarding your astonishing transformation,' Luana said. 'I was about to offer the young lady a position of responsibility in my company for her obvious technical capabilities. But if she had a hand in your metamorphosis, then she's far more than brilliant, she's a sorceress. As another old friend of yours, let me say that your new persona is the butterfly to your previous caterpillar.'

'See,' said Yvette, sounding very much like a young girl in her eagerness to claim correctness, 'I was right. You look just like an English lord, and it suits you!'

'Enough of that. Don't let appearances deceive. Thank you, Yvette, for demonstrating our software. I believe I will "drive" now.'

Yvette slid from her chair with the grace of a mink, and Stone made a mental note that Crandall had referred to 'our software.' Was it possible that the charming woman was involved in the technical details of Crandall's modeling? He made another note when, as Yvette moved to leave the room, Crandall casually remarked, 'No, please stay,' and pointed to a vacant chair.

'Predictive modeling isn't new,' Crandall said. 'Weather and financial modeling are obvious examples that are decades old. In the world of aerospace, probabilities are calculated for detection, track, and kill. The military uses predictions to allocate limited resources around the globe based on probabilities of an imminent conflict.

'Geopolitical and large scale socio-economic modeling are my interests. A staggering amount of input data is required and, of course, the more detail provided in a focused area the more accurate the predictions. The algorithms combine basic stochastic processes, autoregressive techniques, and chaos theory.

'As to the cause of the dramatic change in probability that you saw in the prediction, might I just have your word of honor that what we now discuss must never be shared? Your word as well, Luana. It's somewhat of a formality, but it's all I require. A word of honor from each of you is worth more than most notarized contracts.'

Yvette, sensing she should not be present, moved to leave again, but without looking in her direction, Crandall softly remarked, 'My dear Alice, your continued rustling about is disturbing. You have been invited to stay, and *your* word has been given and accepted long since. Please. Stay.' Yvette once again sat and attempted to be still, her hands in her lap and her head slightly bowed. Only the glow of her cheeks indicated the strong emotions racing through her.

Stone made another mental note as he said, 'I agree, Mr. Crandall. You have my word.'

'Mine as well, Richard. Word of honor,' said Luana.

'Excellent. The cause of the dramatic change in probability is Sir Conrad Smythe-Montgomery,' Crandall said, emphasizing 'Sir' with obvious derision. 'His death, in the near future, would prevent this looming chaos. My dear old friend and I would not shed a tear if this were to occur.'

It was spoken in such a matter-of-fact way that even Stone was stunned.

Crandall made several rapid adjustments to the computer parameters. Clydes flashed, probabilities sprouted, areas on the global map burst out in highlight. 'The man has tentacles worldwide, but his dealings in the Middle East and the Far East are the most relevant. Purchases of businesses. Enormous transfers of capital. Acquisition of friends serving in governments, including former government officials of Iran who would like to be back in power. All very suspicious. His wealth spreads. His influence spreads. But there is a pattern, an overall plan, I'm sure of it.'

'And what would that be?' Stone asked.

'I can't say with certainty. Probabilities change and coalesce daily, but it's hard for the modeling to account for his obvious psychosis and paranoia. He's a peasant playing a lord, and he knows it. In some ways, it is similar to the *apparent* confidence of an extremely insecure person. Simply a pathological overcompensation for massive self-doubt. Difficult on the surface to distinguish from true self-confidence, but far more unstable, far less predictable.'

'You mentioned him hobnobbing with the ousted theocrats of Iran,' Stone said. 'That would put him at odds with Elaya Andoori, wouldn't it?'

'Oh, yes. And it need not be said that when Smythe-Montgomery is at odds with someone, their life expectancy is sadly reduced.'

Luana shook her head slightly and smiled as Stone sat pondering. She knew he had made his decision. When he finally did speak, he said, 'Thank you so much, Mr. Crandall, and thanks to you, Yvette.'

Crandall rose and shook Stone's hand. 'Mr. Stone, you and Luana have roused me from a stupor. My work is exciting to me once again. I've renewed old friendships and I have more purpose in my life.' He glanced at Yvette. 'In some ways, I'm unchanged, but I've awakened into a world full of hazard. I'd not be surprised to see you again, Mr. Stone. We have more in common than I originally suspected.'

Stone and Luana were escorted by Yvette to the front door.

'You really have made his day, you know,' Yvette said to them.

'Good to see you, Yvette,' said Luana as she left.

'A pleasure to meet you,' Stone added. 'You're a lovely and brilliant young woman.'

'And I've heard you have some unique skills, Mr. Stone,' she replied, her eyes twinkling with mischief.

Stone couldn't help laughing.

***

With a sense of fate, Luana turned to Stone on their evening walk. 'So you've decided to help Mr. Johnson.' It wasn't a question.

'I'm that transparent, huh?'

'I'm afraid so, darling.'

'Well, it's reasonable, if you believe Crandall.'

'What I believe is hardly relevant, but it seems you're convinced.'

'Enough so to have the conversation with Chuck. However,' he said with a smile, grasping her shoulders and turning her towards him, 'since you're so good at reading my mind, what am I thinking now?'

Luana looked at him appraisingly and replied, 'Unless I'm badly mistaken, you're considering a course of action that requires us both to be naked. Some unique positioning would also be involved, perhaps requiring the skills of a gymnast.'

'Oh, you know me so well,' said Stone, leaning in and kissing her deeply.

***

Stone put on a robe and slipped quietly out through the sliding door onto the balcony. Luana was sleeping and he didn't want to disturb her. He pulled his cell phone and Chuck's business card from his pocket and dialed the number.

'United Insurance Group,' said a friendly female voice. 'How may I direct your call?'

'I'd like to speak to Sherman Carlyle,' said Stone.

There was a brief pause. 'May I ask who's calling?'

'I recently spoke to Mr. Carlyle regarding some extended-care insurance. He'll recall.'

'Just one moment.'

There was a silent pause.

'This is Carlyle. I take it you've decided on purchasing that very competitive plan we discussed?'

'Yes. Assuming you can give me the answers to a few questions.'

'I can.'

'Excellent. My fiancée and I are traveling to the States soon. Colorado, actually.'

'By a happy coincidence, I too will be in Colorado. I have an associate in London. If you could meet him at the same location as our previous meeting, you can let him know what your travel plans will be. I'm sure I'll be able to join you and finalize your policy. You're making an excellent choice.'

'Sure,' said Stone. 'I'll be seeing you.'

As he ended his call, the balcony door slid open, and Luana stepped out. Unlike Stone, she hadn't bothered to slip into a bathrobe. The diffuse lights of the London metropolis bathed her body in soft amber shades.

'Aren't you cold?' Stone asked.

'Yes. What do you plan to do about that?'

Stone walked up to her, opening his robe, then wrapped it around both of them. He kissed her, then shifted his hands below her buttocks, lifting her gently and carrying her back into the bedroom.

The Reality of Chaos

Stephen Lance / Chuck Markussen

When he received the invitation to meet for further negotiations on board Smythe-Montgomery's yacht, Empire, *docked in Monaco, he was delighted.*

Chapter Eleven

A Night on Empire

Ibrahim al Rahzi was beginning to appreciate the delights of decadence. Since his adoption of the 'When in Rome' philosophy—a move taken more for self-preservation than for pleasure—he had met with Smythe-Montgomery several times. On each occasion, he had been tempted, and on each occasion he had succumbed. It was far simpler (and safer) than resisting, and he had come to look forward with relish to Smythe-Montgomery's invitations. The meetings invariably began with intense, sometimes brutally blunt conversations regarding the business Smythe-Montgomery wished to conduct in an Iran restored to its totalitarian theocracy. Smythe-Montgomery had demanded and had been promised increased latitude for his enterprises.

The epilogues to these discussions were distinctly different. For al Rahzi, it was becoming easier to reconcile his strict religious views with the greatest perversions of the West: alcohol, drugs, and women. As Smythe-Montgomery had put it, 'Our formal personas are ones of culture and civilization. Our appearance to the world—primarily subordinates, family, and the general public—must be governed by the strict behavioral expectations imposed upon aristocracy or, in your case, the truly faithful. But among peers, we are powerful men with a vision for the future. As such, we are entitled to the spoils of life. It is our due. Put succinctly, we take what we want.' And so, on each occasion, formal discussions had ended in nights of decadent pleasure. Ibrahim learned that he could rely on Smythe-Montgomery's discretion, just as Smythe-Montgomery knew he could rely on Ibrahim's. In truth, Ibrahim could not have rejected the temptation even in his earliest association. His elimination and replacement would have been all too easy for Smythe-Montgomery. Now, he no longer had the inclination to resist. Rather the opposite.

When he received the invitation to meet for further negotiations on board Smythe-Montgomery's yacht, *Empire*, docked in Monaco, he was delighted. Smythe-Montgomery had also insisted Ibrahim bring two former high ranking officers of the Islamic Republic's brutal security forces. One had been a chief in the Special Unit of the NAJA, the Iranian Police, and the other a Quds Force commander. Both had a reputation for vicious and unmerciful actions in support of the regime. However, Ibrahim already knew that these men were flexible in their religious zealotry. It was logical to include them in these discussions, as they would control much of the true policing in the restored Islamic Republic and would directly enforce the will of the Supreme Leader, President, and Parliament. Smythe-Montgomery had promised Ibrahim a memorable party following the negotiations. For the sake of privacy, the *Empire* would leave port and the negotiations would be conducted at sea.

It was a warm, golden afternoon, the sun sparkling off the Mediterranean as the three guests arrived. Ibrahim's two companions, Abdul Nasrahni and Barzan Shalah, were both heavily built men with dark beards and suspicious eyes who looked singularly out of place in their ill-fitting English-tailored suits. It amused Smythe-Montgomery as he watched the trio board the ship. It amused him even more to see all three openly ogling the trio of beautiful women sunning themselves on the boat's lounge deck. Long-legged and perfectly tanned, they had abandoned their bikini tops to take full advantage of the afternoon sun. They waved enthusiastically as Ibrahim and his companions stumbled on board. To Smythe-Montgomery's mind, his negotiations had just gotten easier.

Ms. Lister appeared at his side wearing a filmy cover-up over a one piece bathing suit that seemed to be painted onto her body except for the areas where large cutouts exposed her swaying hips. She placed a hand on Smythe-Montgomery's arm and asked, 'Orders for the captain?'

'Yesss,' said Smythe-Montgomery, eyeing her with immense approval. 'As soon as our guests are shown into the conference room we may put to sea. Be sure to introduce them to the lovely ladies, who will enter modestly attired—more or less—for the occasion. Let the men's imaginations whet their appetites for later.'

'And how is your imagination?' she purred.

The Reality of Chaos

He slipped a hand inside her cover-up and caressed her smooth, warm skin. 'Quite up to the task, I believe,' he said with a smile.

Ms. Lister returned the smile and walked away. She turned back once to see her employer and lover staring at the play of the muscles in her long legs as she moved effortlessly down the corridor in her four-inch heels.

***

'Gentlemen, I trust you are comfortable?' Smythe-Montgomery asked. The three men sat awkwardly at the table and looked far from comfortable. They had met the three young ladies, introduced to them only by their first names, Daria, Irina, and Tatiana. 'Modestly attired,' as instructed, the three had been brought in to meet the men, who had only been able to stare at their faces, or catch a glimpse of a tanned leg when the robes the women were wearing swished open teasingly as they walked. The men were clearly thinking of something other than business, their minds trying to complete the images beneath the robes based on the first glimpse they had gotten as they boarded. Ibrahim was the first to recover.

'Yes. Quite ... umm, comfortable. Thank you.'

'Well, well,' Smythe-Montgomery said, nodding to the steward who was standing by, 'please feel free to remove your coats. Loosen your ties. We are all friends here.' He smiled ingratiatingly as the steward offered aperitifs and set out bowls of dates, olives, and sliced cheeses. Smythe-Montgomery made no move to loosen his own tie or to remove his coat. He simply sat and was handed a small glass of Aperol on ice. He sipped it thoughtfully and waited for the others to make a choice. There was no resistance. 'Well, well,' he repeated. 'A toast, gentlemen, to business soon concluded followed by pleasure of a most extended nature.' A distant rumble was heard as *Empire's* engines were throttled up. She headed out to sea and privacy.

***

'Gentlemen, there is but one final point that I must insist upon,' Smythe-Montgomery said. The discussion to this point had been brief, with the Englishman laying out his requirements candidly. It had mostly involved trade with the Islamic Republic of Iran, and assurances that businesses owned by Smythe-Montgomery would receive immediate, liberal licensing agreements and low taxes. He had also announced that he would like to build several large luxury hotels, which would be enclaves of Western culture, suitable for entertaining Russian oligarchs. 'After all,' he had said, 'a country that can produce the beautiful women you just met deserves some latitude, does it not? Other foreign dignitaries of discriminating taste, and—with utmost discretion—the high leaders of Iran, present company included, will also be most welcome.' There had been no argument. The three waited for his final point.

'I have purchased an airline,' he said casually. 'At present, it flies primarily in Indonesia, but I would like to expand its service. Modestly, at first. India, the Phillipines, and so on, but with the goal of a significant hub in Tehran. A jumping off point for western Europe. You can imagine the type of revenue such a venture would bring to your country, not to mention the potential for tourism when combined with my resort hotels.'

'We will see to expedited licensing,' said Shalah, 'perhaps even an expanded and modernized wing of the airport terminal exclusively for your use.' The others eagerly nodded. During the last half hour, the three Russian ladies had seen fit to stroll past the windows of the conference room several times, wearing only their tanning attire. Ibrahim and his companions were willing to agree to almost anything at this point.

Smythe-Montgomery smiled inwardly. These men were such pawns. He realized that nothing said at this meeting was of any consequence. Nothing could be relied upon based on their word alone. But these would be powerful men in a restored regime, and he intended to secure their loyalty and commitment in another way altogether. These discussions were only the window dressing.

'How kind,' said Smythe-Montgomery. 'I accept. But it is imperative that there be no interference—no unnecessary inspections, for instance—with the aircraft or their cargo. I may be doing some discreet exporting of products to Europe and eventually America. It would be less complicated if there was no undue oversight of this, shall we say, unofficial trade.'

The three looked at each other, and Ibrahim spoke. 'I do not understand. Precisely what do you mean?'

'What I mean is that Pacific-Indo-Asia Airlines will have a separate baggage handling facility. Security for this facility will be staffed by my people only. No airport, local, or national security forces will be allowed to be present or to interfere in any way with our operations.'

'But this is impossible!' cried Ibrahim. 'It is the airport of our nation's capital. Security is essential.'

'And you will have my word—along with a very lucrative airport usage fee, with a particular stipend to ... shall we call you the in-country board of directors?'

'We cannot make such a promise. We will need to consult with our leadership.'

'Why?' Smythe-Montgomery asked coolly. 'Will you three not be responsible for the operations of airport and national security? Can you not make arrangements on your own behalf and simply report to your superiors that all is under control? Have I, in fact, been negotiating with the wrong people?' And now there was a stony threat in his voice.

'No, no,' said Ibrahim. 'I assure you. But, perhaps, if there was something we could offer to the Supreme Leader that would solidify his trust in our judgment. Then we would have unilateral authority on such matters as these.'

'You mean more than an economic boom for your country, more than generous fees and license agreements, more even than a stipend to your Supreme Leader's most trusted lieutenants?'

A gentle knock at the door preceded the appearance of Ms. Lister, still dressed in her bathing suit and cover-up. 'Sorry to disturb you, sir, but will you gentlemen be much longer?'

'No,' said Smythe-Montgomery.

Ms. Lister was about to leave, when Smythe-Montgomery halted her. 'Please stay. You may take the gentlemen's dinner order in a moment. I believe we are about to conclude, and you may want to hear how I plan to resolve our current impasse.'

Ms. Lister stood silently, the three men's eyes devouring her body.

But Smythe-Montgomery was no longer trying to seduce the men or weaken their resolve. He had no intention of generously sharing her. However, he knew she had a deep love for violence, finding it extremely erotic—a characteristic he shared—and he wanted her to hear his next words. It would serve as stimulus later.

'Gentlemen,' he said, addressing the two new members of their association, 'Ibrahim is a wise and clever man. Now what could you possibly deliver to your *hypothetical* Supreme Leader that would be of value?' He had stressed 'hypothetical' since, until the government of Iran had once again changed hands, all their talk was merely speculative. 'I know. Let's give him a country to rule? Yes, I think he'd appreciate that.'

The three Iranians sat silently, too focused now on Smythe-Montgomery to see Ms. Lister licking her lips delicately.

'I propose to do you the small favor of returning Iran to your rule. I propose to eliminate Elaya Andoori. She and the people around her will be destroyed—crushed or burned alive by ... but let me not get ahead of myself. These are details that I will not trouble you with for now. So. I return your country to your Supreme Leader, with your aid and your blessing. Who can say? Perhaps it was even your plan. Would that be sufficient to earn his trust?'

'Yes, yes it would, Sir Conrad,' Ibrahim answered, using Smythe-Montgomery's title for the first time.

Smythe-Montgomery glanced over at Ms. Lister and was pleased to see a fire burning in her eyes. It would be a pleasant evening.

***

And it was. A light dinner was followed by music outdoors. Daria, Irina, and Tatiana were accomplished dancers in an erotic style that was part Middle Eastern and part LA strip club. Though they had dressed for dinner, they easily abandoned their outer garments and returned to bikinis afterwards. Generous and unspecific in their attentions to Smythe-Montgomery's guests, they laughed and drank with each in turn. Ms. Lister was quite exclusively with Smythe-Montgomery, and even if the men had been foolish enough to approach her, there was clearly no need. The evening was moving rapidly towards more private activities, as the women were now draping themselves on the men, who were openly fondling them. Ms. Lister slipped away briefly, returning a moment later with what appeared to be a large handbag, and Smythe-Montgomery made the incongruous comment, 'It appears that it might snow.'

Ibrahim was the first to catch on, and he whispered to the other two, 'Cocaine.'

Ms. Lister set out a mirror and carefully created three lines of white powder. Smythe-Montgomery rose, preparing to leave.

'Gentlemen, these three lovely ladies will show you the appropriate method, after which I believe you and they may wish to retire to your private quarters. I believe you will need to burn off some energy. To a successful day and an even more eventful night.'

In his private quarters, Smythe-Montgomery locked the door, grabbed Lister roughly and threw her on the bed. She lay there and made a sound between a growl and a purr, arching her back.

'Are you really going to kill the bitch?' she asked.

'Yes.'

'Tell me how. I want to know how.'

He pointed to the door. 'I'm going to get one of their crazy zealots to pilot an airplane, an airplane from one of my most annoying competitor's airlines, and plow the thing right into the palace while she's sleeping. If the explosion doesn't kill her, the burning jet fuel will.'

'Oh, God, I hope she burns! And the plane, Conrad, it will be full of people?'

'Of course,' he said, flinging his clothes off and walking towards the bar. When he turned back to her he was holding a thirteen-inch-long Yoshihiro Mizuyaki Honjaki knife. A stunning blade with a mirror finish. 'And do you know what I'm going to do to you, Emma?'

'What, Conrad, what?' she panted.

He was on her in an instant, one hand pulling her dress towards him, the other wielding the knife. 'First, I'm going to remove your clothes.'

The blade made a hissing sound as it slit the silk of her dress. He threw the tatters to the floor and proceeded to cut off her bra and panties. He knelt over her and laid the knife blade between her breasts. It felt cool against her skin.

'Now, Conrad!' she rasped.

Smythe-Montgomery pitched the knife across the room. There was a brief tangle of limbs, then her legs were wrapped around him and she was writhing and moaning. The screams of ecstasy that came later were unheard by the six guests on the boat. Neither did Smythe-Montgomery nor Ms. Lister hear the other screams, frantic, and filled much more with pain than with pleasure.

***

Ms. Lister and Smythe-Montgomery were enjoying a late-morning coffee on the balcony of the master suite when the intercom buzzed.

'What is it, Mr. Colpoys?'

'There has been an incident, sir, in the guest quarters. Tatiana is dead.'

Lister stirred at this, but Smythe-Montgomery was unmoved. 'I will be down shortly. Be sure my guests are fed and keep the other two women in their cabins.'

***

Tatiana was lying on her stomach, her wrists tied to the posts at the top of her bed. Several pillows had been stuffed under her midsection, raising her buttocks, and a cord from one of the curtains was tied around her neck—a primitive lasso. It was clear that excessive force had been applied, for her face was purple, her eyes wide with fear and pain.

'Hmm,' was Smythe-Montgomery's first comment. 'It would appear that our guests became somewhat overzealous. Perhaps I had better talk to them.'

'Please,' said Ibrahim, 'it was an accident. The drug …'

'Yes, it can do that if not handled carefully. Out of curiosity, which of you was it?'

'We … we were all there. We had tired of the other two, but this one …'

'I see.' Smythe-Montgomery paused to let the tension build. It collapsed with his next words. 'Fortunately we are in international waters. She might just as easily have fallen off the boat in a drug-induced stupor. In fact, I'm sure that's what happened, wouldn't you agree?'

The three readily nodded.

'Of course, it is likely that the many security cameras on board might have caught something of a compromising nature. Fortunately, once again, I feel no compunction to turn over those videos to authorities. It would ruin our wonderful relationship.'

Ibrahim and his companions immediately agreed and assured their host that they would abide by the terms of the deal they had made the previous day. They didn't dare ask if he intended to destroy the videos, and he had not offered to do so.

At that moment, a large, sleek speedboat came to a halt in the lee of *Empire*.

'Well, then, that's settled,' said Smythe-Montgomery cheerily. 'Please follow the steward to the cabin. I'll join you shortly. It is perhaps best that Tatiana be removed by my security team. I'll make the arrangements.' The three stammered their thanks and followed the steward.

When they had gone, Smythe-Montgomery returned to the cabin where Tatiana's body lay wrapped in sheets.

'Take her on board the *Gryffin*,' he said to his waiting men. 'This really has played out even better than I could have wished, and we now have the leverage we'll need in the new Republic of Iran.'

Colpoys nodded, and turned to assist two other men in removing the body when Smythe-Montgomery placed a hand on his shoulder. 'Get her on board and out of sight, then remove the other two as well. And Mr. Colpoys,' he added, with a sadistic look in his eyes, 'you and your companions may … indulge yourselves. Then dispose of all three.'

Stone and Luana spent the two days before Chuck's arrival visiting properties. Both agreed that their house should be on a large, private lot, be comfortably spacious, have good views, and be reasonably close to skiing.

Chapter Twelve

Case Closed

It was certainly the strangest 'celebration of life' Logan had ever seen, and he had been to more than one wake that had required him to take a taxi home. For Randy, who was not a friend of Steve's but who considered it a duty to attend in order to complete the personality profile of this bizarre character, it was jaw-droppingly peculiar. The celebration was being held at a local hall attached to a handy bar. Many of Steve's friends were musicians, so a steady stream of pianists, bassists, percussionists, and horn players migrated in and out, grouping randomly into ensembles of three, four, or more, and playing short sets of jazz in one corner. Logan and Randy grabbed a drink and listened for a while, Logan pointing out the people that he knew, and Randy making mental notes.

'There were an awful lot of single women at the funeral, and now here,' Randy commented.

Logan shrugged. 'That was Steve. Always out there hustling. Never getting terribly close to anyone. Hey, the piano's vacant for the moment. Mind if I go and play a short set?'

'No, I'll just have another drink and take in the eye candy.'

'Easy there, big fella. Don't forget you're engaged!' Logan said, with a smile.

'Hey, looking is part of my job.'

Logan shook his head and moved off, and Randy resumed looking. It was fairly easy to get a general read of the group. The musicians, of course, were liable to be regular users of recreational drugs, but only a few of the men resembled the meth-head assassin. One or two had the appearance of well-to-do businessmen, in a garish, over-the-top sort of way. Low-level dealers, Randy guessed, and hardly worth pursuing, in his judgment. However, he would add his notes to those of the rather conspicuous undercover officer now working the room. It was part of the deal Randy had negotiated with local law enforcement in order to get easy access to information regarding Steve, and he had picked up a bunch.

Finding the man or men behind Steve's killing was not his job. Confirming or eliminating the killer's possible involvement with a foreign agency was, and Randy was already satisfied as to that score. Attending this little soirée was his final obligation to the investigation, and he planned to brief Chuck tonight. And though he didn't think Chuck would care, Randy was fascinated by the women in the room. It wasn't just that their ages spanned decades or that they were all attractive. It was their behavior. After wandering over to the coffin, a few came away with vindictive smiles as though Steve had gotten his just deserts. A few looked thoughtful but unsurprised. These tended to gather and talk among themselves, laughing and friendly. Apparently they were women who had enjoyed Steve's company as he had enjoyed theirs, with no resentment or jealousy at his short-lived fidelity. A few others eyed each other suspiciously, as though still competing for the man who would no longer charm them with his witty talk or seductive music. One or two of these came away from his coffin in tears. They went singly to the bar to take the edge off their obvious pain. Randy loosely grouped them as haters, users, and lovers. Of course, users had several meanings, and his grouping didn't distinguish.

When Logan finished his set, he spoke a few words to the musicians still gathered at the end of the hall, and came back to Randy at the bar.

'Well,' Logan said, with a crooked smile, 'I've gotten two offers from bassists who'd like to take Steve's place in the Fourth Harmonics.'

'No shit! Isn't that just a little macabre, especially with his corpse lying there?'

'Yeah, I suppose,' Logan replied. 'So, do you want to leave?'

Randy never hesitated. It had been a disturbing gathering on many levels.

***

'So, boss,' Randy began, when he called that evening, 'you wouldn't believe the women at the funeral and the wake, or whatever it was.'

'Yeah, I'm sure, Grasshopper. But I was wondering if you've had time to do your actual job. You know, finding out if our boy was the target of the Quds Force or some other Middle Eastern bad guys.'

Randy had known Chuck wouldn't give a rat's ass about Steve's harem. 'Yeah, I think we can definitely eliminate Middle Eastern bad guys.'

'Enlighten me.'

'Well, first of all, with Steve Eberly, it didn't take much digging to nail down his life story. He played jazz for fun. Didn't earn his daily bread there. He chased women and seemed to be pretty damn good at that. In fact, at that wake—'

'Randy …'

'Right, sorry, boss. Um, so he owned a sleazy dive bar, purchased using money from one of his ex-wives. I'm fairly certain it was part of the deal to get rid of him.'

'And that paid for his daily bread?'

'No, not completely.'

'Ah. Please continue.'

'In a nutshell, he got involved in drugs. Low level dealing. Mostly marijuana, bennies, a little blow. But he'd been getting in deeper. According to one of his bartenders, he'd been using his club as a distribution point, and recently as a place to launder money for dealers—bigger fish. Steve never could manage his finances, and he began cutting the drugs and skimming a little off the top and hiding it from his employers. That's the rumor. Local PD has two clients in mind who most likely discovered what Steve was up to. They suspect one or the other, or both together, put the squeeze on Steve and hired the druggy hitman when Steve couldn't pay up. As for the killer, his story is even less complicated. A couple of drug possession and B and E convictions. He'd do anything for anybody to support a habit that the autopsy doc said was on the verge of killing him. A couple rounds from Becky Amhurst's Smith & Wesson was probably a blessing for the guy.'

'Hmm,' Chuck said. Randy could hear the rasping as Chuck's hand ran over his evening stubble. 'How 'bout Steve's apartment?'

'Fits the profile. Some cash and drugs hidden in the usual places. Ductwork, toilet tanks, dead electrical sockets. Interesting item, the guy had a thing for that '80s scam artist, Barry Minkow. Dude even had a big ZZZZ Best carpet cleaning poster hanging in his living room. Must have admired Minkow's skill at running a massive Ponzi scheme.'

'Yeah, that really didn't work out for Minkow, you know. OK, Randy, I'm tired. Anything else?'

'The guy also had what looked like a lifetime supply of Viagra. Personal use only, I'm guessing. Oh, and he had a photo album that was nothing but pictures of women's feet. Pretty sexy stuff.'

'Randy!'

'Sorry. The nutshell summary is this. The guy was dealing drugs and cheating his suppliers. They found out, got pissed, and had him killed. Not even a whiff of foreign involvement. Not even a whiff that Steve wasn't the intended target.'

'Nice work, Grasshopper. Take the rest of the night off and dine at the finest fast food restaurant you can find. The company will pay.'

'Gee, thanks. And can I just say what a privilege and pleasure it is to work for a kind, reasonable, generous boss, and ... hello? Boss?' Randy smiled and pressed End Call on his cell.

***

Randy was still smiling when Gail walked into the room. 'Finished with your call?'

'Yes—' The words caught in his throat. Gail was wearing one of his old shirts and nothing else, her usual bedtime attire. 'Yes, indeed. Is it really that late?'

'Close enough,' she said. 'Besides, I'm cold.'

The obvious response 'Why don't you put more clothes on?' didn't occur to Randy. Instead he leapt from his chair. 'We can't have that, can we?'

When they were comfortably warm, Gail asked, 'So, I take it the call to Chuck went well?'

'Hmm? Oh, yeah.' He frowned. 'But that means my business in Tucson is done for a while. Guess I shouldn't have been so brilliant and efficient.'

'Guess not.'

'You know, that guy Steve is still a puzzle to me. Women hung on him, but he never stopped playing the field. And that includes the brief interludes when he was married.'

'Maybe he couldn't find the right woman.'

'Maybe. Or maybe he really didn't want one, so he never looked in the right places. Would you still love me if I had women hanging all over me?'

'Of course,' Gail replied. 'But I'm assuming you mean old, grey grammies and dowagers.'

'Exactly what I mean,' he said, pulling her close.

***

Chuck's evening was less warm and cuddly than his young sidekick's. After hanging up with Randy, he dialed an exchange associated with United Insurance Group. With little trouble, he was connected with Jason Stone.

'How's it in Breckenridge, Stone?'

'Nice. Some early powder. Might even get in a run or two. What's the latest word from your partner—you know, the one who wants to kill me?'

'Now I told you he's gotten over that ... mostly. And don't be promoting him. He's my sidekick. At least, until I retire. Then he's me.'

'Kid must be good.'

'Better than I was at his age, but if you tell him I said that I'll drop you like yesterday's garbage.'

He could hear Stone laughing. 'All right, Chuck. But what's the word?'

'Simple. The shooting had nothing to do with Elaya or her "friends," which means Cathie is still flying under the radar.'

'Or, Elaya's "friends," as you call them, are flying lower. This whole thing stinks, and you know it. You've got her walking backwards into a buzz saw and you're telling her not to get cut. Having second thoughts?'

A long silence ensued. What Chuck wanted to say, what his logical mind was shouting, was 'Hell yes!' When he spoke, however, the words were, 'No. Not yet. The risk is manageable.'

'Bullshit. OK, you said what you had to say as a stone-cold agent man. You and I know better.'

'Fine. The risk is more manageable with you directly involved.'

'Humph. Whatever.'

'I'd like to meet you in Colorado, say, day after tomorrow. OK?'

'Yeah. That will give us a day to do a little house hunting without you nervously waiting in the wings.'

'So you're gonna do it, huh? What are you looking for? Nice little secluded cabin?'

'It might suit me, though I'm kind of enjoying some luxury in my declining years.'

'Shit, Stone, if you're in your declining years then I'm already dead. And *do not* reply to that.'

'Anyway, Luana's got us checking out very nice places, all in the seven-figure range.'

'Holy crap, buddy, that's in the upper stratosphere.'

'Well, don't forget, Luana has a good job—a real job. She's put a few bucks away and … we had a bit of a windfall.'

'Some guys have all the luck.'

'No. Not really,' Stone replied grimly, thinking back to the bloody path that had led him to this place.

'Right. Sorry. But you know you don't want to go too high profile, right? Draws a bit of attention.'

'Think about it, Chuck. If the CEO of Infinity Services Group and her consort were to buy a fixer for $130K it would draw far more attention.'

'I suppose you're right,' he conceded.

'If it'll make you feel any better, I'm going to be looking for features of the property that will be more appreciated by you and me.'

'Like what?'

'Let's just say that our pet German shepherd won't be the only security we'll have.'

***

Stone and Luana spent the two days before Chuck's arrival visiting properties. Both agreed that their house should be on a large, private lot, be comfortably spacious, have good views, and be reasonably close to skiing. Luana was also interested in the layout for entertaining. She wanted to host clients and staff, perhaps as many as fifty or sixty at a time, without feeling cramped. Stone was considerably more interested in how security could be managed. After seeing half a dozen homes, they compared notes. Neither was particularly astonished that the same property topped both of their lists: a beautiful two-story home of stone and massive timbers. A huge redwood deck projected out over the sloping ground from the south side of the house. Tables and cushioned chairs clustered around a fire pit, a built-in barbecue, and bar. The living room was an impressive, vaulted affair of large windows and glass doors that opened out onto the deck. A stone fireplace with dark wood framing and mantel dominated one wall while a sunken bar area faced it from across the room. Seated at the bar, they could enjoy the fireplace and the spectacular views beyond the patio. The house sat on a small hilltop, with sloping woods of pine and cedar on all sides—the most desirable feature of the property as far as Stone was concerned. To the east and west, taller ranges of mountains created a stark, jagged horizon, the early snows powdering the upper slopes. Snowy patches surrounded the house as well and blanketed the ground around the trees.

Because the house was relatively new, bathrooms were plentiful and bedrooms large. The vast kitchen was designed for entertaining (assuming a semi-permanent or temporary staff of no more than six). The master bedroom was a self-contained suite, with fireplace, walk-in closet, huge his & hers bathroom and even a minibar. A game room located on the lower level of the house held a pool table, dart board, mini-shuffleboard, a small wet bar, and, off to one side, a cinema room that would seat a dozen in leather-bound luxury.

'Great,' said Stone. 'Done and done.'

'Don't you even want to see any of the other properties the realtor mentioned?' Luana asked.

'Do you? Really?'

'No, darling. This one is lovely. I just wanted to be sure you felt the same.'

'Oh, it's not perfect,' Stone said. 'There are a few unhealthy trees and way too much undergrowth for my taste in the area to the north.'

'And your taste would be most concerned with ...?'

'A clear line of sight, of course,' he said.

'Ah. And do you think it likely a clear line of sight will be required?'

Stone shrugged. 'Better safe. It really will improve the health of those woods if I clear some brush. I'm thinking of putting up woodpecker houses, you know, for woodpeckers.'

'Woodpeckers? You never cease to amaze, love. Tell me, are woodpecker habitats worth'—she glanced at the listing—'$3.7 million?'

'I'd go 3.8 or even 3.9 for good woodpecker lodgings.'

'Very well,' she said, with a wry smile. 'You won't mind if I negotiate the price a bit—just for form's sake.'

'Not at all. But I hope you won't mind if I skip that part. Tell you what, the place being empty and all, Chuck and I may just come by here later this evening.'

'Darling, we don't actually own the house yet.'

'Well, then, damn the woodpeckers. Anyway, we'll just be on the patio.'

'A bit chilly. You do remember I need to fly to LA this evening? Unavoidable, I'm afraid.'

'I do,' said Stone, his face clouding, 'and I wish you weren't. Be careful.'

'I will. Best be off. I still need to run by the realtor's office and purchase your wildlife refuge before I head for the airport.'

***

Later that evening, having gotten grudging, unofficial permission from the otherwise delighted realtor, Chuck and Stone sat on the back patio, huddled as near as they could to the roaring fire pit without melting the soles of their shoes, drinking twenty-year-old single malt scotch and smoking Cuban cigars. A sliver of moon was drifting west across a cloudless, deep-blue sky, causing the mountains to the south to glitter as though a handful of diamonds had been carelessly tossed onto them by a spendthrift god.

'OK,' said Chuck, 'this don't suck too bad.'

Stone smiled and took a slow pull from his Cuban. 'It'll do. Though I don't suppose I'll be here all that often.'

'Kind of nice to come home to, though.'

The two sat in silence, Stone tossing another log onto the glowing embers.

'I've got a few notions of my own on how to proceed,' Stone said, 'but I'd like to hear your thoughts.'

'Buddy, I'd trust your instincts anywhere, but for what it's worth, here's what I've got.' Chuck paused, putting his thoughts into a logical order. 'Since the apparent assassination attempt on Cathie turned out to be no more than a bizarre, coincidental drug dealer's hit, Cathie will be traveling to London soon to meet Conrad Smythe-Montgomery. As I'm sure you already know, he's in league with some of Elaya Andoori's most unprincipled and determined adversaries. So, step one would be to contact Elaya Andoori to let her know some of the details of our arrangement, then proceed to London to keep more than half an eye on Cathie. At the same time, do a little sleuthing into Smythe-Montgomery's activities and associates.'

'Makes sense,' said Stone, 'and it jibes with what I had in mind, though I think another personal chat with Elaya would be better.'

'"Elaya!" Wow! First name basis.'

Stone gave a noncommittal shrug. 'Well, that's her name. Anyway, I know she has a state visit planned to Kuwait. I have a few contacts there. Might be a good place for a second meet.'

Chuck grunted his agreement.

'A visit to London works out well, too,' Stone continued. 'Luana and I have a friend with resources who's very interested in Smythe-Montgomery.'

'What kind of resources?'

'Money and some interesting intel channels. He also has … let's just say some serious history with the man.'

'Friend or foe?'

'Well, if Conrad were to suddenly catch fire, this man wouldn't piss on him to put it out.'

'I think I'll call that a foe. Ready for another?' Chuck added, pointing to Stone's empty glass.

'Sure. We're far from done with this discussion.'

Chuck refilled both glasses, took a drink, and sighed. 'I bought this bottle out of my own pocket, you know? Company per diem wouldn't give me this much money for a hotel room. For a week!'

'Hey, you knew the job was dangerous when you took it!' Stone said, with a grin. 'What other brilliant strategies do you have in mind?'

'We're farming in some pretty played out soil. Information is what we need. You'll have direct access to Andoori and she has her own resources. Cathie Fletcher is only one of mine in London. The other you may not know. Her name is Becky Amhurst.'

'President of ARC Avionics, a recently resurrected company bidding on a job for Pacific-Indo-Asia Airlines, if I'm not mistaken.'

'Shit, Stone, you've done your homework.'

'Yeah, and I also know'—he hesitated and reconsidered his wording—'I don't *know*, but it *smells* like a Company connection. Which means you intend her to win. Which means you're putting her in line for the chopping block just like Cathie Fletcher.'

Chuck sat quietly, swirling the ice in his drink. 'I'd love to know how the fuck you know that.'

'Not important. What is, is that if I can figure it out, you can bet Smythe-Montgomery will—eventually.'

'If that happens—'

'*When* it happens. Don't bullshit me on this, Chuck. You need at least *two* very good plans to extract Becky fast when the time comes.'

'Well, fuck. I've got Randy O'Neil working that, but I figure he'll need your help.'

'You want him to work with me?'

'"Want" has nothing to do with it, brudda. But I believe I've heard that necessity is one mother.'

'That's not exactly how it goes, but close enough. Fine. I presume I get in touch with him the same way I reach you.'

'Yeah. Just give me a day or two to, you know, prepare him for it.'

Stone chuckled and took another long pull on his Cuban, exhaling a thin stream of fragrant blue smoke. 'My new co-conspirator, the guy who wants to kill me. That's super. And beyond that?'

'That's as far as this old man can figure. We need intel before we can move. I get satellite time on Smythe-Montgomery whenever I can, which ain't often enough. But that reminds me. He had a meeting on his yacht—what the hell does he call it? *Big Fuckin' Yacht*, or something.'

'*Empire*, Chuck. C'mon, man.'

'Oh, I'm just trying to add a little humor, Stone. I know the name of the fuckin' thing. Anyway, he had a meeting with some very unsavory types, big dogs in the previous Iranian administration. Their entertainment was a trio of Bolshevik beauties. No official papers. Just invisible people. That is, until one was found washed up on a French beach a few days later.'

'Were you able to get anything from the body?'

'Not much. Other than that she was pretty badly used before she went in the sea.'

'No direct evidence against Smythe-Montgomery, I suppose?'

'Got that right. There was some very official paperwork indicating that all three had passed through Greece on the way back to Mother Russia. All bullshit, of course. My point is, this guy will stop at nothing.'

'But why kill them—and I'm assuming you believe the other two met the same fate—if they were just the entertainment? And what the hell was that meeting all about?'

'Got Randy working that too.'

'He seems to get all the easy assignments. I suppose that leaves you with all the hard ones?'

'Just the ones that require me to shell out for expensive scotch and cigars, and stay out past my bedtime. I think we're on the same page. What're your plans?'

'Stay here for a week or two. We're going to rent the place until escrow closes. That'll give me time to do a little maintenance and start putting up woodpecker houses.'

Chuck sat motionless, his mouth hanging open. 'Woodpeckers? Holy shit, Stone, there's more to you than I'll ever understand.'

Stone smiled a lopsided smile. 'Don't be so sure. Well, I guess I'll just let myself in the house and spend the night. Might as well start getting used to the place.'

'Just one last thing,' Chuck said. 'Luana Chu. You love her, don't you?'

Stone stared straight into Chuck's eyes, wondering what the man was getting at. 'Yes,' he said at last.

'I know I'm dragging you into this, so I shouldn't be saying this, but things could get very bad, very bloody. She *will* be in danger. Can you deal with that?'

'Whoever threatens Luana will not live to regret it. Nor will I hesitate to deal out preemptive justice. There'll be plenty of blood, just not ours.'

Chuck nodded and rose to leave, but he turned back to Stone. 'James, be careful. I would be sorry if anything …'

'Same here, Johnson.'

Stone stuck out his hand and Chuck took it in a firm grip.

The Reality of Chaos

'I'll tell Richard you're here and put on a fresh pot of tea. It's just the two of us this morning.'

Chapter Thirteen

Mother

'Well, hello, Ms. Foster.' Yvette stood looking in surprise at the woman in the wheelchair. 'Forgive me, I ... well, Richard didn't tell me you were visiting today.'

'Good morning, Yvette. Oh, it's an impromptu visit. He called the other day and mentioned you'd received some unique visitors. Mentioned I could stop by at any time for a chat. Of course, I should never have taken him seriously, but here I am.'

'Forgive me,' Yvette repeated, 'it seems my manners are also absent. Won't you please come in?'

'Yes, thank you. It's a fairly typical London day. Which is to say, it's bloody cold and damp out here.'

The corners of Yvette's mouth curled upward and she stifled a laugh at the coarse, colloquial language coming from this rather formal, imposing woman. It was part of Diana's charm. She was trying to put Yvette at her ease.

After helping Diana remove her scarf and heavy coat, Yvette said, 'Excuse me for just a moment. I'll tell Richard you're here and put on a fresh pot of tea. It's just the two of us this morning. Reviewing data from his latest model upgrades.'

Diana glanced at the young woman and held her gaze for a long while. 'You two are thick as thieves when it comes to Richard's predictive modeling, aren't you? That's good.'

Yvette gave her a bashful smile but said nothing. As she left the room, Diana thought, *You've found a gem, haven't you, Richard.*

A few minutes later Yvette returned with a tea tray. 'Richard will be along shortly.' She paused, wondering about the appropriateness of her next words. 'He insists on being presentable these days. It's quite a change, but a good one, don't you think?'

'I do,' Diana replied. 'Will you keep me company while we wait?'

For the next few minutes, Diana listened as Yvette—hesitantly at first, but then more confidently—explained the latest additions to Crandall's predictive chaos models. Scenarios flew across the monitors. Clydes emerged—green, red, yellow—and were highlighted, interrogated, and dismissed in rapid order. Yvette grew more animated and excited seeing the interest and respect in the older woman's eyes, until a sudden pained look invaded Diana's features. Yvette stumbled to a halt. 'I ... I'm sorry, Ms. Foster. Have I said something wrong?'

'What? Oh, no, not at all. And please call me Diana. It's just ...' She pointed to the screen. 'I'm afraid I don't react well when I see this name. Conrad Smythe-Montgomery. I'm afraid it brings back unpleasant memories. The most unpleasant of my life.'

Without thinking, Yvette glanced to Diana's shortened legs. She realized her own indiscretion in an instant, quickly shifted her gaze back to Diana's face, and flushed ruby red.

'I'm so very sorry Ms. ... Diana. I just ...' She hung her head and her lower lip began to tremble.

Diana wheeled her chair closer to Yvette and put a kind hand on her shoulder. 'It's all right. Your conclusion was logical and correct. You needn't feel ashamed.' Diana kept her hand on Yvette's shoulder, squeezing gently, until the young woman regained some of her composure. After what seemed a long time, Diana said, 'I don't suppose Richard ever told you about my unfortunate accident?'

Yvette shook her head, not yet trusting herself to speak.

'No, of course not. He's the soul of discretion. We were schoolmates, you know,' Diana began, wheeling her chair back and pouring herself another cup of tea. 'We stayed in touch even after his welcome break with his family. My own circumstances were ... peculiar as well, but not really relevant. The point was, we trusted each other and could confide thoughts and feelings that we didn't dare share with anyone else. He was ... is ... a very dear friend.

'I was going to university and attending the usual boring social gatherings required of failing aristocracy when I first met Smythe-Montgomery's father: a vulgar, boorish man with delusions of grandeur. He was frightfully wealthy—the only avenue by which he could have entered society. Not to be tedious, but he paid court to me in an obnoxious, mean-spirited way. My parents disapproved but seemed incapable of fending him off. I certainly gave him no encouragement. It was at one of the grander gatherings where his perpetual pawing and lewd suggestions finally became too much to bear. I slapped him publicly and also loudly berated him for his disgusting behavior and for his ... questionable parentage. I also said some rather horrible and truthful things about his family's acquisition of wealth—traitors and pirates to a man—and might have commented on how the apple had not fallen far from the tree. It was quite a scene. He was furious and swore he would make me pay for the insult to his person and his family. But then, nothing.

'For the next several months I would occasionally see him, but he never approached me. In fact, he was already deeply involved with a young, beautiful, wealthy peasant. Another family of dubiously acquired wealth and no social graces. A perfect match. And there was already talk of a merger—that is, marriage. But then I received a series of notes. Ghastly, threatening letters. Impossible to trace, but I was frightened. I asked to meet with Richard in an unlikely setting. An old railroad yard. A place we both knew, where we'd met privately before. I didn't realize my letters were being intercepted and my phone lines tapped. I arrived early—probably a blessing for Richard—but several other men were there. Men I didn't know. Men in disguise. They ... made use of the switching engine, then left. Richard arrived shortly after. I doubt those men intended for me to live, but years later I saw Smythe-Montgomery, and the rapture on his face when he saw me like this showed that he couldn't have wished for a more delightful outcome. Conrad, his son, was four at the time.'

Yvette sat aghast. Her shock from hearing this horrific story combined with her surprise that Diana would be willing to share it—with her!—had driven coherent thought from her mind.

'And unless you should think of this as a case of "sins of the father,"' a soft voice said, 'don't be fooled. The son is as ruthless and brutal as his father ever was, and there is far more to this story. But that's for another time.'

Yvette turned to see Crandall standing in the doorway, impeccably groomed and dressed. A tear trickling down his cheek somewhat spoiled the impression of stoic British aplomb. But he wiped it away with a sparkling white handkerchief and smiled at his young friend. 'Best to say nothing more on this subject for now, Yvette. However, you should stay and chat with us, if you're willing. It would appear that Diana has invited another conspirator into our forlorn group.'

'Forlorn?' Diana asked.

'Well,' said Crandall thoughtfully, 'we are still miserably wretched at times, but perhaps no longer entirely hopeless.'

***

Luana returned from LA—a whirlwind visit of meetings and air travel—two days after Chuck's conversation with Stone. With a temporary rental agreement arranged until the close of escrow, she had begun buying a few crucial items for her new home. A bed and a few basic necessities had already arrived. And though the place was still cavernously empty, it had a tiny feeling of becoming a home. A roaring fire in the fireplace that evening enhanced the feeling, with Luana and Stone drinking wine as they watched a gentle fall of snow. True, they were sitting on folding lawn chairs that Stone had found in one of the outbuildings, but more furniture was scheduled for arrival the next day, and there was a certain air of fun associated with the circumstances. It was a bit like camping out in a mansion.

Stone poured the last of the Cab into Luana's glass and looked sadly at the bottle. 'Must be a combination of altitude and low humidity. This is one of the worst cases of evaporation I've ever seen.'

'Don't despair, darling,' Luana said with a smile. 'There's more in the kitchen.'

'A technical genius, a leader of corporations, a heavenly lover, and a provider extraordinaire! What more could a man ask?'

'Well, *this* man had better not ask for much more. As for "heavenly lover," we do have a large, brand-new bed waiting for us upstairs. I'll ply you with more alcohol first, and then …'

Stone laughed and headed for the kitchen. As he was uncorking the bottle, he heard Luana's cell phone ring. His brow creased and his smile diminished. This was a very untimely interruption. Few people had

Luana's private phone number. As he walked back into the family room, the remainder of his smile vanished entirely. Luana was sitting upright in her chair, tense, her eyes narrowed and staring straight ahead.

'Yes. Yes, I understand,' she said crisply. 'I will most certainly be there. Yes, you may tell my father.' There was a long pause, and Stone could see anger welling up in Luana's expression. 'I am not asking permission! I *will* be there. He may like it or he may ...' Luana struggled to refrain from saying the words that were fighting to escape her. She succeeded, and her final words were as cold as frost. 'He may like it or not. That is his concern. I do not come there for him.' She ended the call and tossed the phone into her purse.

Stone said nothing, waiting. At last, the rigidity left her body. As she turned to him, her anger seemed to melt away. What replaced it was deep sadness. Luana fought to control her emotions, and finally whispered, 'My mother has died. There is to be a ceremony—a traditional Hawaiian ceremony—the day after tomorrow. I must go.'

Stone nodded but continued to watch her intently. He could easily see her grief, but there was something more—far more. It was a look he had seen on the faces of his comrades during battle, particularly after a man had been injured or killed. An expression unrelated to the noble emotion of grief. It was cold fury. Luana was attempting to control it, to bury it deep. But the set of her jaw and her clenched fists showed that she was failing.

'Darling,' Stone began carefully, 'I'm so sorry. You've spoken of your mother. I know how much you loved and admired her. I know it must hurt. But ... is there something more?'

Luana's eyes flashed, but her anger quickly faded and a faint smile painted her face. 'I'd be a fool to ever try to hide something of importance from you, wouldn't I?'

'Yes, you would. Was it something your father said to you?'

Luana's eyes blazed again for an instant. 'No,' she said, the coldness in her voice a harsh counterpoint to the fire in her eyes. 'I was not speaking to my father. He assigned a servant, a lackey, to deliver this news, knowing it would hurt me further.'

'Your father didn't call? Holy ... I mean, that would piss me off, too.'

'That's only a small part. You see, my mother died a week ago.'

'What!'

Luana took a deep breath. 'I mentioned a traditional Hawaiian ceremony?'

Stone nodded.

'There's a custom that after death a period of time must pass before burial. For those of high status—and mother was a descendent of royalty—that period is long. As long as ten days. My father, through his man, felt it unnecessary for me to be present before the burial ceremony. He denied me the right to visit and mourn. He discouraged me from coming at all. But I will go!'

Stone didn't hesitate. He went to her and took her hands as she rose from her chair. 'OK. And I'm going with you.'

***

The following day, Luana made one brief attempt to dissuade Stone from accompanying her. 'Really, darling, it isn't necessary. You could stay here and continue your work on woodpecker houses.'

'Hmph, the woodpeckers can wait. Besides, I'm feeling a distinctly uncomfortable vibe from you.'

'Are you?' she asked, one corner of her mouth quirking up slightly.

'I am. So what gives?'

Rather than answer his question, she turned to look out the window of the master suite. 'You know, I really had wanted you to meet my mother. She has—had—a certain aristocratic charm. The time never seemed right. And now … it's too late.' She sighed. 'Make me some breakfast, would you, love?'

Twenty minutes later, they were feasting on gourmet scrambled eggs and toast—the limits of their breakfast supplies. Fortunately, there was plenty of coffee, and as Stone poured both a second cup, Luana continued her comments as though no time had passed.

'My father is quite another matter.'

'So you've said.'

'Yes, but he would have been quite another matter even before I failed in my filial duty to him. When I first argued that we shouldn't attempt the hack on Alpha Defense he was—how shall I put it?—livid.'

Stone nodded. He had been heavily involved in the plot to break into the Alpha Defense servers—a plot never executed. It was during the early stages of the operation that he had met Luana Chu. *It's a fucked-up world*, he thought. *But sometimes things work out.*

Luana looked at him closely, as though reading some of his inner thoughts, then continued. 'My father reminded me of the appropriate father-daughter relationship, as he sees it, and simply ordered me to proceed. Of course, we didn't.'

'It was a setup. You knew it. You were right.' Stone smiled. 'My old acquaintance and his pal Logan Fletcher had put together a pretty sweet sting.'

'Father does not believe it was a trap. He feels that I failed him. Worse, that I betrayed him.'

'He needs to get the hell over it.'

'Yes. And perhaps in time he would. But now there is no time.'

'He has some knowledge of the role I played? Destroying Alpha's primary servers to force them to use their backups?'

'Yes. And he approves. As to your association with me, he does not. I'm sure he connects you with my decision to abort our operation. It might be best if you didn't come. After all, it's only for the funeral.'

'Whose?' Stone mumbled to himself. But he shook off his grim musings and smiled. 'I'm coming. I could use a little time off in a tropical paradise. Maui, right?'

'Maui. And a *very* traditional Hawaiian funeral. If you insist, I'll have to instruct you on protocol. You wouldn't want to embarrass me, would you?'

'I'll be a good boy.'

This comment brought a genuine smile to Luana's lips, the first since the news of her mother's death. 'Now that I doubt.'

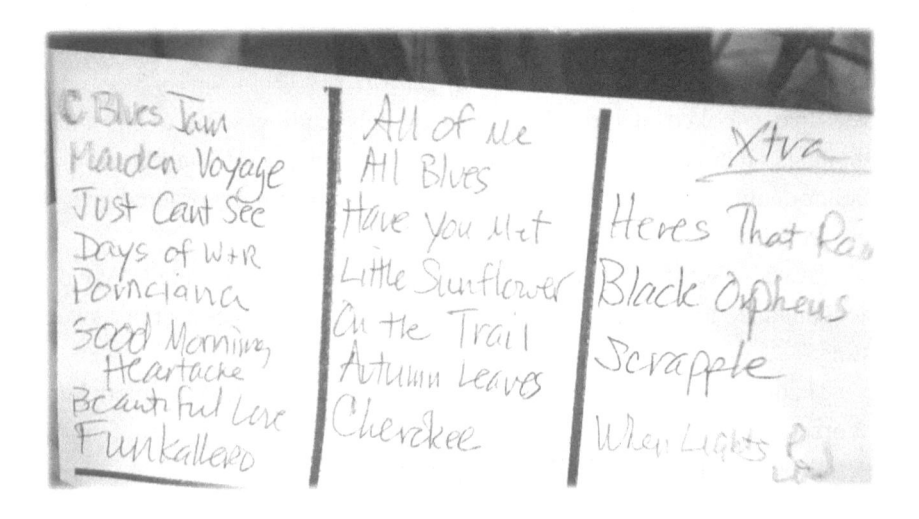

As they arrived, Gina was setting up at one end of the patio. They exchanged greetings and she showed them the playlist for the two sets, pointing out some of Logan's favorites.

Chapter Fourteen

Strange Proposal

'You know, I had forgotten what a dump this place is,' Logan said, as Gary Walkin ushered him down the narrow corridor to his office.

'It's a proposal facility. It's supposed to be cramped, drafty, and dirty. I swear I saw a cockroach near the coffeemaker.'

'Now that's just gross!' Logan replied.

'I could be wrong. It might have been a centipede.'

'Where's Becky, anyway?'

'Oh, she'll be along. I think she was here a little late last night.'

'How late is a little late?'

'Well, the numbers on the digital clock were little, anyway. Single digit for the hour if you know what I mean.'

Logan knew.

'Hey, isn't this your office?' Logan asked, as Gary kept walking down the hall.

'Sure is, but I need a little pick-me-up to get started.' He turned the corner and stopped in front of a coffee station. It was filthy. Grounds, creamer, and sugar were spilled liberally around the two-burner coffeemaker, a half empty bag of chocolate chip cookies and a donut box were shoved to one side, and the two coffee pots looked as though they hadn't been cleaned since—ever. Gary poured coffee into a cup with a Metallica logo on the outside and a thick brown line of grime like a high tide mark on the inside. He grinned and held the pot out to Logan. 'Want some?' Logan grimaced and walked away.

They returned to Gary's office and settled in. Gary shoved papers around to clear a small working space on his desk.

'All right,' Logan said, 'you've succeeded in grossing me out big time. Thanks. But now, do you have anything interesting to show me, or has this been a complete waste of my time?'

'Old and cranky, Fletch. Fine, have it your way,' Gary said, slurping noisily from his coffee cup. He dug through a stack of papers and pulled one out with a grunt of success. 'Current commercial aircraft communicate in a couple different ways: transponder, radio, and ACARS, primarily.'

'Are you planning to start speaking English any time soon, or do I need to get a translator?'

Gary mumbled something that sounded like 'Even the local cockroaches are smarter than you.' He heaved a sigh and smiled at Logan indulgently. 'Sorry. Forgot that you were never really an avionics stud. Let me see. Standard Coms Gear 101. Transponders. There are some standard modes for military and civilian aviation. Mode C, for instance, provides altitude information for civilian aircraft. It can be turned off in the cockpit.'

'Why would someone do that?'

'Umm, I guess if the pilot didn't want other people to know his altitude.'

'Yeah, right,' Logan said. 'Why the fuck didn't I think of that?'

'To be honest, I'm not sure, OK? I'll look into it. Now, there are different types of systems that ask the aircraft for information. They send out an interrogation signal—a couple of electronic pulses with the appropriate spacing—and the transponder on the airplane sends that information back.'

'Like altitude.'

'Exactly. There're a number of modes for civilian aircraft, but a key one is Mode A. It's just a 4-digit code. It's assigned by the air traffic controller, but entered in the cockpit.'

'Seems a bit archaic.'

'Maybe, but it's important. If the aircraft gets pinged in Mode A, it responds with that code, so the person pinging knows what flight is out there. Got it?'

'Yeah, basic ID: "Who are you?" "I'm Delta flight so-and-so." I suppose knowing the code you'd also know the aircraft type, or you could figure it out pretty quick.'

'Were you just sandbaggin' me earlier? You *do* know this shit.'

'I used to be a highly paid aerospace engineer. I have the capacity to learn.'

'So does the roach,' Gary mumbled.

'Look, just give me the top level stuff and then get to what's bothering you. I'll ask questions when I get lost, OK?'

'You've got it, Einstein. So, we talked transponders. Keep Mode A in mind, and also keep in mind that military aircraft have additional modes.'

'Got it.'

'ACARS is pretty straightforward. It stands for Aircraft Communications Addressing and Reporting System. It's a digital datalink for transmitting between the aircraft and ground systems. Reporting the start of major flight events is an important function. The aircraft systems are tied in with sensors on doors, parking brakes, struts, etc. Abnormal events are transmitted as well. It helps the airlines monitor equipment for repair and maintenance.'

'OK. Got that. Anything special to keep an eye on with this one?'

'Yeah. Usually ACARS equipment functions automatically, *but* flight crews can use it to send and receive messages like a request for weather information. Airlines generally customize ACARS for their own needs.'

'Huh. Didn't know that. Wasn't ACARS used in some way when Malaysia Airlines Flight 370 disappeared?'

'Right again. First, the primary system was shut off—a very suspicious action to begin with—but a secondary system kept working and trying to talk to a satellite. Doppler on the signal was used to establish the rough location of the plane.'

'Yeah, I remember now. That's a tough way to establish position. What else should I keep in mind?'

'The fact that the older, secondary system couldn't be shut off. That's important.'

'OK.'

'Lastly, there's standard voice communication between the aircraft and the ground.'

'My recollection is that pilots and ground controllers can manually select frequencies, right?

'Right, and that's the part you need to remember about voice coms.'

'Not bad, Gary. Not bad at all!' said a female voice.

Both Gary and Logan spun around to see Becky leaning against the doorframe, grinning. 'Logan, you were lucky to have a guy like Gary working for you.'

'You too. And now you have him again!'

'Hey, this is too weird,' said Gary. 'Are you guys actually saying nice things about me?'

'I didn't hear anything, did you?' Becky asked Logan.

'Not a word. Probably just your imagination, Gary.'

'Yeah, well, I expect to get paid, anyway.'

'Don't be silly, Gary, you're doing this for king and country!' Becky said, with a laugh.

'OK, break's over,' Logan said. 'Gary, before I forget all the things you told me to remember, don't you think you'd better tell me how they impact the RFP?'

'I'd like to hear that again, too,' Becky said. 'Make it coherent and I promise you'll get paid—something.'

'Worth a shot,' said Gary, searching in his stack of papers once again. He finally fished out a copy of the draft RFP with a handwritten cover sheet stapled to the top.

'I'm assuming you're taking into account that Pacific-Indo-Asia Airlines—or any airline needing to modernize their fleet—would want the latest tech with a few new bells and whistles,' Logan said.

'Yepper. I've even made allowances for the head honcho being a billionaire eccentric looking to wow the industry.'

'Well, OK then. Please carry on.'

Gary became serious as he flipped through the RFP, stopping at the first Post-it he had used to mark a page. 'Let's do the easiest and least controversial first: voice coms. Certainly there are bells and whistles that they want added, but there are two areas that are suspicious. The first, a requirement for higher power than is standard in the business.'

'Sounds pretty innocuous,' Becky said. 'Why *not* ask for a bit more range and clearer communication?'

'Agreed,' Gary replied. 'By itself, it's a whole lot of nothing. The second is more unusual. The ability to use encryption on the voice links.'

'What's the stated purpose?' Logan asked.

'For secure confidential plane-to-plane communications. Company proprietary information exclusive to Pacific-Indo-Asia's pilots.'

'I've heard talk of that in the industry,' Becky said. 'It isn't common now, but more than one airline is considering it.'

'I agree again—mostly,' Gary said. 'The level of encryption is significant. Let's just say that the NSA would take a while to crack this one.'

'That's not so different from a few smart phones,' Logan said, though he sounded unconvinced.

'Such a high level of encryption for this application raises a red flag,' Gary replied.

Logan nodded. 'So that was the easy one. How about ACARS?'

'Ah, now we get more interesting. The ACARS gear would be state of the art, of course. And it would perform its usual duties of transmitting aircraft information and status. However, unlike the Malaysia Air equipment, it would be entirely controlled from the cockpit.'

'Meaning the pilot could turn it off—completely?' Becky asked.

'Yeah.'

'Hmm. Now that's a departure from standard practice. Most airlines are going the other way, making it so the pilot *can't* turn the system off manually.'

'Right,' said Gary. 'But as they say on TV infomercials, that's not all. There's a requirement that would allow minor adjustments to transmit frequency—very minor, very precise.'

'That would take an oscillator and a phase-locked loop,' Logan said.

'Correct. That is, if we were trying to build it, say, a hundred years ago. About the time you were working and the missiles were steam powered. Jeez. Now all it would take would be a small frequency synthesizer chip controlled by an algorithm. But they don't want us to supply the algorithm, just the interface. The algorithm is *not* to be provided by us. Get it?'

Logan and Becky sat puzzling over this. 'Think in terms of Malaysia Airlines Flight 370,' Gary added.

Both realized the implications at the same time.

'They used the Doppler of the ACARS signal to locate the path of Malaysia Flight 370—' Logan began.

'So this chip and algorithm would allow the aircraft to essentially create a false Doppler—' Becky said.

'And create a false track on the aircraft—' Logan added.

'So the world thinks you're in one place when you're actually in another,' Becky finished.

'You two sound like an old married couple,' Gary said, glancing from one to the other. 'Finishing each other's sentences.'

Logan blushed and Becky gave him a sly wink. Gary seemed not to notice, but pressed on. 'That's at least a possibility. Instead of shutting the ACARS off, the pilot just inputs a phony flight path. You let that go on for a while and *then* shut the system off. Voila! And anybody searching for you now is searching in the wrong place! Kind of clever.'

'Still,' Becky reluctantly pointed out, 'it could be they want it for some other purpose.' Neither Logan nor Gary said anything, and Becky finally said, 'Yeah, I don't believe it either.'

'So, Gary, if you've been taking these items in reverse order of suspiciousness, then I presume you've saved the best for last.'

'Yep. The transponder. Here's where things get really murky. The specs call for so much flexibility and programmability—presumably for evolving standards and capability in the future—that it's hard to see what they might have been getting at. But you can certainly imagine wanting to change your 4-digit code. I mean, if you could hide your location you might also want to claim you were someone else. But there's one other aspect that's a little spooky. The guys and I had to dig a little deeper for this one. It looks like, with the appropriate algorithms, this thing could mimic military aircraft modes.'

'What? Why?' Logan asked.

'That's a puzzler. I asked Becky and she agreed that we need to get in a team of operations analysts to evaluate the entire suite to see what might be possible. In particular, I was hoping we could borrow some of Kevin's time. And I have a list of a couple of other guys that we could really use.'

Logan turned to Becky. 'Sounds reasonable,' he said. 'Have you talked to Chuck?'

'I have, and he's greased the skids to pull in this team. But even then …'

'What?'

'Well, even if we can figure out what all this shit is able to do, we still don't know why. What's the bigger picture? What's really going on?'

Logan considered this, exchanging a glance with Becky. 'That intel might have to come from somewhere else. In the meantime, let's get the team in to figure out the "how."'

Becky nodded. 'Gary, you'd better give the guys a call. You know who I mean. Your operations analysis buddies, former pilots, etc.'

'Can I call in Kevin Flahrety?' he asked, looking from Becky to Logan and back.

'Hey, it's OK with me,' said Logan, with a laugh. 'I don't work for Alpha Defense anymore.'

'Call him,' Becky ordered. 'Get him over here. I'll square it with Chuck Johnson and he can schmooze it with Alpha. And we might want to use Alpha's simulation facilities. If you think that would be useful have our contracts guy … what the hell is his name?'

'*Her* name is Colleen,' Gary replied.

'Oooh. First name basis. Anyway, get her to put together a subcontract letter for Alpha. I'll tell Chuck we're bringing in the big guns. As for you, Logan, we should continue our previous conversation. And you can buy me a drink.'

'Right,' said Gary. 'I get Kevin and a bunch of old ops guys in the basement of Building 44 at Alpha Defense. Logan gets the boss lady and alcohol. Hardly seems fair.'

'What have I told you about life, Gary?' Logan asked.

'Bite me, Fletch.'

***

'Exactly what conversation were you wanting to continue, Becky?' asked Logan, as he reached for his beer.

'Oh, I just wanted a drink,' she replied, with a laugh. She looked at Logan and didn't see the corresponding smile she'd hoped for. 'That and the bidders' conference. I guess some of what you said sunk in. I wanted to hear you tell me again how concerned you are for my safety.'

'Ah. That I can do. And given what Gary has dug up, it hasn't caused me to rethink my concern. Incidentally, I hope you and Gary have kept this under your hats. You will have some sort of cover story to tell the guys you're bringing in, won't you?'

'I'm not a complete dolt. Yes, Gary discovered the little quirks, and he's kept that between us. As for the other team, we'll be telling them something like "we're working another advanced avionics program for DARPA." They'll also be signing nondisclosure agreements. You're really concerned, aren't you?'

'I am. A little birdie, whose name I won't mention but whose initials are Chuck Johnson, told me about a Dr. Henry Deacons, now deceased.'

'Didn't he work for Pacific-Indo-Asia Air? Didn't he and his team write this RFP?'

'He did. And he died under the wheels of a London subway. Intoxicated, I've been told. But enough to fall under a train?'

'Christ! Do you suppose—'

'I don't *know* for sure. Neither does Chuck. We do know that his unfortunate accident occurred not long after a meeting with Smythe-Montgomery. Deacons was chief engineer for Pacific-Indo-Asia. If he had a whiff of something wrong about the specs for the RFP *and* he was foolish enough to bring it to the boss's attention ...'

'I'll be sure to tell Gary to keep the lid on. We're just happy to provide whatever capability Pacific-Indo-Asia Air wants. No questions asked.'

'Good plan,' Logan said, taking another pull from his mug.

'I'm ready for another,' said Becky, draining her glass. As she scanned the room for the waiter, Logan noticed her eyes stop briefly on several of the men in the bar area. He smiled.

'So, do women use a one-through-ten scale like guys, or some other rating system?'

'Oh, one through ten is so crude. There are more subtle distinctions. Take the guy at the end of the bar, for instance. He's about forty. Strong jaw. Intelligent eyes. But he just ordered a light beer! I mean, what the hell's the point? The guy at the other end is good-looking enough, and he's drinking straight bourbon. But he's all slouched over, staring into his glass. Under some circumstances, I might enjoy his sad story. Just not

The Reality of Chaos

today. And see the guy walking towards the table along the wall? Check out the clothes. It wouldn't surprise me if he played for the other team, if you know what I mean.'

'Holy shit! A female Sherlock Holmes! Hey, I'll tell you what. If you could pick one guy—if you *had* to pick one guy—you've got to tell me who it is when we leave.'

'Sounds like a crude, boorish men's game. OK.'

The waiter came by, picked up Becky's empty glass, and hustled away for a refill.

'Him?' Logan asked.

'What? Like robbing the cradle.'

Becky returned to a more serious topic. 'So if you're right, we can't rule out murder, with minimal provocation.'

Logan was surprised at this brutal statement, but nodded. 'It's the way Smythe-Montgomery has stayed untouchable for all these years.'

'Chuck still wants me to—how to say it politely—be pleasant to him, if he shows any inclination whatsoever. That part's easy. But I'm going to have to be extremely careful probing for information or sleuthing around.' She grinned suddenly. 'If I'm Holmes, do I get a pipe and a magnifying glass?'

'Sure, why not. I just wouldn't let Smythe-Montgomery see them.'

'Yes, that'll be the trick. And what about Chuck's friend? The scary one?'

'That's a piece of good news, anyway. He should be on duty and available to help.'

'So you say. Any other intel, Logan?'

Logan hesitated. He was planning to meet with Chuck and Cathie to discuss the trip to London and Cathie's meeting with Smythe-Montgomery. He wasn't sure how much of Chuck and Randy's double strategy to share with either Cathie or Becky. It seemed unfair to keep the two prime players in the dark regarding the activities of the other, but it might be dangerous for them to know. Logan's head hurt. He had gone into a career of engineering and program management for very good reason. His talents didn't lie in the area of spying—or keeping information from people he cared about, whatever the reason. As he sat in silence, he gained a much greater appreciation for Chuck's plight. Lies and dissimulation, year after year. Logan knew it would rip him apart, and he was beginning to wonder what was holding Chuck together. He finally forced what he hoped was a carefree smile to his lips. 'Well, Cathie and I may be in London roughly at the same time as you. What a coincidence, huh?'

'To keep an eye on me?' Becky asked. Logan's reaction quickly convinced her otherwise. 'No. Then what? Coincidence my ass, Logan. WTFO?'

Before Logan answered, he pointed to a man in a dark beard, seated next to a tall woman with long brown hair. 'What about him?'

Becky considered. 'I like the beard. He's having a serious drink. And the woman doesn't look like a bimbo. Yeah, he'd be on my short list.'

Logan signaled for the waiter. He returned Logan's glance and nodded, heading back to the bar. 'Actually, the timing is somewhat of a coincidence,' Logan said. 'You know, Cathie and I being in London. Actually, we're sort of meeting, uh, this person. It has to do with research for Cathie's next book. Actually …'

The waiter arrived and a full glass replaced Logan's empty.

'That was fortuitous, Logan. You were on your third "actually."'

'Yeah, no shit. It's just … OK, Cathie has an invite to meet with Smythe-Montgomery to talk about the history of his family, their rags to riches rise, how they raped and pillaged their way to success. That sort of thing.'

Becky stared at him in disbelief, digesting what he'd said. Understanding lit her eyes. 'You've got to be fucking kidding me! Your wife? You're exposing her to that psychopath? Doing a little digging on the side too, I suppose.'

'She got the invite straight up. I was against a meeting. She insisted.'

'And Chuck saw an opening.'

'For what it's worth, I'm the only one of us three who hates this idea. I'm gonna meet with Chuck in a couple of days. My last chance to talk him out of this. Much like I've tried to talk you out of it, once I figured out what the risks would be.'

'It's different with me,' Becky argued.

'It's not.'

Becky sipped her drink. 'It's gotten a whole lot more real, but so have the stakes of this game. Shit,' she said suddenly, looking at her watch, 'I have to get back. There's a review of draft proposal material scheduled and I don't want to miss it.'

'It's almost eight o'clock!'

'I can easily get back, swill some coffee, and be ready for an eight thirty review. You know that's how it's done. We all rest when the proposal is turned in.'

'Right. Becky, I feel like we haven't accomplished a damn thing tonight except to piss you off and to make me feel like shit.'

'Not true. Talk to Chuck. Confirm what you can about his man. Let me know. That's important. And you can try one more time to talk your wife out of the meeting with our friend. Also,' she added, grinning, 'you've taught me a naughty men's game.'

Logan smiled weakly. 'Since you're about to leave, you owe me an answer. Who would you pick? The guy with the beard?'

'Silly boy,' said Becky. She reached across the table and cupped his cheek gently in her hand.

***

Logan's anxiety had grown steadily in the days leading to his meeting with Chuck, and his mental state was in turmoil. At times, he was settled on the strategy Chuck was proposing, provided Jason Stone would be in London. At other times, he planned to adamantly inform Chuck and Cathie that the deal was off. There would be no stupid and dangerous meeting with Smythe-Montgomery. By the day of Chuck's visit, he was in the vague middle ground (as he'd been during most of the time preceding this meeting) where he had no clue what to do or say. He popped an antacid tablet into his mouth, eyed the bottle suspiciously, and popped a second.

When Chuck arrived, around 4:30 in the afternoon, Logan was no closer to deciding on a plan of action. He clumsily opened a bottle of wine, sloshed the liquid in and around the three glasses he had set out, and flopped into an armchair. It had grown cool outside, so Cathie had suggested they all sit around a coffee table in the family room facing the fireplace. Unfortunately, Logan had neglected to light the fire. She gave him a questioning look, snatched the fire starter, and set the kindling ablaze. In a few minutes the fire was crackling pleasantly as she and Chuck sat.

No one wanted to begin the conversation, but as the silence finally grew uncomfortable Chuck softly said, 'OK, brudda. Spit it out or we're not going to get anywhere.'

'Right. Let me start by saying I still don't know my own mind. I realize Smythe-Montgomery is a threat and Cathie has an opportunity to get some intel you could use, but shit, Chuck, this is starting to scare the hell out of me.'

'Why, Logan,' Cathie quipped, 'you must still care about me. This would be the opportune time to get rid of me, otherwise.'

'Yeah, go figure,' Logan replied.

'Here's the deal,' Chuck said. 'The contact has already been made. If Cathie doesn't go now, Smythe-Montgomery may get suspicious—and irritated. If she meets him and things get in the least bit flaky, she can get out. Cathie, you can play it straight up. Flatter his ass, listen to the rubbish he's sure to peddle as his "true family history," and call it a meeting. You may not get an opportunity to do any more than that anyway.'

'I don't know, Chuck,' Cathie said. 'You've seen his letter. He wants his family not only cleared of past sins, but elevated on a pedestal. The stalwart backbone of Jolly Olde England.'

'That's an odd metaphor, dear,' Logan said gloomily.

Cathie raised an eyebrow, but said nothing.

'You think he's liable to want more than one meet?' Chuck asked.

Cathie shrugged. 'Who knows? But if he's as hard over as he sounded in his letter ...'

Chuck considered this. 'Hard to say. He invited you out in the same time period as Becky's bidders' conference. We know he's the keynote speaker at the start of the conference, but that may be his only involvement. Besides, I suppose a man of his abilities can multitask over a week or two. Let's say he does want a second meet. Play it the same way. Flattery, questions, and general agreement with everything he says.'

'What if I'm finding that his family members make robber barons look like choir boys?'

'You'll never find that out from him.'

'But what if his information is just too unbelievable—meaning it's obvious bullshit.'

'You've done research before. Call him on it. Ask for backup, corroboration, whatever. Just keep in mind, however, that in the end you will need to convince him that you've bought his line of BS.'

'I've had decades of practice on this guy.' Cathie tipped her wineglass in Logan's direction. 'Incidentally,' she added, shaking the empty glass forcefully, 'what's wrong with this picture?'

Logan refilled their glasses, but remained stubbornly silent. Chuck ignored him and continued to brief Cathie on all he knew of Conrad Smythe-Montgomery. 'Oh,' Chuck said, as he neared the end of his monologue, 'we also had a company shrink—a hostage negotiator and all around brilliant dude—do a bit of a psychological profile on S&M.'

'And?'

'It's difficult with the subject being so secretive, and, of course, my guy wasn't actually able to interview him.'

'Do you tease Joy this way, too, Chuck? You brought it up. What did your psycho-genius conclude?'

'Megalomania, naturally. Overcompensated insecurity—probably owing to his plebian family roots. Not a hint of aristocratic blood. Extreme narcissism. Pathological paranoia. And, oddly enough, a god complex.'

'So just about as well adjusted as most aerospace managers?' Cathie said, with a glance towards Logan. 'I know the kind.'

'In all seriousness, be careful with this guy. He manipulates people, businesses, and society with impartial brutality. I honestly don't care if you find anything out that I can use … Well, that's not quite true. But the priority is to get you out safe. Incidentally, which characteristic do you suppose my doctor friend told me to be most concerned about?'

'Easy,' said Cathie. 'The paranoia. He might decide to kill me even if I *wasn't* actually spying for the CIA.'

'Right. Reality is whatever he believes.' Chuck took a drink and turned steely eyes to Logan. 'OK, brudda. What are you thinking?'

'My anxiety hasn't actually gone down much, but the wine helps. Answer me this, will Stone be in London?'

'Yes,' Chuck replied, but then shifted uncomfortably in his seat. 'At least, I'm pretty sure.'

'You're what? Pretty sure?'

'The plan is for him to be there. He agreed. But he has this kind of busy schedule. He's trying to meet with Elaya Andoori again. Don't know how or when yet. And, oh yeah, his significant other—'

'Ms. Blue Hawaii,' Logan interrupted, remembering the name he had conjured up for Luana Chu the first time he'd seen her. She had dazzled him with her exotic beauty, appearing in a stunning blue dress and heels.

'Luana Chu, aka Ms. Blue Hawaii,' Chuck said. 'She doesn't hurt the eyes. But if I said that to Stone, I'd be broken into tiny pieces before I could say ouch. Anyway, her mother died, and the two of them are going to the funeral. Hawaii. Maui. He let me know the other night. The schedules still work, but ...'

'"The best laid schemes o' Mice an' Men gang aft agley,"' Cathie said.

'The gang did what?' Chuck asked, astonished.

'Don't forget the next line,' Logan said. 'That's the one that bothers me.'

Chuck looked from Logan back to Cathie, who shrugged and recited, '"An' lea'e us nought but grief an' pain, for promis'd joy!"'

'Robert Burns, "To a Mouse,"' said Logan. 'You can look it up later.'

'And ... look at the time!' Cathie said. 'You boys will need to finish this discussion without me. I'm meeting my friends for dinner, and you two, if I'm not mistaken, have an appointment with some lively jazz downtown. Try not to end up in a place that requires a large supply of singles. And Chuck,' she added, far more seriously, 'I do appreciate the discussion. The dates should be firming up, and I'll let you know. By the way, as this is Company business, I don't suppose I'll get a complimentary first class upgrade?'

'Have a nice evening, Cathie,' Chuck said.

***

Because of Cathie's conflicting plans, Logan had decided to continue his discussion with Chuck at a small venue downtown with an outdoor patio where local jazz artists played on dry evenings—nearly every night in Tucson. The gas heaters would be lit tonight, making the area comfortably warm despite the November chill.

Logan's piano teacher, Gina, was playing this evening, and when Logan had made plans to come here, he was hoping for a nice relaxing evening following a clear and concise discussion with Chuck and Cathie. Like many of Logan's plans, this one had not turned out as he expected. He was still uneasy with everything having to do with Becky and Cathie, and nothing he'd heard earlier had cheered him up much. Chuck's ambiguous answer regarding Stone's presence in London had been singularly unhelpful.

The two parked and walked over to the Trumpet Café on 4th Avenue. As they arrived, Gina was setting up at one end of the patio. They exchanged greetings and she showed them the playlist for the two sets, pointing out some of Logan's favorites. As other tables began to fill, the two took their seats and asked for a dessert menu. Logan cleared his throat to speak. Chuck beat him to it.

'I get it, Logan. This is all a little too real now, isn't it? Look, if I thought there was any significant danger for Cathie I'd tell you. She'll be fine as long as she plays it like we agreed.'

'And exactly how long have you known Cathie?'

'Yeah, well …'

'Exactly.'

'I'll talk to her again,' Chuck said. 'Make her promise not to color outside the lines. It's the best I can do for now. Backing out would be worse, and you know it.'

'My heart and my head are in some disagreement over that point, you know. But fine. You have that conversation, I'll do the same.'

Chuck watched Logan closely, then nodded. 'That's the plan. Best to let it go, brudda. Now what about Ms. Amhurst?'

'Alcohol first.' Logan flagged down a waiter and calmly ordered a double Jack.

'Just pick out a nice Cab for me, would you?' Chuck said. As the waiter moved off, Chuck gave Logan a questioning look. 'Double Jack? You must be uptight.'

'I'm trying to get slightly less uptight, OK?'

When the drinks arrived, Chuck turned back to his friend. 'Alcohol. Now, what's up?'

'My friend Gary has discovered some definite oddities in the request for proposal. He gave Becky and me a full brief. I won't bore you, but the various capabilities ranged from innocuous to "no fuckin' way."'

'That's a broad range.'

'Yeah. But all in all they add up to "suspicious." We agreed to bring in a team of guys to look at the "why." That meeting happened yesterday and I got to sit in.'

'And?'

Logan shrugged. 'Some of it makes sense. Suppose you had an aircraft with onboard electronics that could make another airborne or land-based sensor think the aircraft was someplace else.'

'It would almost be like you were invisible.'

'Then suppose you could electronically mimic any other aircraft flying.'

'So you take on the identity of another aircraft.'

'Yes. If it was a military aircraft, you could cause an awful lot of mayhem: possibly gain access to restricted airspace, possibly threaten other aircraft.'

Chuck shook his head. 'I still don't get it, brudda. There has to be a larger reason for doing that.'

'You're right. The operations analysts we had working this are bright guys, but they're not mind readers. They asked a lot of questions I couldn't answer, and Gary and I steered them away from anything too sensitive. But there were two persistent questions, and they were good ones: What specific aircraft types will be using this gear? What other aircraft modifications is Smythe-Montgomery building into his revitalized personal air force?'

'Shit! You're right. I know there are contracts out for aircraft modification and upgrade, but we had no way to get into that game. I sort of ignored them after we started working with Becky.'

'Might be a good time to reopen the research. Maybe your young sidekick?'

'Good. I'll put the Grasshopper on the job. Depending on what he digs up, I may want to call in a few markers. Jody, a friend of mine, works at a think tank on the west coast. You know the one?'

Logan nodded.

'When we get a few more pieces of this puzzle, I'll see if she can host a little meeting. You, me, Gary, Becky—if she's in town—and a couple of retired three-stars with lively imaginations.'

'You should get Kevin Flahrety from Alpha Defense. He's a smart dude, and he worked with Gary on this analysis.'

'Done. Shit, there are a lot of wheels turning.'

'And the bidders' brief is coming up soon, as well as Cathie's meeting with Smythe-Montgomery.'

'The wild card is Stone. I hope to Christ he can get Luana's mother buried and haul ass back to help us out. *And* he was planning to meet with Elaya Andoori.'

At that moment, the waiter returned.

'I think I'll switch my drink to what my friend just had,' Chuck said, with a grimace.

'Best bring me another,' Logan said.

Not long after, the club manager announced their guest performer for the evening, Gina.

'I think we can afford to take a break from worrying and listen for a bit,' Logan said. 'She plays "Good Morning Heartache" like nobody's business. It'd be a shame to miss out.'

'That's allegedly why we came, brudda.'

***

In a small, secluded home in a quiet suburb of London, a very different type of entertainment was unfolding. Yvette's body shook and her breaths came in harsh gasps, while Crandall sat watching in silence. The last time he had seen her like this, satisfying his desires while she satisfied her own, he had been calling her Alice, and there had been two others there: part of his own strange fantasy. But something had changed. It had been many years since he had critically examined himself and the aberrant behavior that had split him from his family. Many years. He had accepted himself and moved on from there. But—

'Richard,' said a soft voice, 'hand me that.' Yvette pointed to one of several devices nearby.

He did as she asked, and she was soon moaning with pleasure until she suddenly stopped. Her back arched off the bed and she let out a long-drawn, high-pitched sound between a wail and a shriek, then collapsed, panting heavily with her chest heaving. Droplets of sweat covered her body.

Crandall sat quietly, staring at the lovely young woman as her breathing slowed and she turned to him with a smile. His self-examination could wait.

The Reality of Chaos

Stephen Lance / Chuck Markussen

Stone had been to Luana's family home on Maui once before, but under entirely different circumstances.

Chapter Fifteen

The Funeral

Stone had been to Luana's family home on Maui once before, but under entirely different circumstances. They had been alone except for the staff who maintained the property, Luana's parents being in China. At that time, Stone and Luana were already in love, but not fully committed, each still cloaking the darkest secrets of their lives. It had been a short, sweet vacation, a time away from the shadows and ghosts. This time was different.

As Stone drove out of the rental car lot at the small Kahalui Airport he figured he had about an hour's drive to Luana's home in Kaanapali. A few things still needed to be discussed, but he was reluctant to begin. After the first initial shock, Luana had handled the news of her mother's death stoically. What she hadn't handled well was the behavior of her father. She was seething with unabated anger, a fire in her eyes every time Stone mentioned the funeral. Days of delay before notifying her of her mother's death and the disdain her father had shown by delegating this sensitive message to an employee had infuriated her. Being told she was not welcome for the burial ceremony had been the supreme insult. Naturally, neither her father nor his minions offered to send a car to the airport to receive them. And while this slight stoked her anger, Stone was actually happy. A chauffeured ride with a driver loyal to Luana's father would have squelched any private conversation, a conversation he desperately needed to begin—now.

'Talk to me,' he said. 'Tell me what you're feeling. Or if you're not ready for that, tell me about what to expect at a Hawaiian funeral.'

Luana said nothing at first, but just stared out the car window as they approached the mountains of the island's western lobe. She began with the easier of the two topics Stone had offered. 'As to a traditional Hawaiian funeral, that's hard to define. In former times, royalty and high chieftains were often taken after death to a room of waiting. This could be for ten or more days. Blood relatives were called upon to attend the body. My mother has two sisters, so they will be there. But they are old, and I expect they will allow one or two of my mother's household who have been with her for a long time to be present. I will be allowed to enter the house, you will not.' She grimaced. 'But as my father deliberately delayed in informing me, the waiting period will be almost at an end. Those attending to her will be required to undergo a cleansing ritual after the burial. Are you sure you wish to know all this? It may seem brutal or superstitious.'

Stone turned a serious face to Luana, but didn't speak. His look communicated all she needed to know. She sighed. 'If the true traditions have been followed—and Mother would have insisted—then during the process of preparation, her internal organs would have been removed and her body filled with salt for preservation. The inner parts would have been burned, very privately. They are not considered important. Her body will be positioned in a certain way using ropes, and then wrapped in kapa.'

'Kapa?'

'A type of cloth. The burial will be at night. You will be able to observe, from a distance, but not participate. Those participating will undergo the washing and purification by the kahuna pule heiau—a priest. And it will be over. The household may wish for a ceremonial farewell at the sea—a modernized and less brutally archaic ceremony with candles and flowers. This will be at sunset the following day. But mother's body will not be there.'

'Where exactly will she be?'

'Many of the great kings of Hawaii are buried at a mausoleum—a more modern affair, and mindful of their conversion to Christianity. My mother too was a Christian, but she preferred to use the family cavern on our property rather than a public cemetery or crypt. Just a small cave in a cleft of the mountain facing the sea, enlarged over the years. Sealed now with a massive iron door. There is really nothing cheerful about the tomb. It's a place of death, and that's all.'

'I had no idea,' Stone said.

'You're disappointed?'

'Of course not, if it's what she wanted. Hell, I know a guy who wants his ashes dumped in the sand trap of the 7th hole at Pebble Beach.' It was a bit of an offhand comment, but it struck exactly the right tone, taking Luana away from her dismal thoughts.

She took a deep breath, smiled, and reached a hand out to stroke his face. 'I like your friend's way better.' But her face fell immediately and she added, 'I fear my mother's funeral will be the least depressing of my experiences on this trip.'

The ice had broken, and Stone gently took the opportunity to say, 'Talk to me about it.'

'As you know, my father is extremely disappointed in me. He lost considerable prestige with Chinese military leadership when he failed to produce the codes to crack secure U.S. datalink systems.'

'The codes we were trying to steal from Alpha Defense,' said Stone. 'But that was a trap, and we both knew it. Why won't your father accept it?'

'Possibly because the loss of the codes and his prestige was not the worst outcome of that situation. I was. I was not an obedient daughter.'

'So you were supposed to be obedient and execute a compromised operation? He wanted you caught? Arrested? Thrown in jail for a very long time?'

'He didn't see it that way.'

'Maybe he needs glasses.'

Luana smiled. 'Maybe. But then I refused to meet with him after ... after what happened in the Middle East. We haven't spoken since.' She laughed humorlessly. 'I suppose we still haven't, since it was not he who told me of Mother's death.'

'So what's the plan?'

'Exactly what I've been contemplating since I received the news. James, I'm so furious with him. But ...'

'Uh-oh.'

'I'll be polite to him—as one adult to another. I would like to reconcile, but not at the cost of my independence. I will no longer be the obedient little Chinese girl of the last century.'

'Then that's the plan.'

***

Their arrival at the house caused a stir. Those household staff who had truly loved and respected Luana's mother glanced sympathetically at the two—a mere nod. But there was no doubt they were cowed by the presence of Luana's father and his huge Hawaiian bodyguard. The bodyguard frowned slightly, his nearest approximation to an emotional outburst of disapproval, as Luana and Stone entered. And then there was Luana's father. He stood in the entranceway, his arms crossed and a fierce scowl on his face. He ignored Stone and spoke directly to Luana.

'You should not have come. Was my message to you unclear?'

'Hello, Father,' Luana said. 'Mr. Stone and I have come to pay our respects to Mother. I would like a private word with you as well.'

'You should not have come,' he repeated. 'But as you are here, you may stay for the ceremony.'

Stone saw Luana stiffen at this comment, knowing she would argue her father's authority to approve or deny her visit. He touched her hand gently and he saw her draw a shallow, controlled breath.

'Alani, Waiola,' Wan Chu said, speaking to two timid staff women, 'see to the needs of Luana and her guest. Ikaika, with me.' He turned on his heel and left.

The large Hawaiian gave Stone one last appraising look. He seemed unimpressed. He turned away slowly and deliberately and followed his employer.

'Ee ki ca?' Stone asked.

'It means "man of strength,"' Luana replied. 'His look alone terrorizes the household staff. He is not a man to be trifled with.'

'Trust me, darling, I would never trifle with a brick shithouse like that guy.'

'Charming, my love.' She turned to the two women, Alani and Waiola. 'It's so good to see you.'

Wailoa, by far the younger of the two, was a willowy, clear-skinned woman of perhaps twenty-five. Even so, she had been with the household for nearly ten years. She smiled and nodded her head shyly. Alani was a woman well into her sixties, with tired, sad eyes. But these brightened slightly as she stepped forward to welcome Luana.

'My little goddess. Welcome. And welcome to you also, sir.'

'Thank you,' Luana and Stone replied.

'I only wish it were under happier circumstances. It's a sad time, and I'm afraid your father is displeased.'

'I gathered as much. Perhaps later, when we talk, things may improve.'

Alani nodded politely, but her eyes did not offer any encouragement. 'Please come with me.'

***

That evening, Stone and Luana sat together on a small patio north of the home. 'Do you see it? In the deep cleft at the end of the path?' she asked.

'Yeah, I do. Is that the entrance to your family's burial vault?'

'Yes. You'll probably not find a better location to observe than here.'

The path from the house to the entrance of the tomb was roughly a quarter of a mile long. Stone scanned the surrounding hills. Luana was right. This location was ideal for watching the procession and the entrance to the vault.

'Was Alani able to help me out?' he asked.

'No, but Wailoa was. She's an avid bird watcher.' Luana reached into a large bag at her side and pulled out a pair of powerful binoculars. 'Try these.'

Stone did, and he was amazed at how the cave entrance sprang nearer. The resolution was excellent.

'Good glass,' he said, placing the binoculars on a small table. 'I was beginning to wish I had brought some night vision gear with me on this trip, but from what you've told me, the entire path and entrance will be lined with torches. They would have screwed things up anyway. The binocs are better. Give Wailoa my thanks.'

'You can do so yourself. She and Alani will remain here. And now, darling, I must go and prepare. When it's fully dark we will begin.'

Stone rose with Luana and hugged her. 'Watch your step ... on the path,' he said.

She gave him a knowing look, then smiled. 'You too. Here.'

***

The black of night had settled in. Stone sat on the patio with Alani and Wailoa. Though they had repeatedly rejected his offer to join him, they had finally relented. 'After all,' he'd insisted, 'you seem to be an important part of this household.'

They'd been sitting quietly for a half hour when orange lights appeared on the trail. The procession had begun. Stone leveled the binoculars and carefully scanned the group. There were two older women that he guessed were Luana's aunts. Several younger men and women followed. Perhaps cousins. One man had the accoutrements that marked him as an official of the ceremony—the *kahuna pule heiau*. Luana walked near her mother's body, her father ahead. He was apparently unwilling to join his daughter even for this ceremony. 'Huh!' Stone said with some surprise. 'I thought only family were allowed, plus maybe the priest.'

'Yes, that is tradition,' Alani said.

'Then what is Wan Chu's bodyguard doing there?'

'What?' Alani said, shocked.

'See for yourself,' Stone said, passing the binoculars.

Alani took the binoculars and stared. With a look of disgust, she returned them to Stone. She muttered a long string of what Stone took to be Hawaiian invective and then turned to him. 'The man has no shame. His guardian does not leave his side even to this ritual ceremony. And a half-breed at that.'

'Half-breed?' Stone asked.

Alani said nothing directly, but muttered more words to herself.

Stone turned inquisitive eyes to Wailoa. 'Half-breed?' he asked again.

'Yes,' Wailoa replied. 'Ikaika is half Hawaiian, yes, but also half Tongan.'

'And that's bad?'

'No. Not always. But this one has a black heart. Black Tongan heart.'

Stone refocused on the procession. 'He's not allowed inside the chamber, at least.'

'They will be within for a period of time. Perhaps as long as an hour. Then those participating will be purified. I will go now. Good night, Mr. Stone,' Alani said. 'Come along, Wailoa.'

'Good night, Mr. Stone,' Wailoa echoed quietly.

'Good night to you both. May I return these in the morning?' he asked, holding up the binoculars.

'Of course.'

When the two had gone, Stone refocused on the big 'half-breed' standing like a silent Buddha at the entrance to the vault. 'That man's a piece of work, and no mistake,' he said in an undertone. 'And never leaves the boss's side. Something to keep in mind.'

***

The house was somber the next day. It wasn't just the aftermath of the funeral that made it so. Luana had approached her father early in the morning and asked to speak with him privately. At first he had refused but had finally agreed to meet briefly in the room that he called his study.

This room was as dark as the rest of the dwelling was light, being more reminiscent of an old English library. Heavy furniture filled the room. A massive oak table—designed for meetings rather than meals—dominated the room. Ornate oak chairs upholstered in dark leather surrounded it. A desk sat beneath the only window in the room, but the shades were drawn and the morning's light was muted. On two walls were wooden bookcases stuffed with musty volumes. Hawaiian artifacts, including a few relics of Lahaina's early whaling society, were displayed on another wall. Other smaller tables held items of Hawaiian historical significance.

When Luana and Stone entered the room, her father stood at one end of the great table, arms folded and a scowl on his face.

'We were to meet privately,' he said.

'And yet, there stands Ikaika,' Luana replied, pointing to the man as he stood like a carved statue near the Hawaiian artifacts. He was so still that he himself might have been mistaken for part of the display if not for the tiny, amused curl of his lips. 'Jason may hear any words between us.'

'Are you mistress of this house?' Wan Chu asked. 'Your mother is buried for less than half a day, and you have the temerity to assume her duties? No! My word is law here! You have been disobedient and arrogant. You will apologize now, once this man has left, and then I will remind you of your proper duties.'

'Father, I came here to be reconciled with you. I am here to speak with you and resolve our differences.'

'No!' Wan Chu bellowed. 'There is nothing to discuss. You will apologize. I will decide your punishment and determine your role in the future. And yet this man remains! Ikaika, remove him!'

The huge Hawaiian moved towards Stone with surprising speed, but Luana was faster. She stepped between the two. 'Father, stop this foolishness. If you will not reason with me, then Jason and I will leave together.'

But Wan Chu had passed beyond reason. His eyes shone with anger, and his body shook. 'Ikaika, I have given you a command! Remove this man. My daughter will stay!'

Ikaika reached a hand out to move Luana aside, but quicker than she could see, Stone had intercepted it, grasping the man by his wrist and moving out from behind her.

'Easy there,' Stone said. 'You don't want to be doing that.'

Ikaika looked at Stone and then down to his own wrist where Stone's hand gripped him. He then spoke the first words Stone had ever heard him say. 'Yes, I do.'

In a single swift move Ikaika brushed Luana aside with his free arm and chopped upward, aiming for Stone's throat. Stone leapt back and the blow whistled by an inch from his windpipe, but he had been forced to release Ikaika's wrist. He countered a series of additional blows as Ikaika moved more swiftly than Stone could have imagined. The big man used an economy of movement that was a pleasure to observe, if you were not the subject of the attack. But Stone was swifter still, dodging strikes, deflecting others, and connecting twice with blows to Ikaika's midsection. Unfortunately, as solid as those strikes were, they didn't faze the big man.

Stone backed away and assessed the situation. In the hallway, two terrified women held their hands to their mouths, their eyes wide in horror. As Stone changed his focus, one of them turned away. Inside the room, Luana was standing near her father, shock on her face. Stone gave her a quick shake of his head to warn her to stay out of the conflict. With a man of Ikaika's size, a random blow could be fatal. He turned back to face his foe and was surprised to see a tiny smile on his otherwise impassive face. The man was enjoying himself. Stone considered trying to reason with this behemoth, but immediately rejected the idea. He stole

The Reality of Chaos

a glance at Luana's father, who was snarling like a madman. The older man grabbed Luana's arm and pulled her back roughly. Stone hesitated, then moved to go to her, but Ikaika saw his opportunity and attacked again.

For a few minutes there was chaos. A solid blow to his stomach sent Stone crashing into a bookcase with such force that books rained down on him. Luana cried out in alarm.

Stone grabbed a heavy wooden carving from a side table and flung it at Ikaika's head. The man simply slapped it aside and advanced again. Stone feigned a frontal attack with his fists, but Ikaika had grown overconfident. He stepped in closer and moved to block. As he did, Stone spun on one foot and landed a solid kick on the side of Ikaika's head, dazing the man and driving him back a step. Blood trickled from his lip and the tiny smile had been replaced by icy rage, but he recovered quickly and was already in a defensive posture before Stone could follow up.

Another series of rapid strikes and blocks occurred. Ikaika had learned not to underestimate his opponent, however, and Stone was unable to land another blow. But then Ikaika stumbled on the edge of the heavy rug under the oak table. For just a moment he seemed off balance. Stone moved in to take advantage and swung his leg once again at Ikaika's head. But it had been a ruse. Ikaika caught Stone's leg with an arm as thick and powerful as a python and twisted violently. Stone grunted in pain and went down. Before he was able to rise, a kick to the midsection sent him flying. A staggering, sharp pain ripped through his chest. *Dammit!* he thought. *Ribs again!*

It was a fleeting thought since another kick came flying towards his head. He was a fraction too slow, but managed to avoid a direct strike that might have broken his neck. The glancing blow was bad enough, splitting the skin above his left eye. Ignoring the screaming pain in his chest, he rolled away then sprang to his feet, blood running down the left side of his face. He wiped it from his eye. The large man stood at the other end of the room and casually brushed a few drops sweat from his brow. During the brief respite, Stone considered. So far, his opponent had shown surprising speed as well as enormous strength, but the last few exchanges had convinced Stone of something more. This man had training—possibly years of training. When he was able to draw an easier breath, he said simply, 'Afghanistan?'

The big man's smile returned. 'Not such a tame place as that. Chechnya. Somalia. Syria.'

'I'll bet the pay was good.'

Ikaika shook his head. 'This job pays better. And is more fun.'

'Enough!' Wan Chu bellowed, still in a paroxysm of rage. 'Dispose of him immediately!'

Ikaika shrugged as though he were being robbed of a rare treat. But before he could even begin to reach inside his jacket for his concealed weapon, Stone had smashed an ornamental glass bottle and sent a heavy shard flying. The jagged edge pierced the back of Ikaika's right hand. He bellowed in anger as Stone launched himself, leaping in the air and catching Ikaika full in the upper chest with both feet. Ikaika crashed into the wall of Hawaiian artifacts, and several fell around him with a clatter. Once again, he reached inside his jacket and was pulling out a .45 caliber Sig Sauer that looked small in his hand. Stone kicked again and hit the back of the injured hand. The gun went flying, sailing across the room and sliding under the desk.

Ikaika struck like a mongoose with his left hand, knocking Stone back again, then snarled in anger. 'Good!' he shouted, looking in the direction of the missing gun. 'This way is better.'

Stone took a defensive posture, expecting a sudden and violent attack from the injured man. But with an uncanny self-possession, Ikaika regained control of his emotions. He turned briefly away from Stone to face the wall of artifacts and removed a large Hawaiian club. It was a beautiful and lethal piece of work: heavy, dark, polished koa wood, the head shaped like a large spade or leaf, wide at the base and coming to a point at the end. Around the head, shark teeth were attached in a deadly perimeter. Ikaika swung the club and made several swift, chopping motions. It whistled fiercely as it slashed through the air. 'Better,' he repeated.

Stone realized he was in trouble. The blood running down his face clouded his vision, and his ribs were screaming. He had barely managed to keep up with this man when he was unarmed. And now Ikaika had a formidable weapon with which he was apparently quite familiar. Stone glanced around the room. There were a few items that might have been useful, but they were still on the wall behind Ikaika. Stone doubted the big man would graciously step aside and allow him to choose one.

Ikaika strode across the room, and Stone desperately looked for anything he could use. He grabbed a heavy book and used it to block Ikaika's first vicious swipe. But the book was neatly severed almost to Stone's fingers, and he tossed it aside. A small wooden statue survived two glancing blows before it was knocked from his grasp. Ikaika took a scything sweep that cut through Stone's shirt like a razor and left a bloody track a foot long on his chest. Stone countered with a blow to the lower ribcage near the kidney. A second swing connected with the man's head, just above the ear, but to Stone it felt like he had just struck a brick. Still, it knocked Ikaika to the side slightly. Stone aimed a savage blow at the Hawaiian's throat, but realized at the last instant that, once again, Ikaika had deliberately shifted to induce Stone into a foolish attack. Stone twisted violently and leapt back just as a sweeping backhand of the koa club came shrieking at him. *Bad idea*, he thought, as he raised his left arm to protect his face. But he had no choice. The club's teeth sliced through his sleeve and forearm, cutting to the bone. Stone grunted in pain as blood poured from the wound. He kicked out and struck Ikaika's knee with satisfying force. This time, the big man did stagger, but he didn't fall. He roared in pain, rebalancing his weight to relieve his injured knee.

Then Stone saw it. A real weapon he could use, on the floor below the wall of Hawaiian artifacts. It was a heavy whaling spade—a head spade. Many types of spades were used in whaling, primarily for removing meat and blubber from the dead animal. The head spade was the largest of these. Roughly four feet long, the rounded metal shank expanded at one end to accept a long wooden pole for use at sea. The opposite end was similar to a flat-bladed shovel, though it tapered back to the metal shaft. Three edges of the blade were sharpened. The chisel end could be used to flense away flesh, or, with the pole in place, the spade could be used like an axe to cut through large bones.

Yes, a serviceable weapon, knocked from the wall in the early struggle. The only problem being that Ikaika still stood between it and Stone. *It's going to cost some blood to get to that thing,* Stone thought. *He's fooled me twice. Maybe I can fool him once.*

Stone backed away from Ikaika, circling around the table. He picked up a chair, smashed it across the table's top, and tore one wooden leg away from the remains. It was short, no more than eighteen inches long, but it had some weight to it. It would have to do. He circled back to face Ikaika, who took two whistling swings with the club. Stone resisted the temptation to rush in behind the final sweep. He would not be fooled a third time. But as Ikaika resumed his fighting stance, Stone attacked. A series of swings of the chair leg were deftly blocked by the big man. Stone's arms were growing heavy, his ribs shrieked, and the blood still ran from his many wounds. It was now or never. He feinted to the right, swept back to the left, and swung downward. Ikaika stepped easily to his left, and allowed Stone's momentum to carry him past, striking Stone a blow on his back and shoulder. It connected, but without the strength it might have had, since Stone was already lunging in the same direction. He went sprawling on his stomach, and Ikaika stepped around behind him to deliver a killing blow. But Stone was now nearest to the display wall, and his fingertips had found the end of the spade shaft.

'You fight well. But now you die,' Ikaika said.

The big man positioned himself astride the prostrate Stone.

Stone waited. It seemed like an eternity. Then he sensed Ikaika drawing the club back. Luana screamed. Stone snatched the whaling spade and rolled onto his back. There was Ikaika standing above him, the bloody club poised above his head. Stone swung with every ounce of strength he still possessed. A dull thud, like an axe biting wet wood. A look of surprise on Ikaika's face. He collapsed to the side, his neck sliced halfway through, his spine severed. The spade, stuck fast in the vertebrae of Ikaika's neck, pulled from Stone's grasp.

Stone lay there breathing shallow, painful breaths. A scuffling noise on the other end of the room caught his attention and he rolled over onto his side. Wan Chu had released Luana and was groping beneath the desk, Luana tugging at his arms and back. He shoved her away savagely, gave a yell of triumph and pulled himself from under the desk. Stone tried to rise, but had barely gotten to one knee when the old man was there, gun barrel pointed at his chest. With his teeth clenched in a grimace of victory, Wan Chu pulled the trigger. But Luana barreled into him at the last instant, and the shot whistled past Stone's ear. He grabbed hold of a

The Reality of Chaos

chair and pulled himself upright. Luana and her father were on the ground, wrestling furiously for the gun. Before Stone could force his exhausted body to move, the old man had rolled on top of his daughter, one hand clenched around her throat. A second shot, and the fighting suddenly halted. Luana's eyes were wide and her face deadly pale. Her father rolled to one side, blood pouring from a wound in his chest, and collapsed. He let out a few gurgling breaths and then was still.

Stone staggered over to Luana and offered a hand covered in blood. She took it and rose in disbelief to a sight of hideous carnage, but in a moment, her attention returned solely to Stone.

'Oh, James, James,' she said, rushing to hold him, to ease him into a chair. 'Oh, God, what has he done to you?'

Stone attempted a weak smile. 'I think I need a Band-Aid. Maybe two. Also a nap.'

At that moment, Alani entered the room. 'We have seen. The police are on the way. And an ambulance. Wailoa is bringing hot water, towels.'

'God bless you, Alani,' Luana said, tears streaming down her face. 'God bless you.'

Stephen Lance / Chuck Markussen

This had been a quiet Thanksgiving. Only the two couples. Their grown children were in other parts of the country. Even Randy and Gail had regretfully declined Logan's invitation—a previous commitment to Gail's parents in Nebraska.

Chapter Sixteen

Thanksgiving

'Christ, Stone, you look like warmed-over shit!'

It was the third time since his arrival in Maui that Chuck Johnson had made this astute observation. He was sitting at Stone's bedside in a bright, airy room of Luana's parents' house. Except, of course, it was now *her* house since both her parents were dead. Stone had insisted on remaining here and not spending time in the hospital. Doctors—well paid and carefully selected for their discretion—had come to the house and strongly argued the point with him, but when he had been adamant, they had treated him as best they could and wished him well.

'You're no picture of manly beauty yourself, Johnson,' Stone replied. 'And you weren't in a fight with a humpback whale.'

'Yeah, no kidding. So what did the docs have to say?'

'Oh, stitches above the left eye, which you can plainly see, and stitches in my shoulder. Miscellaneous cuts and bruises. But the winner has to be my forearm. A whole bunch of stitches there and—this is pretty funny—the doc had to remove a shark's tooth that had lodged in the bone.'

'You've got a strange sense of humor, brudda. Shark's tooth! How about the ribs?'

'Only one broken. I must be getting soft. I would have guessed two or three. Still hurts like a son of a bitch, though.'

'The ribs do hurt,' Chuck said, with an emphasis that made it clear that he understood—personally. 'So how long will you be laid up?'

'I could whip your sorry ass right now. But I'll give it another day. Should be up and about by tomorrow.'

'Are you fuckin' serious? I would have thought a week at least.'

'I won't be playing any rugby for a while, but I'll definitely be mobile. I've got that meeting with Elaya slated for next week in Belgium, then it's on to London.'

'Holy shit, Stone, I didn't realize you already set up the meeting with Madam President. Are you sure you can cover the bidders' brief, too?'

'Oh, yeah. And keep an eye on your friend Logan and his wife. Besides, Luana will be in London and I can continue to recoup there and visit with a friend.'

'The one with the interesting intel?'

'Yeah, that one. He's got an unusual sidekick—a young lady. Sharp as hell. And he has another friend I haven't met yet who has a long history with Sir Conrad. I'm hoping to meet her on this trip.'

Chuck nodded, thinking over Stone's words. 'Well, the timing should be good. You'll get the best part of a couple of weeks in London for R&R before the conference.'

'Man, you know as well as I do that those days are priceless. Survey the field of battle *before* the fight. That's what I learned in soldier school.'

'You're not going to a fight,' Chuck said.

'From your lips to God's ears, Johnson. And give me an "amen!"'

'Amen ... And Ms. Chu is OK with all this?'

'Hell no! She thinks I'm pretty much acting like an idiot. I told her I agreed with her, but, surprisingly, that didn't calm her down.'

'Crap. Sorry to hear that.'

'Oh, don't sweat it. She's coming around. She did like the part about me spending time with her in London. And before I forget, thanks for everything you've done to smooth things out with the authorities here. Neither of us would have the luxury of traveling if we were involved in a rat's nest here.'

Chuck waved that aside. 'The two ladies—what were their names?'

'Alani and Wailoa.'

'They were fantastic. The backup from some of the other household staff confirmed Ikaika's general temperament and Wan Chu's irrational anger towards his daughter.'

'Yeah, well, I know you smoothed a couple of rough edges. Especially knowing Wan Chu's connections with Mother China.'

'Some of the boys did do a little polishing, it's true. As for Luana's rightful inheritance, that could be trickier.'

'I suppose killing your father, even in self-defense, must look mighty suspicious.'

'True enough. But the real issue is how much of the old man's estate will revert back to his Chinese handlers. Luckily, Ms. Chu's mother left many things directly to her. Still, once you get lawyers involved, everything becomes a cluster. It may all take a while to straighten out.'

'Not to worry, Johnson. Luana has a well-paying job and I think I've mentioned that we've put a little coin aside.'

Chuck smiled.

***

'So Stone is off to London?' After Logan asked the question, he took a sip of the Courvoisier in his snifter and turned his attention back to his cigar.

'Yeah,' Chuck replied. 'With a quick stop in Belgium. He mentioned something about waffles.' He took a pull on his own Cuban. 'Crazy SOB. *Tough* crazy SOB.'

'That's good, right?'

'Sure. As far as it goes. I'd prefer he stay alive.'

They were seated in Logan's backyard digesting the usual heavy Thanksgiving meal. An outdoor television had the football game on, but the volume was off, and neither man seemed particularly interested. The day had grown chilly, with thick clouds scuttling past the setting sun, and Chuck's wife, Joy, and Cathie were indoors. But Logan had stoked the chimenea to a crackling glow, and the two men were comfortably warm, the fine brandy adding a fire within.

This had been a quiet Thanksgiving. Only the two couples. Their grown children were in other parts of the country. Even Randy and Gail had regretfully declined Logan's invitation—a previous commitment to Gail's parents in Nebraska. It was a good opportunity for a quiet discussion, and Logan had a lot on his mind. For the moment, though, he couldn't help pursuing his thoughts on the enigma that was Jason Stone.

'Was the guy even planning to have a Thanksgiving turkey?'

Chuck shook his head. 'Not sure. He and Luana went back to their "little cabin" in Breckenridge. Who knows? Maybe they'll have a big shindig, but I doubt it. They're an odd couple.' He paused thoughtfully. 'Naw, that's not right. They're a bit of an *unusual* couple.'

'Well, she's drop-dead gorgeous, and he's at least tolerable to look at.'

'Not beautiful men like the two of us, you mean?'

'Precisely.' Logan swirled the brandy and took another drink.

After a brief silence, Chuck asked, 'Did you and Becky have your follow-on meeting?'

'Yeah, we did. Oh, and that intel you gave me on the other upgrades Smythe-Montgomery is making to his old aircraft fleet, and on the new equipment he's buying, raised quite a few eyebrows.'

Chuck sat back in his chair and adopted a regal expression. 'We are the government. We're here to help!'

Logan smiled wryly and muttered a few words that might have included 'bull' and 'shit.'

'So, seriously, what did the bright boys have to say?' Chuck asked.

'They said Sir Conrad could end up with a fleet of unique planes in his airline. Capabilities include takeoff and landing on rough fields, some highly unusual and difficult-to-access cargo storage, and additional electronics that can only be described as radar warning and jamming gear. I'm assuming Smythe-Montgomery didn't actually associate the latter with his commercial ventures.'

'True. It's supposedly a separate contract to support Indian Air Force upgrades. But Randy suggested—and I agreed—that it wouldn't take a leap for Smythe-Montgomery to integrate that equipment on any of his planes. Anything else?'

'Oh, hell yeah. The best parts. Some of the auxiliary cargo bays can be opened in flight, and there are cockpit-controlled release mechanisms.'

'Now I wonder why he would want that?' said Chuck, with a knowing smile.

'Exactly,' Logan said. 'You could actually drop cargo in flight.'

'Why did your guys think you might want to do that?'

'Well, the advertised reason—those bays could hold hazardous material, lithium batteries, or whatever, that could be dumped if sensors detected fire—actually made them laugh. Their best guess was that the pilot would be able to jettison illegal cargo if you discover the airport you're about to land at has gotten suspicious. Or—and I really like this one—you can drop cargo for pickup in a remote location and never need to touch down at all.'

Chuck grunted his agreement. 'Makes sense. So—'

'That's not all,' Logan interrupted. 'A few seemingly innocuous structural mods to the fuselage and wings of some of the aircraft could be used as hard points for mounting standard military gear.'

Chuck sat up straight. 'What kind of gear?'

'This is all speculation, right, but the guys thought that a flare-launching pod or some other electronic gear was possible. One guy even suggested you could mount the Chinese equivalent of a small UAV or even an air-to-surface missile. A small one.'

'Fuck me,' Chuck whispered. 'What in the hell is this maniac up to?'

'That discussion was even more interesting, though, of course, no one knew who we were talking about.' Logan smiled. 'When I told Kevin, my Operations Analysis guru from Alpha, what Gary thought, he just laughed and said, "I see a forest. Gary sees a bunch of stupid trees." Things got pretty wild after that. In the end—' Logan stopped abruptly and refilled drinks. 'Did you ever meet Steve Nahna? Interesting guy. He's a maniac for detail, but he can zoom up to fifty thousand feet easy and see things more clearly than almost anyone I know.'

'Name's familiar. Was he part of your old crew?'

Logan nodded. 'His opinion is gold. His first comment was that every damn thing we talked about could be explained in a perfectly reasonable way, if one didn't mind taking the long road to do it. Then he brought up Occam's razor.'

'His what?' Chuck asked, stunned.

'Seriously? It's a problem-solving principle. If there are two or more explanations for an occurrence, the simplest one is usually correct.'

'No shit? Learn something new every day, though Razor Boy could be describing good old police investigation principles.'

Logan shrugged. 'Maybe Occam worked for the LAPD.'

'OK, give me the punchline. What did your friend say was the simplest explanation?'

'He said—let me get this correct—"This stinks."'

'Wow! Any other gems?'

'Actually, his definition of "stinks" was also simple. And here I'll paraphrase: Someone is trying to smuggle highly illegal items. They want to hide their aircraft and cargo, detect trouble in advance, and defend themselves—passively or kinetically—if the shit really goes down.'

Chuck sat rubbing the stubble on his chin nervously. 'Sounds like your boy is on to something. Fits in with some other intel I've gotten.'

Logan looked questioningly at his friend, who squirmed a bit and then said, 'What the hell. They can only fire my ass once. Anyway, it's just a rumor, but apparently Smythe-Montgomery's representatives have been negotiating with President Andoori's people, trying to get some sort of an airport terminal deal. Details are vague, but if he gets a solid hold in Tehran, it would open up possible destinations for his illegal product.'

'Shit!' said Logan. 'How is his proposition being received by Andoori's people?'

Chuck snorted derisively. 'What's Farsi for "fuck you"? A stupid, unnecessary provocation. They should have kept Smythe-Montgomery's people talking. Played for time. But no. "Fuck you!"'

'That means—'

'Obviously!' Chuck said. 'Smythe-Montgomery will go to the opposition. Probably has by now. Andoori already had one foot on a roller skate and one on a banana peel. Now she's trying to dance a tango. I've talked to Stone and he agrees, but it may be too late to reel this fish back in.'

'You're sadly overburdened with metaphors, brother,' Logan said.

'Nah. That's Cathie's department. I'm just a burned out old agency dude with retirement on his mind.'

Though Logan was concerned at his friend's words, he had heard them before. But there was a difference in tone, and he felt it. Chuck was serious.

***

Stone certainly agreed with Chuck Johnson's assessment. And though Stone had mentally shrugged off Andoori's belligerent response to Smythe-Montgomery as water under the bridge, he knew it would

The Reality of Chaos

make his job more difficult. He had also been very blunt about that with Chuck.

'She's as good as dead, you know that, don't you?' Stone had said.

Chuck thought to argue, but what the hell was the point?

'Unless …' Stone had added teasingly.

'Have you got an idea? If so, lay it on me.'

Stone shook his head. 'Just a notion. A dangerous one. But it depends on Smythe-Montgomery to make his move. Trouble is, his options are wide open and there's only the two of us.'

'And Randy,' Chuck had countered.

'Yeah,' Stone replied with a smile, 'my good buddy Randy.'

'So how do we play this?'

Stone considered briefly. 'I'll have my chat with Elaya. Have your people keep their ears open and report back anything they pick up on Smythe-Montgomery, no matter how trivial it seems.' He suddenly gave Chuck an odd smile. 'Hey, Johnson, ever heard this one? "You can't kill a dead man."'

Chuck stared at Stone for a minute, then shook his head. Whether it was a negative response to Stone's question or disbelief at his peculiar sense of humor was never clear.

Stephen Lance / Chuck Markussen

He had promised Luana he'd meet her in London tonight.

Chapter Seventeen

Meeting with Elaya

Stone shifted in his airplane seat. Even in first class he couldn't find a comfortable position. Too many things still hurt. He checked his watch. Just under two hours until he landed in Brussels. Then a limo ride to an obscure location, a short meeting with Elaya, back to the airport. He had promised Luana he'd meet her in London tonight. He smiled at the thought that he wouldn't be good for much more than dinner and conversation for the next couple of nights. That damned half-Hawaiian had been pretty good at his job. Almost good enough.

***

The obscure location turned out to be even more obscure than Stone expected. It was the penthouse suite in a hotel—an empty hotel, soon to be demolished. A few folding chairs and a card table were the hastily acquired furnishings in what had once been a vast sitting room with a view of the Royal Palace, Brussels Park, and the Parliament Building. Ornate moldings along the floor and ceiling and a huge, equally gaudy mirror at one end of the room still hinted at gothic luxury. Peeled and chipping paint and a water-stained ceiling indicated the neglect this old building had suffered in recent years. Once beautiful hardwood flooring creaked under his feet as Stone paced the room. Of no particular historical significance, and occupying an extraordinary piece of prime real estate, this building had been doomed. In a few months, the steel skeleton of a modern monstrosity would begin to rise over its forgotten gravesite.

Stone was just pondering why this thought should disturb him when he heard footsteps in the hallway. Elaya Andoori entered with two guards. She gave them and Stone's driver brief instructions and they moved back into the hallway, closing the door behind them.

'First let me apologize, Mr. Stone. It was quite impossible to arrange an acknowledged meeting or even a more civilized one, as we had in London. At this moment, I am stuck in traffic between the Iranian embassy and the civic auditorium where I am scheduled to speak in just under twenty minutes. I am afraid I will be late. This brief detour is known only to you and the three men outside. I might add that those three men, still quite loyal to me, have an unfortunately short life expectancy if recent history is a guide.'

'Please don't apologize, and call me Jason.'

Elaya smiled, but it was a haunted look. 'As you wish, Jason.'

'I gather there have been assassination attempts?'

'Yes. Two in the past three weeks. In both cases, I was close enough to hear gunshots.'

'That's far too close.'

'Closer still for my men. Three killed, one grievously wounded.'

Stone shook his head. 'I have a plan, but it will require two things: the right opportunity and your full cooperation.'

'My cooperation is yours for the asking, but what of this opportunity?'

'That, I'm afraid, is in the hands of your adversaries. For now, please pass on any information on their movements or actions. Anything at all. I have other resources working this, and I hope to give you some news soon. When I do, you must be ready to act quickly. I'll be more specific as soon as I have more information.'

'Very well. Anything else?'

'Well, yes. Try very hard to stay alive until I contact you.'

***

At least the flight from Brussels to London had been short. Stone began to wonder whether he ought to have spent more time in Hawaii or Breckenridge recuperating. *I'm just gettin' old*, he thought. Though what he might mean by that comment was uncertain.

As he trundled his luggage to curbside at Heathrow, he was surprised to see Luana standing there and a large SUV waiting. 'Darling,' she said, gently wrapping her arms around him and avoiding the more damaged areas. After he released her, Stone looked inside the vehicle and was

The Reality of Chaos

surprised to see a lordly-looking gentleman, Richard Crandall, sitting beside the driver. Crandall nodded with due dignity.

'What's this?' Stone asked.

'Oh, Richard insisted. He wants us to use his house—the one where you met with President Andoori—for as long as we like. It's a bit of a drive from town, so he sent his car.'

'With him in it?'

'It's just his way. Besides, he hopes you're up to meeting a friend at the house. A special friend.'

Understanding lit Stone's eyes. 'Sure. But then—'

'The house is ours. A few staff people will take care of things, but we'll have complete privacy.'

'And if I need to spend time in London?'

'If *we* need to spend time in London, I've booked our same hotel for three weeks. We're rather wealthy, you know.'

'May I take your bags, Mr. Stone?' the driver asked.

Stone looked at Luana, a warm gleam in his eyes. 'Sure. Why—' The word 'not' died on his lips. 'What the hell is that?' he asked, pointing.

Not far down the road, near an enormous red kettle, a four-piece brass ensemble had begun a lively marching tune. A number of airport travelers stopped and listened appreciatively.

'Ah,' the driver said perfunctorily, 'that would be the annual kettle drive. The Salvation Army, you know. They do some very good works here, and it wouldn't be the Christmas season without them, would it?'

'In the States, when I was a kid, my mom would never pass by a Salvation Army kettle without dropping in a buck or two. But back then the kettles were 'kettle-sized' and there was a bell ringer, not Chicago's brass section.'

'The Army was started here, and perhaps we do get a bit carried away. I'm sure Mr. Crandall could tell you more if you were interested. Shall we go, sir?'

'Hello,' Stone said, as he entered the SUV. 'It's nice of you to let us use your country home and to come pick me up.'

'Think nothing of it. It's good to see both you and Luana again, and I particularly wanted you to meet a very close friend of mine. From what

Luana tells me, it's possible that all four of us may have something in common. Yvette insisted that she be allowed to bring her to the house, so she'll be there as well.'

'Yvette, the rather brilliant young lady who was so proud of Clyde?' Stone said.

'Precisely. I think part of her enthusiasm to escort my friend might have had something to do with seeing you again. You and Luana add a bit of mystery and intrigue to her existence. She fantasizes that you are both spies of some significance. A bit like John Steed and Emma Peel of *The Avengers* fame. But I'm sure neither of you would remember that show.'

'I *did* see the movie,' Luana said.

'Oh,' said Stone, 'when I was a kid, someone—maybe my grandma—kept raving about the TV series. I watched a few episodes online. If Yvette thinks that's us, she's in for a disappointment.'

Crandall just laughed.

'He was asking about the enormous kettle, sir,' the driver said.

'Yes, a wonderful organization, The Salvation Army. Perhaps you'd like to hear a bit of history, Mr. Stone.'

'Absolutely,' Stone replied.

Crandall proceeded to describe the founder of the Army, its goals, its history and growth in England, and its expansion to other countries. He was surprisingly knowledgeable and was a good story teller. Stone listened intently. At last Crandall paused, and with embarrassment added, 'I'm sure I've gone on long enough. I apologize. I do have a certain fascination with their organization, and a deep respect. A bit out of character for me, I suppose.' He fell silent, withdrawing into some internal reflections that he chose not to share.

***

When they arrived at Crandall's country home, Stone went around to the back of the SUV to get his and Luana's bags. Crandall stopped him gently. 'Alex will take care of that.'

The driver, Alex, nodded and smiled.

Stone relented without protest. He was still stiff and sore. *Besides*, he thought, *there's nothing critical in any of my luggage. My equipment will arrive later, a bit more discreetly.* He ran through a mental checklist: a laser microphone, a compact high-frequency satellite linking station, a good-old parabolic mike, several encrypted radios, and an excellent computer-hacking laptop. Other equipment was more of the kinetic variety: several handguns, a sniper rifle, and miscellaneous explosive devices. He had many connections in England, and his unique property would be left at various bus terminal lockers in London.

As he walked into the somewhat familiar house, he was pleasantly surprised to see it fully decked out for the Christmas season. Two large wreaths with bright red bows hung on the front doors. Strings of holly decorated the upper moldings of the entryway. Decorations of ribbon and fir branches were placed on end tables, cabinets, and bookshelves. Colored lights and painted glass balls had taken up residence in windows and on fireplace mantels. As they were led into the large study, Stone realized that the decorations were not quite complete. In the corner of the room near a large bay window was a beautiful Christmas tree. Yvette stood on tiptoe to one side, adding tinsel and ornaments handed to her by a serious but attractive woman in a wheelchair. Stone guessed she might be about sixty.

Seeing the guests, Yvette muttered something that sounded like 'drat.' She hastily hung the ornament in her hand, a beautiful glass bird resembling a peacock, and turned to face Stone and Luana.

'Never mind,' the older woman said. 'You can finish later.'

Yvette stepped forward, her demeanor a curious mixture of shyness and self-confidence. She remembered her manners at the last moment and waited for the older woman to wheel herself forward.

'Mr. Stone,' said Crandall, 'let me introduce my longtime friend and confidante, Lady Diana Foster. Diana, this is Jason Stone. Luana you know, of course.'

Yvette stood gape-mouthed at this introduction, but just as she was about to conclude that 'Lady' was an eccentric jest on Crandall's part, Diana spoke up. 'It's just Diana, Mr. Stone. And if Richard persists in his formality I'll be forced to call him Lord—'

'Yes, yes, all right Diana,' Crandall said hastily, 'there's no need for that.' But Yvette's look of astonishment grew as she turned towards him. Her face was an incredible confusion of astonishment and fear. Had she really been friends with a genuine lord and lady? Had she really chatted away for hours with both of them? Had she really been calling them by their first names all along? She blushed scarlet.

'Now look what you've done, Richard,' Diana said, smiling gently at Yvette. 'Never mind the silly old man, dear. It's just us. Your friends.'

She turned back to Stone who held out his hand. 'Pleased to meet you, Diana. Call me Jason.' He turned to Yvette. 'I guess we've both gotten a surprise, but I'll bet these two would prefer we continue to treat them casually. I suppose I can do that if you can.' He held out his hand and Yvette took it solemnly.

'It's good to see you Mr. Stone. And you, Ms. Chu.'

'Since we're all adults, Yvette, I'm sure we can go by first names,' Luana said.

'I doubt that I can,' Crandall said sourly. 'But enough of stilted greetings. The sun is long since over the yardarm. Drinks, anyone?'

***

When everyone was situated comfortably, sipping on their respective aperitifs, Crandall began.

'Let me see, I believe everyone knows a little about the others, but perhaps not enough. Let me briefly summarize the situation. Chime in if you'd care to add to or correct anything I say. And for heaven's sake, Yvette, stop your fidgeting. You're welcome to go—or stay. I'd much rather you stayed. Please fetch the keyboard from the side office and turn on the monitor. We may need to give Clyde some exercise.'

'Honestly, Richard, I think you're confusing the poor girl,' Diana whispered as Yvette left the room.

'Am I?' he asked wearily. 'Perhaps I am. I will look to you for counsel in the near future.'

'Diana,' Stone said, 'it would help me if I understood your position in all this. I've received only the barest intel ... information. Luana told me you have a serious grievance against Conrad Smythe-Montgomery and that you're willing to help our motley group.'

'And I would like to learn more of you and your background, Jason, though Luana tells me there are closet doors best left unopened.'

'Simply crammed with skeletons, I'm afraid, and not all of them figurative. But fair is fair, and I'll tell you all I can that's relevant to our collaboration.'

Yvette returned and handed a small keyboard to Crandall, then turned on an 80-inch TV monitor on the other side of the room. In a short time, a huge purple Clyde filled the screen. Beneath it were words, written in fiery letters, that read, 'And just what the hell do you want?'

Crandall shook his head slightly, but there was a smile on his face. 'Apparently Yvette has too much free time on her hands. I'll have to correct that.'

'Later, Richard. Stories first, I believe.' Diana paused to collect her thoughts. 'Yes, this will do,' she said briskly. She briefly retold the tale she had shared with Yvette not long before. When she finished, Yvette was once again crying softly, her head hung down.

'I'm truly sorry, Diana,' Stone said. 'I can understand your feelings towards Smythe-Montgomery's family.'

'No, you really can't. It may be hard to believe, but I never held Conrad accountable for this.' She motioned to her legs. 'But he grew in his father's shadow and became, if anything, crueler and more vicious than the old man himself. When I refused to die, Conrad's father was furious. But when he realized the full extent of my injuries, he simply gloated. He'd done worse than kill me; he'd inflicted perpetual torment for refusing him. Things had worked out far better than he could have envisioned. But the universe does not turn on the Smythe-Montgomery whim.' Diana sighed, and took a sip of her Chardonnay. 'Oh, sod it,' she said, banging the drink down on the end table. 'Yvette, please get me a Beefeaters on the rocks. Easy on the rocks.'

With her new drink in hand, she continued. 'This part of my story only Richard has ever heard before.' She sighed. 'Well, we all grew older over the years, as is often the case. Smythe-Montgomery the elder grew sickly and bitter. The younger was barely in his twenties, already indulging in the brutality and decadence of power. I had grown accustomed to my situation. I spent many hours with my friend.' She reached over and patted Crandall's hand. 'Then one day Richard introduced me to—well, his name hardly matters. A kind and gentle man. Wonderfully intelligent and humorous, but with horrible taste. You see, I fell in love with him and he with me. It was rather a miracle. We had such plans ... Not to be tedious, the old man found out, and his fury was renewed tenfold. He died not long after, and so might his grudge have died with him, but for his loving son, Conrad. He ... I ... Oh, Lord.' She took an enormous gulp of her drink. 'Richard, would you?' she managed to croak out.

'Yes.' He passed Diana a box of tissues and turned to the others. 'The poor man, my friend, Diana's fiancé, was brutally murdered. No direct connection could be made to Smythe-Montgomery, of course. But there can be no doubt he was to carry out his father's wish that Diana continue to suffer. The information I've uncovered I will gladly share, including the confession of one of the killers. I was able to extract it, with some difficulty, but the man escaped my custody, only to find himself floating in the Thames, half eaten by fishes, some days later. Perhaps that's enough for now.'

Yvette sat in stunned silence, Luana with a look of disgust. Diana had regained her composure, but her eyes were gleaming, sharp enough to cut diamonds.

Crandall attempted to bring the group back to a sense of the present—back to an assessment of their future actions. 'Luana, Mr. Stone, as you can imagine, if it is your goal to undo Smythe-Montgomery, you have two zealous allies. Independent of his previous sins, which are legion, you have seen my projections for the future and the role that evil man will play.'

'You'll forgive me,' said Stone, 'but those are just models.'

'Just models!' Yvette yelped, jarred back to the discussion in an instant. 'I don't believe it of you, Mr. Stone. An intelligent man—as you clearly are—must see the truth of it. I know you must!'

Stone turned to her with a serious expression and finally nodded. 'I meant no disrespect. And I've been impressed with the accuracy, as demonstrated in the previous world crisis. But it is, after all, the future.' He saw Yvette readying herself for a brisk defense, so he quickly added, 'I am, however, willing to plan accordingly, under the assumption that the models are one hundred percent accurate. It's likely that Smythe-Montgomery is up to no good. Will that do for now?'

'Yes,' Yvette said.

'Too much time on her hands,' Crandall repeated, shaking his head slowly. But his smile told another story entirely. 'So, Diana and I—and,

The Reality of Chaos

of course, Yvette—have been open and honest with you. What can you share with us?'

Stone had known this question would be coming. Though he had given considerable thought to the matter, it always came out the same. His betrayals, his lies, his brutal actions, his cold-blooded killing haunted his thoughts. He longed to surrender, to confess his sins and be done with it. No. It couldn't be. Even Luana had only the slightest notion of the man he was before he met her. Without any premeditation, he began with a story he would never have consciously chosen.

'I was always a bit of an odd kid. Proud. Independent. Not resistant to discipline, but to authority. Especially foolish, ill-informed, and autocratic authority. My father disapproved. My mother approved. I joined the military and spent some time in the Rangers—with mixed success. Then I did some freelancing. During the latter part of that period in my life I met Luana. Because of my experiences and unusual capabilities I recently was asked by Iran's leader, President Elaya Andoori, to head up her internal security forces. I declined. But after some further consideration, I've agreed to help her. I made that decision after discussions with Luana.'

'They were rather brief,' she said, with a smile. 'But I agreed.'

Stone hesitated. 'I should also say that Smythe-Montgomery—' He stopped abruptly. 'You know, I'm getting tired of rattling off that geezer's name. We should pick a nickname. It might come in handy for casual conversation, say, over an open phone line. Something snappy.' He grinned. 'Like Clyde. Any ideas, Yvette?'

She considered. 'Monty is way too obvious. How about Jack? I've known several Jacks, and they've all been wankers.'

Diana stifled a chuckle. Stone looked at the others, then nodded. 'Jack it is, then. Well, Jack has been meeting regularly with some of the least savory men from Iran's previous administration. It doesn't take a genius to conclude that these meetings must be good for him and bad for Elaya. So that's the nexus for me.'

'Nexus?' Yvette asked.

'The link. The connection between Elaya and Jack. It means I have an interest in Jack by virtue of my deal with Elaya. But also ...' He paused, and Luana gave him a probing look. 'I feel I should say this, but

I won't be able to add much. There are others interested in both Jack and Elaya, or at least in the success of her fledgling administration in Iran. I've also agreed to investigate Jack for that reason.'

'You've left very little time for a decent game of squash, Mr. Stone,' said Crandall, impressed.

'Handball, please,' Stone countered. 'Better for symmetrical conditioning.'

'I sit corrected. And I will refrain from any questions regarding your other commitment, assuming you can assure me that the entity to whom you are committed is no friend to ... Jack.'

'I can,' Stone said firmly.

'Very well.' Crandall glanced at a mantel clock nearby. 'Since it's almost dinnertime, I believe I have only two more points to cover. The first is devilishly easy to ask. Perhaps harder to answer. How are we to collaborate on our joint venture?'

'Ah,' said Stone, 'I plan to do a little discreet surveillance in London. There's a bidders' conference in a few weeks. Jack will undoubtedly be present. I plan to—'

'Case the joint!' Yvette interrupted.

'Well ... yeah, I guess that's about the size of it. The venue, the hotel where Jack is staying, and so on.'

'I may be able to help you, Mr. Stone,' Diana said. 'There are a few local establishments that Jack is known to frequent.'

'That would be great,' Stone replied. 'Right now, that's the extent of my plans. Gather intel.'

'Wise,' said Crandall. 'And with that in mind, I'd like to make a request. As I'm sure you know, my modeling predictions are only as good as the data I input. I propose we review the results.' Yvette rapidly pulled up the most recent modeling data while Crandall answered questions. When these were exhausted, he said, 'Every bit of public information on Jack—a pathetically meager supply—has been entered. With the astonishing predictions you've just seen.'

'And you'd like a little more input data. Something a bit harder to come by,' said Stone.

'His corporate empire is privately held, which means his financial statements are private and unpublished. But a sneak peek at his accounts would be exceedingly helpful.'

'I damn well bet it would,' Stone said. 'How do you propose to get that peek?'

'I have an idea,' Luana said, 'but I'd like to think it through. Since it's dinnertime, maybe we could meet again in a day or two.'

Dinner went by quickly, and, true to his word, Crandall gathered up Yvette and Diana and left shortly after, with just one last word to Luana. 'I would be very interested in whatever idea you have regarding Smythe-Montgomery's finances. And I would, of course, share any modeling results based on that information.'

***

Later that evening, Stone was struggling to remove his T-shirt, and cursing under his breath.

'Here, let me,' Luana said, gently lifting the shirt over his head. Looking at his injuries, she sighed. Some of the man's more recent scars still had an angry, red look, but there were others—quite a few—that were older and that spoke of a violent past.

'Thanks, darling,' he said, turning and kissing her. But there was little passion in his kiss, and his eyes were clouded. Luana immediately guessed the cause.

'You have far too much on your mind, far too much to manage. You may be the only person in our group today who has the entire picture clear in his mind.'

'*You've* got a pretty good notion,' Stone said, with a crooked smile.

Luana brushed this off. 'Perhaps a notion, but not the responsibility to make decisions and to take action. Let me help.'

'I really don't want you involved in this at all,' Stone said.

'Well I am. So I repeat, why not let me help?'

'I don't suppose I really have a choice, do I?'

'None.'

'Fine. Then get me a soft flannel shirt—one that buttons in the front!—and a couple of drinks. Let's reconvene in the study. I seem to remember a couple of comfy chairs and a fireplace waiting to be lit. It's gotten cold in here.'

'Drafty old English country houses. Of course, the weather has turned ugly—cold, windy, and rainy.'

'Then let's warm the place up and talk. You're right about one thing, darling, I have too many thoughts bouncing around inside my tiny mind. You can help me sort them out.'

A few minutes later they were seated in the study, each holding a snifter of cognac. The fire popped and crackled pleasantly, sending dancing shadows across the bookcases. Rain pounded the leaded-glass window at one end of the room, and the wind gave a low moan as it coursed past the old building.

Stone swirled the neat brandy in his glass. 'Smythe-Montgomery. He's the key to all this.'

'Oh? What of the former Islamic Republic of Iran? Their threat against Elaya is very real. They need her eliminated to regain power, so they hardly need any urging from Smythe-Montgomery.'

'That's true. And I'm sure they've been trying. But there's something else. Chuck told me about Smythe-Montgomery's meetings with key former members of their police and military. He's helping them or they're helping him or both. Something just stinks. If they have an alliance, it will be a lot harder to keep Elaya safe.'

'Why is that?'

'Smythe-Montgomery! He has resources and a deep network. And Chuck has never been able to lay a glove on him.'

'Is that a fashion reference, dear?' Luana asked dryly.

'Boxing.' He ignored her attempt at humor. 'There's a connection there, I know it, and I'd give a lot to know the purpose.'

'Won't you find out something more when Chuck's friends arrive here?'

'First of all, they're not really Chuck's friends. They're the friends of *Chuck's friend* Logan Fletcher. Well,' he added, 'one of them is Logan's wife. I presume they're friends.'

'Like us?'

'Not like us! Far more civilized.'

'Cathie Fletcher is the author, isn't she? I've read some of her books. She and Logan seem like unlikely people to be involved in this.'

'You've got that right! Logan's wife, Cathie, and his work acquaintance, Becky, shouldn't be involved at all. I've told Chuck this. They're amateurs.'

'Perhaps that's exactly why Chuck can use them. Smythe-Montgomery is too clever to allow a professional into his confidence.'

Stone nodded reluctantly. 'Suppose so. But there's going to be blood on this one. There's no avoiding it. These people are in over their heads, and if they start playing spy they're going to get hurt.'

'They must be aware of the dangers. You can't protect everyone.'

The statement was true, but it grated on Stone nonetheless. A moment later a hint of a smile crossed his face as he remembered something Chuck had told him. 'I may not need to protect everyone, at least not alone. Chuck has coerced his trusty sidekick, Randy O'Neil, into helping. He should be in London in a couple of days.'

Luana frowned. 'Isn't he the young man who threatened to kill you?'

'Yep. That's the one. But I'm sure he's gotten over it.'

'Really? What makes you think that?'

'Chuck has explained to him—several times—why I needed to shoot his fiancée.'

Luana's eyes widened.

'Oh, I just grazed her,' Stone said innocently. 'I thought I'd mentioned the incident before.'

'I believe you may have glossed over it, darling,' Luana said icily.

'Well, if he's as smart as his boss claims he is, he'll get it—intellectually. I'm afraid if someone shot you I'd be hard to convince.'

'Yes? I'll try to avoid being shot, then, so as not to leave you with a conundrum.'

'Thanks.'

Outside, the storm continued unabated. Rain pounded down and the wind increased, whipping trees and bushes outside and coaxing more low moans from the old house. Luana shivered. 'Stoke the fire, would you, darling? I'll get us a refill of Richard's fine cognac. There's one more thing I'd like to discuss with you.'

'Your idea on how to help Richard Crandall get his information?'

'Clever man. Yes.'

The fire was blazing once again and the warmth it radiated was extremely welcome. Luana set their brandy glasses on a small table.

'The algorithm we were to use for extracting data from Alpha Defense would be ideal for capturing information from Smythe-Montgomery's financial data,' she said.

'You mean the little worm that was never installed on Alpha's servers?'

Stone was referring to a bit of malicious software that Luana, with his help, had planned to install on Alpha Defense Electronics' servers. The software was intended to capture critical technical information on datalinks and networks of U.S. military systems. At the last moment, they had chosen not to initiate the attack, sensing a trap. Their instincts had been correct, as Chuck Johnson and Randy O'Neil had planned a sting operation to catch the perpetrators. Stone smiled at the recollection. Circumstances made for surprising enemies—or allies.

'Yes. With minimal modification, it could seek out the data Richard needs.'

'But don't you need access to the servers? I doubt they're linked to the internet.'

'No. Richard has already made that attempt—with Yvette's help.'

'So she's learning how to hack computer systems. What other interesting skills is she acquiring?'

'It's best not to ask,' Luana said.

'I suppose not. So how do we get access?'

'Logan's business associate, Becky Amhurst, is president of one of the companies bidding for a contract with Smythe-Montgomery's airline. Perhaps there's a way through her. An electronic submittal of their proposal, for instance.'

'But you also need to get the information out.'

'Yes. It's just the kernel of an idea. Do you suppose I could meet with her? Is she fully committed to this endeavor?'

'She is, according to Chuck. And yeah, I have contact information. But if you talk to her then I guess you're fully committed to this endeavor as well.'

'I already am, for the sake of Richard and Diana.'

'OK. She rolls into town in a week or ten days. You go ahead and get your tricky computer bug ready. I'll set up a meet with her. But this may not pan out.'

'We'll see. But enough business. Let's enjoy the fire and talk of other things. Our home in Breckenridge and your interesting woodpecker houses, or …'

'We could watch a movie, I suppose. Something light and funny would be a nice change.' He stood and walked over to a flat screen TV monitor built into the bookcase and opened the drawer below it. Suddenly, he burst into laughter—an odd sound after their serious discussions.

'What have you found, darling?' Luana asked.

Stone turned to her with a huge grin. 'I believe Yvette has left us some entertainment and a rather unsubtle message.'

Luana looked puzzled until Stone held up a box set of DVDs. It was the complete set of the old *Avengers* TV series. Their laughter filled the room.

Stephen Lance / Chuck Markussen

Two days later, Stone was walking alone in St. James's Park ...

Chapter Eighteen

London Town

Two days later, Stone was walking alone in St. James's Park and he wasn't particularly amused. Randy O'Neil was going to meet him here and Stone felt strangely nervous.

'Gettin' old, Kulwicki,' he said to himself. 'He's just a guy. Just a guy who wanted to kill me.' He snorted in irritation. 'Guess he wouldn't be the first.'

He caught movement out of the corner of his eye and saw Randy approaching, trying too hard to look casual, which made him look even more nervous. 'Shit, we both need to relax,' Stone muttered.

Randy walked up to Stone but didn't offer his hand. *Now that would have surprised me*, Stone thought. 'Mr. O'Neil, I presume?' he said, in what he hoped was a professional and non-threatening tone.

'That's me,' Randy assented. The two stood regarding each other. Stone was taller and heavier in build, but Randy looked tough in a wiry sort of way, and was clearly the younger man. 'Look,' he finally said, 'let me get it off my chest. You shot my fiancée, and I was pretty fuckin' pissed. I mean, how would you feel?'

It was exactly what Stone had been thinking the other day, and he answered honestly. 'I would have killed you—or given it a good try.'

'Chuck tells me that trying usually works for you. So answer me this. Why?'

Stone had considered this many times over the past months, but he had no feelings of guilt. It had been a highly fluid situation and there had been no time to weigh options. In hindsight, he was quite proud of an elegant solution that had eliminated a troublesome member of his little terrorist group, boosted his status with the remaining members, and spared Chuck's friends from pain and death. Above all, it had allowed him to continue his mission—his bloody sacred mission. After more deception and more death he had succeeded, years after he had begun. He pondered how to put this into words to this still-angry young man. He already liked Randy, who had been open and direct, wanting to clear the air. Stone decided to use the same approach.

'Mr. O'Neil, I'm sure you saw what I saw. Your fiancée was about to be raped by a brutal man. Then she and you and your friend Logan Fletcher would have been killed. You weren't expected at the air force base and I had no contingency plans for you. I had roughly—what would you say?—ten seconds to formulate a plan and act. As I'm sure Chuck told you, the three of you were expendable to my primary mission. I surprised myself at being unwilling to accept that. In retrospect, I'd say it worked out rather well.'

'But you could have missed,' Randy said. 'You might have killed her.'

Stone looked at him incredulously. Then the tiniest hint of a smile crossed his lips. 'You don't know me, so I'll take that into account. Let me say this once.' His look hardened. It was the look of a killer, an assassin. 'I don't miss.'

Randy considered a challenging response, but Stone had spoken the words without a hint of a bragging tone. To him, it was a simple, undeniable fact. He didn't miss. To Randy's surprise, he found himself asking, with some deference, 'Are you serious?'

Stone nodded, then shrugged slightly. 'Depends on conditions, but I've been trained never to take a questionable shot. Sometimes the targets refuse to cooperate.'

'The coyotes in the San Bernardino National Wildlife Refuge. There was one guy shot through the eye and not square in the forehead.'

'You saw the bodies? You were there?'

'No. But Chuck and I know a couple of awesome Border Patrol agents who were. They told us that each of the coyotes was dropped with an unbelievably clean shot, except for one guy. Don't get me wrong, he was just as dead.'

'He moved slower than I expected, and, of course, the lighting wasn't ideal.'

'You are serious, aren't you?'

'Look, Randy, I put the smallest scratch on your fiancée—'

'Gail. Her name is Gail.'

'Well, I tried to do the least possible harm while still preserving my status with the rest of those ass-clowns.'

Randy considered all he had heard, then stuck out his hand. 'Name's Randy. I suppose it will be easier if we use first names.'

'Good thought,' Stone replied, taking his hand. 'Call me Jason. What do you say we continue this conversation over a couple of nice warm British beers?'

Randy smiled. 'That would be great. Hey,' he added, as Stone turned to go, 'Gail knows you did what was best. She's told me about, oh, a jillion times, that I'm being unreasonable. I think the word she used was "jerk."'

Stone laughed. 'C'mon, Randy. First round is on me.'

***

For the next week, Stone and Randy surveilled critical areas in London, gradually growing more comfortable with each other. Their primary focus was a complex of buildings near London's Gatwick Airport, south of the city. A hotel and convention facility owned by Smythe-Montgomery was to be the site of the bidders' conference. Next door to these facilities was a private hangar and taxiway. When Smythe-Montgomery traveled, he flew a private jet. There were rumored to be no fewer than three Gulfstream G6 aircraft and two Learjet 60s at his disposal. Larger aircraft might have been roomier, but couldn't have been more luxurious than his personally outfitted fleet, nor would they have been practical out of a private facility. And, of course, Smythe-Montgomery preferred discretion in his travel. He usually stayed in the huge top-floor penthouse of his hotel when in England, and would come and go with the silence and unpredictability of a ghost.

Randy and Stone had taken lodgings in an older, shabbier establishment whose only recommendation was a clear line of sight to both Smythe-Montgomery's hotel and the hangar.

'I still don't get it,' Randy said, as he set a powerful pair of binoculars down on the room's small desk. 'According to Becky, the briefings are all being held in the main conference room. But the reception—the big bash after everyone is done—is in the hangar. Seems pretty downscale for a guy like Smythe-Montgomery. He's supposed to be at this shindig, right?'

'He is. But I wouldn't be so sure about the actual event. He's been known to give some unorthodox and lavish parties.'

'In a hangar?'

Stone shrugged. 'What's that?' he asked a moment later, as Randy began to assemble a tripod structure. A tube at the pivot point of the tripod had cables that ran to a laptop computer that was booting up.

'Cool, huh? It's a laser listening device. But not like the crappy ones you can get online. I'm going to take a shot at Smythe-Montgomery's windows, see if I can pick up a conversation.'

The principle of these devices was simple: Shine a laser beam on the window of a room where you were eavesdropping. Soundwaves within the room would cause the glass to resonate, which in turn would modulate the laser light reflected from the glass. The received signal was stripped of the carrier, leaving only the audio—the sounds from inside the room. They could be astonishingly effective. However, they did have a few weaknesses.

'Damn,' said Randy. 'There's a whole hell of a lot of noise. They must be using countermeasures.' He made a few entries on his laptop.

'You mean those little gadgets you stick to your windows? I bought some from Amazon for my house in Breckenridge.'

'You've got a house in Breck?' Randy asked, though he stayed focused on his computer. 'Sweet.'

'I haven't spent a lot of time there. I've really neglected my woodpecker houses.'

This time Randy paused. He turned to Stone, a look of disbelief on his face. 'I didn't know people put up houses for woodpeckers. Don't they, like, peck their way through the wood?'

'That may be why they're not really working out,' Stone said, with an ironic smile. 'So are you giving up on that gadget?'

'Not just yet. There's some cool stochastic filtering that I'm going to try, but it takes a longer collection interval.'

'You don't actually know what stochastic filtering is, do you?' Stone asked.

The Reality of Chaos

Randy smiled. 'Hell no. But it does take a while to run. Might work, might not. There are lots of other windows to try. I'll bet they're not all protected. I've gotten some pretty good intel from staff people, hotel workers, live-in mistresses.'

'That sounds like a story worth hearing.' Stone checked his watch. 'We should get going soon. It's after 5:00. You may have to try again tomorrow.'

'Damn. What with the fog and the short days you could have told me it was midnight. Still, what's the rush?'

'Dinner plans. For both of us.'

Randy gave Stone a puzzled look, but didn't object when Stone began packing up their gear.

***

Letty Green was *north* of London, hence the need for an early start. After they had been driving for some time, Randy asked where they were headed, and Stone merely replied, 'To the house of a friend where Luana and I are staying, when I don't need to be elsewhere.'

Randy sat silently, processing this information. Luana had been described by Chuck Johnson. Both her personal appearance and her corporate achievements had made quite an impression on Randy. But when Chuck informed him that she and Stone had been behind the attack on Alpha Defense Electronics, Randy had been stunned. Now, Stone and Luana were allies against Smythe-Montgomery, and Randy felt as though he'd fallen into one of Cathie's novels—the one titled *A Tangled Web*. He also pondered the words of Chuck Johnson when he'd asked Randy to take this assignment:

> *'Look, Randy, in our business we often live by the old saying "the enemy of my enemy is my friend." But I'll go you one better. Sometimes the enemy of my enemy can truly become my best friend. It doesn't make sense, but it's a bizarre, fucked-up world.'*

As Randy glanced over at Stone, he acknowledged the logic of what Chuck had said. Randy was reluctantly beginning to like Jason Stone. It wasn't any particular thing, but their previous adversarial relationship didn't seem to matter now. He was beginning to understand the man, and with understanding came respect.

***

As Stone brought the car to a stop, Randy gazed at the lovely English home surrounded by large, beautifully manicured grounds. It was winter, so the lawn, trees, pond, and garden didn't show to full advantage as they would have in summer. Nevertheless, Randy was impressed. The feeling intensified as they entered the front hallway and he took in the Indian carpet, the Elizabethan furniture, and the beautiful paintings.

'Is … is that a—'

'Monet? As a matter of fact it is. Ah, Luana,' Stone said, as she entered the hallway from the sitting room, 'come meet our guest. Luana Chu, this is Randy O'Neil.'

All thoughts of English gardens and Monet paintings were driven from Randy's mind. Though it could have been argued that Luana was modestly dressed, she still appeared stunning in an ankle-length dress that looked as though fresh cream had been poured over her body. Her dark hair flowed over her shoulders, and her large, beautiful eyes sparkled with lively intelligence.

'Um, hi,' Randy said after an awkward moment where he was too inclined to stare. 'I'm very happy to meet you.' He held out his hand and Luana shook it with a firm grip. 'And please call me Randy.'

'And me Luana.' She glanced at an ancient mantle clock. 'You must be tired and hungry. Dinner will be ready in about twenty minutes, but I'm sure you'd like a drink. Our host has some extraordinary single malt scotch. Also, a great wine cellar.'

'Well, when I can't get a Town Drunk—it's a local connoisseur beer in Oakland—I do like a good scotch.'

'Come and have a look, then,' Stone said. 'The bar is pretty well stocked.'

Randy stared in reverent silence at Crandall's selection. He recognized a few brands: Glenfiddich and Laphroaig. But even these were of a vintage he wouldn't have dared touch at the liquor warehouse in Oakland for fear of dropping one and owing the five-hundred-plus dollars it was worth. Some of the others had names he couldn't even pronounce. At last he spotted one in an unassuming bottle and pointed.

The Reality of Chaos

'Good choice,' said Stone. 'I think I'll join you.'
***

A few minutes later, Randy and Stone were enjoying their drinks and a cheerful fire. The day had been grey, damp, and cold, though no rain had fallen.

'I hate to mix business with scotch,' Stone began.

'I find it usually helps,' Randy replied. 'And as this is darn fine scotch, I'm going to assume the business is serious.'

'The scotch is thirty-year-old Glen Skyre at a cool $1500 a bottle.'

Randy almost gagged and Stone chuckled.

'Don't worry, Crandall is generous to a fault—and he has another case of this stuff in the cellar.'

'Man, do I not work for the right people,' Randy said.
***

Luana joined them for dinner, and once again Randy had to concentrate to avoid staring. He succeeded more gracefully this time, then asked a question that had been bothering him for quite a while. 'I understand that your company, Infinity Services Group, is doing very well. How do you manage to run a corporation and still do so many other things?'

Luana smiled. 'Thank you. The company *is* doing well, thanks in part to a competent board of directors and the management chain through all levels. Our primary product—cybersecurity—is in high demand, for obvious reasons. The other key to our success is in employing some of the most brilliant cyber experts from around the globe.' She laughed lightly. 'On a small scale, it's reminiscent of the Howard Hughes empire. Howard eventually disappeared from all direct operations, but his people—management and technical—were outstanding, and the company continued to thrive. I, fortunately, have not become entirely superfluous. I attend board meetings, visit with key clients—'

'And pick up the big check!' Stone added.

Luana inclined her head towards him and smiled.

After a brief lull in the conversation, Stone asked, 'How much do you know about predictive chaos theory, Randy?'

Randy took a slow drink of his scotch. 'Some. A little. Chuck gave me a briefing and I did as much research as I could. I'm told Mr.

Crandall is the leading man in the field, but his publications are, well, nil! Everything I found was written by others, some of it flattering, some of it rudely skeptical.'

'Does Chuck Johnson believe it works?'

'He's heard the evidence—through you. Let's just say he's *politely* skeptical.'

'And how about you?' Luana asked. It was a casual question, asked with a smile, but there was an intensity in her eyes that caused Randy to consider carefully before he spoke.

'I don't believe that anyone can predict the future. Not in the absolute sense of a mythological Sybil. However ... A lot of what a Company analyst does isn't so far removed. It's a logical extrapolation of known facts in order to plan and act in the future. The more facts, the better the extrapolation, the better the result. Now *that* I believe in.'

Luana exchanged a glance with Stone, who smiled and said, 'Told you he was bright.'

'Well, Randy, you've summarized our collective faith in Richard's new science rather nicely,' Luana said. 'Perhaps you may not be aware that it points to Conrad Smythe-Montgomery as the focal point for grievous changes to our world in the near future. The modeling is emphatic on that point. The current leader of Iran, Elaya Andoori, is also a key player.'

'Chuck told me about your uncanny guesses regarding those two,' Randy said, glancing at Stone. 'Were you relying on the model?'

'Relying, no,' Stone said. 'But the model agreed with my own logic—my own extrapolation of facts. And my gut agreed with those two. It was pretty convincing.'

'We're now trying to use Richard's models to dig deeper,' Luana added, 'to understand the specifics of Smythe-Montgomery's plans and his ultimate goals, which he has kept well hidden. As you say, Randy, the more facts, the better the extrapolation.'

This is it, thought Randy. *This is the crux of tonight's conversation.*

'How can I help?' he asked.

Stone smiled at Randy's directness, but it was Luana who answered. 'My company, in learning how to protect our customers from cyberattack, has naturally learned many techniques for launching such attacks. However, the internal financial workings of Smythe-Montgomery's corporate empire—which we strongly desire to see—are protected more securely than the secrets of most major governments. He has not merely firewalled the information, he has physically isolated it from any exterior access. It's quite impressive, for such a large enterprise. A completely closed network. Un-hackable. If it were possible to access the server, even briefly, the information could be discovered and extracted without leaving a trace. A small thumb drive and less time than I have taken to describe the process.'

'You have no one on the inside?'

'Sadly, no. ISG *was not* selected as Smythe-Montgomery's network security provider.'

'Becky Amhurst and the bidders' brief,' Stone interjected. 'It's our possible entrée. At the moment, our only possibility.'

'Becky Amhurst,' Randy repeated, musing. 'Well, shit. But—'

Luana rose from her seat. 'If you gentlemen don't mind, I believe I'll retire for the evening. I have an early conference call with my COO tomorrow,' she added, with a playful smile in Randy's direction.

When she'd left, Stone turned to Randy. 'Why don't you get us both a refill while I stir up the fire.'

A minute later Stone accepted the drink and sat heavily back into his seat. He took a measured drink of scotch before continuing their previous discussion. 'Sometimes I think Chuck is mad to put a couple of green amateurs—*enthusiastic* green amateurs—into this cauldron. And I hate like hell to ask anything more of Becky.'

Randy gave this some thought. 'Chuck is damn worried about Smythe-Montgomery, Jason. He wouldn't do it otherwise. We're here—at least, I am—primarily to keep an eye on Becky and Cathie.'

'Randy, don't take this wrong, but you're good and so am I—'

'You're a damn sight better than good,' Randy said, with feeling.

Stone acknowledged his comment with a twisted smile. 'Sometimes good isn't good enough. Somebody's getting bloody this time, and we won't be able to stop it.'

'See that pub over there?' She pointed to an establishment at the base of a four-story building that looked even older than its neighbors. An ancient gilded sign identified it as The Hartshorne Pub – Est. 1742.

Chapter Nineteen

A Family History

Becky Amhurst stared at the empty baggage carousel, muttering curses to herself. Gary Walkin stood at her side with both of his battered Samsonite bags and tried not to look superior. The carousel clattered to a halt. There would be no more bags coming from this flight. Which meant that somewhere between the bustling metro airport of Tucson, Arizona, and London's Gatwick, the airline had succeeded in losing Becky's bags.

'Maybe,' Gary said, 'there's a special place for the luggage of people who flew first class across the pond, instead of, you know, cattle-car class, where I was.'

'Gary, my brothers taught me how to choke the life out of an enemy in hand-to-hand combat. Don't get me thinking you're my enemy.'

'No way, boss. Just trying to be helpful.'

'Fine. Just go and fetch me a double espresso while I wait in line and try to explain to the fine people of this fine airline that I really can't go to this bidders' conference naked!'

'The guys wouldn't object, boss.'

'Nice save. Now ... fetch!'

By the time Gary returned, Becky was done at the customer service counter. She held out her hand for the coffee and muttered thanks, a thoughtful look on her face.

'So?' he asked, when they were seated in a cab heading for the hotel.

'Well, it's funny. The gentleman at the counter was mildly sympathetic to my plight, but regretted he couldn't offer more than £200 to tide me over. Certain my luggage would show up by tomorrow. Stiff upper lip and all that.'

'Two hundred pounds! That ain't squat.'

'Yes. But then I told him the purpose of my visit and the gentleman hosting the shindig. It was like I'd bitch-slapped him into another dimension. He tore up the chit for £200 and gave me a slip of paper with a seven-digit code that was access to a line of credit at three major department stores and a fine shop specializing in ladies' intimate apparel!'

'Hell!' Gary said in wonder. 'Wish my luggage had been lost!'

'Tut, tut, no sour grapes now. Excuse me, driver,' Becky said, 'a slight detour, I think. How far is it to Harrods?'

***

Winter suited London. Or perhaps, more accurately, the Christmas season suited London. The busy thoroughfares were still hectic, but the traffic appeared to have a more benign purpose. Aging light poles wrapped in artificial holly or fir boughs and red ribbons looked charming. Tall brick buildings of a bygone era came alive, each window wrapped in lights and decorations. Leafless trees sparkled with strings of lights: white, red, green, or blue. It seemed that every street corner was graced with a Salvation Army band, large or small, playing songs of the season and doing a brisk business at their charmingly festooned kettles. Even the weather was cooperating, and a gentle snow was falling as Becky exited the last store on her list. She and Gary were now heavily burdened with holiday-spangled bags carrying Becky's Christmas booty.

'Do women really wear that stuff underneath their regular clothes?'

'Why, Gary, I believe you're blushing. The answer is: only on special occasions. Surely on your wedding night—or was it nights?—you saw something of the sort.'

'That was a long time ago. Best not to stir up those memories.'

'C'mon,' she said, with a friendly smile. 'See that pub over there?' She pointed to an establishment at the base of a four-story building that looked even older than its neighbors. An ancient gilded sign identified it as The Hartshorne Pub – Est. 1742. Strings of colored bulbs cluttered the entrance and a fine, lively sound escaped into the chill evening air every time the front door was opened, along with a heavenly aroma of shepherd's pie. 'Drinks and dinner on me. You've been a hell of a good sport.'

The Reality of Chaos

A grin lit Gary's face. 'Logan was right about you. You are a better boss than him!'

Becky laughed and they headed for the Hartshorne.

***

Logan and Cathie were enjoying a similar pleasant holiday scene. They had flown in through Heathrow and were hailing a cab at about the same time Becky and Gary headed into the Hartshorne.

'I can't believe I'll actually get to meet Conrad Smythe-Montgomery this Friday!' Cathie exclaimed.

Logan had heard this refrain repeatedly over the past several days, and it was wearing thin. 'Honestly, dear, you'd best lose your groupie-like adoration or you'll embarrass yourself. He's just a guy.'

'Oh, yes, just a devilishly handsome billionaire who happens to enjoy my books.'

'Don't forget narcissist, egomaniac, and, oh yeah, suspected stone-cold murderer.'

'Well, I suppose there's that. Still, don't be a killjoy. You can buy me a nice dinner and a drink or two. Tomorrow we'll roam this lovely town and enjoy the sights, then on Friday …'

'We get to meet Brad Pitt.'

Cathie swatted Logan's arm, her smile of anticipation persisting. But as the cab maneuvered its way through the throng of the metropolis, Logan's sense of gloom rose steadily. This was all too serious. He wondered how he'd let Chuck talk him into this. Of course, Logan hadn't gotten the slightest bit of support from Cathie or Becky, both of whom had been not only willing but eager. So, to Logan's deepening gloom, another layer was added. *I really am getting old. At least, too old to see anything but danger in this insane exercise. Is it just me? I need to talk to Randy. The kid has his head screwed on straight despite his constant exposure to Chuck. He'll tell me whether I'm justified or whether I've become a terrified old man, no use to anyone.*

***

Cathie and Logan rode the express elevator to the building's top floor, which was exclusively occupied by Smythe-Montgomery—his executive suite. An exceptionally well-dressed man named Colpoys had welcomed them in the lobby and punched in the elevator code before stepping back and resuming his post. Logan was as nervous as a cat turned loose in a dog pound. He fiddled with his sport coat. He fiddled with his tie. He tightened his belt a notch. Cathie finally turned to him, completely exasperated. 'If you don't stop that right now, I'll send you back to the hotel and meet with Conrad alone.'

More than anything else, Cathie's use of Smythe-Montgomery's first name jarred Logan back to something nearing equanimity. 'Fine,' he grumbled. 'But when the guy with the elevator code is wearing a $2000 tailored suit, it does tend to be just a bit intimidating.'

'You look lovely, dear,' she teased, kissing him on the cheek.

When the elevator doors opened, the two found themselves looking into an unusual waiting room. A large mahogany desk dominated the room, and there were several large chairs of an Elizabethan style off to one side. A similarly styled table sat on a Persian carpet facing the chairs. Tall brass lamps gave off a mellow light on either side of the room. To the left of the desk were two heavy wooden doors, clearly the entrance to Smythe-Montgomery's offices. With the exception of the phone and other electronics on the desk, there was little to indicate this room belonged in the 21st century.

'Ms. Fletcher, Mr. Fletcher,' said a throaty female voice. 'I'm Ms. Lister, Sir Conrad's assistant.' She rose from behind the desk and stepped out, greeting both with a firm handshake. 'I know how very excited he is to meet you, Ms. Fletcher. Thank you both so much for visiting. I'll let him know you're here.'

Logan's eyes involuntarily followed Lister's swaying hips as she went through the large double doors. Cathie elbowed him, but was no less impressed by the tall, stunning woman who had greeted them. 'Steady there,' she muttered.

'Easy for you to say,' he whispered back as the door reopened.

Lister hardly seemed surprised at Logan's reaction. Or Cathie's. She had been doing this job for quite a while. She smiled a brilliant smile. 'Would you please come in.'

Smythe-Montgomery met them just inside his office as the two doors closed behind them.

'Ms. Fletcher,' he said, beaming at her. He took her hand in his and brought it to his lips. 'What an infinite pleasure.'

'Just Cathie, please,' she managed to say, in a voice that trembled slightly.

'Ah, then you must call me Conrad. And Mr. Fletcher, thank you so much for coming and, of course, for granting me some time with your lovely and talented wife.'

Logan quickly assessed Smythe-Montgomery. Most men had to look up to meet Logan's eye, but Smythe-Montgomery was an inch or so taller. He was well-built—not thin, but with no apparent excess fat. Logan unconsciously pulled in his stomach. Smythe-Montgomery's pale blue eyes were brilliant as diamonds, sparkling in the bronze tan of his face. And, Logan noticed with irritation, the man wore his three piece suit (a suit that made Colpoys' look like something from a rag fair) with such ease and nonchalance that he might have been born in it.

'Logan, please,' he said, with a smile.

'Excellent!' said Smythe-Montgomery. 'Like old friends, wot? Now please sit. Drinks? I have a small selection here'—he pointed to a well-stocked bar—'but anything you'd like can be arranged. Ms. Lister, please step in for a moment.'

She did, causing Logan to wonder what it would take, this late in his life, to become a billionaire. Whatever it was, it might be worth it. He raised an eyebrow as Cathie requested a Cosmo.

'A scotch on the rocks for me,' said Logan.

'A man after my own heart,' Smythe-Montgomery said. 'I'll take care of the gentleman, Ms. Lister, if you will see to the lady.'

When Lister had left, Smythe-Montgomery quickly poured out two glasses of scotch, then reached behind his desk and pulled out what looked like several old journals, bound in leather.

'These are from my collection. Records dating back to the crucial period in history when my family came into its own. They're just a sampling of all that's available. Here, slide closer and let me show you.'

Within minutes, Cathie was genuinely engrossed in the historical record of the family Croker. Logan sat back in his chair and sipped his delicious single malt scotch, staring out the wall of glass at the Thames and the swirling humanity far below. Periodically, he had an even better view, as Ms. Lister re-entered and brought a fresh drink for Cathie or handed Smythe-Montgomery a note and received a quick response. On each occasion she smiled pleasantly at Logan, well aware that he was more than a little distracted by her presence. Again, this was commonplace for her, and she took it as the natural state of things. Logan's eyes followed Ms. Lister while he occasionally picked up fragments of the animated discussion between Cathie and Smythe-Montgomery.

'… so it was your great-great-great-grandfather's plan that led to such an easy victory?' Cathie asked.

'Precisely!' Smythe-Montgomery replied. 'It was glorious, but it could easily have been a bloodbath if his plan had not been adopted. Months later, General Bernard—or General Barnyard as his troops referred to him for his slovenly dress—claimed it had been his plan all along. Pure jealousy, of course. Then the Chinese made protests to government, with highly exaggerated claims of brutality, clouding the entire victory. The general staff—goaded on by that incompetent fool Bernard—needed a scapegoat. They blamed my great-great-great-grandfather!'

'But he was never convicted at a court martial?'

'They didn't dare bring charges. Their case had no merit, and they knew it. He was harassed and bullied into resigning his commission, and so left the military under a cloud—a very false cloud indeed! But his brother would have none of it …'

Logan's attention wandered. He stood and walked over to the huge window and stared down on the city scene. The Thames, brown and drab, dominated the landscape, though he could also see St. James's Park, Waterloo Station, and the London Eye. Everywhere was a mass of humanity, crawling in ant-like obscurity several hundred feet below. Logan wondered how a perpetual view of the world, with people reduced to anonymous insects, would affect the psyche of a man like Smythe-Montgomery. If one were already inclined to see most of mankind as insignificant, perhaps even parasitical, this daily view of them scuttling about would enforce that impression. As Logan watched, the late-afternoon fog closed in, obscuring much of the view like a shabby curtain dropped at the end of a sad and pointless play. Logan was well in tune with the mood of the day.

'Extraordinary!'

The Reality of Chaos

Cathie's exclamation broke in on his dismal musing.

'Logan, Conrad has shown me direct evidence that his great-great-great-grandfather was robbed of credit for a splendid victory and blamed for military abuses that were clearly not his fault. Letters from before and after the battle absolutely prove it! What I don't understand, though, Conrad, is how he did so well following the Opium Wars given that the military establishment of the day had cast such a blemish—albeit false—on his actions.'

'Ah, that's a story for another time. But he had established a rapport with a powerful Chinese industrialist, Shin Lee, who was never fooled by the false accusations of the British military. Our families joined forces and established a mutually beneficial trading alliance. In time, the influence of my family grew. Wealth and power are bosom companions in the British Empire.'

'Extraordinary!' Cathie repeated.

Jeez, thought Logan, *I know Chuck said to butter this guy up, but come on, Cathie. He may be a narcissistic egotist, but he may start to smell a rat.*

'And so now, here you are,' she continued, unaware of Logan's apprehension. 'You've built your own empire—'

Logan noticed Smythe-Montgomery twitch at the words, but he quickly recovered, smiling complacently and murmuring modest denials.

'—so in addition to understanding your past, I would love to write an epilogue to your family's story, or rather a prologue to your own. What monument to history do you hope to leave behind, Conrad? Where will your dreams and ambitions take you?'

Smythe-Montgomery laughed. He glanced at his watch. 'Sadly, in the near term, only to a dreary business meeting in my offices near Gatwick in eighty-three short minutes. I can't tell you what a pleasure it's been discussing my family with you, Ms. Fletcher.'

'Cathie.'

'Forgive me. Cathie,' he said. 'Much more material is available for your perusal at my country estate in the southwest near the coast. Arrangements can be made for you to visit at your convenience, and I would love to meet with you at some future time. Is it too much to hope that you will take on the challenge of writing the truth of my family's history?'

'On one condition,' Cathie said playfully. 'I absolutely insist on that final chapter: The future empire of Sir Conrad Smythe-Montgomery!'

Again Logan noticed the involuntary twitch at Cathie's words. It would make an interesting point of discussion later.

'I'd be honored,' said Smythe-Montgomery. 'Perhaps in a few months you might send along some draft material for your book? An outline perhaps?'

'I'd love to. And I look forward to seeing the family records you spoke of and to meeting with you again.'

With no obvious signal from Smythe-Montgomery, Ms. Lister entered the room.

'Your limousine is waiting, sir,' she said. 'As the weather has turned rather nasty, I've taken the liberty of ordering a limousine for the Fletchers as well.'

'Excellent.' He waved off Logan's attempt at a protest. 'I won't hear of it. My guests will not stand in the cold and wet trying to hail a taxicab. Well,' he said, shaking their hands, 'I must go. When we meet again, perhaps we can toast your future Pulitzer Prize winning book, Ms. Fletcher.'

In an instant, he had left the room through another heavy wooden door, leaving both Logan and Cathie breathless.

'He has tremendous energy,' Ms. Lister said, in a serious tone. But Logan thought he caught the flicker of an impish smile as she spoke.

He and Cathie rode the elevator down in silence, Logan once again pondering a strategy to become a billionaire.

***

The next evening, at a quiet pub on Duke Street, Becky slipped into a secluded booth where two men were already seated. Both rose slightly, but she waved them back into their seats.

'No ceremony necessary, gentlemen. I'm a Marine brat. Hello, Randy. And "Mr. Shirley." Really?' she said, with a grin. 'Why on earth "Mr. Shirley."'

'Because it's a lot harder to be just "Shirley" when I'm in public and not online … Inside joke. You'll have to ask Luana sometime.'

The Reality of Chaos

'Luana Chu, CEO of Infinity Services Group. I wish to God my company's name was that cool, and that my company was as successful.'

'Hmm. Careful what you wish for. Just call me Jason, by the way.'

'Jason it is.' She scanned the table quickly. 'Excuse me for mentioning it, but there's something wrong with this picture.'

Randy laughed. 'Chuck warned me about you. Drinks are ordered and on the way, along with some scotch eggs that look like meatballs and something that appears to be a cheese sandwich, but that the menu called Welsh rarebit. God knows what the English version of a quesadilla is called.'

'I'm pretty sure it's called a quesadilla,' Stone said.

'Excellent,' Becky said. 'I'm famished from another busy day shopping.' She gave a lighthearted laugh and looked at Stone, who was evaluating her with a professional eye.

'Well, Jason, I'm five foot nine, age forty-three—though I usually lie about that—still run half marathons in a respectable time, enjoy a variety of sexual positions, some of my own invention, and would not resist stooping to picking up either of you gentlemen under the right circumstances. Also, I'm relatively intelligent, professionally successful, and a complete amateur in the field where I'm reliably told you excel.'

Stone laughed heartily. 'And clearly you're shy and withdrawn, not to mention hard to get.'

She shrugged at this, then pointed to Randy. 'Is that a genuine blush? Gail is such a lucky girl.'

'Easy, Randy,' Stone said, 'I doubt that Becky bites.'

'I wouldn't bet money on that, Jason,' she said, with a wink.

The drinks arrived just then, saving Randy from continued teasing.

After the waitress had taken dinner orders and left, Becky turned back to Stone. 'What were you actually trying to assess?'

'Well, you're clearly attractive enough to turn the head of our Smythe-Montgomery. You have the gift of comfortable, sexy banter, which should also be an asset. I just wonder if you realize the danger of this game you're so eager to play. Specifically, do you know when to pull the ejection handles and cut your losses, or are you going to ride it in to a spectacular, flaming finale?'

'Well phrased. Have you ever punched out of a disabled fighter?'

'I'm more accustomed to hard helo landings. Wrong branch of the military, I guess.'

'Aren't you just a puzzle,' she said, nodding with appreciation. 'To answer your specific question—what was your specific question again?'

'Do you want to stay alive?' Stone asked blandly.

'That should be obvious. I enjoy life immensely. I intend to keep on enjoying life and robbing the cradle until I'm at least eighty. Good enough?'

'Good enough for me,' Stone said.

'I'm not sure it's good enough for me.'

The two turned startled faces to Randy, who eyed them seriously.

'Becky, you sound like a high schooler taking a dare to swim across Devil's Lake in the dark, or to stay overnight in old Jensen's haunted farmhouse. Chuck's given me the authority to pull the plug on this little outing,' he lied, 'if I decide the risk unacceptable.'

Becky's face grew suddenly stern. 'Just what part of "I want to stay alive" failed to fire in your synapses? I'm not like you, all serious and professional, but I'm *deadly* serious about my life. Got it?'

'Yeah,' said Randy. 'Sorry about that. But I really did need to hear you say it seriously, at least once. For what it's worth, Chuck would have my nuts if I squelched this operation.'

'That would be a terrible loss—for Gail,' Becky said, the easy smile returning to her face.

The food arrived and the three settled in, Stone with bangers and mash, Randy with shepherd's pie, and Becky with a rare-to-the-point-of-mooing steak.

'Way to blend in, Becky,' Randy said.

'Pooh! I'm a good red-blooded American with a decadent taste for cow.'

Halfway through the meal, Stone casually placed an innocuous black thumb drive on the table.

'The family photos you asked for.'

Becky didn't immediately reach for the drive, but turned incredulous eyes to Stone. 'A thumb drive? Really? I mean, isn't there some other more, I don't know, high tech, cooler gadget?'

'I'll tell Luana,' he said. 'She'll be crushed.'

The Reality of Chaos

In a flash, Becky realized that Stone and Luana were the adversaries Chuck had expected to hack the Alpha Defense servers. She stared into Stone's eyes. He seemed to understand the unspoken question and nodded slightly.

'Yep,' Randy said, also having intercepted the silent communication. 'Strange bedfellows, hey?'

'Yes indeed,' Becky said. 'I'd like to meet Ms. Chu.'

'You will,' said Stone. 'She's asked to meet with you as well.'

'So ...' Becky said, pointing to the drive.

'It may not be as mundane as you think. Have you ever seen the stylized pictures of snakes eating their own tails?'

Becky said nothing, and Stone continued. 'It isn't actually a crappy old 64 gig thumb drive. You plug it into the computer. That's it. It searches, finds what it wants, emits a nonrepeating mini-burst of RF energy with 256 bit encryption, then proceeds to eat itself. There will be no sign of the embedded software or the information it found.'

'The RF transmitter?'

'Someone might find its remains with X-ray. An unidentifiable blob of fused circuits.'

'Cool,' said Becky. 'And all I do is plug it in? What about login passwords, stuff like that?'

'That's handled,' Stone said, 'but don't ask me how. Luana could explain.'

'How about some kind of cover? You know, some random files that are meaningless if someone picks up the thing later and just looks inside.'

'Thought of that. The remains of the drive are accessible. Right now they're loaded up with various pointless spreadsheets and downloaded news stories. Files with a few tourist snaps of London.'

'Seems pretty slick.'

'It's all of that,' said Randy. 'But if the computer you plug into isn't connected to Smythe-Montgomery's insider network, there won't be much to find. Wasted effort. Don't bother with any of the machines at the bidders' conference.'

'Duh,' said Becky, rolling her eyes.

'Fine,' Randy said, with a yawn. 'The only other thing I have to say is *please* be careful. It's way more important that you come away from this in one piece. Screw the data.'

'That was hardly my intention,' Becky replied, but she immediately banished the grin from her face. 'I'll say it seriously for you, Mr. O'Neil. I will be *very* careful. But it doesn't mean I can't have some fun, right?'

'Right.' Randy fished in his pocket and pulled out a wad of bills, which he carelessly tossed on the table. 'British money is weird. That should be enough. Sadly, I must now go and connect with my slave-driving boss and give him a full update. Goodnight, Stone. Goodnight, Becky.'

'I should probably head off too,' Stone said.

'Oh, just stay and buy me one more drink, would you Jason? I have a couple more questions.'

Randy left and Stone flagged the waitress. 'Two more, please.' When she had left, Stone turned a questioning face to Becky.

'The thumb drive. Can I add a few photos to the cover files?'

'Sure. Just be sure to boot the computer with the drive already plugged in. It will accept data normally then. Otherwise—'

'It will transmit all my nasty files to Chuck Johnson. Got it.'

The two sat in silence, enjoying their drinks, until Becky spoke again. 'You and Luana are well matched. Both intelligent. Both a little wild—or so I've been led to believe. I wouldn't mind hearing a little more of your backstory some time.'

'Hmm, that might be a long ways off. But I wouldn't mind a relaxing evening at our place in Breckenridge, once the dust settles.'

'I'm curious, of course. But I'd settle for that relaxing evening.' She seemed to be considering her words carefully before she continued. 'I could really use your help acquiring a few critical items—mostly girl stuff—that I couldn't easily transport on commercial airlines.'

'Girl stuff that won't survive TSA security. I'm all ears.'

Becky rattled off her short list of needs as Stone's mouth gaped wider and wider.

'Holy shit!' he said, when she was done. 'I wasn't expecting that. But yeah, I've got a few ... unusual friends who might have what you need. Should I ask why you need them?'

'No,' Becky said tersely, with a wry smile. 'If you don't already know, don't ask.'

***

Later that evening, Stone sat in Crandall's study jabbing at the logs in the fireplace. He would randomly add a log and then fuss with its position for the next five minutes. Luana, sitting in a loveseat nearby, finally asked him the obvious.

'What's troubling you, James? And you may save time by skipping a weak denial and simply telling me. You may also get me a cognac.'

Stone turned to her and smiled. 'That obvious, huh?'

'You've just about worried the poor fire into oblivion.' Luana put down the book she had been reading, an ancient Dickens tome from Crandall's library. 'Come sit and tell me.'

Stone returned with two snifters of cognac and sat down beside her. 'It's this whole business,' he said. 'I keep warning people—Chuck, Randy—that it's going to get bloody. I feel it in my gut. This guy Smythe-Montgomery is brilliant and ruthless, and he has the resources to do a lot of damage. That's unusual in an adversary.' He shrugged. 'At least, in an adversary that isn't a foreign government. And because he isn't a foreign government, he can move faster and with more efficiency. He's also far less predictable.'

'That's where Richard and his models come in.'

'Yes. Maybe. But I can't shake the feeling we're outmatched on this one.'

'Darling, have you considered your alternatives?'

Stone looked at her uncertainly. 'What do you mean?'

'It's simple. You and I and others, including Richard and Diana, know how dangerous this man is. Your alternatives are limited. Oppose him as we are. Oppose him in some other way. Or simply cut and run.'

'I didn't mention running,' Stone said harshly.

'No, but I did. It's an alternative and you must face it. That is, *we* must face it.'

'How?'

'Simply consider. What would the likely result be if Smythe-Montgomery were unopposed? Or put another way, given his nature, what is the risk of allowing him to proceed with his plans without resistance?'

'Pretty grim, I'd say. Even without knowing his ultimate goals.'

'If we step away, could you live with the outcome?' Luana asked.

'No.'

'So running is not an option. Very well. Can you think of a better way to oppose him?'

'Hell yeah. A small army of Rangers or SEAL Team Six guys. A little recon. A little stealth operation. Maybe some targeted hits.'

'Now that you've indulged your fantasies, James, can you think of another way to oppose him, *given the actual constraints of the situation*?'

He considered. 'No.'

'So, to worry about a choice that doesn't exist is unproductive, is it not?'

'You know,' he said, with a smile, 'in addition to being disturbingly gorgeous, you're annoyingly logical. So what do you suggest, my love, to distract me from my fruitless worry?'

In answer, Luana stood and dropped the heavy bathrobe she had been wearing. 'This usually works.'

He stood and took her in his arms. 'Yes, it usually does.'

***

Cathie was still irritated with Logan. After their meeting, he had repeatedly criticized her for her obvious stroking of Smythe-Montgomery's ego. Her rebuttal, that this had been the plan all along, was not well received. She had finally reduced him to silence by pointing out that he had been more interested in Ms. Lister's 'assets' than in Smythe-Montgomery's. Two days later, the discussion was still rankling both of them. Unfortunately, they were both expecting moral support and affirmation from Randy O'Neil, whom they were meeting for dinner.

Randy joined them at the Park Terrace Restaurant, overlooking Kensington Palace. He sensed the mood, and quickly ordered a well-aged Bordeaux as a sop to both. Perhaps it worked, or perhaps he had just gotten lucky. After their second glass, a cordial truce was in place, which Randy hoped to seal as he frantically flagged the waiter down and ordered another bottle.

'So, what now?' he asked, after meal orders had been placed.

The Reality of Chaos

'We stay a few more days,' Logan said, 'do a little sightseeing—'

'And a little shopping!' Cathie interrupted.

'Like she said,' Logan added. 'Then we head home and Cathie begins to craft her wonderful fictional history of Sir Conrad Croker.'

Cathie gave him a dirty look. 'Fictional history indeed!' she said, the truce broken in an instant. 'Tell us, Randy, what is the point of my interaction with *Conrad*? Am I to flog him in the public square, or inveigle him into another meeting, using my keen observation skills to uncover his nefarious plots?'

'Oh, gawd,' said Logan, 'sounds like one of your novels.'

'You, sir, are officially in the doghouse! Randy,' she said sweetly, 'please give me your *professional* opinion.'

Randy looked from one to the other. He was no fool, and he recognized a no-win situation when he saw one. 'I wouldn't mind a little light buttering up.'

'Coward,' Cathie whispered, but she smiled.

'So other than being high in cholesterol, how'd it go?' Randy asked.

Cathie gave him a brief rundown, emphasizing the potential for a meeting at Smythe-Montgomery's country estate.

'Well, good enough. How about you, Logan? Any observations?'

'Just one.'

'Hold that valuable thought until I get a drink, would you?' said Chuck Johnson, as he slid into the remaining seat at their table.

'Holy ... Chuck. Boss,' Randy quickly amended. 'Umm ... what the fuck are you doing here?'

Chuck laughed humorlessly. 'My Spidey sense was tingling, and it was telling me you guys could use some help.'

'Amen,' said Logan. 'Ah,' he added, as the waiter arrived at the table, 'it appears there will be four for dinner. So, another bottle of wine, and our new arrival will have the same thing as me.'

'What would that be?' Chuck asked.

'I've kind of forgotten, to be honest with you.'

'Beef Wellington, darling,' Cathie said. 'You're not getting senile on me, are you?'

'Not a bit. By the way, who are you?'

243

'You guys really ought to have your own comedy act,' Chuck said, shaking his head. 'But if you don't mind, I'd like to hear your one and only observation from your meeting with Smythe-Montgomery.'

'Yeah, well, it's simple and probably meaningless, but every time Cathie mentioned Smythe-Montgomery's future empire, he gave a twitch as though his comely assistant, Ms. Lister, had touched a delicate spot, if you know what I mean.'

'Crude, dear, but accurate,' Cathie said. 'I noticed that also. It seemed a bit odd. Any notions?' She looked from Randy to Chuck.

'Sounds like delusions of grandeur to me,' Randy said.

'What if they're not delusions?' asked Chuck.

Randy began to laugh, then grew quiet as he watched his boss. 'Are you serious?'

'Yes ... No ... Maybe. I've talked to Stone. Sounds like you two'—he nodded towards Randy—'had an interesting meeting with Ms. Amhurst. It also seems that Stone has confidence in Richard Crandall's geopolitical predictions. I'm hoping for some intel we can feed into his models. Empire. I doubt it's a coincidence that that's the name of his yacht.'

'So what's the play, boss?' Randy asked.

'Same as before. The bidders' conference is coming up this week. Stay close to Becky, make sure you and Stone keep a receiver tuned to her ... gadget ... and that you're as close as possible. We'd hate like hell to miss an interesting broadcast ... of BBC news,' he added, as the waiter arrived with a packed tray.

The Reality of Chaos

Smythe-Montgomery glanced at his watch. 'Come,' he said cheerfully, 'we have just enough time to catch the train and make it back to the Christmas tree by 9:00.'

Chapter Twenty

Bidders' Conference

Most bidders' conferences are deadly dull. Technical briefings, pontificating on the scope and value of potential future contracts, and the pointless interplay between contractors, trying to extract a few crumbs of competitive intel. This conference was no exception. One difference might have been that the value of the contract was significant. The current contract also specified that the winning bidder would have any subsequent work: there would not be another proposal.

The first morning, a cold and dreary Tuesday a week before Christmas, was taken up with customer briefings. There were the obligatory contracts briefs, a program executive summary by an anonymous VP of Pacific-Indo-Asia Air, and the much more technical briefings by the new chief engineer, a thin, nervous man with sandy hair and an ill-fitting suit. As Becky watched his choppy, anxious performance, she wondered how much the man knew (or guessed) about the fate of his predecessor. By the time he finished, it was lunchtime.

'For the love of God,' Becky whispered to Gary, 'don't embarrass me with a horrible briefing like that tomorrow.'

'Like you haven't seen me practice it—fourteen times!'

'Just make number fifteen solid gold. We do want to win this thing.'

'Oh, we should be a shoo-in if Smythe-Montgomery gets a look at you.'

Becky smiled. She was dressed in a stylish grey business suit, the skirt just reaching the top of her knees. Her black shirt was cut low enough to accommodate a gold chain and black pendant. Black nylons and heels completed the picture. Her long, golden hair, normally done in a utilitarian manner, was loose about her shoulders. The overall look was professional while leaving little doubt that she was a woman, and a very attractive one at that. But it was far from alluring, at least by her standards, which is why Gary's comment made her smile.

'Thanks. I wonder what all the commotion is about?' she asked. There was a buzz as the contractors exited the large conference room for an adjacent hall that was set up for a buffet lunch.

'I'll go and find out,' Gary said. He shuffled off and asked a few questions of the staff who were guiding the participants as they left the conference room. When he returned, he looked stunned. 'The guest speaker at lunch. It's him. Smythe-Montgomery.'

This was a surprise. Becky had expected a typical motivational speaker, perhaps a former athlete or celebrity, but this was far better. *Game on*, she thought.

***

Lunch was surprisingly good for an event of this kind. Even better, there was no American taboo against alcohol being served. The wine was excellent. But Becky drank only a small amount. She wanted to be sharp when Smythe-Montgomery spoke.

His speech was brief and focused almost entirely on the opportunity for the company that won the contract, promising a fulfilling working relationship in a robust, expanding enterprise. She was intrigued by his allusions to the former British Empire: its strengths and weaknesses, its rise and fall. 'In our own small way,' he had said, 'we are a mirror to the past and an example for the future of the limitless possibilities of a successful collaboration.' To Becky, this comparison provided an irresistible entrée.

After the speech, Smythe-Montgomery went briefly to each table, welcoming the proposal participants. He was gracious and friendly, but never spent more than a minute with each group. That is, until he came to Becky's table.

'Becky Amhurst,' she said, rising and shaking his hand firmly, 'ARC Avionics. This is my chief engineer, Gary Walkin.'

'Charmed,' said Smythe-Montgomery, never taking his eyes off Becky. Gary muttered a few words, then fell silent, watching the interplay between Becky and Smythe-Montgomery.

'I wasn't horribly impressed with your speech,' she said, with a brilliant smile.

The Reality of Chaos

'Indeed?' Smythe-Montgomery responded, trying to hide his pique.

'That is, until your absolutely captivating words regarding the parallels of a successful business venture and the most successful empire the world has ever known.'

'Ah,' he said, smiling in return. 'Could it be that you are both a successful businesswoman and a student of history?'

'On a very modest level. But I believe strongly in the principles of focus, cooperation, and discipline—in any endeavor.'

Only a blind fool could have missed the playful implications of her comments, and Smythe-Montgomery was neither.

'Ms. Amhurst, I believe you may be a kindred spirit in many ways, and I would very much like to continue this conversation. Sadly, I will be preoccupied for the next day or so, but … you will be attending our little party Wednesday evening, after the conference is concluded?'

'Absolutely,' Becky said. 'I wouldn't miss it.'

'Excellent! I'm sure you'll enjoy it. Please don't be put off by the fact that it takes place in one of my hangars near here. I promise something … special. And, of course, I will be counting on resuming our discussion.'

'You'll be there?'

'I certainly was planning to attend, but now my motivation is greatly enhanced—anticipating our discussion.'

'I should ask, then,' Becky said, with a look of girlish shyness that Gary had never seen on his hard-bitten boss, 'the proper way to address a knight of the realm. Is it Sir Smythe-Montgomery, or—'

At that moment, Becky's purse slipped off the back of her chair and tumbled to the ground. In an instant, Smythe-Montgomery was picking it up and handing it to Becky, a smile on his lips and a spark in his eyes.

'Conrad,' he said. 'Please call me Conrad.'

Becky nodded, and a blush flashed across her face, once again amazing Gary. 'As you wish … Conrad. It's only fair that you call me Becky.'

'Would that be short for Rebecca?'

'Yes.'

To Gary's everlasting amazement, Sir Conrad Smythe-Montgomery took her hand to his lips and kissed it. 'Until tomorrow evening, then, Rebecca.'

'Holy crap!' Gary whispered, as Smythe-Montgomery moved off, with a final turn and a smile, 'I don't believe I just saw that!'

'Oh ye of little faith!' Becky replied.

'And when your purse fell and he just stooped down to grab it …!'

'Don't be a hick from the sticks, Gary. The purse fell because I wanted it to fall. And he knew that before he went to pick it up.'

'Holy crap!' Gary repeated. 'I bow to your phenomenally superior abilities, boss. My parents must have been holding out on me in the social skills department.'

'Don't you believe it. I learned everything I know through practice—and some unfortunate experiences.' She was thoughtful for a moment, considering her past. 'I don't know that it was all worth it. I sometimes really envy what Logan and Cathie have.'

Gary gave her a puzzled look.

'Never mind,' she said, her effervescent spirit quickly resurfacing. 'Water under the bridge, or over the dam, or under the damn bridge. Anyway, past and gone. Top up my wine glass, would you, there's no point in staying sharp for the rest of this day.'

***

The following afternoon, Becky met Gary outside the entrance to the conference room. He had changed his tie, but was otherwise wearing the same clothes as the previous day. But he stared at Becky in surprise. She was in a different business suit: pinstripes this time, and slim, straight pants instead of a skirt, a white button-down shirt, and a simple gold chain high around her neck.

'Wow!' he said. 'Did you buy all these clothes in London?'

Becky shrugged, looking only slightly guilty. 'A woman has to appear especially sharp and professional in a business environment dominated by men. What else was I supposed to do?'

'Well, hell' was all Gary could say. He checked his watch. Nearly 1:00. The other two contractors had already presented: one the previous afternoon, and one in the morning. Naturally, only the briefing contractor and the customer were present for each of these briefings. Becky was delighted that ARC Avionics would be last. The customers would have her messaging most clearly in their minds after two days of drudgery. And she had a few special twists—approved with enthusiasm by Chuck Johnson—that would get their attention. An offer of a huge independent research and development investment for related technology was the biggest sweetener. The contractor was not allowed to use their own funds to pay for contract tasks, of course. That was an easy way to wind up in jail, and Becky knew several program managers and CEOs who'd gotten into a world of trouble. But on related technology, the field was clear. The fact that this related technology would fit perfectly with the potential future contracts from Pacific-Indo-Asia Air was, as she thought, a happy coincidence. It was perfectly legal, but it would allow Pacific-Indo-Asia Air to reduce the scope of future work knowing it had already been done using someone else's money. There could be no contractual commitment, but Becky had the funding in a long term plan—approved by her board.

She opened her briefing briskly, walking through cost, schedule, and technology, before passing the baton to Gary. She would save her surprises for her closing statement.

This wasn't Gary's first rodeo, and though he'd complained about the many times he had reviewed his material with Becky, he was a firm believer in the adage that the secret to a good briefing was practice, practice, practice. This philosophy and his years of experience paid off, and his only stumble occurred when a customer asked a business-related question that was out of his area of expertise. Becky stepped in with a crisp, satisfying answer, and Gary returned to his briefing, unruffled.

Becky stood up and gave her closing remarks, casually dropping her deal sweeteners on a pleasantly stunned audience. As the meeting concluded, she could see several executives from the airline talking among themselves. At one point, the nervous chief engineer was collared and dragged into the discussion. She could see him nodding vigorously as the others pummeled him with questions. *The fish is nosing the bait*, she thought.

After a brief adjournment, the CEO of Pacific-Indo-Asia Air invited all three contractors back in for a final word. It was an obligatory, nearly pointless formality, but Becky was gratified to see the representatives from her two competitors eyeing her suspiciously during the comments. Apparently, rumors had spread quickly.

When the CEO finally completed his banal remarks, the audience rose and began their retreat back to their rooms. It was nearly 5:00, and the party, hosted by the gracious Smythe-Montgomery, would begin at 7:30. A host of rare butterflies began to dance in Becky's stomach. *Wow,* she thought, *haven't felt that since senior prom! Scary—but good!*

'So, do you want to get some dinner, boss?' Gary asked, stifling a yawn.

'Not for me, but you go ahead. Besides, I need a little time to get ready for that party. What?' she asked, as Gary scanned her immaculate outfit in confusion. 'You can't expect me to wear this to a party! It's a'—she waved her hands in exasperation—'party! And one hosted by Sir Handsome himself. Oh, you look fine,' she added, as he inspected his slightly rumpled suit. 'It's a girl thing. Besides, I know you saw the Indonesian woman, the deputy chief engineer if Indo-Air, giving you the eye. Her name is Devi Idrial, by the way. Just meet me in the lobby at 8:00 and we'll catch the shuttle over to the hangar.'

'The party starts at 7:30.'

'Gary ... hick from the sticks! Fashionably late! Makes your arrival that much more special. Go on now. Get your dinner.'

***

Gary had been waiting in the lobby since 7:35. Most of the other contractors had come through and caught the shuttle, as had some of the customers. He was nervous to be on his way, as he had exchanged a few words with Devi earlier, and she had seemed eager to continue a discussion on the advantages of a federated avionics suite.

People came and went as the time approached 8:00. Gary did a double take as a tall, striking woman in tight-fitting black dress and wearing a sparkling diamond necklace entered the lobby. He began sweating as she walked towards him until he suddenly realized that this gorgeous stunner was none other than his boss, Becky Amhurst. He took the next few moments to carefully look her over. It was hard to believe that this was the same woman who had so competently briefed the customer earlier in the day. Her dress, held up by a single sequined strap on her left shoulder, highlighted her curves wonderfully but reached below her ankles so that Gary wondered how she could walk so easily. This problem resolved itself as she neared: Gary could see a slit down each side of her dress that reached to her upper thighs and gave tantalizing glimpses of long legs. When she sidled up to him, a slow smile creeping onto her face, she was several inches taller than earlier in the day. Clearly, she was wearing some impressive heels. Her face was made up just to the happy side of overdone, highlighting her high cheekbones and full lips. Gary just stood and gaped.

'Haven't you ever seen a woman before?' she asked.

'Apparently not! Holy smokes! My boss, the fashion model!'

'Oh, enough of that boss crap. Give me your arm and escort me to the shuttle. It's time to party.'

***

The Smythe-Montgomery complex included his hotel, the conference center, three smaller office buildings, and the operations building located between his two private hangars. This cluster of buildings was located at the northeast corner of the airport, near the end of Gatwick's main runway. A small taxiway connected the hangars to the main taxiway of the airport, giving Smythe-Montgomery's aircraft easy access. Ideal for the billionaire who needed to rapidly leave or return to England.

The outside of the larger of Smythe-Montgomery's private hangars was uninviting to say the least. The large structure was the color of lead and only a few colored lights surrounded the windows—all shuttered—on the side of the building opposite the taxiway. Only the appearance of several of his staff near a small, unassuming side door gave any hint of activity inside. Had Logan been present, he might have recognized Mr. Colpoys in a tuxedo. In the dark room of another nearby hotel, Jason Stone had already made that identification. He would also be able to comment on the steady procession of delivery trucks for several days prior, and on the small army of workers who had only finished their task—still a mystery—just the day before.

'Well, Becky, it looks as though you may have gotten all dressed up for nothing,' Gary said, with just a hint of 'told you so.'

'We'll see,' she said. 'Keep in mind who's hosting this little get-together.'

The shuttle stopped near the hangar and one of the well-dressed attendants came to the door. The man offered a hand to Becky, and she and Gary stepped across the pavement and entered ... the world of a Christmas fantasy.

Absolutely nothing about the inside of the building reminded them of an aircraft hangar. The entryway was a snow-covered forest, the fir trees blazing with Christmas lights and ornaments. Large trees and small trees on man-made hills covered in snow. Above, the twinkling of stars, the only other lighting in this bizarre woodland setting. Though each tree was bathed in color, illuminating the area immediately surrounding itself, other areas were mysteriously shadowed, as if the fairies who had created this scene might be hiding somewhere in the darkness. Up ahead, at the end of the twisting path, was an arched doorway, with the hint of silver light beyond. Music drifted through the woods to add a surreal melody to the illusion of the woodland. And another sound—a train whistle?—haunted this magical scene.

The two walked slowly along the winding path until they passed through the archway into a fantasy world of ice and snow. Pathways led in various directions. One towards what appeared to be a frozen pond, with Christmas elves as ice skaters. One to a busy table, where drinks were being poured. Contractors and customers from the conference were drinking, talking, and pointing everywhere. An eight-piece band, dressed in full costume and seated on a fanciful ice-block bandstand, were playing seasonal music with an Elizabethan flare. Other paths led to tables of food, chocolate fountains, fondues. A man at a small table was making rosette cookies to order, sprinkling powdered sugar or a dust of chocolate on the hot pastries. Decorated trees, strings of holly, colored lights, and animated characters were everywhere. In one corner of the building, a Christmas castle, drawbridge down, invited visitors to come and explore. A small village at the base of the castle was also attracting conference participants. Between the village and the castle was a town square that featured an enormous Christmas tree, whose base was crowded with brightly-wrapped presents of all shapes and sizes. Everywhere, men in suits and impeccably dressed women were exploring, entranced. A small train looped around the entire scene, stopping at a platform to allow guests to board.

'You were saying?' Becky asked.

'This is unbelievable,' Gary said solemnly.

Before they had gone more than a few steps, a tall man in a splendid tuxedo emerged from behind a cluster of large candy canes.

'Why there you are, Rebecca!' he said. 'I had begun to despair.'

'Gary, best you go and find Devi now,' Becky whispered.

Smythe-Montgomery arrived just as Gary drifted away.

'Stunning!' he said, looking Becky over with admiration.

'As are you, Sir—'

'Tut, tut,' he interrupted, wagging a finger.

'Sorry. Conrad. But you look every inch the British nobleman.'

He bowed. 'Would you care to join me for a cocktail?'

'I'd love to. By the way, this place …!'

'Do you like it? I must show you around. Though I shouldn't say so, it was built primarily for the homeless children of London. It will open tomorrow. The presents under the tree are for them. But I felt it might add a bit of seasonal fun to close out what I suspect were two days of rather dull meetings. And, of course, the first day's speaker was appallingly uninspiring.'

'Oh, you just aren't going to let me forget that, are you? Is there anything I can do to make amends?'

Smythe-Montgomery smiled charmingly. 'Why, Rebecca, what a delightful offer. Let me consider while we have that drink and explore my whimsical little world.'

They walked, drinks in hand, around the fantasy world, Smythe-Montgomery pointing out particular features he had personally insisted upon, and Becky obsequiously commenting on his creativity and generosity. 'What a wonderful, magical gift to give to children, Conrad. I've never seen anything like it.'

Smythe-Montgomery glanced at his watch. 'Come,' he said cheerfully, 'we have just enough time to catch the train and make it back to the Christmas tree by 9:00.'

'What happens at 9:00? Don't tell me Santa is going to make an appearance.'

Smythe-Montgomery laughed. 'Not hardly, but you'll see.'

As the train pulled away, he said, 'Now, when we get to the birch tree forest, keep an eye out for cardinals. That was one of my ideas!'

The train made its slow excursion around the entire hangar: past the village and the castle, through the birch tree forest, across a small bridge with a snow-banked creek splashing noisily below, past elvish workshops, through a part of the darkened fir-tree forest of the entrance. At this point, Smythe-Montgomery leaned close to Becky and placed his hand on her bare shoulder.

'You'll love this next part,' he said.

Becky edged closer on the small wooden seat until she was pressed tightly against him. A moment later they were in a woodland scene full of animals: squirrels, foxes, bears, bobcats, martins, rabbits, owls, deer. All turned to look as the train passed, chattering, growling, or hooting, as appropriate.

'Wonderful!' Becky exclaimed, reaching across and squeezing his hand. 'It's like a dream.'

'Isn't it?' he replied, smiling. 'Ah, but sadly, we are near our stop.' He released her shoulder and she slid away slightly, giving his hand one final squeeze.

'There,' she said, with a sigh, 'we've had our fantasy, and now we have to behave with proper decorum.'

'For now,' he whispered, as the train came to a halt. 'Quickly, we have just time to get another cocktail and walk to the Christmas tree.'

Becky gave him a puzzled look.

'Just wait,' he said.

When they arrived at the tree, he checked his watch. The seconds ticked down, and it was nine o'clock. And it began to snow.

Everywhere in the transformed hangar, people were laughing and pointing upward as a light snow fell everywhere.

'Another of your ideas, Conrad?'

He inclined his head slightly. 'As a matter of fact. There are several snow machines—'

Becky put a cool finger to his lips. 'Don't spoil it. Let's just say it's magic.'

The snow lasted only briefly, but when it ended there was spontaneous applause from all around the hangar.

As the applause died out, Ms. Lister walked up and waited several paces from where Smythe-Montgomery and Becky stood.

'Ah,' he said. 'Excuse me for just a moment.'

Becky eyed Ms. Lister carefully while she whispered to Smythe-Montgomery. She was stunning in a short, midnight-blue dress, her long hair cascading down her back seductively.

Definitely more than a working relationship, thought Becky, as the two conversed. *Well, all's fair ...'*

As Smythe-Montgomery turned away, Becky saw Ms. Lister giving her an equally appraising stare.

'It seems I have a little business to attend to,' Smythe-Montgomery said, frowning.

Becky was about to protest, but he stopped her. 'I will return shortly, but I must mingle with all my guests, as Ms. Lister rightly points out. However, there will be a smaller, more exclusive party for the presidents and CEOs of our contractors and Pacific-Indo-Asia Air, plus a few other executives of my global operations. You are most cordially invited. I would be *very* disappointed if you chose not to attend,' he added.

'I'd be delighted, Conrad.'

'Excellent.' He pointed to a man in a tuxedo standing nearby. He was clearly not a guest. 'Mr. Colpoys or one of his assistants will direct you at, say, 10:30.'

'I'm looking forward to it!' Becky said, her eyes gleaming.

'Until then, Rebecca,' Smythe-Montgomery replied, then walked off at a brisk pace.

When he had gone, Becky found her hands were shaking. *What the hell have you gotten yourself into?* she wondered. *But this is exactly how I wanted things to work out. If I'm not having sex with that man by midnight, I'll be astounded.* She smiled nervously at that. *I guess I've still got it. Now, where the hell has Gary gotten to? I need another drink.*

***

In their darkened hotel room, Randy and Stone talked quietly.

'Well, there's only one security man standing outside now,' Randy said. 'Apparently all the guests have arrived. The others have all moved in now.'

'Including my personal friend with the Uzi,' said Stone.

'What?' Randy asked. Stone briefly related his first encounter with Colpoys.

'Great first impression, Stone. Wish I'd been there to see it.'

'It happened pretty fast. Luana thought I'd overreacted.' He shrugged.

'So what now?' Randy asked.

Since their first tense meeting, the relationship between Stone and Randy had grown to one of mutual respect, almost admiration. In the early days, Randy would never have asked Stone's opinion, but would have offered suggestions or acted independently. Stone was flattered, but he reflected the question with equal grace.

'What do you think?' he asked, with a smile.

Randy considered. 'We've probably got some dead time now. Maybe a couple of hours, but we can't count on it. You might want to try a few random shots with the laser. See if there's any useful chatter in Smythe-Montgomery's tower. I suppose I'd better get the mobile receiver into the car and start driving aimless loops around the hotel. You've got the primary here, but if for some reason Becky leaves the area, I'd better be ready to pursue. How's that sound?'

'Just about dead nuts on to what I was thinking,' Stone said. 'But I'll tell you what, give me about twenty minutes. I want to go up to the roof, see if I can get a better line of sight to some of the windows that don't have countermeasures. I should have done it before, but ... let me give it a try. I should be back soon.'

'Got it. Better bring a scarf. It's getting kind of brisk outside.'

Stone just smiled and noiselessly left the room.

***

Though he might have been joking about the scarf, Randy hadn't been joking about the weather. It was cold and damp, and the persistent drizzle had become almost indistinguishable from the pleasant indoor snowfall inside the hangar. Stone had brought only a light jacket and was regretting the choice as he secured his headphones and positioned the laser. Just as he was preparing to sample a few random windows, a light flickered on in an office on the floor below Smythe-Montgomery's penthouse suite. Stone and Randy had long since determined that this floor was used by Smythe-Montgomery's senior staff and advisers. He adjusted the laser and was rewarded with voices, barely intelligible over crackling static. Stone adjusted his aim point and pushed a few buttons on the electronic controls, adding some narrowband filtering. The voices sounded flat, as though speaking through mud, but the static was significantly reduced.

'… ready by 10:30,' said a female voice. 'The guests will come up through the private elevator. There will be—' Interference briefly obscured the voice. '—and, of course, surveillance. Also,' the voice added, in a low grumble, 'he will likely have a guest for the ni—'

Damn it! Stone thought.

'—hurst.'

'Competition?' asked a male voice. There were a few chuckles in the background.

'If you want to keep your job, and your insignificant balls attached to your body, you can shut the—'

And now I miss the best part, thought Stone, with a grin.

'—goes for every one of you. Am I making myself clear?'

A humble chorus of 'Yes, Ms. Lister. Absolutely, Ms. Lister.'

'Oh, jolly good! Now get out of here and do your jobs!'

The light went out a short time later, and Lister's undecipherable mumbles ended with the slam of a door.

'Not a happy camper,' Stone said to himself. 'I suppose since I'm up here, I should check a couple other rooms for the sake of duty.'

For the next few minutes, Stone scanned every window—dark or lit—on the two floors directly below the suite. He thought he picked up the grumbling of two male voices briefly in one, and distinctly heard the word 'bitch.' But that room soon went dark. Stone glanced at the slushy mix that continued to fall from the sky and shook his head.

'Enough of this shit.'

He packed his gear and headed back to the room.

***

'Well?' Randy asked, as Stone stripped off his sodden jacket.

'You were right. It's kind of brisk out there. But I picked up one useful crumb. Sounds like an after-party in Smythe-Montgomery's suite starting at about 10:30. It's possible that Becky has landed her fish.'

'What do you mean, possible?'

Stone played back the recording of the conversation he had intercepted. When it finished, Randy nodded and said, 'I see what you mean. Still, an after-party would imply bosses. I'm sure she'd go if invited. I'll check to see if anyone else's name might end with "hurst." Presumably a female.'

It took Randy no more than two minutes to peruse the list. 'Nope,' he said. 'So I'd say possible has moved to probable.'

'But not certain.'

'Sadly, no. I'd better saddle up just in case. If you can confirm she's there, let me know and I'll head back.'

'Then that's the plan,' Stone said. As Randy was about to leave, Stone added, 'Better take your jacket.'

Randy grinned and went out as quietly as Stone had.

The Reality of Chaos

Stephen Lance / Chuck Markussen

'I have just the thing, a lovely 1985 Dom Perignon.'

Chapter Twenty-One

After-Party

A little after ten, Gary appeared, looking sheepish. He and Becky had gotten a drink over an hour ago, but he had left her immediately after, in search of Devi once again. This had forced Becky to make the rounds of the others at the party. It was a usual thing after such a conference, but her nerves were on edge and she kept checking her watch.

'Oh, for heaven's sake, just have her come over.' Becky was looking over Gary's shoulder at a respectful and deferential Devi, obviously waiting in the wings. Gary motioned and Devi walked over. 'Hello,' Becky said cheerfully. 'Enjoying the party?'

'Oh, yes, Ms. Amhurst. Very much.'

This seemed to be the extent of her desire to talk, so Gary took over. 'I hope you don't mind, but I … that is we … were thinking of leaving. We might, you know, stop off somewhere for a drink—'

'It's OK, Gary,' Becky said, sounding to herself like a mother being asked by a shy boy if he could date her daughter. She took a deep breath. 'Go on. Have a great time.'

The two shuffled off, still with a guilty demeanor, and Becky checked her watch. It was 10:17.

Crap, she thought, *might as well take another train ride. What the hell is the matter with me?*

Well, she answered herself, *I've never seduced a billionaire before. That is, a psychotic, murderous billionaire.*

And you won't, either. Not in your present state. Now, what would I do if I had finally managed to coax Logan into a fling?

Easy. I'd get another drink and lighten the fuck up! This is either going to be fun or it isn't.

And the other thing? The super-sleuth spy stuff?

Probably never even get an opportunity. So shut the hell up!

Becky's advice had been sound. She spent the next twenty minutes having a drink with the CEO of Pacific-Indo-Asia Air, a portly businessman from Singapore, and watching the elves skate on the icy pond. She was enjoying the conversation when the man named Colpoys came up to the two and politely reminded them that it was now past 10:30, and would they care to join their host.

'Well, Mr. Yee, we really should, I suppose. I'd hate to be rude.'

'It would be a fatal slight to my employer, Sir Conrad.'

The word 'fatal' caused a brief chill to sweep up Becky's spine, but the Cosmo she had been drinking had calmed her, and the chill passed quickly, replaced with excited anticipation.

That's my girl. Now for some fun!

Smythe-Montgomery's suite was beautifully decorated for the season, though, as always, he opted for an Elizabethan style: Wooden desks and tables, ornately carved. Couches and love seats with stuffed cushions in extravagantly designed material. Heavy carpets with elaborate designs of castles, lions, and griffins.

Guests were shown in to a large room that took up one entire end of the top floor. There were glass walls on three sides with the exception of a fireplace bisecting the windows of the end wall. Surrounded by dark, heavy wood and with a deeply carved mantel, it looked as though it had been removed from an ancient castle and brought here. It had. A garland of holly and mistletoe stretched across the mantel and hung down the sides, framing the blazing fire.

Large, brightly lit Christmas trees were stationed in either corner of the room. Chairs, sofas, and tables, scattered everywhere, held a few guests who were already holding drinks, talking, and pointing in disbelief at the marvelous setting. Many of the furnishings were not only of an Elizabethan style, but were truly of that era, restored to glory and scattered almost carelessly in this 21st century setting.

Becky scanned the room several times, no less impressed than the others. *Wonder what his bedroom looks like?*

***

Stone was amazed as Smythe-Montgomery's suite blazed into light when heavy curtains were drawn to allow guests a full view outside. He tried the laser microphone on every window, but the noise-generating devices were doing an excellent job, and no combination of filters or algorithms was able to clear up the signal. He had anticipated this, and switched to binoculars. After scanning the room for about fifteen minutes, he saw Becky arrive.

'There's our girl. Wow! Smythe-Montgomery would have to be made of stone to ignore that.' He watched Becky for a while as she circulated in the room, talking to other guests. He continued watching until Smythe-Montgomery appeared, greeting each of his guests. Though he was careful not to show too much particular attention to Becky, there was no doubt he preferred her company.

Stone reached for a two-way radio. 'Randy, you copy?'

'Ten-four, Stone. What's up?'

'Our lady is at the party. Come on back. Whatever is going to happen will happen right here. And by the way, you might want to buy Gail a dress like the one Becky is wearing. Just don't tell her where you first saw it.'

'That good, huh?'

'Come on back. Judge for yourself.'

When Randy returned, he grabbed another pair of binoculars and watched the scene for the next twenty minutes. Finally, he turned away with a sigh.

'It looks like a terrible party. I only saw one caviar station, and they're running low on champagne.'

'Nope,' Stone said, 'I see another case rolling in.'

'Crap! Now that's just mean. And I'm getting hungry.'

Stone pointed at the counter in the kitchen. 'Still got some leftover pizza, champ.'

'I should have specified hungry for *food*,' Randy replied sourly.

***

It was after midnight, and the party had begun to break up. Some of the guests had flights the next day. One by one they said goodnight to their host and were escorted to the elevator, either to exit the building or return to their own rooms below. At last, only Becky and Yee, the Pacific-Indo-Asia Air executive, remained.

'Goodnight, Sir Conrad,' said Yee. 'I have a long flight home tomorrow, and much work when I arrive there.'

'Goodnight, Yee. I'm so glad you could come.'

'I really should be going, too,' Becky said sadly. 'But what a wonderful evening. Thank you so much.'

'Surely you aren't flying home tomorrow, Rebecca?' The way he asked made it clear that he was well aware of her travel plans.

'No, not until next week.'

'Then please stay a while longer. A nightcap perhaps? Or a lively discussion of the British Empire?'

Becky flushed. 'I'd love to, but ... would it be appropriate, in light of the competition?'

'I assure you Mr. Yee will spread the word that you and he left at the same time. The last guests to go.'

'Why, Conrad, that's ... lovely. I'm not above a little deception to be able to accept your offer.'

'Just a little?' he asked, a mock-disappointed look on his face. 'Come, let's grab that drink and I'll give you a tour of the remainder of my little domicile.'

The rest of Smythe-Montgomery's staff vanished within two minutes, and so did Smythe-Montgomery's deferential reserve. He placed his arm around Becky's waist. She smiled and melted against his side. They had moved into an anteroom at the far end of the suite when he halted. He took her shoulders in his hands and turned her to face him.

'You are quite beautiful, Rebecca.'

'Why don't you kiss me?' she asked.

He pulled her body to his and kissed her passionately. His right hand ran down her hip and found the slit on the side of her dress. He grabbed her thigh, raising her leg, and ran his hand along its length, squeezing.

'I see you're fascinated by my silk stockings,' she said huskily.

'I really have very little interest in silk.'

She pushed him back slowly and placed her foot on the seat of a chair. The back of her dress fell away exposing her from her foot to a point two-thirds of the way up her thigh. She lifted her dress slightly higher and disengaged her garter belt from the top of her stocking, watching his reaction as she slowly slid it down her leg.

'*Quite* interesting,' he said. He turned and pointed to a set of heavy wooden double doors. 'Do you know what's in there?'

She pulled herself back into his arms. 'It had better be your bedroom.'

In a few moments they were inside. Becky kicked off her shoes and threw her purse onto a chair, making sure it was near the bed. The bed: a massive four-poster with a fabulously carved headboard. Curtains of deep purple hung at each corner and the same material was woven into a latticework of dark wood slats above. Off to one side was a heavy dresser, and beyond that, facing a heavily draped window, a massive desk. A large computer monitor dominated the desk, an erotic screensaver fading in and out, offering tantalizing glimpses. In an alcove below the desktop a large tower hummed quietly. *Jackpot!* thought Becky. *But first things first.*

Smythe-Montgomery pulled her close again and covered her face with kisses. A blur of rapid motion, he unzipping her dress, she tugging at his belt. The dress was tossed onto a chair, his tuxedo, shirt, and pants following. Then he was naked, on his knees, unfastening her other stocking and sliding it down with both hands past her knee, her calf, her foot. He reached up again and grasped the sides of her panties and eased them down to her ankles. She reached down and pulled him to his feet.

'Get in bed,' she whispered.

Another blur of motion as she pushed him onto his back and then straddled him. His hands reached up, cupping her breasts. For the next half hour they wrestled, sometimes gently, sometimes with surprising violence. Becky had temporarily forgotten any notion of spying and was simply enjoying the wild sexual experience. She was once again on top as Smythe-Montgomery let out a deep growl of ecstasy. Becky relaxed from her concentration and allowed herself to be overwhelmed with pleasure. Her moans joined his. It lasted for long moments, then she collapsed into his arms.

In what seemed a very short time, Smythe-Montgomery rolled her off him and stood up. 'A drink, Rebecca?'

'Please.'

He bent over and kissed her. 'I won't be long. I have just the thing, a lovely 1985 Dom Perignon.' He walked through another doorway at the end of the room.

It took nearly half a minute before Becky realized that this was her opportunity. She quickly slid from the bed and retrieved the thumb drive from her purse. Her hands shaking, she inserted the drive into a front-side USB port.

***

A frantic beeping brought Randy upright in his chair. Stone beat him to the laptop by inches. He keyed in an access code and a custom display popped up. A status bar was filling with blinding speed. And then—done. Stone turned to Randy with a grin. 'Got it! Every damn data bit worth having.'

***

Smythe-Montgomery's face was an evolving picture of surprise, embarrassment, and fury as he stood in the doorway, a drink in each hand. Becky turned hastily and stood up from her kneeling position near the computer tower.

'Oh, fuck,' she said, grimacing. 'I wish to hell you hadn't seen that.'

'I imagine you do. I also imagine you'll be found, possibly, with an extremely high blood alcohol content floating in the Thames.'

'Ooh, Conrad,' she said, as she retrieved her purse, 'no torture first? I may have overestimated you. I was certain there was a kinky, wild side to you.'

Time for some of the 'girl stuff' that Stone so obligingly got for me. In an instant she had reached in and pulled out a Walther PPK, dull black in the dim light of the bedroom.

'Are you a fool?' he snarled.

She reached in again with her other hand, careful not to let her eye or her aim drift away from this furious man. She retrieved a small object made of leather about the size of a wallet. She flipped it open, exposing a very unflattering photograph of her as well as official inscriptions and insignias.

'Interpol,' she said blandly. 'One of my very best assignments, I assure you.' She carefully surveyed his naked body. 'Yes, one of my very best.'

'You are a fool,' he said, 'and perhaps some torture would be appropriate after all. You know you'll never leave this building alive, but I will need to know how you managed all this, plus everything you and your people know. I think you'll be begging to cooperate.'

'Not bloody likely, as you would say.' She tossed her ID to one side and reached into her purse for the third time. 'Put the drinks down.'

Smythe-Montgomery barely had time to do so before a set of handcuffs came sailing across the room. He caught them deftly.

'Put one end on your right wrist.'

'Absolutely mad!'

'Do it. Now snap the other cuff around one of those lovely iron bars in the headboard. That's right.'

She pulled out another set of cuffs, and in a moment, Smythe-Montgomery was lying on his back, naked, with both arms cuffed above his head to the heavy ironwork of the bed.

'Now I wonder ... what should we do next?' Becky asked.

'You might try praying. Some of my enemies have,' he continued, thinking of the traitorous zealot, Ahmed, and his final ending at the pork processing plant. 'I can't believe you turned out to be my enemy.'

'You may be mistaken,' Becky said, 'but for curiosity's sake, how would you deal with an enemy? A powerful enemy.'

'Oh, I expect I'd be gracious—to a powerful enemy. Perhaps burning her ... or him ... to death in their own bed. Exquisitely painful, but in the comfort of one's home. You see the irony?'

Becky began to shake, as though suddenly realizing the gravity of her situation. 'Would you do that to me, Conrad?'

'No. Something far slower, I think. Perhaps my men might contribute an idea or two. I rather enjoy the notion of you screaming.'

Becky's shaking grew more severe.

'And if I begged for mercy?' she said.

Smythe-Montgomery wasn't certain, but he thought that a tear was tracking its way down her face. He sensed victory.

'Hah! I might enjoy that, Rebecca.' He spat out her name. 'But I'll tell you what, release me now, tell me everything you know—*everything*—and perhaps I'll kill you quickly.'

'Oh no! What the hell have I done? I can't. I can't.'

To Smythe-Montgomery's astonishment, she turned the Walther towards her head and put the barrel in her mouth—and bit the end off. Then she burst out laughing.

'I love licorice, don't you? How well you played along! Torture, burning, my body in the Thames! Finally a man who understands what a woman needs. What *I* need!'

Smythe-Montgomery felt he had woken from a dream. This mad woman was really after more sex! He felt a stirring deep in his gut and his groin. This was game-playing taken to its most extreme. His fantasies with Ms. Lister were tame by comparison.

Becky looked down between Smythe-Montgomery's legs and smiled broadly. 'Now there's my Conrad. But I have been a very naughty girl, and naughty girls deserve to be punished.'

'You've been very naughty indeed. I don't suppose you've brought anything in your purse with which I could suitably administer punishment?'

'Oh, I believe I might have. But first …'

She slipped below his level of vision. A moment later an electric thrill shot through his body.

***

The sky was turning a filmy grey as Becky gathered her things.

'Where are you off to?' Smythe-Montgomery asked.

'My rooms. A little sleep.'

He got up quickly and went over to the computer.

'And this?' he asked, pointing to the thumb drive. There was a slight edge in his voice.

'A little something to remind you of me if you ever again tire of Ms. Lister. Take a look.'

Smythe-Montgomery tapped the screen and it came to life. On the desktop was a folder labeled 'Naughty Girl.' He opened it to discover astonishing photographs of Becky in various levels of exposure, looking wild, sultry, and very sexy.

He turned to her. 'Thank you. As I know you are not leaving until Sunday, might it be too much to hope that you would join me for … ah … dinner this evening?'

'And why do you suppose I would need a little sleep?' she answered teasingly.

'Excellent!'

She turned to go, but he stopped her. 'The thumb drive?'

'Keep it. Share it with a friend if you like. Or with Ms. Lister,' she added brightly.

***

'Becky?' Randy exclaimed. 'We were about to send in the cavalry. It's nearly 7:30 ... a.m.!'

'Oh?' she said, with a yawn. 'I thought it was later. And how was your evening? Anything good on TV?'

'Yeah, thanks for asking,' said Randy bitterly. 'But, yes, some excellent shows came on last night.'

'Oh, good. I'm going to sleep now. Maybe we can talk later.'

'How about this evening?'

'No can do.' She smiled to herself. 'I've got a date.'

***

That night, Becky enjoyed a few more of her fantasies as well as several of Smythe-Montgomery's. His conversation had become far less guarded and far more graphic, and Becky was certain the thumb drive had been thoroughly probed and he was satisfied that it contained nothing more than the photos of the 'naughty girl.' As she'd hoped, she was suitably punished for her previous behavior, but her mind was already far from the game.

A meeting at Crandall's home was then possible for several hours before Becky very publicly returned to her hotel, burdened with the spoils of her travels.

Chapter Twenty-Two

Debrief the Plan

Stone and Randy were eager to pass on the data that had been transmitted two days before, but they were equally eager to debrief Becky. Smythe-Montgomery had abruptly left the country the Friday after the conference, but brief communications from Becky had indicated concern that she was being watched. Chuck had suggested a series of trips to shopping malls—crowded at this time of year—and several random rides on the tube to throw off any potential observers. A meeting at Crandall's home was then possible for several hours before Becky very publicly returned to her hotel, burdened with the spoils of her travels.

'And this little shopping spree …?' she had asked.

Randy had anticipated this, and his reply of 'On the company' was well received.

Saturday afternoon, three days before Christmas, Becky was ushered into the study of Crandall's house only to find an extraordinary and eclectic group of individuals waiting for her.

She spotted Randy and Stone, and waved. When she noticed Chuck Johnson near them, she remarked, 'Wow, it's like old home week!' But then her eye took in a few others. A stunningly beautiful woman with an exotic look, but wearing a modest English dress, something Becky had seen on Sloane Street, walked calmly up to her and extended her hand.

'We meet at last,' she said. 'I'm Luana Chu. Let me introduce you to the others.'

Becky had noticed the disparate trio off to one side of the room: an attractive mature woman in a wheelchair, her legs gone below her knees; a dignified older man in a tweed smoking jacket who seemed somewhat ill at ease; and, most astonishing of all, a pretty young woman, clearly nervous and blushing crimson.

Luana introduced them one by one.

'This is Lady Diana Foster—though she absolutely insists on just Diana. She has a very long history with the family of Smythe-Montgomery and her interest in the affairs of Sir Conrad is quite significant.'

Diana nodded politely, and Luana turned to the man. 'This is our generous host, Mr. Richard Crandall, though I blush to introduce him so informally. He too suffers from an overabundance of modesty.'

'Ah,' Becky said, gripping his hand, 'the father of predictive chaos theory. You surely must take pride in that accomplishment, at least.'

'You've found my soft spot,' he said, with a smile.

'And this brilliant and lovely lady,' Luana continued, 'is his protégé, Yvette.'

Becky reached out her hand, and Yvette took it hesitantly. 'I ... I should like to know how you wish to be addressed. I've not always been completely correct in the past. Is it "Miss" or "Mrs." or "Dame"?'

'Yvette, I'd be horribly insulted if you didn't call me Becky.'

'There,' said Chuck, with a sigh, 'now that's all settled. And I want to go on the record as saying that I was not in favor of this group gathering.'

'Oh, what a sourpuss!' Becky said, with a wink in Yvette's direction. 'Communication is the key to success in any endeavor.'

'Not always in my business,' he countered.

'Randy? Jason?' Becky said, hoping for support.

Randy squirmed uncomfortably, but Stone jumped in. 'For good or bad, we're all here. And for what it's worth, I agree with Becky. So let's talk. The lady is on a timetable.'

Eager to get back to business, Randy produced a thumb drive—an innocuous device—and handed it to Crandall. 'A copy of everything we got.'

Without a word, Crandall passed the drive to Yvette, who plugged it in and began downloading data.

'You're sure Smythe-Montgomery wasn't suspicious?' Chuck asked Becky.

'Suspicious? He caught me at his own personal computer with the drive plugged in.'

The Reality of Chaos

Chuck looked grim, but Stone smiled. He could smell a setup.

'I was putting erotic pictures of myself onto his computer,' Becky added.

Yvette's head shot up, her eyes wide, but she quickly looked down again and concentrated as hard as she could on her task.

'And you're sure he bought that? Absolutely sure?'

'He was still suspicious ... then. But by the next evening, I was quite confident he'd put any lingering doubts to rest.'

'How's that?' Chuck persisted.

'Because we had another night of extraordinary sex and he didn't kill me.'

This time Yvette couldn't help herself. She stared at this enigmatic woman, her mouth gaping.

Chuck couldn't help a choking laugh. 'That's some good reasoning. What did we get?' he asked, turning to Randy.

'It's good stuff, boss. Stone and I took a quick look. Lots of financial data, travel plans, contact lists, all sorts of M&A information.'

Diana looked puzzled, but Becky laughed. 'If I didn't know that M&A stands for mergers and acquisitions, I'd think Randy was being lewd.'

'Precisely the information we'd hoped for,' Crandall said. 'Yvette, let's see what Clyde has to say.'

It was Becky's turn to be puzzled.

'Long story,' Stone said. 'It's connected with Mr. Crandall's chaos-based predictions. Yvette can explain.'

'Can she?' Becky asked, watching the young woman eagerly entering information at a computer terminal.

'While Yvette finishes loading the data, what else can you tell us?' Randy asked. 'Other than it was a great party.'

'It was that,' she said. 'By the way, Jason, thanks for all the girl stuff you picked up for me. I used every single thing.'

'No kidding?' Stone couldn't help asking. 'Even the handcuffs?'

'*Especially* the handcuffs!'

Crandall nudged Yvette. 'Carry on, please.'

She tore her eyes away from Becky and, with considerable effort, got back to work.

'So here's the thing,' Becky continued, collecting her thoughts, 'without getting too graphic, it's clear that this man is into violence.'

'Like father, like son,' Diana whispered to Crandall.

'On our first night, he let something drop that I almost ignored. We happened to be talking about dealing with a powerful enemy. He was a bit miffed with me at the time. Actually believed I was with Interpol. But he mentioned being gracious, and burning her ... or him ... to death. The "or him" was definitely an afterthought. At the time, I was a bit preoccupied, then later I thought he might have used a female gender there because of me. But during my second evening ...'

'Keep working,' Crandall whispered to Yvette, unable to hide his smile.

'... he specifically mentioned, and I quote, "the bitch who is making my life so irritating in Iran." Then he referred to his previous evening's comments. Something like "burning her alive in her own bed." It was pretty gruesome. I think he means to do it, but I'm not sure how.'

'Perhaps—' Yvette began, but immediately choked off her own words and looked guiltily towards Crandall.

'Please continue, Yvette,' Crandall said. He caught her eye, transmitting total confidence in that one glance.

'Well, as you've been talking, I've been looking at his recent e-mail. One caught my eye. It's to several men with Arab names, but it alludes to paying a pilot and his family.'

'He owns an airline, so paying a pilot doesn't seem odd,' Chuck mused. 'But his family?' He looked towards Stone who nodded.

'Also,' Yvette said, 'he mentions the airline the pilot works for.'

'Pacific-Indo-Asia Air?' Randy asked.

'No. It's Arabian-World Air, a joint Saudi-Kuwaiti airline. A competitor of Pacific-Indo-Asia in the Middle East, according to Clyde.'

'The payment,' Stone said, through grated teeth. 'Does it say how much?'

'Yes. That was another other peculiar part. It was for $200,000 U.S.'

'A bit steep,' Chuck said, 'but how did you make a connection—'

'That's the last part,' Yvette added. 'Jack ... that is, Smythe-Montgomery, replied that he accepted the deal, but he grumbled about the "high price of fire." He also gave instructions to use the EMPR1 account for payment. It doesn't make any sense, unless ...'

She faded to silence and the room was speechless until Becky finally said, 'I think you owe me an apology, Chuck. Communication *is* the key to success in any endeavor.'

'I apologize,' Chuck said softly.

'I really need to spend some time with this data,' Stone said, his thoughts spinning. This was the opening he'd been waiting for. A thin, unpleasant smile appeared as he remembered the words 'You can't kill a dead man.'

Randy saw the look on his face. It was cold—the look of an assassin. Randy coughed suddenly and turned pointedly to Crandall.

'How long do you need for the rest of the data?'

Crandall shrugged. 'A day or two for a preliminary assessment ... with the right help,' he said, glancing at Yvette.

'But, Richard, that's Christmas Eve!' she said, like a young girl about to be deprived of her holiday.

'Well, perhaps if we *focus* we may have that assessment by tomorrow at this time. Then we can enjoy Christmas.'

Yvette nodded.

'We'll take our leave and return tomorrow,' Crandall said. He held up the thumb drive. 'Is there anything else?'

'Just a quick comment from Cathie Fletcher's meeting with Smythe-Montgomery,' Randy said. 'As expected, Smythe-Montgomery was *extremely* defensive about his family's shadowy rise to power during and after the Opium Wars. My full report is on the drive. But I wanted to emphasize his reaction to the word "empire"—both Cathie and Logan noticed this. And, of course, that's the name of his boat.'

'Interesting,' said Crandall. 'In light of the man's megalomania it may be significant. Thank you.'

'I'll take my leave also,' said Diana. 'Becky, a pleasure.' She paused and memories of the past clouded her eyes. 'You're a courageous woman. Be very careful. I should like to speak with you again before you return to the States. Can that be arranged?'

Becky nodded.

As they were about to leave, Yvette turned to Becky. She straightened her back and asked, in a firm voice, 'Might I have a word … a private word?'

'Of course.'

Becky followed her into the deserted dining room.

'Thank you for not treating me like a little girl,' Yvette said. 'A prudish little girl.'

'I'll treat you the way you deserve to be treated: like a brilliant young woman who enjoys the respect and trust of everyone you know.' She smiled ruefully. 'It's more than I had at your age.'

'I … I'd like to …' Yvette broke off, her throat suddenly too constricted for speech.

Becky fished into her purse and pulled out a business card. She searched a bit more and retrieved a pen. Turning the card over, she wrote a phone number.

'My cell. Call. Anytime, OK?'

Yvette sniffed and turned huge, brimming eyes to Becky, then swiftly left the room.

'Hey,' said Randy, poking his nose into the dining room, 'Chuck wants me to ride back with you to the tube station.'

'But I—'

'Oh, just let me come along and don't argue for once,' he said, with a grin.

***

When the others had left, Stone tended the fire while Luana poured drinks.

'So I take it you wanted to have a quiet chat,' said Chuck, accepting his drink from Luana.

Stone swirled the scotch and ice in his glass. His face still had a cold, killer's look about it, but there was something else. Could it be fear? Chuck could hardly believe it.

'I wanted to leave you both out of this,' Stone began, 'but I need your help, Johnson.' He turned to face Luana and his features softened. 'And I need your help more. People are about to die …'

***

Chuck was on his third drink by the time Stone finished explaining his plan. 'Damn, Stone, it's taking a hell of a risk.'

'Not to mention the cost, even if it is successful,' Luana said, shaking her head sadly. 'Is it really necessary, James?'

Stone shrugged. 'I'd say yes—pending an examination of Crandall's predictions. It isn't easy to put the cost of one life against others. I've had to do it and so have you, Johnson. What do you say? Is one life worth ten? Twenty? How about a million?'

'If you're right—and I haven't reached that conclusion just yet—then we'll have to sit back and watch people die. People whose deaths could have been prevented.'

'I've done worse,' Stone said softly. 'Far worse.' Luana gave him a penetrating look, but remained silent. 'I'll do it again if the mission warrants it.'

'It may not be as clear cut as before,' Chuck said. 'But it may be more so once we've seen Crandall's data.' He glanced at his watch. 'Fuck. Never enough time. I'll call a cab.' He rose from his seat, looking grim and exhausted.

'Luana, I'll wait with Chuck in the front lobby if you don't mind.'

'That's fine. I'll be in our room. Perhaps we might have time for a brief talk.'

Stone nodded, though he doubted the talk would be all that brief.

**

'What did you mean, darling, by saying you've done far worse?'

It was the question Stone knew was coming. When he had first met Luana, he had been working with Ivor Vachenko. What she hadn't learned until later, when they had come to trust each other totally and had broken with both Ivor and Wan Chu, was that Stone had another mission, given to him years earlier by Chuck Johnson: Find and destroy a Russian nuclear weapon that had gone missing at the end of the Cold War. Do anything necessary to complete the mission. Anything.

The instructions were meant literally, and Stone took them as such. In order to gain access to information that might lead him to the weapon, he had taken extreme steps. He had faked his own death, resurfaced as an anonymous gun for hire and assassin with a grudge against the U.S., and wheedled his way into a terrorist cell. During that time, he had betrayed

American soldiers, fought alongside the terrorists, killed many innocent people, and witnessed atrocities that he could have prevented. All for the mission. In the latter part of this involvement he had met Luana, and through a twist of fate, she had been able to provide key intel allowing him to locate the weapon. From that point on, they had worked together to ensure its harmless destruction. They had fallen in love in the process and were now crafting their own lives, out from the shadow of their past. A past they rarely spoke of.

'In case you're wondering,' she said, breaking in on his thoughts, 'there is nothing you can say that will change how I feel about you. I know you and I love you. I ask only to share the burden you still carry from those times.'

'A nightcap, then, and I'll be brief.' He smiled, but seemed nervous. 'A historical accounting of my scars and what I was doing when I got them should provide a suitable summary. Now this one,' he said, pointing to an old, pale line across his arm, 'is from a state championship football game ...'

***

Incredibly, Chuck postponed the meeting with Crandall until the 26th. Doubly confusing to Randy, when Chuck met with him the morning of Sunday the 23rd, he insisted that Randy catch a flight back to the States immediately. 'You've done a great job,' Chuck said, 'but everyone is heading back home for Christmas: Logan, Cathie, and Becky. Why not you? It'd be a nice surprise for Gail, wouldn't it? Assuming you've gotten her a very nice, very special London gift. You have gotten her a gift, haven't you?'

Randy was shocked.

'There you are,' said Chuck. 'Do some shopping and get on the 2:30 flight out of Gatwick. I think Becky is also on that one.'

'But Crandall's analysis?'

'No one is taking any action until after Christmas. I'll be home shortly after or I'll set up a secure call. Don't worry, Grasshopper, I'll keep you in the loop.'

He turned away as he spoke the last words. He had come to hate the necessity of lying, and it was doubly repugnant to lie to a promising Company man and—he had to admit—a friend. Telling himself that it was better if Randy didn't know about Stone's plan didn't help, and Chuck felt a cold lump in his stomach: one part bile, three parts guilt. *Decision made*, he thought grimly. He forced a smile to his lips. 'Go on, get out of here. Wish Gail a merry Christmas for me.'

Still puzzled, but delighted about being able to share Christmas with Gail, Randy shook his boss's hand and headed out, turning his thoughts to finding a suitable gift in less than three hours.

***

'I'm getting far too old for this shit, Stone.'

It was still black as midnight, though the clock in Crandall's study said 6:00 a.m.

'You realize you've said that three times now, don't you? That is, in the last fifteen minutes,' Stone said. He took a careful drink from a steaming mug of coffee while he scrutinized Chuck Johnson. The man looked old and worn. Creases in his face were partially hidden, but in a very unflattering way, by a nascent beard, mostly grey. 'Come on, drink your coffee. You wanted to meet bright and early before Crandall and his sidekick roll in.'

Chuck grunted and sat down heavily near the blazing fire Stone had stoked. 'This fucking London damp just gets into my bones.'

'Here,' said Stone, tipping a modest tot of brandy into Chuck's cup and then his own, 'for the cold.'

'Thanks.'

'Judging by the note of excitement in Yvette's voice, I'd say she and Richard think they've found something. Got any guesses?'

Chuck shrugged. 'Our own operations people suspect illegal cargo. So illegal that Smythe-Montgomery's aircraft may carry countermeasure gear or weapons in some cases. Or they can jettison cargo if things get too hot. The most obvious cargo is drugs, though blood diamonds or some other small, precious commodity is also possible.'

Stone nodded. They had discussed this previously. 'But what's the endgame? The man hardly needs more cash. He's rolling in it. And why is he courting the Iranian theocracy?'

'Let's hope Crandall has some sort of answer. In the meantime, we'd better talk more about your plan. You said the clock was ticking.'

'It is. Double time. I absolutely need to arrange a private meeting with Elaya. Maybe you can help there.'

'What do you need?'

***

By 9:30, grey light filled the room, and Chuck and Stone had the beginnings of a plan.

'Chuck, you'd better borrow my razor and have a shave before Crandall and Yvette arrive. You look like someone who should be typing a manifesto in Montana.'

Chuck ran his hand across the rough stubble of his face. 'Shit. You're right.'

Some twenty minutes later, Chuck appeared, shaved, washed, and looking somewhat more professional. A moment later, a car rolled into the driveway and voices were heard.

'Just in the nick of time. Thanks, Stone.'

As always, Yvette gave Stone a long, inquisitive look as she entered. The more she learned of him, the more he remained a mystery. But Crandall coughed tactfully and she returned to her duties. She seemed comfortable at the keyboard, loading the results from her recent day's efforts, and Crandall was confident in her abilities. It might have made her laugh to know that she was almost as much of a puzzle to Stone as he was to her.

'So, Mr. Crandall,' Chuck said, setting a steaming cup of coffee on an end table, 'have you got any revelations for us this fine day?'

'Indeed I have, Mr. Johnson. The information that Ms. Amhurst was able to obtain was extraordinary. The risks that woman must have taken.' He shook his head. 'To be brief, it contained all the strategic financial data for his worldwide operations: mergers and acquisitions, controlling interest in corporations, debts and assets, unusual bookkeeping. Well, I'm not being brief, am I, but just the financials took a while to incorporate into our system.'

Stone mentally noted the use of 'our' versus 'my' in Crandall's description. Another indication of his trust and respect for Yvette.

'There are a number of private communications similar to the one Yvette commented on at our previous meeting,' Crandall continued.

'Most are cryptic and perhaps require some precursor information to make them intelligible. Perhaps you may have that.'

'I've examined all of them,' Stone said. 'You're right, some make more sense than others based on what we already knew. Randy and I will continue to assess them.'

'From my perspective, I was able to glean more from the interconnections. To whom were letters written? What level of deference or disdain was used in the verbiage? If there was a reply, how was it written?'

'Your model can take that into account?' Chuck asked, impressed.

'Yes, to a degree. His communications with a few colleagues whom I took to be in the hierarchy of the former Iranian government, for instance, were quite instructive. His deference is completely artificial, despite whatever their exalted rank may have been. Smythe-Montgomery'—he shot a look towards Yvette—'or Jack as we refer to him, clearly has some serious leverage over these men. Perhaps they are being blackmailed.'

Chuck and Stone exchanged a glance. Both were thinking of the peculiar incidents aboard Smythe-Montgomery's yacht, *Empire*.

Crandall grinned. 'I see I may have confirmed a suspicion. Many other miscellaneous documents—travel plans for instance—are also quite intriguing. But as you might have guessed, nowhere within his files is a document titled "Details of My Evil Plots and the Stratagems for Their Execution." And yet ... perhaps we may be able to shed a little light on that as well. Are you ready?' he asked, turning to Yvette, whose fingers had been flying over the keyboard while he spoke.

'One moment. Yes. Ready.'

The large monitor now displayed a world map. Colored lines—red, green, or yellow—connected cities over much of the Far East, India, and the Middle East. Stone smiled wryly. The city of Ashgabat, Turkmenistan, was part of the network. This fascinating former Soviet-controlled city had played a prominent role in his previous mission to find and destroy the lost nuclear weapon. He rubbed his ribcage, remembering a wound he had gotten during a vicious firefight in the desert seventy-five miles north of there. As Stone studied the screen, he wondered why the red line connecting Kuala Lumpur in Malaysia to Tehran was dashed.

'As I'm sure you realize,' Crandall said in a matter-of-fact tone, 'our Jack receives a sizable amount of income from the illegal drug trade.'

'What?' Chuck asked, stunned. 'Can you prove that?'

'Certainly not. So if you were hoping for a quick arrest and conviction I'm afraid I must disappoint you. But the probability is remarkably high. Surely you've guessed the same?'

'We have,' Stone replied.

'And the aircraft modifications—specifically to the electronics, cargo bays, and even hard points on the wings—as well as the purchase of a not-insignificant number of aircraft designed to operate from short, unpaved runways clearly indicates a desire to expand his operations.'

'Yeah, that jibes,' Chuck said gloomily.

Crandall pointed to the screen. 'Naturally we aren't able to display all the routes of his airlines without making a sad spaghetti bowl of the display.'

To illustrate the point, Yvette typed in a command and the screen filled with web of lines that made the display unreadable. Two things could be easily seen, however. A new color of line had been added—grey—and these lines went mostly to areas where there were no large cities; some apparently into empty parts of various countries. The other item of note was the addition of more dashed lines.

'Clearly, the aircraft designed for short, undeveloped airfields will be used here.' Crandall pointed to the end points of several grey lines. 'The dashed lines indicate potential routes not currently in operation. So you see, Jack has notions to expand. Previous screen please, Yvette.'

The original display returned to the screen. 'The route into Tehran is of great importance to Jack, as you'll see in a moment.'

Chuck studied the screen intently. 'This is like a drug dealer's road map connecting sources of supply to points of distribution.'

'Yes,' Crandall said. 'Particularly if one focuses on the red lines, which indicate a high probability of use for drug transport. Greater than 80%. Those in green seem more like legitimate civilian routes, while those in yellow are of an elevated but inconclusive probability.'

The Reality of Chaos

'Even the ones in green could be used to spread the product, though,' Stone said, pointing to various routes.

'Indeed,' Crandall replied.

'This is extraordinary,' Chuck said. 'You've added a lot of confidence to our vague suspicions and given us places to focus our future investigations.'

'Surely you can't imagine this is all we have to offer?' Crandall asked. 'I'm mildly insulted.' He turned to Yvette who nodded severely.

'No. I mean—' Chuck began. He stopped abruptly and a knowing look crept onto his face. 'You're playin' me. Nice. I feel like I'm back in Philly listening to Fat Louie Gargiano spinnin' a tall tale.'

Crandall exchanged a confused glance with Yvette. 'If you mean to imply I'm joking about having more information, then I assure you I am not.'

Chuck was incredulous. 'You have more?'

Crandall turned to Yvette, who said, 'Predictive chaos algorithms are tailored to predict future geopolitical events! What we've shown so far is nearly all in place today.'

'OK, fine,' Chuck said grumpily. 'What's it look like in five years?'

Luana, who had been quiet up to this point, turned to Stone with a sad smile. 'Chuck has never heard the expression "When you're at the bottom of a hole, quit digging."'

'In five years, it looks like this.' Yvette typed a command and Chuck sat bolt upright, shocked. Lines had branched out from Tehran to Paris, Moscow, Brussels, Vienna, and London.

'You're just guessing. You can't know this.'

'We don't "know" anything. However, based on Jack's travel, investments, standing offers to acquire currently failing airlines, and actual inquiries into airport facilities, the probability is above 50%. Would you care to see a prediction with only a slightly lower probability?' Without waiting for an answer, Crandall turned to Yvette. 'Please display the eight-year prediction.'

She did, and Chuck saw lines connecting Singapore to San Francisco and Paris to Atlanta. 'There are others—potential connections, that is—but I refuse to show probabilities below 30%.'

'Christ,' said Chuck, rubbing at his newly shaved chin, 'why is it that every time I come here I feel like a kid getting schooled?'

'They say humility is good for the soul,' Stone remarked.

'Huh,' Chuck snorted, 'like you'd know. OK, Mr. Crandall, you've made your point.'

'What I still don't understand is why,' Luana said. 'What would be Jack's motive?'

'That's simple enough,' Chuck replied. 'Money.'

'But the man can make billions through legitimate business,' Luana countered.

'Luana is quite right,' Crandall said. 'The accumulation of wealth is only important in that it allows him to pursue his true goal.'

'And that would be ...?' Chuck prompted.

'Empire,' Yvette said.

Chuck turned to her with irritation. 'Seriously? Empire?'

'Still digging, Chuck?' Stone asked. 'Listen to the young lady. Please continue, Yvette.'

'We really aren't guessing on this, Mr. Johnson,' she said. 'If you consider Jack's psychological makeup—paranoia, megalomania, gross insecurity, inferiority complex—and combine those with his passion for history, his own family's history, for instance—'

'Wait just a minute,' Chuck interrupted, 'how can a tall, handsome guy worth billions have an inferiority complex?'

Yvette smiled crookedly. 'Because he still does not possess what he and his family have so coveted since the time of the Opium Wars. It can't be bought, though his family did purchase a rotten borough and usurp a name. But he will never have what Diana Foster has. Or Richard,' she added quietly, glancing towards Crandall.

Chuck Johnson still had a blank look on his face.

Yvette drew a deep breath. 'Conrad Smythe-Montgomery is a commoner and he wants to be a lord, a peer of the realm. Despite all his wealth, he will always be a poor man. He'll always be a Croker.'

'Never forget that Napoleon crowned himself, Mr. Johnson,' Crandall added. 'Ask Ms. Fletcher for her impressions of the man. I believe she will agree with our assessment of his obsession.'

'But suppose I buy all that. How does running drugs help?'

The Reality of Chaos

'What motivates drug lords, Mr. Johnson? What is their desired goal?'

'Money. Power. More damn money,' Johnson said.

'And Smythe-Montgomery's desired goal?'

'Well, I would have said the same, but you're telling me he wants an empire. With money he can buy mercenaries, take over banana republics. It ain't no empire!'

'Consider history,' Crandall countered. 'Particularly his family's history.'

'Now I really do feel like the class dunce. I suppose you two have figured this out?' He looked from Stone to Luana. 'Well, fine. OK, his family history really begins during the Opium Wars. No doubt they began to build their fortune back then, probably through some very dirty deals. But they weren't nobody in the British hierarchy—the British *Empire*. Now why were the Opium Wars even being fought? Because the British were trying to extend their empire to China. But the Chinese wouldn't trade fair and square. No. They wanted cash for their goods. The British had nothing they wanted. Until those sneaky Brits—no offense intended—got the Chinese people all hooked on opium. Now they had something the Chinese really wanted, now they had—' He stopped suddenly, looking as though he'd been slapped. 'No fucking way! There's no fucking way!'

'You may be right,' Crandall said softly. 'His is, after all, a paranoid *delusion*. But how much damage can this man do by forcing an addictive product on the world? Think of the impact on the global economy, not to mention the human suffering. He is aping the British Empire of the 1800s. Corrupt governments will support him. Buying mercenaries? What if he buys governments? Iran. North Korea. He spreads his poison and consolidates his power. He does not have to fully succeed, Mr. Johnson, to destroy the world.'

Chuck grimaced. 'Uncle. I get it. Got any more predictions? How 'bout the winning lottery numbers?'

'I believe you have plumbed the depth of our knowledge and struck bottom,' said Crandall. 'For now.'

'Many thanks,' Chuck said. 'And thanks also to you, Ms. Yvette. A masterful performance.' He turned to Jason Stone. 'Hadn't we better get busy?'

The Reality of Chaos

Stephen Lance / Chuck Markussen

A frantic TV announcer was describing a scene of horror and death ...

Chapter Twenty-Three

Attack on Elaya

Within twenty-four hours of meeting with Crandall, Chuck and Stone were flying towards distinctly different destinations. Stone was heading for Istanbul where he hoped for a brief, private meeting with Elaya. Time was slipping away. Further examination of e-mail traffic captured from Smythe-Montgomery's computer had made that all too clear. If the meeting went as he hoped, then he would be busier still with no definite date for returning to the States. Luana decided to visit her family home in Hawaii to assess the status of her tangled inheritance before returning to Breckenridge.

Chuck Johnson had flown west to Washington, D.C. He was hoping for a meeting with the Secretary of Defense if it could be arranged. His boss in Oakland wouldn't be too pleased, and he'd have to deal with that later. Worse yet, his ulcers had been acting up and the physical discomfort wasn't helping his attitude. Nor was having to explain to his wife, Joy, that he'd be missing New Year's Eve with her. Their son, Marcus, would be in town, which was some consolation to her, and when Chuck suggested she should take a week or two and visit her longtime friend, Cathie Fletcher, she had been nearly mollified. His offhand comment that he had purchased her a rather unique Christmas gift of a sparkly nature—a complete lie at the time—had completely restored her equanimity.

***

Elaya made a brief stop at the British embassy during her visit to Istanbul, and through a series of connections, Chuck had arranged for Stone to be there as well.

'Jason, it's good to see you,' she said, 'though I doubt this meeting will bring either of us much pleasure.'

'I'm afraid not, Madam President. However, perhaps something good can come of it. If you remember our last conversation, I mentioned that two things were needed to protect you from constant attack and stabilize your position: the right opportunity and your full cooperation. The opportunity is about to present itself.'

Elaya Andoori shuddered. 'I do remember. At the time, it all seemed theoretical, and the remoteness was comforting. But the seriousness and danger of what we discussed is much more disturbing when it becomes an imminent reality.'

'Yes. So my first question to you is, are you still willing? We've discussed the dangers and they're quite real. If you want to take another path, now is the time to choose.'

'You really don't beat around the bush, do you, Jason? Is there another path open to me? A better one? One we haven't previously discussed?'

'No.'

'Eloquent,' she said. 'Very well. What must I do?'

'First, it's imperative that you stick to your usual schedule. Any change is almost certain to invalidate our intel.'

'I understand. Tomorrow I return to Iran. In roughly a week I will kick off an initiative I've been planning for a long while. I will be staying in Tehran for at least two months, living in the presidential palace.'

'Excellent. I'll be nearby, but we'll have no contact after today. Now here's the tricky part …'

***

Chuck spent ten days in Washington and never even managed to get on the SecDef's calendar. Frustrated by offers to meet with various undersecretaries—offers which he had forcefully declined—he left D.C. and headed back to Oakland, knowing that Joy and Marcus were already gone: Marcus back to training at Camp Peary in Virginia and Joy to visit Cathie Fletcher in Tucson. He sat grumpily on the packed airplane heading across the country. *Well, fuck the SecDef*, he thought. *He'd probably think I was feedin' him a pack of lies anyway. This way is better.* As for missing Marcus, he truly was disappointed. His son had become almost as busy as he was, and he regretted the lost opportunity.

The Reality of Chaos

But he brightened slightly thinking about Joy. She and Cathie had been friends since their sorority days at USC. The beginning of a friendship with Logan had come from their relationship. Years of working with Logan on highly sensitive programs—Chuck with the CIA, Logan at Alpha Defense—had brought them very close. A few of Logan's more esoteric gadgets had saved Chuck's ass when he was a young stud working in the field. Decades later, they remained best friends, as did Cathie and Joy.

The heavyset man next to him shifted in his seat, bumping into Chuck's arm for about the twentieth time with a grunt of apology. Chuck slid over as far as the cramped seat would allow, his gloom returning. It would be a long flight.

***

Stone still had many contacts in Iran, but most of them were of an extremely unsavory sort: dregs left over from his days working with Ivor Vachenko. There were few in Tehran he trusted and no one he could thoroughly rely upon. Perhaps another approach. He would travel under his old guise as a free-lance geologist from Ottawa, Canada. He still had a close friend in Kuwait, Ganesh Bhatia, whom he had contacted as soon as Elaya Andoori had agreed to his plan. Ganesh would make a few crucial arrangements to account for different eventualities. Stone always kept several options open, a policy that had saved his skin more than once. There might be one or two people in Tehran he could trust to find him a discreet house near the palace where he could wait. It was the best he could do.

***

Stone waited. By mid-January, he had fallen into a routine, rising late in the day, eating alone in the tiny, crumbling home he had rented through a third party. He would approach the palace from one of four distinct routes, randomly shuffling them from day to day. There he would spend most nights surveilling the grounds. They were poorly guarded, despite Elaya's best efforts, and Stone thought grimly how easy it would be for a talented assassin to kill her in her own home. With the first grey light of dawn, he returned to his dusty house. Only occasionally would he venture out during the day, visiting mining offices or oil company business buildings and inquiring about potential work for a man with his skills, often leaving with a business card and a website where he could apply for a job.

Stone also tracked Elaya's movements and activities. He was one of the few who were not surprised when she announced a new age of women's rights in Iran at her palace news conference. In a move that was sure to further infuriate the imams and ayatollahs, she rolled back, as she put it, 'the archaic restrictions on the rights of women that make them second-class citizens, hardly better than property.' She was trying to restore the Western culture that had been growing during the time of the Shah and had been crushed shortly after the revolution. It was a bold move, and Stone admired her for it.

***

In Tucson, Cathie Fletcher called to her visiting friend, Joy Johnson.

'Come look at this. You can't believe what our former sorority sister is doing now.'

Joy joined her friend in the family room and was soon gaping at the TV. Elaya stood at a podium in a courtyard of her presidential palace reminiscent of the White House Rose Garden. A translator's voice overrode the Farsi of her actual speech.

'… equal opportunity, equal justice, and equal rights for all the women of Iran …'

'Holy shit!' Joy exclaimed. 'Look at her! Ms. Women's Lib in 21st century Iran! Our wild little Pi Beta Phi sister, once the wife of a Saudi prince, now leader of Iran and turning their whole culture upside down.'

Logan walked into the room and stopped to watch. At the conclusion of Elaya's speech, the small group gathered in the palace courtyard was silent, their disapproval palpable. Elaya, head held high, returned to the palace and that was that. The endless chattering of postmortem news panels now began.

'What do you think, darling?' Cathie asked. 'I guess our little friend from college did good.'

'Really?' Logan asked. 'Maybe. But if she wanted to make a mortal enemy of every religious zealot in Iran, she just succeeded. That woman is sticking her neck out a mile. And poor Chuck is supposed to be looking after her.'

'Chuck will take care of her,' Cathie replied. 'And he has some help, as you know.'

'He's gonna need it,' Logan said, shaking his head as he left the room.

***

A few more days passed. January 29. Elaya had another ceremony to oversee today, a slightly more popular one. General Zareb, a colonel and faithful ally to Elaya through the chaos and collapse of the previous regime, was being promoted once again, this time to commander of the Iranian Air Force. Zareb was popular in the military: a man who had risen through the ranks, flown combat, and, most importantly, had survived the changing of regimes over decades. His political alliance with Elaya—well known in Iran—was less of a hindrance in a branch of the military that tended to favor reform.

That night, Stone performed his usual surveillance. It was cold but clear, the stars blazing away. The moon rose late, a waning crescent, and Stone was troubled by the sight. It seemed to portend an ending, a descent into blackness as the new moon approached.

'Superstitious, Stone?' he whispered to himself. 'Maybe it's time to consider retiring from this line of work.'

***

Passengers shuffled bleary-eyed aboard the regional jet boarding from Tehran's Khomeini International Airport. Despite her best efforts to date, Elaya had been unable to purge the name of the former leader. It was 4:00 a.m., a horrible time for a flight unless you needed to connect with a major European hub for a transcontinental or transatlantic flight. Thirty-seven passengers had felt that need, and they were cared for by two flight attendants. The pilot and co-pilot checked their route to today's destination: Paris.

They were wheels up at 4:37, turning onto a designated track to clear the airport as they climbed. Passengers had already begun to pull out laptops and fiddle with electronic notepads, though no announcement permitting this had yet been made. The flight attendants had just released their seatbelts and prepared to go to work. Plenty of hot coffee and tea would be needed to prepare this group for a long day.

The captain turned to pass a casual word with his copilot, a last-minute replacement whom the captain had never flown with before. As he turned, the copilot shoved a long, thin blade between his ribs, piercing his heart. The captain's eyes widened in shock and his mouth moved noiselessly for a few moments, but the spark of life was already fleeing his body, and his eyes became dull and empty.

The copilot checked to ensure the cabin door was securely locked and then began to change course.

***

The last half hour before dawn was always the worst. If a man had demons, they would visit him then. Stone had many, and he stared with growing gloom at the palace. Without warning, the unthinkable occurred. The unmistakable roar of jet engines, far too low, cut through his musings like a sword. He turned to the east to see a small plane on a steep descent heading for the palace. Stone automatically jerked upright, but there was nothing he could do. In less time than he could have imagined, the roar grew and was suddenly eclipsed by a massive explosion as the plane crashed into the living quarters of the palace. Full fuel tanks burst, and the entire palace was soon engulfed in scorching flame, a scene from hell.

Stone watched briefly, feeling the heat of the flames on his face even from the distance. There could be no survivors. He turned and hurried away.

***

Joy and Cathie were enjoying a drink on the patio near the warm chimenea when Logan threw open the sliding glass door. 'You'd better come in here. Quick!'

The two looked at each other in confusion, but followed Logan into the house. A frantic TV announcer was describing a scene of horror and death, with the images showing a large, ornate building engulfed in flames. The banner scrolling across the bottom of the screen mentioned a plane crash—possibly a terrorist attack. As awful as it all was, the women were surprised at Logan's distress. He turned to them and blurted out, 'It's the Iranian presidential palace. They're saying it was a deliberate terrorist attack. Elaya was in that building! She's dead and the country's in chaos!'

Joy and Cathie turned back to the television and stood watching intently while casualties were reported. No hope for anyone on the aircraft. No hope for anyone in the living quarters of the palace. Yes, the president was sleeping there the night of the attack. The conclusion was obvious.

The reporting was in its early stages, and when the announcer began to repeat the same information, the two women turned stunned faces back to Logan. Joy's look suddenly turned from shock to fear. 'I have to call Chuck!' she said, dashing for the cell phone in her room.

***

Joy's first attempts to reach her husband went directly to voice mail, an obnoxious recording saying he was currently not available, and telling her to leave a message and have a nice day. Johnson's boss in Oakland had beaten her by a few minutes.

'Johnson,' Chuck had answered, knowing by the ringtone who was calling.

'What in the unholy fuck is going on!' a voice bellowed.

'Still gathering information, boss,' he replied calmly.

'Still gathering— Are you fucking kidding me? You were supposed to keep an eye on her! Keep her safe! Do you call "dead" safe?'

Chuck took several deep breaths. Had his boss been in the room at that moment it was likely that Chuck would have pulled his gun and dropped him like a sack of trash. 'As I said, information is still coming in.'

'Have you seen the fucking video? Do you think she's going to walk out of there wearing a singed nightie?'

'What do you want me to do?' Chuck responded, an edgy, angry tone creeping into his voice despite his best efforts.

'Listen carefully. I want you to stand the fuck down. You are officially on administrative leave, from which you are unlikely to return. By God, you'll be lucky if you can take the easy way out, but I'd suggest polishing up those retirement plans.'

'Do you mind if I come home first?'

'Come home? Where the fuck are you?'

Well, I'm obviously not in the office, you jackass, Chuck thought, *or you'd be skinning my ass in person.* 'I'm in Iceland, boss.'

'Iceland!' he bellowed. 'What the fuck are you doing in Iceland? You know what, never mind. Just get your ass back to the States. Now!'

'Yes, sir.' Chuck disconnected the call, then added, 'And fuck you very much!'

***

'I just can't believe it.' It was barely more than a murmur. Crandall looked over at Yvette. She was watching the BBC news and her reaction was not so different from many all over the world. But her statement held a hidden meaning, and Crandall knew it.

'Turn it off, Yvette,' he said softly.

'But it can't be true,' she replied. 'He was working for her.'

Crandall sighed. He knew she was referring to Jason Stone, a man who had grown to almost superhero proportions in her mind.

She turned to face Crandall, her eyes brimming with tears. 'How could he have let this happen?'

The Reality of Chaos

Stephen Lance / Chuck Markussen

The general scrambled for the sidearm he kept in his desk, but a knife came whistling across the room, catching him in the shoulder.

Chapter Twenty-Four

A Bad Deal

'What now?' Zareb grumbled to the harassed aide standing in the doorway of his office.

'It's the British delegation, General. They insist on seeing you.'

'Well, show them in,' he said, muttering a curse.

Zareb had gotten little sleep for over a week and he could feel himself growing slow and stupid. Few members of his staff, or Elaya's for that matter, had been seen since the disaster of her death. He was attempting to keep her government running from his office at the Defense Ministry, but even many men whom he had counted as allies were taking a cautious, wait-and-see attitude. He could hardly blame them. The ayatollahs and mullahs were in the streets inciting crowds, demanding the return of the former theocratic government. Zareb did not have the forces to suppress them and the balance of power was very fine indeed. His aide had only gotten the job a few days before, when most of the usual staff had failed to report in. The man was an obedient fool, but he was here and that counted for something.

The general had called in every marker he or Elaya had among the leadership of foreign governments and businesses. Mostly in vain. Like his local 'friends,' they preferred to wait until the dust had settled a bit. *When the dust settles, they might find me beneath it*, he thought grimly. Few options remained. This British delegation, for instance. He couldn't remember whether they represented the official government, were unofficially connected, or were simply businessmen. He had rejected seeing them for several days, but as his list of allies had shrunk—polite refusals to help and deep regrets being the most common response of his desperate phone calls—he felt he must take what was offered.

His aide showed two impeccably dressed English gentlemen into his office, and announced nervously, 'Representing Mr. Conrad Smythe-Montgomery, Mr. Richardson and Mr. Coppers.'

'Colpoys,' one of the men corrected, with a sneer.

'Representing Smythe-Montgomery,' Zareb said, scowling. 'Had I known, I would have refused to see you.'

'And why is that?' Colpoys asked.

'I know enough of him to realize I should not associate with his lackeys.'

'General, I'm wounded. And we've come all this way to make you such a generous offer.'

'You have nothing I want.'

'No? Not even your own life?'

Zareb blanched. 'Speak your offer,' he said softly.

'Let me not beat around the bush, then. As you may have guessed, our employer may have had some ... influence ... over the unfortunate airline accident that has deprived this country of its most beloved leader.'

'You dare to come into my office and admit this?'

'I admit nothing. However, you may draw your own conclusions. I've been instructed to make you this very generous offer only once. The old regime is returning. They will want a strong military. You have surprising influence within the air force and the other services. You can discreetly guide your fellow officers to support the new government. In return, you will remain in your current station and enjoy the gratitude of your country's leaders and my employer.'

'Or ...'

'My dear General, is it really so difficult to deduce? We'll expect your reply by tomorrow morning. Choose wisely.'

Richardson and Colpoys left the room and the junior aide returned, pale as milk. 'Sir?'

'I'll be staying in the offices tonight. Have a bed brought in and send in Sergeant Amir immediately. I will weather this storm.'

***

By noon the next day Zareb was beginning to believe he had done just that. He was about to call in his aide when he heard sounds of a struggle in the hallway. He rose from his desk, but before he could walk to the door the man staggered in, followed immediately by Colpoys. The general scrambled for the sidearm he kept in his desk, but a knife came whistling across the room, catching him in the shoulder. In an instant, Colpoys shoved the aide to the floor and sprang at Zareb, knocking him down and pinning him with a knee in his gut.

'You really should have accepted our deal, General. Now I'm afraid your sergeant and several others have had to pay the price. As will you. That is, unless you'd care to reconsider. I have no orders to make you this offer, but I'm feeling generous today.'

Zareb spat in his face.

'Foolish,' said Colpoys. He reached over and casually pulled the knife from Zareb's shoulder. The man screamed in pain. 'Since you have remained intransigent to the end, however, I am authorized to do the following.' Colpoys drove the knife under Zareb's chin, then wrenched it quickly to the side. He stepped back hastily to avoid the gurgling blood spouting from the general's throat. 'And you?' he said, turning casually to the terrified man on the ground.

'I will serve you! Command me!'

'Excellent.'

***

Joy had been calling Chuck nonstop since the day of Elaya's assassination, but had been unable to get anything more from him than 'I'm in the States, but there're a few things I have to work out. I'll be home in a couple of days.'

The day he arrived was the day the American news media began reporting on the murder of General Zareb, loyal confidant to former president Elaya Andoori. By all accounts he had struggled to keep Andoori's government functioning, appealing both to loyalists within the country and to sympathetic leaders around the world. It appeared he had been gaining traction until his sudden and mysterious death after meeting with a private delegation from Britain. The news media hesitated to make a correlation, and no explanation was given. Iran descended into chaos. The loyalist faction was hunted down and imprisoned. The suppressed agents of the old theocracy re-emerged and began seizing power at all levels.

***

After an evening of intense carnal pleasures, Smythe-Montgomery and Emma Lister shared a drink and watched the evening news with profound satisfaction.

'I believe I'll be making a few phone calls tomorrow,' he said. 'I'll start with my good friend Ibrahim al Rahzi.'

'Hmph,' Lister responded. 'He's a bit of an imbecile, isn't he?'

'Now, we must be gracious towards our business associate, mustn't we? Though, as you say, he is a bit of an imbecile. But so pliable. So useful.'

'As you say, Conrad.'

'Perhaps another drink,' he said, holding up his glass.

Lister immediately rose from her chair and moved off gracefully, her open robe billowing out behind her. She stepped behind the bar and began to mix another martini.

'And Emma, when you return, you may leave your robe … and bring the handcuffs.'

***

Chuck watched the news dejectedly. Things were going pretty much as he'd expected, though he regretted being unable to help Zareb. He picked up his phone, wondering if he should try to get in touch with the SecDef again, but the last twenty or so calls had been efficiently rebuffed by his staff. Clearly the Secretary did not wish to speak to him. Chuck tossed the phone down.

'You ready to talk about it yet?' Joy asked. He hadn't even heard her enter the room.

'Not much to say. I fucked up big time, and now it looks like the end of … well, it never really was a very promising career, was it?'

'Why are you saying that? And why won't you talk to me? Or to Randy? He calls about five times a day.'

'No point talking to him. I'm on official leave, and he'll just get splattered with the same shit if he associates with me. The dumb kid knows better.'

'He ain't no kid, and he sure as hell isn't dumb. He's your friend. And so am I. Along with being your wife. You know, the one you can share things with?'

'It doesn't work that way in my business, and you've known that for years.'

'Yeah, but now you're about to become "Chuck Johnson, ordinary citizen," and not some damn agency robot. Won't you tell me what's going on?' Chuck remained silent, but Joy could tell by his body language that he was aching to share something. She suddenly had an idea. 'OK, sugar, I know how the game works, but here's what I'm going to do. I'm going to make a guess. If you don't contradict me, I'm gonna assume my guess is a good one. You don't have to say shit, so you can technically keep to your masochistic code.' She considered her next words very carefully. 'I've been watching the same news as you. If it's all true, then you screwed up big. But something stinks. For one thing, you've *never* screwed up big before. For another thing, the only calls you've been making are to your mysterious friend, Jason Stone. Now, you want to know how I know this? I've got eyes and ears, that's how, so don't even think of interrupting me. I'm on a roll. Well, the news is usually three parts bullshit to one part truth on a normal day. Nothin' about this is normal. So here's my guess. There's more to the story—maybe a whole lot more—and only you and brudda Stone really know the score. So there. I'll leave it at that. Tell me I'm wrong!'

Chuck had been listening intently, and now a slow smile crept onto his face. He rose and took Joy in a crushing embrace. 'How'd I get so damn lucky? Go get the bottle of scotch I was savin' for company. The 18-year-old single malt. Let's get drunk and have sex.'

Joy laughed. 'Oh, darling, I know you better than you think. We'd better reverse the order of those two activities or you'll be sound asleep before I get my fill.'

***

Diana Foster had joined Crandall at his London home to consider their plans going forward, given the unhappy turn of events. He would need to update the modeling, and then ... Well, she doubted the future predictions would improve.

'Yvette, we have work to do,' Diana said to the brooding young woman. 'I realize you ... that is, none of us can understand what could have caused these tragedies, but we must still fight, and here we are with the tools to do so at our disposal. We should proceed.'

At first there was no response, but Yvette finally squared her shoulders and said, 'You're right.'

'Please,' Crandall said kindly, pointing to the keyboard. 'You're so much more adept than I am.'

This drew a tiny smile from Yvette and she took her place at the keyboard. At the end of an hour, Crandall nodded. Updating the models for Elaya's and General Zareb's deaths had resulted in the expected outcome: the return of the theocratic regime in Iran. It wouldn't take long. Crandall rubbed his forehead in frustration. 'Clearly the e-mail Yvette discovered referred to the attack on the presidential palace. The "high price of fire" makes it rather clear—in hindsight.'

'Richard, you've said that four times already,' Diana remarked, with irritation. 'Where are you trying to go?'

'Sorry. It's just ... we really need more insight. Ms. Amhurst had a few acute observations after her evening with him. Perhaps there is something else she could add.'

'We could contact her,' Diana suggested.

Yvette squirmed uncomfortably in her chair. 'I have her private phone number,' she said. 'Would you like me to call?'

Diana smiled at her, considering the beneficial influence that a call to Becky might have on Yvette, regardless of whether any new information was gained for Richard's investigation. 'Yes, that would be excellent. Let's consider what we might specifically want to ask her. And you can have a private conversation with her at the same time.'

***

'Yvette, is that you?' Becky asked cheerfully.

'Yes. Is this a good time to talk?'

Becky sighed audibly. 'It sure is. I'm just driving home from the proposal area and I could use a little friendly conversation.'

'Just driving home? It's nearly 9:00 p.m. your time. Or do I have my time zones confused?'

'No, you're exactly right. But as it turns out, this is the earliest I've left work in weeks. Proposals are a pure bitch, you know.'

Yvette smiled. There was something in Becky's blunt, rough-edged talk that she liked. Oh, she liked the formal English banter that would often flow between Diana and Richard well enough, but this was different. Plainer. Stronger in a way.

'And you're up bright and early,' Becky added. 'Funny. I kind of had you pegged for a night owl like me.'

'I am! It's a bit torturous getting up at this hour, but I really wanted to talk to you. The time difference is such a pain in the bum. Still, I've failed to catch you at home.'

'Close enough. And who knows if I'd be coherent in another hour? That's the usual proposal drill. Up at 4:00. Roll in to work at around 5:30, guzzle gallons of coffee, have endless meetings, read endless tedious pages of technical drivel, drive home, slam down a scotch or three. Crash and burn. Repeat. Thank God it's only a forty-five-day proposal.'

'Sounds hideous!'

'It is. But if you win, it gets even harder. So, to what do I owe the pleasure of hearing your voice?'

Yvette blushed suddenly, though no one was there to see it. 'Actually, it's two different things. One is what you might call business, and the other much more ... personal.'

'I usually put pleasure before business, but perhaps we'd better do business first. Just this once.'

'It's about your, umm, evenings with Smythe-Montgomery.' As Yvette spoke, she considered the concise questions that Diana and Richard had prepared. For some reason, she ignored them and instead asked the question she'd been aching to put to Becky. 'Did you enjoy it? The time with him?' The minute the words left her mouth she regretted her temerity. *What on earth possessed me?* she thought.

There was a burst of laughter. 'Now that's a great question! I think old Chuck Johnson was dying to know that, too, but didn't have the nerve to ask. The answer is yes. I enjoyed the hell out of it. Not just the sex, but playing Conrad S&M like a fish. It was fun. I was also more terrified than I've ever been in my life.'

'Would you ... would you do it again?'

'Maybe. Yeah, probably, if I knew people like Randy and Stone were looking out for me.'

The mention of Stone's name brought Yvette painfully back to the primary reason for her call. 'Richard would so angry with me for departing from the script. I have much more serious questions to ask.'

'We'll keep it our secret, then, OK? What did Richard want to know?'

'He's delighted, of course, with all the data from the thumb drive, but also maddeningly frustrated. With the death of Elaya—' She stopped suddenly. 'I'm sorry, it's just that I can't believe she's dead. I really thought, with Jason looking out for her ...'

'I understand. But he was only one of a few—Chuck and Randy being the others—trying to protect her, and you know the scope of Smythe-Montgomery's organization. Have you heard any news from Stone or Luana?'

'Nothing. It's like they've both disappeared. I can hardly believe it.'

'Then don't,' Becky said simply. 'My gut tells me we'll see them again. Now, go ahead and ask those carefully prepared questions, then we'll have a nice little chat while I'm guzzling a drink.'

'Richard and I have programmed the death of Elaya and her friend General Zareb, and it's very likely their government will fall and the theocratic regime will return. And we have a rather good picture, at a high level, of Jack's plans.'

'I thought that was the goal of predictive chaos. It seems to be working if you ask me.'

'Yes. But now I'm puzzled. It appears Richard is trying to extract more specifics. He asked if you might possibly have any information, more from a behavioral perspective, on Jack's desire for an empire.'

'Ah. That's a good one. You know, I was a little startled that Cathie Fletcher found that to be so significant.'

'It is.' Yvette related her discussion with Chuck and the projected behavior of a man who wanted to be a lord.

'No kidding?' Becky said. 'Back where I come from they call that being too big for your britches. That's an American colloquialism for pants. But I thought Conrad Big Britches was a "sir." Doesn't that count?'

'Oh, no. A knighthood does not make one a peer. Even movie stars and musicians receive knighthoods.'

'People far below Conrad. I see, sort of. Are peerages handed out just for being filthy rich?'

'Not as such. It's a bit complicated, and I won't bore you. There are new barons and baronesses galore. Most of the new titles are granted to politicians who serve in the House of Lords, and many of these are life peerages where the title is not passed on. Wealth alone, particularly new wealth, is not enough.'

Becky considered this. 'You know, he did make a few comments in the course of our evenings together, and you and Richard are welcome to them, but Cathie Fletcher's next meeting with Conrad would be an opportunity to probe more deeply. If you and Richard have anything specific in mind, you should pass your questions on to her. I think she plans to see him again in March.'

'An excellent thought. Thank you, we will.' Yvette couldn't help being flattered that she had been lumped in with Crandall as a source of questions.

'So here's what I remember,' Becky said, 'but it's pretty thin.' She passed on a few offhand comments, which Yvette dutifully typed into a Word file.

'As I said, not much,' Becky repeated. 'What else?'

'Did he ever mention a General Zareb? He was an ally to President Andoori and he was killed a week or so after her death.'

'No. I don't recall hearing that name. Sorry.'

'Oh, that's all right.'

Yvette heard rustling sounds and a door closing.

'OK, I'm home now. I've kicked off my shoes and poured myself a stiff drink. Now let's talk about something that matters.'

Yvette only hesitated for an instant. 'It's complicated. My relationship with Richard. I enjoy working with him on his wonderful modeling, and I believe he values my help. But I also enjoy the other part of my relationship with him. I mean, it really doesn't bother me at all, a bit like your time with Smythe-Montgomery. But lately, Richard seems less comfortable with that part of our—'

'Whoa!' Becky said, with a chuckle. 'You have me at a disadvantage. I think you'd better start from the beginning. Take your time, I have plenty of scotch!'

By the time the four reached the 7th tee, they were deep into the politics of the day.

Chapter Twenty-Five

Golf with Generals

With the proposal finally complete and delivered, Becky decided it was time to relax. She and Gary had long been planning the ARC Avionics TGIO (Thank God It's Over) Open golf tournament in Tucson. Along with her dedicated staff and employees, she had invited a few special guests including Logan Fletcher, who knew most of the folks on the team, and two other high level consultants: retired three-stars who served on several boards of local companies, taught a few business classes at the local university, and had low handicaps. Tom Knaggs was a retired Air Force lieutenant general, SR-71 pilot, and base commander. Quiet and subtle, he was a keen observer of political events and had a knack for brilliant insights in a near vacuum of information. Marty Bamford had been a vice admiral in the Navy, responsible for Advanced Weapon Development and Kill Chain Performance. He was also a student of world affairs, though, unlike Tom, he could be hot-tempered if provoked. He had known Tom for years, and it needn't be said that Tom enjoyed provoking him just to see the fireworks. The two had served on the proposal Red Team, a group of experts hired to find flaws, omissions, or outright errors in the overall proposal strategy. Though they tended to ignore the bulk of the technical data, they had liberally bled red ink on Becky's executive summary, fraying her nerves, but significantly improving the critical opening section of the proposal.

Becky had arranged for Logan, Tom, Marty, and herself to be on the same team, though Gary had grumbled.

'Tell you what, Gary,' Becky had said. 'Why don't you take Quint? He's got like a minus-two handicap.'

'Seriously? Didn't he play the pro tour for a while?'

'He did indeed, and he's all yours. Sound OK?'

'We are so going to wipe your sorry butts! Boss,' he added quickly.

'Run along now and see if you can do something about shortening the rules. I swear the thing is written as a three-volume set. This is supposed to be fun!'

'Will do,' he said cheerfully. 'Oh, you are so smoked!' he added in a stage whisper as he moved off.

***

It was a beautiful winter morning in Tucson. A clear blue sky, a light breeze, and the promise of a day in the low seventies. Logan stared out at the Catalina Mountains from the back of the pro shop and spoke his usual mantra: 'This doesn't suck! If I didn't already live here, I'd become a snowbird. I wonder how the greens are playing in Chicago on this fine February 15 morning?' But he already knew. He'd checked the weather forecast for the Windy City just for fun: expected high, twenty-eight degrees, winds west at twenty to thirty miles per hour, heavy snow expected later in the day. He chuckled to himself and tipped his face up to the warm sun. 'Nope. This doesn't suck.'

He wandered over to the cart area and saw that Tom and Marty were already loading their clubs.

'Jeez, Marty,' Tom said, 'did you get those clubs at The Salvation Army? They look like they were brand new—in 1958. I hope you don't expect me to spot you strokes out of sympathy.'

Marty turned red and launched into a full-throated defense of his 'classic' equipment. Tom turned and smiled at Logan as he approached. He was getting an early start.

A short time later, Becky joined the trio. 'Gentlemen. Logan,' she added, with a wink.

Logan smiled. 'I thought you *didn't* want me to be a gentleman! I'm so confused.'

'You are that,' Becky replied. 'But so loveable.'

Marty checked his watch. 'Hey, hadn't we better get moving? Shotgun start and we're off on the 4th tee.'

***

By the time the four reached the 7th tee, they were deep into the politics of the day. Marty lit a cigar and handed one to Tom and Logan. A loud cough caught his attention and he saw Becky staring at him, hand

The Reality of Chaos

extended. With a raised eyebrow he fished around and found a fourth cigar.

'So, Tom,' Marty said, as the two waited for Logan and Becky to take their second shots, 'didn't you know Zareb?'

Tom nodded as he blew a fragrant cloud of smoke downwind. 'Met him a few times. Can't say I really knew him. But his men liked and respected him, and that says a lot.'

'Destined for big things under the former government.'

'He was. He was all for embracing Western ways, and not just in the running of the Iranian Air Force. He had a bright future under a leader with the same goals.'

'And no future at all under a theocratic regime. Still, I'm surprised they got him so easily. There's still a lot of chaos over there. I thought he'd put up more of a fight.'

'It won't be long,' Tom said glumly.

'What won't be long?' Logan asked as he returned.

'Won't be long till Marty's clubs are put in a museum.'

'Enough with the clubs! We were talking about regime change in Iran—again. What do you think, Fletch? I give it a couple more weeks before the beards are back in charge.'

'Yeah. That sounds about right. With Zareb gone, there aren't any more high level leaders of Andoori's regime left.'

'And before long, the Iranians will become a thorn in our collective sides once again,' Tom said. 'What do you think, Marty? Another carrier group deployed to keep an eye on things?'

'One's on the way already. But you didn't hear that from me.'

'What did I miss?' Becky asked, as she walked up.

'The fall of Iran,' Marty said roughly.

The smile that had been on her face melted away.

***

Tom's and Marty's assessment of Iran's political situation was quite accurate. By early March the ayatollahs and mullahs were consolidating power and the streets were running with the blood of Andoori loyalists or suspected loyalists. There was a purge of high leadership in the Iranian Air Force. Anyone who had ever spoken a kind word about Andoori or Zareb was suspected. A few escaped. Most did not.

Stephen Lance / Chuck Markussen

***

In the London office of Smythe-Montgomery, Ibrahim al Rahzi tapped his glass to his host's. 'To our great success!' al Rahzi said.

'Indeed,' said Smythe-Montgomery. 'And to our future collaboration and its success as well, I hope.'

'Yes, yes. The Supreme Leader is overflowing with gratitude, as am I. While he is aware of your support—your generous and crucial support—you have graciously allowed my colleagues and me to take credit for the idea. We are now, as you had foreseen, in a position to grant every request you made of us. And more, I swear it!'

'Excellent! Then we have achieved quite a success. I propose a small celebration aboard my yacht, once you and your friends can free yourselves from the duties of state. I can promise you another entertaining excursion.'

'When in Rome,' al Rahzi said, with enthusiasm.

'But perhaps a little business first. Might I expect to be able to begin operations at Khomeini International Airport by month's end?'

'No!' al Rahzi said. 'You may begin almost immediately! Within two days. We will clear a terminal for the exclusive use of Pacific-Indo-Asia Airlines, and all shall be exactly as you requested.'

'Why, my dear friend, I am grateful. But you know, another little thought occurred to me. I'm sure that in his brief exile in Paris your leader must have made a few contacts within the civil aviation world. An encouraging word from a highly placed official, such as yourself, might put me in a position to accelerate my plans to expand my em'—he coughed suddenly—'that is, my airline.'

'I am yours to command, my lord.'

Lord, thought Smythe-Montgomery. *Not just yet, but very soon.*

***

Yvette had relayed Becky's excellent advice to Richard and Diana. After a brief discussion they had decided it would be best if Randy contacted Cathie Fletcher and passed on their questions regarding Smythe-Montgomery's family.

He'd done so cheerfully, but had been surprised at Cathie's response.

'I just don't know if I can do this, Randy. It's not that I'm afraid … OK, I am a little. But if what everyone tells me is true, then he murdered my friend! Not to mention innocent people on the plane and on the ground. And now look what's happened! The country in chaos, people being murdered for supporting Elaya. How can I just sit and chat with a psychotic killer about his stupid family history?'

'Hey, listen, Cathie, if you say no then it's no. The potential intel might be useful. Richard Crandall thinks so, but no pressure, all right?'

Cathie laughed. 'You sound like Logan. "It would really be helpful, but it's OK if you chicken out." Don't either of you realize I just need a little encouragement? I feel like shit for Elaya. I still can't get over it. And it'll take all my self-control not to slap that stupid Limey into another time zone. But what I need is a "you can do it" pep talk, and not people holding the easy-exit door wide open.'

'Then how about this? I'll travel with you to London. We'll work out a game plan. Obviously, I can't be associated with you officially, and I sure as hell can't go to Smythe-Montgomery's home with you. But Logan will be there, and if things go sour, he can say a few clever, gracious words and you both exit.'

'Clever and gracious? Do you actually know my husband?'

Randy laughed. 'Is it a deal? Come on. Stiff upper lip!'

'Good pep talk! It's a deal. Hey, you wouldn't want to role-play Smythe-Montgomery? You know, let me vent on you and get it out of my system?'

'Will there be violence?'

'Maybe.'

'Uh ... no.'

'Fine. I'll just have to do without. I'll send you our travel itinerary. You do know I'm scheduled to meet with Smythe-Montgomery on the ides of March?'

'Super,' Randy replied. 'Well, I'll be in a pub, but I will be nearby. You and Logan can "beware."'

***

The day before their flight to London, Logan came down with a cough and fever that his doctor feared was a precursor to pneumonia. He was forbidden from leaving the house, let alone flying overseas. Randy was in favor of canceling the trip, but his pep talk had been too effective. Cathie assured him that she'd be just fine.

'In any case,' she had said, 'Conrad may not even be there, or, if he is, it may be just to say hello before he lets me dig through his archives.'

'I think that's unlikely,' Randy had replied. 'If that guy has a weak spot, it's his fascination with his family and its imaginary glory. I think he'll be around to soak up the adulation.'

'He may be disappointed. In any case, I'm going.'

'Then I guess I'm going too.'

***

A limo picked Cathie up at her hotel for the long drive to Smythe-Montgomery's country estate. Once there, she was impressed despite herself. A private drive nearly a half mile long led through two long rows of century-old beech trees, bare now, but some early buds promising a long, green tunnel in summer months. Beyond a wrought iron gate set in tall stone columns, a large circular drive wrapped around a massive fountain, the spraying water sparkling in the cool afternoon air.

The mansion was an imposing structure of old, mellow brick, partially ivy covered. Huge pillars supported a high roof that sheltered the end of the drive and a flight of stairs leading to the large oak doors of the main entry. Tall windows looked out from the first two floors. The third floor boasted a series of gables protruding from a severely pitched roof. Cathie counted at least a half dozen chimneys standing proud above the roofline. At each end of the house, square towers reached skyward another thirty feet, crenelated stone at their tops.

I wonder what his property taxes are, she thought. It was an attempt at self-distraction. Her best efforts at remaining calm had failed and she was sorely wishing that Logan had been able to come with her. She had spoken to Randy the night before and he had done his best to reassure her, but now, she was on her own.

Ms. Lister met her at the foot of the stairs, looking seductive even in the severe business suit she was wearing.

'Ms. Fletcher, so good to see you again,' she said, extending her hand. 'Please come in. I'm afraid Sir Conrad has been delayed, but he asked me to show you to the study and to provide you with everything you need until his arrival.'

Cathie politely acknowledged the greeting, and the two ascended the steps and entered the house. The entry was striking, with marble floors,

The Reality of Chaos

wood-paneled walls, and a decorative plastered ceiling some twenty-five feet above. A huge chandelier hanging from a heavy chain added a sparkling aura to the natural light—dingy by comparison—entering through banks of tall windows on either side of the door. Stairways at both ends of the room led to a second floor balcony that surrounded three sides of the entry. Heavy wooden tables held vases full of fresh flowers, and portraits of women and men looked down pompously from the walls. The room was beautiful in a formal, Elizabethan way, but to Cathie it felt overdone, as though it were designed to bludgeon visitors into a state of awe rather than charm them.

Lister motioned to her right and led Cathie down a long hallway, rooms and other smaller halls opening on her left, a line of windows on her right. At last they arrived in a large square room.

'The east tower is Sir Conrad's private library. I think it's rather impressive.'

'It certainly is,' Cathie agreed, scanning the room in astonishment. Where the stained-glass windows did not intervene, every wall was covered with built-in bookshelves and glass-doored cabinets. Books and manuscripts filled every space. Three massive dark wood tables sat around the interior, a handful of chairs upholstered in a heavy burgundy fabric placed around each. A large cabinet that seemed to be a card file stood at one end of the room. Various reading chairs sat conveniently near windows or near one of the two fireplaces, both blazing away cheerfully on this chilly late-winter day. Thick rugs covered much of the stone floor, adding splashes of color and softening the look of the room to more of a study rather than a library. Most impressive of all: narrow stairways leading to a second and third floor, with balconies that swept around all four walls. These too were filled with bookcases and cabinets containing more books, folders, and documents.

'It certainly is,' Cathie repeated. 'Impressive and beautiful. But where to begin?'

'We've taken the liberty of selecting a few documents, letters, family histories, and so on, and having them brought out from the vault. Because of their age, we keep them in a temperature- and humidity-controlled environment.' She guided Cathie to one of the tables strategically placed near a window and a fireplace. Several stacks of documents were clustered at one end along with notepaper, pencils, and a laptop computer. 'We weren't sure whether you prefer an old-school approach or were more of a technophile in your research. The laptop can be used to search for documents in our library. But as you might have guessed, we have a traditional card catalogue and lists of periodicals, letters, etc. Use whichever you prefer. Either will guide you to a floor, section, and number of whatever book or document you wish to study. Those that are secured are indicated as such, but our librarian, Ms. Guillfeld, is available to bring you anything you desire.'

As if by a magic trick, a small paneled door opened, and a rather portly, silver-haired lady entered the room and bowed. The room behind her looked like a functional modern office, with a desk, chair, and several computer monitors just visible through the open door. The woman smiled and said, 'I'll be just in there, working. There are quite a few new acquisitions, you see, that must be sorted and catalogued before they find their way to a proper place in the library.'

'Thank you,' Cathie replied. The woman bowed deeply once again and returned to her office. *And I'll bet part of your job is to keep an eye on me,* Cathie thought. *Make sure I don't get too nosy or start digging in the wrong pile.* A grimace found its way onto her face, which she struggled to banish. She was at least partially successful as she turned back to Lister. 'You've been more than kind. Just one other crucial question.'

Lister smiled. 'Just back down the hallway where we entered,' she said, pointing. 'First door on the right. If you need anything at all, please ask Ms. Guillfeld. She can also summon me at any time if I can be of service.'

'Thank you so much. Now, I should probably get to work and take advantage of every minute.'

Lister gave her a sharp look as if sensing something in Cathie's words, but it dissolved quickly into her usual pleasantly professional smile. 'Yes. Well, I'll be on my way then.' She turned and walked back down the long hallway.

Cathie eyed her as she left and couldn't help thinking, *Logan, you don't know what you're missing.*

***

At the end of an hour, Cathie found herself thoroughly engrossed in her work, forgetting for a short while her disdain and loathing for her host. She had decided to go old school, scribbling numerous notes and questions on the paper pad and shuffling through the old card catalogue like an excited school child—a rather geeky, excited school child with a passion for books and research. She had found several thorough histories of the Opium Wars, compiled by competent British historians, and not generally available to the public. She was now in the process of developing a detailed timeline, correlating letters and documents (military, commercial, and personal) from the period 1830 to 1870 against the baseline of the histories.

She frowned slightly. What was becoming apparent was that only a totally biased individual could attribute courage, loyalty, and genius to the family Croker. It could be done if selected documents—particularly military and government records—were interpreted as being hostile towards Smythe-Montgomery's family and if the letters of friends (or even cousins, for the love of God!) with a definite prejudice in favor of the family were taken at face value. Yes. With the correct assignment of credibility, one could make a case. But taking that approach stretched credulity to the bursting point, and no serious historian (or writer) could accept the word of those who owed allegiance to the family against official accounts. Cathie also noticed that, in many cases, corroborating documentation of military men or businessmen referenced in *negative* assessments were not to be found within the library, whereas every *supportive* letter or journal referenced had been dutifully collected.

'Please forgive my tardiness, Ms. Fletcher.' Smythe-Montgomery's smooth words sliced across her thoughts like a paper cut and she felt her hackles rise.

Steady, girl, she thought. But she wondered how this meeting would play out.

'Hello, Sir Conrad,' she began, with a forced smile.

'Tut. We've been over this before. Just Conrad, please.'

'Well, hello, Conrad. I hope you haven't abandoned anything important just to see me.'

'Nonsense. What could be more important than putting my family's history into a proper light?'

Cathie stifled a sniff of disbelief and continued to smile.

'Are you quite all right?' he asked. 'You seem disturbed.' He glanced at his watch. 'Ah, perhaps it's time for an afternoon cocktail.'

A few minutes later, both were sipping drinks. Smythe-Montgomery a gin and tonic, Cathie a glass of Chardonnay.

'So, how goes the research? I see you've made some extensive notes.'

'I have. And I do have a few questions, if you don't mind?'

'Please, ask away!' Smythe-Montgomery said cheerfully.

Cathie shuffled through her notes. 'In May of 1841, during the battle of Canton, your great-great-great-grandfather Lieutenant Rolf Croker participated in the capture of a fort, Yung-Kang-Tai. He was only a young man then, barely twenty.'

'He was indeed a young man, but I must quibble a bit with your characterization of "participation." His commanding officer, recognizing his leadership potential, gave him a key role in the capture. In fact, the officer followed Rolf's plan and essentially gave him operational command.' Smythe-Montgomery scanned the neat piles on the desk, and gently pulled a letter from the stack. 'Here, indeed'—he took the letter from the envelope and scanned the contents—'is the detailed description of the action. Perhaps you've missed this.'

'But that letter was written by him.' Cathie said, the words leaving her mouth before she had time to consider them.

Smythe-Montgomery gave her a puzzled look. 'Yes?'

'Well, there really isn't any corroborating documentation,' she said nervously.

'Surely you wouldn't question the account of my great-great-great-grandfather?' Smythe-Montgomery asked. The pleasant smile on his face seemed forced now and not in keeping with the flintiness of his stare.

'No, no, of course not.' Cathie attempted a casual, offhand laugh. 'I guess it's just the historian in me looking for confirmation.'

'Have you found any contradiction?'

Cathie hadn't, but it wouldn't do to mention that one of the distinct gaps in official records involved this particular attack.

'Absolutely not. But some reports—completely false, I'm sure—allege misconduct by the men under his command. Pillage and rape are mentioned.' Cathie did not add that the accusations had not excluded the lieutenant in command.

Smythe-Montgomery's face grew hard. 'Surely the letters and journals'—he waved at the stack—'serve to debunk these vicious lies. In any case, it was simple jealousy by the other lieutenant involved in the attack for being placed in a subordinate role to Rolf.'

Cathie had read the accounts, but they were all written by Rolf Croker. She felt strong resentment for having to countenance this vile man's twisted fantasies, but she reminded herself why she was here and put the most pleasant, deferential smile on her face. 'Forgive me, Conrad, but I've only been investigating for an hour or so. I fully accept the veracity of your great-great-great-grandfather.'

This seemed to satisfy him. Fortunately, the period between the Opium Wars had been one of success for Rolf Croker. During the peace he had gained a certain reputation in the military: dedicated, strict, and a stickler for the rules. He had also succeeded in ingratiating himself to his superiors, eager to praise or support them in their endeavors. It wasn't particularly evil, though it certainly wasn't particularly impressive, but it had resulted in the desired outcome.

'Rolf did quite well during the interval between the wars,' Cathie said truthfully. 'He rose rapidly to the rank of colonel, and he was well respected by his men.' The evidence for this last claim had been only Rolf's word, but Cathie felt it wouldn't hurt to simply accept it for now.

Smythe-Montgomery was pleased by her comment. 'Yes, his career was proceeding brilliantly, and he was much loved by his officers and men.'

'In 1857 he found himself once again at Canton. Apparently, the Chinese had not adhered to the treaty of 1842.'

'Quite so. There had been attacks on the British and the seizure of a foreign vessel. The British had no choice but to send forces back to Canton. Of course, they chose one of their most seasoned and successful officers, and one with previous fighting experience to play a critical role.

'The bombardment began just three days after Christmas. On the morning of the 29th, French forces climbed the city wall. The British under Rolf's command broke into the city by the east gate. By January 5th, British and French forces moved into the city.'

'There were accusations of excessive force by the invading British,' Cathie said. 'Thousands of Chinese killed, tens of thousands of homes burned to the ground.'

'Rubbish,' Smythe-Montgomery said, with a dismissive wave of his hand. 'The usual claims of the incompetent losers, who were cowardly to boot.'

'But, Conrad, claims were made by General Bernard.'

'I've already explained to you that his claims were pure jealousy. The ease of the victory was clearly due to Rolf's superior tactics. It was only after his friends at court pressed Queen Victoria for a peerage for Rolf—as was his due—that Bernard wrote his scurrilous lies, denying that it had been Rolf's strategy that had won the day and blaming him for civilian deaths and destruction that were never proved.'

'Even so, your own father vigorously pursued the peerage based on an attempt to disprove Bernard's claims, with no success.'

Smythe-Montgomery was startled by this comment and glanced at the documents. Something was puzzling him. 'But naturally, the same prejudice exhibited during Rolf's time persists to this very day. Pure jealousy and politics.'

Cathie remained stubbornly silent. She was not going to accept this nonsense when even the records of Smythe-Montgomery's own private library made the falsity of his claims evident.

'Perhaps it's time for a brief break,' he said, when the tension had grown unendurable. He pressed a button on an intercom. 'Please send in drinks and snacks for myself and my guest.'

During the course of their half-hour recess, Cathie handed Smythe-Montgomery a draft outline of her book. Smythe-Montgomery inspected it, his equanimity and good humor returning as he saw the flattering spin Cathie was putting on his family's history.

But as he became more cheerful, Cathie grew furious. This man had killed her friend! The thought sprang irresistibly into her mind, and try as she might, she couldn't banish it.

It was in this rebellious mood that she asked, 'Now, Conrad, you promised me that if you approved of my outline you would help furnish me with details of your own goals as an epilogue to your family's history. Your own personal plans for empire!'

Smythe-Montgomery stiffened, but Cathie had passed beyond the point of caution. She asked questions about his airline, his other business ventures, his successes, his failures. He answered many of these tersely, and some he deflected. He became more uncomfortable and taciturn, but Cathie recklessly pressed on.

'For a man of your global reach, world events must come into your daily calculations. For instance, how does the death of Elaya Andoori affect your plans?'

Smythe-Montgomery's eyes grew hard as diamonds and he glanced at his watch. 'I am terribly sorry, but I'm afraid I have a pressing appointment.' He rose and shook her hand coldly. 'Please keep me posted on the progress of your book. Good day!'

After he left, Cathie remained seated. She was shaking, and wondering to herself how she could have been such a fool as to antagonize this powerful, psychotic man. And how would Logan react when he heard the results of this meeting?

'I am so fucking screwed!' she whispered to herself.

Not ten minutes after Smythe-Montgomery left, Ms. Guillfeld emerged from her office. 'The bulk of these documents must now go back into storage, Ms. Fletcher. But I'm sure arrangements can be made for you to visit with us again.'

That'll be a cold day in Tucson, Cathie thought, as she gathered her things and took the long walk down the hallway to the mansion's exit and the waiting limousine.

***

Before he left his mansion, Smythe-Montgomery spoke to Ms. Lister.

'Something isn't quite right,' he said. 'I know you've run a background check on Cathie Clark Fletcher. But something isn't right. Actually, several things. She mentioned my father's crusade to correct the faulty history from the Second Opium War and to obtain a peerage, but none of the documents she had access to would have mentioned that. And she spoke of Elaya Andoori's death completely out of context and with a barely veiled anger. There may be something about Ms. Fletcher that we've missed. Dig deeper.'

Lister nodded, a look of malicious energy on her face.

***

Late that evening, Cathie was working on her third Cosmo—dangerous territory—while Randy listened to her story.

'God, I screwed up!' she said. 'All I had to do was behave, do some buttering up, ask a few questions, finish up with more butter, and get the hell out. Why, why, why did I let him get under my skin?'

'Because he's an arrogant jerk and a pathological liar with delusions the size of a planet.'

'I just couldn't stand listening to that crap about his family!' she continued, ignoring Randy. 'I should never have come. What was I thinking?'

She reached for her drink and Randy gently placed a hand on her arm. 'Slow down. And listen for a minute. What's done is done. I know it wasn't the plan to piss him off, but you weren't intending to meet with him again, and you did get some of Crandall's questions asked. Who knows, maybe Smythe-Montgomery's answers were more unguarded while he was angry. I'll pass along the intel and we'll just see, OK?'

'Thanks. But I know a FUB when I see one.'

'Sorry. A FUB?'

'Fucked Up Big. Oh, shit, what will Logan think?'

'Now that's enough,' Randy said. 'Logan wasn't here and you were. You did your best. Now get up to your room, try to get some sleep, and go home tomorrow.'

Cathie patted his arm. 'If you're this understanding with Gail, and she with you, you two will be the happiest couple in history.'

'Now that I'll drink to!' Randy said, with a grin.

***

Twenty-four hours later, Cathie was home. Logan, still recovering from his flu, was far more understanding than she had predicted.

'Forget it, babe,' he croaked out. 'I'm just glad you're home. I'd give you a hug, but I may still be conta ...' He sneezed loudly, and then slipped into a fit of coughing. 'Still sick,' he finished weakly.

'Typhoid Fletcher,' she said, with a soft smile. 'Did I ever tell you how lucky I am?'

Logan smiled back, but gave up trying to speak.

***

The Reality of Chaos

At roughly the same time, Smythe-Montgomery carefully read the page of information that Ms. Lister had just handed him. 'Are you absolutely certain this is accurate?'

'Yes,' she said, 'and let me just say that I deeply regret not having uncovered this sooner.'

Smythe-Montgomery waved her to silence. 'A shared responsibility. We knew she was a successful author. We knew her husband worked in aerospace. What we didn't know was that his best friend works for the CIA. And we certainly didn't know that Ms. Fletcher and her best friend—the CIA agent's wife, no less!—knew Elaya Andoori in college.'

He continued to study the information. When the silence had grown to several minutes, Lister offered, 'The most likely conclusion is that the relationships are entirely coincidental and innocent. Ms. Fletcher's prickly attitude can easily be attributed to sadness and anger at her friend's death. And Mr. Fletcher's connection with a CIA agent is hardly unusual for a man in his profession.'

'All true, Ms. Lister, all true.' Another long period of silence ensued.

'There is one other thing,' Lister said hesitantly.

'Well?' Smythe-Montgomery snapped.

'It may be nothing, but one of Andoori's former bodyguards, now a loyal employee of al Rahzi, claims that a secret meeting took place between Andoori and several other persons at a country home belonging to Richard Crandall.'

'Crandall! Is it possible that he and that bitch Diana Foster are meddling? Ah! They would certainly know of my father's pursuit of a peerage. Is there a connection between Crandall and Ms. Fletcher?'

'Unknown. Again, it could be nothing but coincidence.'

'Nevertheless,' Smythe-Montgomery said, 'it would be best to be certain. Let's start with Ms. Fletcher. I believe that our friend Ibrahim should make a few discreet inquiries. Have Mr. Colpoys make the arrangements.'

Lister nodded. 'And if he is satisfied?'

'It hardly matters. We can't be having any loose ends, can we?'

Crandall sat studying a detailed screen he had arrived at through four layers of Clydes.

Chapter Twenty-Six

Reworking the Simulation

While time doesn't heal all wounds, it can certainly dull the pain. Several weeks had passed since Cathie returned home and she was beginning to put the events in London behind her. Logan had nearly recovered from his illness, and there was a new, much anticipated event on the horizon: Gail and Randy's wedding.

'You know,' Cathie said suddenly, interrupting Logan's piano practice, 'I just realized we haven't gotten a wedding gift for Gail and Randy.'

Logan stopped playing and looked across the room at his wife. It was the first time in a long while that she hadn't been consumed with thoughts of her last meeting with Smythe-Montgomery. While the topic, choosing a wedding present, didn't really thrill him, he did his best to appear interested and eager.

'You know, you're right. But I'll bet you have a few things in mind.'

'I do, but it needs to be something special, don't you think?'

'How about an all-expenses-paid vacation to Kotor, Montenegro? No, wait, that's where they're getting married! Jeez, I guess they already have everything!'

'Very funny. You know having the wedding there was really all about pleasing Gail's parents. Wedding in Kotor, reception in Venice. Now why didn't we think of that?'

'Because we didn't have a spare quarter-million laying around to blow on an extravagant luxury, that's why.'

'"Lying," dear.'

'Am not.'

'Oh, you're hopeless. Besides, the Grasshoppers did manage a compromise. Another ceremony in Vegas for their friends in the States who couldn't go overseas. Paid for by the happy couple. I think that's a nice gesture.'

'All I know is that Randy's in hock for the rings. He'll be working at the agency for two hundred years just to pay them off.'

'You're such an old stick-in-the-mud. But quit distracting me. We *were* going to talk about gifts. Clever, unique, special gifts.'

'In that case, let me open a bottle of wine. A wine guaranteed to provide inspiration for selecting clever, unique, special gifts.'

***

'Well, now, this is interesting.'

Crandall sat studying a detailed screen he had arrived at through four layers of Clydes. It was unusual for him to dig this deep for two reasons. The first was that he was generally more interested in global trends. Smythe-Montgomery, as an individual, had only begun to appear regularly because the man's influence exceeded that of most countries with a small-to-average GDP. Crandall's knowledge of statistics was the second reason. He knew very well that the deeper he went, the larger the uncertainty. At some point, much like a long-term weather forecast, the predictions became useless.

'Yvette, have you noticed this?'

She came up to stand beside him and examine the screen. 'It appears to make a correlation between the *particular* airline used in the attack on Elaya and a secondary—no, a tertiary—objective of Jack's.'

'Must you use that nickname? I always have to stop and remember who we're talking about.'

'His stupid name is too long,' she replied, with a pout. 'And "Jack" suits him for so many reasons.' She smiled brightly. 'Suppose his last name were "Ass."'

Crandall laughed despite himself. 'Fine. Jack of the family Ass.'

He brought her attention back to the screen. 'This inference came as a result of the information from Ms. Amhurst. Comments about his airline competitors in the region.'

'But this is a level four prediction.' She reached around Crandall and grabbed the mouse. With one click she displayed the confidence interval on the prediction. 'There,' she said, 'the standard deviation is nearly three times what we normally consider acceptable. An awful estimate.'

'How did you do that?' Crandall asked, ignoring her comment and focusing on the process. 'I would normally have to run a separate subroutine to obtain and display that information.'

'Oh, I created a shortcut,' she said nonchalantly. 'If you click on this little image of a normal distribution—here—it accesses the subroutine and displays the results. This little eraser'—she clicked on the icon near the results—'returns you to the original screen.'

'Excellent,' he said. 'Quite efficient. We should incorporate this at the other levels, don't you think?'

'Now, Richard,' she said, with a wry look, 'why on earth would I introduce this on the least significant layer only?'

'You mean—'

'It's available on all levels, of course.'

'Well, I'm afraid "excellent" is the only word that comes to mind quickly enough to match your wit. Really!' He paused, staring at her until a faint blush appeared on her face. He coughed and turned away. 'But to my original point. Look at the information. Never mind the statistics.'

Her eyebrows shot up. It was not what she expected to hear from this man. She glanced back at the screen and said, 'It's a bit of a clue, isn't it? A reason to connect Jack to the attack. An obvious motive.' She considered further, then shook her head. 'But this really is paper thin.'

'Nevertheless, we should pass it on.'

'To whom?'

'Why, Jason, of course. As we haven't seen or heard from him in quite a while, I suggest Luana. She can forward the information as she sees fit.'

***

Though unreachable, Jason Stone had not been idle. The attack on Elaya *should* have exposed threads, tendrils that led back to Smythe-Montgomery. At least, that had been his and Chuck's hope. They needed to find hard evidence to tie him to her murder and the overthrow of her government. But he was a slimy devil and nearly always used layers of subordinates and surrogates to carry out his plans. The strategy was sound, though Stone could hardly believe that an operation of this magnitude—assassination and the overthrow of a government—could be flawless.

He had been spending much of his time in the Middle East, tugging at threads. A few were promising. He had an 'interview' arranged with the lackey who, rumor had it, had been a witness to Zareb's murder. Under the current circumstances, 'interview' meant he had discovered where the man lived. Stone would pay him a visit tonight and ask a few pointed questions. Stone knew he should kill the man following the questioning. It was the only thing that made sense. But it brought back unpleasant memories. True, he was still alive, and that was a testament to his past practice: leave no loose ends. Stone would not have been surprised to discover Smythe-Montgomery shared an identical philosophy. It was beginning to sicken Stone, however. He had begun to wonder at what point his tactics made him a truly evil man. 'Kill a few, save millions' had made some kind of sense for a long time. But he was covered in blood, and it sickened him.

His phone rang, belying the notion that he was unreachable, but there were only two people who had this number. He glanced at the display. His second-favorite caller, Chuck Johnson.

'What's new, Johnson?'

'Hello to you too, Stone. I finally got hold of the SecDef. He told me I had exactly twenty seconds of his time, so I had to unload our plan on him without any soft soap to ease the pain.'

'I'll bet that went well. How'd he take it?'

'Well, we talked for nearly half an hour, and at the end he told me I was fucking insane. But being as how he had no other options, he said he'd let things play out—for now.'

'Do you trust him one hundred percent?' Stone asked.

'I don't trust anyone one hundred percent, and that includes my wife—and you.'

Stone listened with growing gloom.

'Are you getting any support?'

'Hell no! I'm still on leave, and as far as he's concerned, our conversation never happened. He also made it clear that no matter how things play out, I'm done. I'll be lucky if I don't end up in jail.

Retirement with benefits if I'm *very* lucky. How's things in your neck of the woods?'

'Fair,' Stone replied. 'I'm following up on one lead tonight. Might be useful. Plus I got some intel from Luana—via Becky Amhurst, via Yvette, via Richard Crandall.'

'Quite a pedigree. But is it worth a shit?'

'Maybe. It's a possible tie-in between Smythe-Montgomery's EMPR1 bank account and a more obvious motive for him to bring down that jet. His *competitor's* jet. Luana is working the banking angle. There may be a way to get more information.'

'A hack?'

'Johnson, please! A "less-than-fully-authorized perusal of the account."'

Chuck grunted. 'When did you start being such an eloquent bullshitter?'

'There's a lot about me you still don't know,' Stone said seriously.

'Amen. And I'm glad to keep it that way. But the question is, when do we pull the trigger on our brilliant plan?'

'Can't say. Let's see how my interview and Crandall's data pan out. I tell you what, though. I'd love to have a couple of hours to sweat one of Smythe-Montgomery's friends, like Ibrahim al Rahzi.'

'You'd need a small army to get near the SOB now that the old regime is gearing up.'

Stone couldn't disagree. 'That reminds me, how is the consolidation of Elaya's supporters going?'

'Better than we'd hoped,' Chuck replied. 'After Zareb's death, the rest of her loyal followers made a mad dash for the borders. A few more made it than we thought at first. They're organizing now—quietly—in one of your favorite vacation spots, Ashgabat.'

'Does that make sense? The place is hardly secure.'

'Nowhere is secure. The point is, no one knows they're there. Not even the SecDef.'

'Leaks, Johnson, leaks.'

'I know,' Chuck barked. 'Everything has a time constant. They're safe for now. We need to hurry, or get lucky, or both.'

'"Both" is good.'

'Speaking of good, will you and Luana be attending Randy's wedding?'

'Hmph. I'd rather not. Kind of busy, for one thing. How 'bout you?'

'I said no. Then Joy said yes. So I'll be there. It's a small affair, at least. But, you know, I just feel like I'm stinking of skunk right now.'

'No,' Stone said dryly, 'that's your normal odor. No one will notice.'

'Fuck you, Stone!'

'Likewise, my friend.'

***

'Don't tell me you're packed already?' Randy asked, as he stared at the two suitcases and one backpack lined up neatly at the door of Gail's apartment.

'Of course I am. We're leaving tomorrow, you know. Besides, you're packed.'

'That's 'cause I just flew in from Oakland. With my bags. You know, packed.'

'Well then, we're both ready!' she said.

Randy drew a deep breath. 'Are we?'

'Not having second thoughts, are you?' she asked playfully.

'About getting married? Hell no!' he said, as he wrapped her in his arms. 'But here's an idea: let's run down to city hall right now and then vacation in Flagstaff.'

'Really? And give up a beautiful wedding and honeymoon in Montenegro, Venice, and points beyond?'

'No. I suppose not. It sounds pretty awesome, actually. But you know I'm a beans and burgers kind of guy. This type of luxury makes me nervous.'

'Don't get used to it, darling.' She kissed him lightly on the nose. 'A struggling agency drone and an aerospace grunt can't keep up that lifestyle. But Dad proposed to Mom on a wild fling in Montenegro and always wanted to see me married there. I guess that's why they're being so generous.'

'They certainly are. My folks about dropped when they saw the wedding invitation.' He smiled at the recollection of their subsequent phone call. 'They accused me of being a gold digger!'

'Too bad it's not true,' she said. 'Say, you wouldn't leave me for a rich Hollywood starlet, would you?'

'Not a chance.'

'Good! So, since I'm already packed, how should we spend the rest of the day?'

Randy smiled. 'We could do some honeymoon rehearsal.'

Gail swatted him on the arm, but a moment later she walked to her bedroom. She turned back to Randy and mirrored his smile. 'Well?'

Stephen Lance / Chuck Markussen

The day could only be described as spectacular, with temperatures in the upper 70s and a gentle breeze that brought both land and sea fragrances to the tiny islet of Our Lady of the Rocks.

Chapter Twenty-Seven

The Wedding

The sun sparkled off pearly blue water in the Bay of Kotor, a large, winding bay of the Adriatic Sea. Past a narrow inlet, a dual-lobed inner bay opened wide. Just inside the inner bay were two islets, dots of land that seemed to be floating on the calm water. The day could only be described as spectacular, with temperatures in the upper 70s and a gentle breeze that brought both land and sea fragrances to the tiny islet of Our Lady of the Rocks. The guests had already arrived and were touring the church and the attached museum.

Legend had it that the islet had been made over centuries by local seamen who, returning from a successful voyage, would lay a rock in the bay. The current islet was the result of such offerings begun in 1452. The copper-domed Roman Catholic church was the principle structure. The interior of the church was gorgeous and contained beautiful artwork from the 17th century, but Gail had preferred that the ceremony take place on the grassy, triangular courtyard facing St. George, less than a quarter of a mile distant. The St. George Abbey, a stone structure with a red tile roof, dominated that minute island. Unlike Our Lady of the Rocks, which had very little vegetation, the abbey was surrounded by several dozen cyprus trees, as tall as the bell tower.

Small towns, clinging to the feet of tall steep mountains, dotted the perimeter of the bay: Risan, Donji Stoliv, Orahovac, and others. White houses with red-tiled roofs climbed in rows from the shore. To the southeast, Mount Lovćen rose to over 5600 feet above Kotor, largest of the bay's coastal towns. Tucked at the southern end of a narrow tongue of water, it wasn't visible from the islands, but many fishing boats from that town made their way past them on a daily basis, adding territory to Our Lady of the Rocks on each successful return.

Logan and Cathie walked out of the church and into the tiny courtyard where a guitarist and a harpist were setting up. Gail and Randy had chosen nontraditional music for their ceremony, despising the idea of a wheezing organ thrumming out the 'Wedding March.'

Logan scanned the handful of chairs set out. Few enough. Gail's and Randy's parents would be here soon along with the young couple. The bride had invited her two best friends from college, Randy a single individual from his high school days. Chuck, driven reluctantly by Joy, had come, and that pleased Randy. But he couldn't hide his disappointment when he'd received the polite negative response from Stone and Luana. He had come not only to respect Stone, but to think of him as a true friend. That little irony made him smile since Stone was the only man who had ever shot Gail.

Logan did the mental count. Thirteen. Unlucky. Though he didn't intend to mention this to anyone. He too wished that Stone were here, and not just to move the wedding count to a happier number. Cathie had been nervous since their flight landed, swearing that she was being watched and constantly glancing around her. A small fishing boat passed between the islet and the mainland town of Perast where Logan could see the wedding party assembling.

Cathie tugged his sleeve. 'Look at the guy on the boat. The one driving. Don't be obvious, but just glance over.'

Logan did.

'So?' Cathie asked.

'So what?'

'I'm certain he's the same guy we saw at the airport. He kept staring at us when we were picking up our bags.'

Logan looked again, but the boat was already moving away.

'Not sure.'

Cathie gave him a vicious look. 'I'm going to tell Chuck about it.' She marched back to the church, where Joy and Chuck were still touring.

'Well this is going to be fun,' Logan muttered, but he kept an eye on the boat. By the time Chuck came out to talk to him and smoke a cigar, the boat had made a slow turn and, not leaving the inner bay, was now sailing slowly past the islet's southern side. Logan thought he caught the glint of sun off glass. Was someone on board using binoculars to observe them?

'Cathie mentioned the boat,' Chuck said, lighting up and offering Logan a cigar. 'It seems odd. Not going out fishing, I mean.'

'No. Could just be curiosity, I suppose. Can't be many weddings on this rock.'

'Maybe,' Chuck replied. 'But the wedding hasn't started and that guy is burning fuel to watch a couple of old men smoke cigars.'

Logan grunted, then pointed to the north. 'Wedding party's pushing off. I don't think we'll have time to finish these.' He held up his newly lit cigar.

'Shit. I needed a smoke.' Chuck snubbed out his cigar and jammed it back in his inner pocket. 'Later.'

Logan did the same, glancing to make sure Cathie wasn't watching him.

The shuttle boat made a quick passage between Perast and Our Lady of the Rocks, and soon Gail, Randy, and the two sets of parents stepped onto the islet and entered the church before proceeding to the courtyard. The harpist struck up a lovely tune that sounded Celtic to Logan. The guitar quietly joined in as Randy's parents came out and took a seat. A moment later, Randy escorted Gail's mother from the church and took his place facing the guests. He looked decidedly uncomfortable. The priest came out, a broad grin on his face, followed a moment later by Gail and her father, who led her to stand beside Randy and went to his seat, tears trickling down his cheeks.

***

From a grassy ridge high above the town of Perast, Jason Stone adjusted his binoculars and stared down at the unfolding scene. Though he smiled and quickly commented to himself, 'Randy's a braver man than me, though he looks more like he's heading for the gallows,' his primary focus was on the town below and the boats in the bay. He'd been worried for Cathie ever since hearing the story of her meeting with Smythe-Montgomery. It had been a bad idea letting her go alone. Very bad. The man might be delusional, but he was a crafty, perceptive viper. Stone was certain that Smythe-Montgomery no longer trusted Cathie.

He was also certain she and Logan had been followed, and he didn't like the fact that the same fishing boat was now passing the islet for the third time. A two-man operation. One man driving the boat, another observing with a pair of binoculars. If these were nosy locals, then Stone was a Buddhist monk. He had no fear for Cathie at the moment. It was a public place, and Randy was there. Stone was gratified when he detected a slight bulge under Randy's tux. 'Carrying. Good man,' he whispered.

***

Cathie elbowed Logan and inclined her head slightly towards the fishing boat, passing by once again. This time Logan was convinced that someone was observing the ceremony. But it turned out to be the boat's last pass; it turned east and headed back towards the town of Kotor. It was just as well. The ceremony was moving quickly, and Logan wanted to focus. Cathie gave him a nervous smile and also turned her attention to the young couple, who were whispering their way through their vows.

***

'It's official,' Gail said, holding up her hand and staring at the thin band of gold tucked alongside her engagement ring. 'Any regrets?'

Randy laughed. 'Not a one. Though I don't think I've been that nervous since I did my handgun qualification for the agency.'

'How romantic,' Gail said, with a crooked smile.

Her father joined the two. 'Well, Mrs. O'Neil, the first shuttle boat is loading. Would you and Randy like join us?'

'Oh, gawd yes,' Gail said. 'I need to change into something that doesn't feel like a cross between a fairy princess dress and a medieval torture device.'

A small group, gathered near the dock, showered the newlyweds with flower petals and good wishes as they boarded.

'See you all at dinner,' Randy shouted, as the boat's motor roared to life. Of the wedding attendees, only Chuck, Joy, Cathie, and Logan remained. It wouldn't be long before the boat returned for them. Joy was already deep in conversation with Cathie, reliving the ceremony. Chuck tugged at Logan's sleeve and led him towards the other side of the islet, simultaneously retrieving his barely used cigar.

'C'mon, brudda. I definitely need that smoke now.'

The Reality of Chaos

The two stood leaning on the courtyard's stone wall and staring across the glistening stretch of water to the abbey. 'Don't know about you,' Chuck said, blowing a cloud of blue-grey smoke into the clear air, 'but these events always leave me feeling a little flat. Don't get me wrong, I'm glad the Grasshoppers tied the knot. They both seem really happy.'

'You're just getting unromantic in your old age,' Logan said. 'I hate to admit I kind of feel the same. But hell, it's meant to be done when you're young. Sort of like having babies. Not a game for the old.'

'Say, what do you suppose two grasshoppers have for babies? Crickets?'

Logan laughed. 'Little grasshoppers, dumb ass.'

Chuck leaned back and stretched, letting out a soft grunt, then ran a hand on his chin, already scratchy though it was only midafternoon. Logan recognized the gesture.

'OK, Chuck, what's on your mind? You look like you just bit a worm-infested lemon.'

'Nothing really. Except for the fact that there's a crazy megalomaniac plotting the rise of a new empire. And insane theocrats are in charge of Iran and driving it back towards the 7th century. Not only do I have no solution to any of this, but my ass is about to become unemployed.'

'Just think of all the free time you'll have,' Logan said.

Chuck laughed humorlessly. 'You know, it's kind of pretty here. Might be a good place to retire.' The bay was dazzling, with only a few small boats out. Behind the tree-crowded islet of St. George, tall, green mountains rose steeply from the water's edge. The buildings of another small town to the southeast clustered along the shoreline.

'It's pretty, I'll grant you that,' Logan said, taking a pull at his cigar. 'But I can't see you out fishing every day. You'd be bored.'

'Yeah, well I wouldn't mind it once in a while. Plus I think a little boredom would be good for the ulcer, if you know what I mean.'

Logan turned and looked at his friend seriously. 'If it comes to that—retirement, I mean—stay busy, at least part time. Do some consulting. You'd have your pick of aerospace companies and think tanks. Do three days a week. Go fishing on two.'

'And take care of honey-dos on the other two,' Chuck said.

'Not all retired people are comfortable sitting on their asses and drinking wine. It takes a certain kind of guy. Me, for instance.'

'Thanks, brudda,' Chuck said, putting his hand on Logan's shoulder. 'Thanks for trying. Hey, here's the girls come to fetch us.'

***

A late afternoon breeze was kicking up small, white-topped waves in the bay, a distinct smell of salt water, fish, and seaweed haunting the streets of Perast. Gail had gotten into comfortable clothes and was off shopping with her parents. Randy had shed his tux and cummerbund and was thinking seriously of smoking a cigar. He finally decided this would be a good opportunity, as Gail would be gone for a few hours and then they'd all be off to dinner. He stepped out of his room into a small grassy courtyard overlooking the bay, a drink in one hand and a Monte Cristo in the other.

'I don't suppose you'd have two of those,' a voice said.

Randy nearly dropped his drink. He hadn't seen the man lazing in the chaise lounge facing the bay. In fact, the man was sunk so low—obviously quite relaxed—that the chair's back still prevented Randy from seeing him until he twisted in his seat and looked back, grinning.

'Oh, and a drink too? Thanks. Don't mind if I do.' It was Jason Stone.

Randy simply passed his drink and cigar to Stone. In a few minutes he was back and seated in the chair next to Stone. He took a sip of his scotch and put the cigar to his lips. As the blue smoke drifted off he said, 'Jeez, Stone, a little warning would be nice.'

'What? And ruin my surprise?'

'Good thing I wasn't still carrying. I would hate to have shot your ass.'

Stone grunted. 'Messy. Probably spoil your dinner.'

'Speaking of surprises, if you just happened to be in Montenegro, why not drop in on my wedding? I did invite you, you know?'

'I do,' said Stone seriously. 'I really appreciate that, by the way. And I did enjoy it—from up there.' He pointed behind himself to the looming mountain. 'Even heard it. The harp was a nice touch.'

'So binoculars and a parabolic mike. But why eavesdrop on my wedding when you could have been there? Do you hate wearing a tux that much?'

'I wasn't only spying on *you*.'

'That so? So what's up?'

'Not sure, but something's not right. Since Cathie's ill-fated meeting with Smythe-Montgomery I've been worried.'

'Yeah, that didn't go well, though I tried to get her to forget about it. Water under the bridge.'

'Maybe,' Stone said. 'But there was one party on a boat who was overly interested in your nuptials. Two guys circling your wedding island. Unfortunately, they didn't talk much, and when they did ... Well, my Farsi isn't all that good.'

'Farsi? I would have expected English with a cockney accent.'

'He's too careful for that. Too subtle. It's always intermediaries with him, two, three layers removed.'

Randy took a pull at his drink and frowned. 'It's why the old snake has never been nailed.'

Stone nodded. 'Luana sends her best, by the way.'

'How's she doing?'

'Busy. She has this thing—I think it's called a company. She keeps telling me it needs her constant attention. In reality, she's been busy on something else. Something a little more on topic.'

Randy turned in his seat and stared at Stone expectantly.

'Luana, Crandall, and Yvette have been working the financial angle on Sir Snake. It seems the EMPR1 account Yvette discovered in his e-mail is both fat and multi-tentacled. Sort of a bloated squid. Some of the tendrils go to very unusual places.' He shrugged. 'A lot of it is speculation. Most of the e-mails are encrypted or use code words that they've only partially cracked.'

Randy relaxed back into his lounge chair.

'Actually, that's not even why I'm here.'

'It's not?' Randy asked, surprised.

'No. I need to tell you something. It's a little angle Chuck and I have been working. He should've been the one to tell you, but he thinks he'd be dragging you into something that might hurt your career—or get you killed. I forget which. He carelessly failed to swear me to silence, and I think you should know. I'll tell you straight up, we're gonna need your help.'

Randy's eyes grew rounder and his jaw sagged lower as Stone explained. When he was finished, Randy drained his glass in one massive gulp. He rose from his chair and headed for the minibar in his room. 'Holy shit! I need a drink!'

When he was seated again, he attacked his new drink with the same energy as he had his first.

'Steady, Randolph,' Stone said, with a smile. 'It's your wedding night. Wouldn't do to disappoint the bride.'

Randy ignored the attempt at humor. 'Are you serious? About all of it?'

'Straight up,' Stone replied.

'So, what's your plan?'

'Plan?' said Stone, his head cocked to one side and a wry smile curling one corner of his mouth.

'Funny. At least, I hope you're still joking.'

'Only sort of. Things are in flux. I need to be three places at once: here, London, and Tehran.' He sighed, and Randy could see the stress and weariness on Stone's usually energetic face: dark circles under his eyes, forehead wrinkled, jaw tensed. 'I'll have to keep you posted.'

***

The following evening found the happy couple, their parents, and guests seated around a large table at the Restaurant Terrazza Danieli in Venice. Palm fronds softened the glistening marble of pillars and floor, while gorgeous paintings in elaborate gilded frames surrounded the room. The table was beautifully set on dazzling linen, and flowers adorned its entire length. The setting sun filtered in through curtains swaying in the gentle breeze, sparkling off china, silver, and cut glass. Randy and Gail sat at the center of the table facing the windows, adding their own glow to the room. They appeared to be a bit tired, but undeniably happy.

The dinner was a sumptuous affair, with a steady flow of courses and paired wines. Much to Logan's delight, the 'coat-and-tie casual' promised in the wedding invitation rapidly devolved to 'coat draped over the back of chair, and ties loosened or removed.' By the time the third (or was it fourth?) main dish arrived—calamari in a creamy sauce with spices that defied identification—there was a steady buzz of conversation. When all were stuffed and taking a break prior to indulging in dessert, a few speeches were made. Randy's best friend from college, acting as best man, led off, delivering a workmanlike if unoriginal oratory, wishing the new couple health, happiness, and success. Drinks were refilled and others stood to offer their best wishes. Even Chuck, who had been somewhat gloomy during the proceedings, stood and waxed eloquent.

'To my partner and my friend, and to the lovely woman at his side, what can I say? In our business, there's no greater compliment than to say "I'd trust him covering my back," which means, of course, I'd trust him with my life. Randy, I'd trust you covering my back as I hope you trust me covering yours. I also believe that a true friend is a friend for life. I have few enough of those, but I'd be proud to call you one.

'Gail, for as short a time as I've known you, we've had some unique experiences together, haven't we? And I can honestly say that you personally prevented your rash husband from murdering me not so long ago. Thank you for that! It's funny, isn't it, how things work out.'

Chuck paused, and the smile on his face melted to a thoughtful, introspective expression. But he shook his head slightly and grinned at the couple. 'Live long and love each other like every day is a gift, 'cause it is. Congratulations!'

Applause filled the room, and Logan rose to speak.

'I remember the night you two met. It was random luck, Randy and I meeting up with Becky Amhurst and her posse at a restaurant in Tucson. That night, her posse had a new addition: a beautiful, intelligent woman who stole Randy's attention right from the start. You two took some serious teasing but lived to tell the tale. Who knew you'd end up stealing each other's heart?' He lifted his glass. 'Here's to Mr. and Mrs. Grasshopper! Health, happiness, and loads of little grasshoppers!'

More applause and laughter. Randy and Gail rose together to thank their friends and families. As they spoke, Logan quietly slipped from the table, Cathie giving him a private, knowing smile. When the young couple finished, they began to sit down, but Cathie quickly said, 'I believe you should share your first dance.'

Gail and Randy looked at each other in puzzlement. There had been no arrangements for music, and the room really wasn't large enough for dancing. But there was a small open area near the arched entryway from the hall, and Cathie motioned to that area. Randy was about to argue when the first chords of Billy Joel's 'Just the Way You Are' filled the room. He and Gail turned in surprise to see Logan seated at a Steinway Victorian upright piano tucked in an alcove at one end of the room, his head down, concentrating on the music. Everyone clapped and shouted encouragement to the bride and groom, and, both blushing, they stepped out into the open area and began to step through the dance. The wedding party watched happily, cameras flashed, and even the serving staff of the restaurant stood grinning.

When the song ended, Randy kissed Gail and hugged her fiercely while cheers erupted all around. Tears streamed down Gail's face as Randy led her back to their seats. A moment later, the staff lit candles, refilled glasses, and brought in trays loaded with pastries and confections. Eating and drinking resumed.

***

It was nearly 11:00 p.m. and Gail's parents were saying their goodbyes. Randy's parents had left a short while earlier. Joy and Cathie were talking to Gail and her friend at one end of the table when Chuck came up to Logan, tapped significantly on the pocket of his sport coat, and motioned towards the hall leading to the main lobby of the hotel. A few minutes later, the two were looking out over the Grand Canal, smoking cigars and enjoying the fresh night air. The Riva Schiavoni was still alive with tourists, and the hotel lights bathed the walkway with amber light. Out on the water, lights from dozens of boats sparkled and reflected off the canal's smooth surface.

'So you and Cathie are sticking around for a couple of days?' Chuck asked, after a long, silent interval.

'That's the plan. It's not like we get here all that often. A little sightseeing, a little shopping. Well, maybe a lot of shopping. You?'

'I'm out tomorrow. Got a few things I need to keep an eye on in the States.'

The Reality of Chaos

'Really?' Logan was about to add 'Like what?' but realized that in Chuck's line of work this type of question never got an answer—an honest answer.

Chuck sensed what Logan was thinking. He smiled crookedly. 'Yeah. Just some stuff to keep an eye on. Joy just about wants to hang me.'

'Hell, let her stay! She can hang with us or go solo. She can fly back with us, anyway, and it would give her some time away from your grouchy old ass.'

Chuck rubbed his hand over the stubble on his chin. 'You know, that ain't a half bad idea. I'll go tell her.'

As Chuck started to move off, Logan grabbed his arm gently and pulled him back. 'Cathie already talked to her, and Joy changed her flights earlier today. My job was to make sure you were OK with it, which I knew you would be. So you and I can finish our cigars in peace.'

'My friend the conspirator. You missed your calling, brudda. You could have made a good agent.'

'I'll take that as an insult,' Logan said. He looked from side to side and pulled a small silver flask from his coat pocket. 'Single malt. Eighteen years young. Sorry I didn't bring the whisky glasses.'

'I take it back. My friend the genius.'

Logan took a drink and then passed the flask. 'To Randy and Gail. May their marriage be as long and happy as both of ours.'

Chuck accepted the flask and took a deep swallow. 'Amen, brudda. Amen!'

Stephen Lance / Chuck Markussen

Logan and Cathie had decided to have one last meal at an open air café overlooking the Grand Canal.

Chapter Twenty-Eight

Bad Evening for the Fletchers

Randy, Gail, and most of the wedding party left Venice the following day on various flights depending on their respective destinations. Joy, Cathie, and Logan spent the day wandering up and down the Riva Schiavoni alternately shopping and visiting some of the fascinating historical and cultural sights. Logan had been puzzled by the stacks of wide composite planks and the curved metal tubing found at intervals along nearly every street until he was told that they could be assembled into temporary walkways to aid foot traffic during unusual times of flooding. Cathie and Joy had dragged him on, muttering something about 'engineers and their weird interests.'

They took the obligatory gondola ride, passing through the narrow canal under the Bridge of Sighs, the covered limestone bridge that connected the interrogation rooms in the Doge's Palace to the prison. Despite the legend surrounding the name—that prisoners would sigh at their last view of beautiful Venice as they were taken to their cells—the bridge was built long after the days of the Inquisition. And as Logan discovered, the view through the small, grill-covered windows was severely limited. Like most legends, however, this one refused to die, even in the face of contrary evidence. The trio also took a tour of the prison, with its tiny, stone-walled rooms. These were clearly places of despair and suffering, and no passage of time could add a charming patina to their form or function.

St. Mark's Basilica, on the other hand, was a place of glorious, ornate beauty. Its Byzantine architecture, opulent design, and gold mosaics had earned it the nickname Church of Gold, and it did not disappoint. Marble floors, statues, and glistening mosaics were crowned by five enormous domes, each decorated to its apex with religious figures amid shimmering gold. When the three finally exited onto the

Piazza San Marco, Logan was rubbing his neck, stiff from so much head-tilted gazing, and his comment 'nice place' was understatement taken to the extreme.

The next day followed a similar pattern, leaving three exhausted but happy tourists ready to head home to recover from their vacation. Logan and Cathie had decided to have one last meal at an open air café overlooking the Grand Canal. Joy had declined. 'It's not a good idea for me to eat heavy the night before fourteen hours of plane rides, if you know what I mean.'

'We do,' Logan said, with an imploring look towards Cathie.

'But we're going out anyway,' Cathie said firmly. 'You promised. Besides, you can always order something light.'

Joy chuckled. 'I'll just let you two work it out. I think I'll take a hot shower, order a little room service, and hit the sack early. Meet you in the lobby in the a.m.'

Logan nodded and he and Cathie strolled off down the canal-side walkway, heading for their restaurant.

The sun had already set, and a cool, moist breeze wafted up to the second floor restaurant. Seated at a corner booth with a fabulous view of the canal, the Basilica, and the Riva Schiavoni, Logan felt much more comfortable with their decision not to miss this dinner. His only disappointment had been the wine—a Cabernet from a local winery with a somewhat peculiar flavor. Cathie had noticed it as well, but after a few sips both had agreed that it was actually quite good, though different from their usual favorites.

When the main course dishes were cleared and dessert menus deposited on the table, Cathie excused herself. 'I'm feeling a little odd. You go ahead and order while I go and powder my nose. I'll be right back.'

But Logan was also feeling lightheaded. In the end, he ordered nothing but a cup of coffee. *Must be getting too old for three days in a row of partying*, he thought. *A little caffeine should help.*

As he drank the hot brew, he realized Cathie had been gone for a long time. He was finding it impossible to think straight, and the coffee wasn't helping. He was on the point of asking one of the female wait staff to check the ladies' room when a well-dressed man walked up and placed a folded piece of paper on the table beside Logan's coffee cup. He was gone before Logan could get his sluggish mind to react. The lights in the restaurant were blurring as he reached for the note and opened it.

We have your wife. Please come to the front of the restaurant. No trouble please. Your bill has been paid. Leave now.

A surge of adrenaline shot through Logan and he rose hastily from his seat. Too hastily, and he had to pause and steady himself, holding the table. A few other patrons eyed him knowingly. Apparently the large man couldn't hold his liquor. It happened often enough.

Logan blinked his eyes and tried to focus as he descended the stairs of the restaurant, crossed the entryway, and stepped out onto the walkway. Two men came up on either side and guided him down a short set of stairs to a boat bobbing in the canal. Cathie was there, a large man at her side. She seemed drunk or half asleep.

'Logan, no,' she whispered, but he was already on board. He felt a sharp stab in his upper arm. He turned and stared stupidly as the syringe was pulled out. Someone gave an order in a language he didn't understand, and the boat's engine roared to life just as his leaden eyelids closed.

***

'Can you at *least* get me a pad of paper and a pencil? I'm a writer and I want to write.'

The words filtered into Logan's torpid brain, and he had a momentary notion that they were aimed at him. Cathie had wanted him to do something or get something for her and he had fallen asleep on the couch. Now he was in the doghouse. But as his eyes came back into focus, he realized that he wasn't in his living room in Tucson, and he certainly wasn't lying on his comfortable couch. He was seated on a cold, hard floor, his back and head resting against an even harder, rougher wall.

'Whass going on?' he mumbled.

'Ah, Sleeping Beauty awakens,' Cathie replied, leaning over and kissing his forehead. 'We've been kidnapped, dear. Whether for ransom or some other nefarious purpose, I've been unable to discern. The imbeciles guarding us are unable or unwilling to say which. Oh, I know you're out there listening,' she bellowed at the heavy wooden door of their cell.

'Kidnapped? What the hell!' Logan tried to stand, but toppled back down, cracking his head on the stone wall. 'Shit! Where are we?'

'Not sure. Reminds me of one of the cells in the prison connected to the Bridge of Sighs, but there haven't been many tourists.' She lowered her voice. 'There are three of them that I've seen. They speak English well enough, but they're clearly Middle Eastern. And I've heard a smattering of Farsi when they think they're out of earshot.'

'What do they want?'

'I'll make allowances for the double dose of anesthetic they gave you, but I've already told you, I don't know. They seem to be waiting for someone else—their head honcho, I suppose. You've been out for about eight hours, by my best reckoning. They took our watches, but I can guess by the sunlight coming in our one, lonely, barred window. I've been up for a few hours.'

'Were you just asking for something, or was I dreaming?'

'I was asking for paper and pencil. The cretins refuse to provide a laptop, of course, but my fingers are twitching and until I can put them to better use—like throttling the greasy bastards—I figured I might just write something.'

'Good plan, dear,' Logan said, slowly raising himself to a standing position. 'You know, this really wasn't worth it for a free dinner.'

A key ground in the door's lock and the door swung open. One of the guards tossed in a pad of paper and a pen. 'What do you write?' he asked, unable to hide his curiosity.

'Oh, you'll see,' Cathie said archly.

The guard grunted and left, locking the door noisily.

'We're kind of screwed, aren't we?' Cathie asked, a far more serious tone in her voice.

Logan rubbed his head. 'Well, if your time estimate is right, we should have met Joy in the lobby by now. She'll check our room, see that we never returned last night, and contact Chuck—'

'Who's already in the States. I think I'll stick to my "we're kind of screwed" position.'

'There is someone we haven't seen recently.'

'He could be anywhere in the world—literally,' Cathie whispered.

***

Joy's phone rang, and she snatched it up. Events had gone exactly along the lines Logan had predicted, and she had been waiting impatiently for a callback from Chuck. She was more than a little surprised when she heard another voice entirely.

'Joy, this is Jason Stone.'

'Jason, what—'

'Don't worry. I talked to Randy who talked to Chuck and it turns out I'm in the neighborhood. I have a notion as to what's going on and I told Randy I'd handle it. Do me a favor, though, tell me all about your last day with the Fletchers.'

Joy did. 'So what should I do?'

'Stay in your hotel. Don't go to the airport, and definitely don't take a cab anywhere. If there's a bar in the hotel with lots of people, stay there, or go back to your room and don't open up for anyone. If all goes well, I'll be in touch soon.'

'"If all goes well"?'

'Don't worry,' he repeated. 'I'll call you soon.'

***

Stone had continued surveilling the Fletchers after their arrival in Venice. Their decision to stay after the others departed vexed him, but he had felt more comfortable while they kept company with Joy. Their dinner alone had been an obvious opportunity for their kidnappers. Stone had underestimated the cleverness and careful planning of his adversaries, but he had anticipated an escape by boat, should they attempt anything, allowing him to make arrangements to have his own boat standing by. He followed at a safe distance, though he was certain the kidnappers believed they'd made an unobserved getaway. Unlike the Fletchers, he was positive that ransom was not the motive for the kidnapping, having even discussed the possibility of an incident with Chuck long before the wedding.

***

'It's not a great idea for them to travel overseas. Not if Cathie Fletcher has succeeded in making Smythe-Montgomery suspicious,' Stone had said.

'Blame the Grasshoppers. Randy and Gail have had this little extravaganza planned for a long time, and Cathie and Logan sure as hell aren't going to miss it. What if I just hang out with them till they leave?'

'We've talked about this, Chuck. I've got this covered. You've got another obligation back home—a big one—remember?'

'Yeah. But I'm gonna have a sour stomach till everyone is safe back home. Including you.'

And Chuck had been right.

***

It had been simple to follow the kidnappers, who hadn't gone far: a grubby abandoned prison now used as warehouse in the town of Cabrina, barely a dozen miles up the coast on the spit of land that pointed towards Venice like a finger from the mainland. Only three men were guarding the Fletchers, but Stone would need to move quickly. They were clearly waiting for one or more others, and Stone was certain that when they arrived, they would begin to question Cathie and Logan. The questioning was likely to be violent and brief.

Stone checked the time. Nearly noon. The roof of a nearby building made a good vantage point, and he watched as food was brought to the prison, indicating that Cathie and Logan would be here for a while. Stone decided he could wait until evening. Fighting at dusk suited him, and over the years he'd found that others tended to be at their most relaxed, their most careless at that time. He would wait until all three were there. It would be easy enough to take them all from this location, but he had other plans.

***

That evening, the man brought food and water for the two captives, but stared at Cathie after he had placed it on the ground. 'You still write. Why? What is it?'

Cathie looked up with an evil smile. 'I'm bored, so I write.' She didn't add that she was also nervous bordering on terrified. She and Logan had dismissed the idea of kidnapping for money and were

The Reality of Chaos

convinced that these men, though certainly not British, were connected with Smythe-Montgomery. And if that were so, the two of them had scant hope of a pleasant outcome.

'But *what* do you write?' the man insisted. 'You might as well tell me, for when Ibrahim arrives, you will tell us that and much more.'

Logan took a step towards him, but the guard raised his gun, and the shadow of another man lurking in the hall moved forward. 'Do not be foolish. She will be sufficient if an accident should befall you.'

The open door was tempting, and Logan was wavering until Cathie interrupted his inner debate. 'Sit down, dear.' Logan reluctantly did. 'So you want to know what I'm writing?' she said, turning back to the guard. 'Very well, I'll tell you. I'm writing our rescue scene. You know, where our friends come to get us out of this shithole. Oh, I'm afraid it ends badly for you. I'd say I was sorry, but I'm not.'

The guard involuntarily took a step back, but stopped, his mouth widening in a grin as he considered a mocking reply. Before he could utter a word, the man behind him grunted and suddenly collapsed. There was a knife sticking from his back.

The guard's grin vanished as one bloomed on Cathie's face. 'I see it's beginning now.'

The guard froze. Should he kill the prisoners? Call for Hamid, the third man and the leader of their group? Lock the cell door? Stone resolved the situation for him, arriving like a ghost and moving with the speed of a mongoose. As the guard raised his gun, Stone stepped in close, grabbed his wrist, and gave a violent twist. Logan could hear bones snap as the gun tumbled from the guard's hand. Stone covered the man's mouth to stifle the scream of pain and shoved him roughly to the ground, face down, twisting the man's arm behind him. He transferred his grip to the man's hand and gave it a slight twist. He could feel the man's body buck as the excruciating pain of bone grinding on bone shot through him.

'I'm going to take my hand from your mouth, and you're going to calmly call Hamid—yes, yes, I know all your names. If you do, you may live, though that's not my preference. If you call a warning, you'll die—painfully.' He twisted the man's wrist again and felt the involuntary spasm. 'Nod if you agree.' The man did. Stone's freed hand slid silently to his belt.

'Hamid! Come here. Hamid. We must talk.'

'Good boy,' whispered Stone. 'Now shut up and behave.'

'It's funny,' Cathie breathed into Logan's ear, 'I really didn't imagine this one living.'

Footsteps were heard in the hallway. As Hamid rounded a corner, he saw one man down. In the fading light, only unidentifiable shapes were silhouetted in the cell. A silver blade sparkled in the dim corridor as it flew, plunging into the muscle above Hamid's knee. The man gave a shriek of pain and dropped to the floor. In an instant, Stone was up and running towards him.

The man in the room, frightened but desperate, decided to disobey Stone's command. He rose with difficulty. Logan leapt across the room, trying to trip him up. Barely missed. The man clumsily pulled a knife from his belt with his left hand, and charged towards Stone, whose back was turned as he dealt with Hamid.

With uncanny speed, Stone kicked away the gun Hamid had been fumbling for, rose up, and twisted his body to the side. The blow aimed for his back missed. In one fluid motion, Stone grabbed the guard's arm, and, using his momentum, continued to pull the knife forward, changing its course and swinging it back. As the man stumbled forward, the knife plunged into his neck. His eyes grew even wider and he collapsed bonelessly.

'Should have behaved,' Stone muttered.

Cathie and Logan rose to their feet. 'Now that's pretty much how I wrote the scene,' she said, her voice shaking.

Stone dragged Hamid down the hallway into what had at one time been a jailer's booth. Logan and Cathie followed.

Stone ignored the man's groans and sat him in a chair, the knife still protruding from his knee.

'Thanks,' Cathie said, placing a hand on Stone's shoulder.

'Yeah, thanks,' Logan echoed, but then frowned as he looked at the knife in the man's leg. 'I'm surprised, though, I thought you never miss.'

'I don't,' Stone said, with a wry smile. 'But I'm going to need a few answers from this man. This place is extremely secluded. A good place

The Reality of Chaos

for getting answers even if the people giving the answers are … fussing a bit. There are a lot of nerve clusters in and around the knee, and I'll bet that stings like hell.' His eyes were locked on Hamid as he nodded towards the knife.

'Please—' Hamid began.

'None of that, now,' Stone said coldly. 'I doubt you intended to be gentle with your captives. I know your techniques.' He eyed the man balefully. 'I'm going to ask questions, and you're going to answer. How uncomfortable you're going to be depends on you.'

'My father will—'

'That will be the first question, then. Just who the fuck are you? Then, who do you work for? What's your favorite color? And so on.' Stone turned to Logan and Cathie. 'I suggest you wait in the courtyard outside. This might be upsetting.'

Cathie gave Hamid one last look, with eyes that held no sympathy whatsoever, then took Logan's arm and headed down the hallway.

***

They stood in the open courtyard watching the last yellow and orange light in the west fade to greens and blues. Occasionally, they heard what might have been the howl of a dog, but they knew it was not. Neither spoke.

Before their grim thoughts were able to transform into images of what was going on inside, Stone reappeared, shepherding a now-gagged former guard who was pale and beaded with sweat, but otherwise surprisingly undamaged.

'He was remarkably forthcoming,' Stone said.

A van appeared at the entrance of the former prison, heading their way. Logan and Cathie stiffened. Stone casually glanced at his watch. 'Right on time. They're friends of Chuck's, come to take custody of this fellow. Who'd have believed he was the only son of the head of the new Islamic Republic's state security forces? Imagine our luck. He'll have a lot to discuss with Chuck's pals, I'm sure. We'd love to take the old man himself, since sonny here says he'll be arriving tomorrow to question you two. But sadly, he'll be coming with a substantial security detail and we don't want an international incident. However, since Chuck plans to keep the son in custody indefinitely, you two will be free from future

355

harassment. I imagine that if you're even in a minor car accident, Chuck's friends will send this boy back to his father—one tiny piece at a time.'

Logan glanced over at their captive, who was wide-eyed with terror. He assumed Stone was speaking for the young man's benefit—coldly threatening him to keep him pliable for future questioning—but he wasn't entirely certain that it was a bluff.

The van pulled up and the front seat passenger stepped out. 'Stone?'

'Right. And you must be Vincenzo?'

The man nodded, then glanced over to Stone's prisoner. 'So here's our VIP guest, huh?' He turned back to the van and waved. The side door slid open and two others emerged, quickly taking custody of the man and hustling him into the van. A short time later, Vincenzo was shaking Stone's hand and heading back to the van. The entire exchange had taken less than a minute.

'Well, that's that,' Stone said. 'I hope you two don't mind a short boat ride back to your hotel? It's a pleasant evening, and I've packed a few goodies assuming you'd be hungry. There's also a nice bottle of wine that hasn't been doctored with sedatives.'

'I wondered about that,' Cathie said.

'Yes. It helped to disorient you. Made things easier for them.'

'Yeah,' Logan said, 'my brain felt like molasses when the guy dropped off the note. I take it the man you questioned told you the whole story.'

'He did, but it was hardly the most significant information he gave up.'

'Really?' Cathie asked.

'Really. Come on, let's get you back to my boat. It's time you heard what's going on.'

***

Within a half hour, the three had walked to a small, lonely pier where Stone's boat was tied up. Before long, they were underway, eating snacks and drinking wine. The air was cool, with the scent of fish and seaweed. It felt cleansing after the confinement of the dusty prison.

'OK,' Cathie said, 'you've piqued my interest. What about that story?'

The Reality of Chaos

Stone smiled. 'Chuck and I have been working a plan for a long time. A plan to take down Smythe-Montgomery. The encounter with the son of Iran's security head is the break we needed.'

'Can you really bring him down? He's a slippery devil,' Logan said.

'Yes. And more.'

'Do tell,' said Cathie, leaning forward with impatience.

'In order for you to understand what's going on, I need to rewrite a little history. Think back to the night Elaya's presidential palace was attacked. I was nearby when the plane hit …'

After a rough approach, when the small aircraft pitched and rolled in the buffeting wind, the Gulfstream landed in the icy dark at the Reykjavik Airport.

Chapter Twenty-Nine

Rewriting History

The night of the attack on Elaya's presidential palace ...

Stone turned away and hurried from his location. He had only a few minutes now and he moved swiftly down the streets, cloaked by the last dark hour of the night. As he neared the palace grounds, an angry orange light illuminated his surroundings fitfully, casting wild, jagged shadows that leapt from side to side like a drunken dancer. He came to a set of sloped double doors, set at roughly a forty-five-degree angle from vertical—a merchants' entrance for bringing food into the cellars below the palace. Stone glanced up and down the narrow street. It was deserted. Not far away, sirens howled. He had used his previous evenings wisely, and had fashioned a crude key for the heavy padlock holding the doors secure. He opened the lock and slipped in, easing the door shut behind him.

As his eyes adjusted, he saw a pale glow at the far end of the cavernous room. He pulled out his own small light and moved forward. Empty crates were stacked along one wall, a large refrigerator occupied the other. Another large metal door led to a frozen storage area. A long, heavy table ran down the middle of the room, used for sorting the meat and produce brought in from the street. Two large utility sinks stood off to the side, one dripping steadily. At the end of the room, near a narrow flight of stairs, was a large stack of boxes. The light glowed from behind them.

Stone drew his gun. 'Madam President?'

'Jason, praise be to Allah!'

A moment later, a noticeably trembling woman appeared, tears running down her cheeks. Without thinking, she hurried to him and he took her in his arms. He held her tightly and she gradually grew calmer, her breathing slower and more regular. He released her and she stepped back. 'Did everything go as planned?' he asked.

'Yes,' she replied, in a quavering voice. 'The kitchen staff are on holiday, and each night for the past several days I have removed myself to their quarters after everyone has turned in for the night.'

'The guards above?'

'Ran immediately after the horrible crash. A few to investigate, but most, I fear, to flee. I entered the cellar unobserved.'

'Excellent. Sadly, however …' He held up a satchel which Elaya took with a grimace. She retreated behind the boxes and emerged again a few minutes later wearing a grubby burka. Stone had slipped into an old hooded cloak. 'Now we're a pair.'

Noises from far above—crashing of collapsing beams, the approaching roar of flame—quickly doused any feelings of amusement at this bizarre situation.

'We should go quickly,' Stone said, and Elaya nodded.

*

The drive from Tehran to Kuwait City was long and boring but for the constant, dramatic news of President Elaya Andoori's flaming death in what could only have been a suicide attack. Elaya listened intently to the car's staticky radio, translating for Stone when the talk became too fast for him to follow. She listened with manic eagerness, only to fall into black depression when the newsmen would discuss casualties on the ground and on board the airplane. Then she would slip into melancholy silence, pondering what she and the man beside her had *allowed* to happen to facilitate her escape. When the news switched back to politics, she would listen eagerly again, stating more than once her belief that her loyal man, General Muhammed Zareb, would surely hold her government together. Stone said nothing, but Chuck and he were convinced of the exact opposite.

After nearly ten hours on the road, Elaya finally collapsed into the sleep of exhaustion. Stone was relieved. He switched the radio to play music from his iPod and selected an oldies collection of Simon and Garfunkel tunes that he and Luana often enjoyed. He shifted in his seat and settled in for the final four hours' drive. Ganesh would have

The Reality of Chaos

arranged for a swift crossing of the border for a Canadian freelance geologist and his newly acquired assistant and translator, Rashida Najjar.

*

Ganesh met them at the private terminal of Kuwait International Airport, some sixteen kilometers south of Kuwait City. Again, the way had been smoothed by Ganesh, and the requisite paperwork was ready. He stared curiously at the woman in the black burka, but asked no questions. A virtue Stone deeply appreciated.

'My friend,' Stone said, grasping his hand, 'I am once again deep in your debt.'

Ganesh smiled but shook his head. He pulled up the sleeve of his left arm. There was a crisscross pattern of scars from wrist to shoulder, and the arm itself was slightly crooked. 'But for you, this would have been the end of me.'

'That was a long time ago, and just look at the fine result of my stitching. I think you'd have been better off with a blind seamstress.'

'I think not,' Ganesh replied, firmly gripping Stone's shoulder with his left hand. There was no absence of strength. 'I'd wish you safe travels, but, after all, it is you! Go. Board your plane. I will impatiently await my next opportunity to repay an unpayable debt.'

'Take care, my friend.'

Ganesh raised a clenched fist to his heart and tapped it several times, then turned and left.

A little while later, Elaya climbed the Gulfstream 5's short flight of stairs. The pilot and copilot were busy at the controls, going over flight plans, and there was no flight attendant. But as Elaya and Stone moved back into the cabin, a woman appeared from behind a panel near the rear. She smiled and walked towards Elaya, holding out her hand.

'Luana Chu,' the woman said. She glanced knowingly towards the cockpit. 'A pleasure to meet you, Ms. Najjar. As for you,' she continued, facing Stone, 'I see the fates have spared you yet again.'

Stone and Luana exchanged a few words, then he turned back to Elaya. 'I'll be leaving you now,' he said, 'but only for a short while. I need to gather some intel back in London, but you're in good hands with Luana. She'll see you safe to the halfway point where you'll meet a friend of mine—' Stone stopped abruptly and glanced at Luana with a wry smile. 'Man, I don't get to use that line very often! Anyway, a friend, Chuck Johnson. He'll have some new papers for you and he'll be with you until you arrive at my house in Breckenridge, Colorado. There won't be any staff there, but you'll be safe. Make yourself at home. You'll find an ample supply of Beefeater and tonic, and some excellent wines, selected by Luana. We'll join you in a few days.'

'With your permission,' Elaya said, nodding to Luana, who just smiled. Elaya turned back to Stone and hugged him. 'Thank you, Jason. Thank you so much. And I'll echo your friend's words: travel safely!'

'I'll see you both soon,' he said.

*

After a rough approach, when the small aircraft pitched and rolled in the buffeting wind, the Gulfstream landed in the icy dark at the Reykjavik Airport. Luana had provided her passenger with suitable clothes, so a few minutes after the plane taxied to a halt, two heavily bundled forms walked down the stairs and into the executive terminal. They were escorted directly to a security office—a small, austere room with a desk and three chairs—where Chuck Johnson sat waiting.

'Thanks,' Chuck said to the airport security officer. When the man hesitated, Chuck fixed him with an icy stare and he reluctantly departed.

'Madam President,' Chuck said, when the three were alone, 'it's good to see you safe and well.'

'I'm certainly safe,' Elaya said, 'but I can't get over the horror of that night and the thought that so many had to die.'

'Well, let's just make sure their sacrifice wasn't in vain,' he responded harshly.

Luana coughed slightly, and Chuck realized he was being rude.

'I do apologize, Madam President. I know you've been through a lot. I'm on a short fuse lately with all that's been going on. To top it off, I am now officially exceeding my authority.' He shrugged. 'It hardly matters. I only managed to make it on this trip before my boss in Oakland essentially fired me—for failing to protect you! So you see the irony.'

'The arrangements?' Luana asked, with a look of concern.

'Already made.' He brought out a large manila envelope and tore off one end. Inside was a letter, which he put to one side, and a smaller envelope. He dumped its contents onto the desk: a passport, a Colorado driver's license, and several other documents.

'You are now Connie Hadley, a high-end real estate agent from California who's recently moved to Breckenridge. You're staying with friends of your family, Ms. Chu and Mr. Stone, while you become acquainted with the area. They've graciously asked you to remain until you are completely comfortable in Breck. At that time, you will purchase a home and open your own real estate office, but until then you will be occasionally visiting local properties to become familiar with pricing, etc. The paperwork documents your previous activities in California. Anyone calling the numbers listed will receive full confirmation.' He handed her a business card with the number crossed out and a new number written in. 'My personal cell,' he said, in answer to her questioning look. 'My work number may not be useful much longer.'

'But it says that you sell long term care insurance.' Elaya said.

'Yeah?' Chuck replied.

'His usual discreet phone exchange,' Luana said. 'Has it really gotten so bad, Chuck?'

'Yes it has. And it's liable to get worse before it gets better. The good news is I may be happily retired soon. Don't worry,' he added, seeing anxiety on Elaya's face, 'I'm damn good and ready. But until you're solidly back in charge in Iran, you can count on me.'

'Jason and I as well,' Luana said. She looked at her watch. 'Hadn't you better be going?'

'Ah, crap,' Chuck said, checking his own. 'Yeah, we'd best head out. There are few enough flights out of this place at this time of year, and it wouldn't do to miss this one. I sprang for a couple of first-class upgrades, so we can have a quiet conversation and you can get a little more sleep. I get the feeling you haven't had that luxury lately.'

'It seems like months, Mr. Johnson. Luana, will you be joining us?'

'I need to return to London. With luck, Jason and I will see you in a few days. Goodbye for now.'

*

Nearly a week passed before Stone and Luana returned, the day of Zareb's assassination, but it would be several days before official word of his death would be released from Iran.

Chuck had stayed with Elaya the entire time, but was eager to return home.

'I need to get back to Joy,' Chuck said. 'She knows that I'm on administrative leave for botching my protection of Madam President and she understands what that means. It looks like retirement for me—if I'm lucky.'

'C'mon, Chuck, what about the SecDef?' Stone asked.

'Surprisingly, it's quite difficult to get on his calendar when one is on administrative leave.'

'His loss, the dumb ass. You'd think he might want to know the president of Iran is still alive. And he *should* realize you don't screw things up. That should count for something after … how long?'

'Twenty-seven years, if I was counting. But you know as well as I do that you're only as good as your latest fuckup.'

Stone nodded, but a smile slowly crept onto his face.

'You look like the cat that ate the canary,' Chuck said. 'Now why's that?'

'Cause you've got an ace in the hole, Johnson. Tell me you see it?'

'Feels like London all over again. Guess I'm still about as clueless as a box of hammers. Enlighten me.'

'You'll have the eternal gratitude of a major world leader. Someone who can put in a good word for you with, say, *our* president, at some snooty state dinner. Even the SecDef has a boss, and our friend is acquainted with him.'

The light was slow to dawn, but when it did, it put a boyish grin on Chuck's face. 'Yeah! That's right. My good pal, the President of Iran. I just call her Elaya when we're hangin' out.' His happy mood faded quickly. 'But that only works if we can keep her safe and put her back in power.'

'That's the plan, isn't it?'

'Yeah, that's the plan. Speaking of plans, what're yours and Luana's?'

'Luana will be coming and going. She does have a business to run. Becky wants Infinity Services Group to provide data archiving and backup services for ARC. Plus Luana will be making several trips to Maui—'

The Reality of Chaos

'Poor girl.'

Stone frowned. 'Trips to Maui to clean up the mess with her family's estate. You know, the mess we kind of caused? Turns out most of her mother's property goes to her. Her dad's holdings—and they're extensive—are bequeathed to anonymous organizations in China. Her parents' joint assets are the real tangle. I should be going with her, and not just to deal with that. Having to kill her own father to save my ass—'

'Was probably the easiest decision of her life.'

'You think so?' Stone said, his frown deepening. 'It's not the decision she regrets, anyway. It's having to do it at all. She isn't like us.'

'Sorry, Stone. I'll shut the hell up and let you finish.'

'Well, those are her plans. She'll be back and forth. I'll be in Breck for a while unless you need me somewhere else. I plan to keep working on my woodpecker houses.'

'What's with you and woodpecker houses?'

Stone smiled. 'What about you?' he asked.

'I've got to keep working channels and see if I can at least get a secure call with the SecDef. In the meantime, Randy and a couple other good men are working the "assassination." With luck, there'll be a link straight back to Smythe-Montgomery.'

'If not, we always have Plan B. By the way, when are you going to let Randy in on our little gambit?'

'Probably about the time glaciers cover Tucson. My neck's on the chopping block. If I involve him in this and it all goes south, he'll wind up sittin' on a street corner with a sign that says "Will kill bad guys for food."'

Stone shook his head. 'He's gonna hate you when he finds out.'

'He can join the club. Damn, I do wish I could bring him in, though. He's a good man.'

'He is,' Stone agreed. An idea occurred to him, and he almost said more. Instead, he stuck out his hand. 'Guess we've both got our plans. Stay in touch and try not to get fired just yet.'

Chuck grunted and shook Stone's hand. 'Try not to get killed.'

***

'So far, so good,' Stone said, as he concluded his astonishing revision of history. He smiled with amusement at the dumbfounded expressions on Cathie's and Logan's faces.

For a brief interval, there was no sound but the steady purr of the boat's motor and the lap of water along its side, then both of them began talking at once.

'You mean Elaya is still alive?'
'But why keep all this secret?'
'Who knows all this?'
'When will she reappear?'
'What's this got to do with Smythe-Montgomery?'
'How does the guy who was guarding us play into the picture?'
'What should we do?'

Stone glanced at the coastline and made a slight adjustment to the tiller, waiting until Cathie and Logan lost some of their manic energy. When both stopped, he said, 'Yes. To set a trap. The SecDef, Randy, Luana, and you two. Soon. Everything. He gave up the connection. Relax.'

The Fletchers shared a look of bewilderment while Stone laughed. 'Fine, I'll explain it more slowly. Both of you can calm down. To your last question, you should fly home with Joy, go back to Tucson, and do absolutely nothing else except relax. There's likely to be an ugly period soon, and there's no need for you to be involved. Chuck or I will stay in touch and share what we can when we can. This is not negotiable,' he said, his features hard. 'I'm counting on you to accept my conditions if I tell you what's going on. I *don't* think Chuck would agree with this deal.'

'Got that right,' Logan mumbled.

'Here it is in a nutshell. We couldn't keep Elaya safe. *I* couldn't keep her safe. Not in her role as president. Not living in Tehran. I estimated she would have been dead in a month or less. Well, you can't kill a dead man. Allowing her enemies to think they'd succeeded was the only way to take the pressure off. Obviously, after being killed, she couldn't continue popping up in Tehran. She's living in my home in Breckenridge. Which reminds me, I've got to finish those woodpecker houses. Never mind,' he added quickly, seeing their confusion.

'But, Jason,' Cathie said, 'so many people died. The plane crash, the purges. Surely there was … another way.'

Stone looked pained. 'What you have to remember,' he said, 'is that there was very little time and no good option. The purges would have come, perhaps a bit later. As for the innocent people on the airplane and the ground? Yes, we allowed that to happen and we could have stopped it. But it's the action you *don't know* in advance that usually kills the greatest number of people. Smythe-Montgomery was behind the attack, and he would not have stopped even if we had thwarted him.'

'Oh, Jason, you can't be certain.'

Stone nodded. 'True, but it was our assessment at the time. I know it sounds coldly calculating and indifferent. Maybe it is. It's one of the reasons I involved Luana in all this. My life for many years has been nothing but a series of calculations just like this one. People have lived or died based on my decisions and I was worried I'd lost the ability to feel anything but devotion to an objective. It was a terrible burden to share, but I did. Luana agreed that there was no other choice. So did Chuck.'

Cathie reached a hand back to where Stone was seated at the tiller and squeezed his shoulder.

'I take it the guy you interrogated back there knew there was a connection to Smythe-Montgomery,' Logan said.

'Better than that. He had names, and they jibe with what Randy had already dug up.'

'So you can finally connect Smythe-Montgomery to a criminal act, and a big one,' Logan said. 'The assassination of the president of Iran!'

'Ah,' Stone said, 'wouldn't that be lovely. Maybe we can—eventually. Richard Crandall and Yvette have done wonders interpreting the intel Becky Amhurst was able to gather. However, it isn't really necessary to connect *all* the dots.'

'It isn't?' Cathie asked in surprise.

'No. It's only necessary for him to *believe* we have. And, of course, convincing the rest of the world will help. I doubt that he fears prison as much as he fears the collapse of his empire. If I'm not mistaken, it will goad him into some precipitous action, and that's where we'll get him.'

'"Precipitous action,"' Logan repeated. 'Exactly what kind of precipitous action?'

'Kinetic.'

***

The last thing Stone had said to Cathie and Logan before he returned them to their hotel was 'Say nothing about Elaya, but when you get home, keep an eye on the news.'

Joy had been alerted to their rescue and was waiting for them in the hotel lobby. Stone left soon after, and the three others retired to Joy's room where several bottles of wine were waiting. Once each had a glass in hand, she sat the two down. 'Now, tell me what happened, and don't leave out anything.' The bulk of the night was spent with Logan and Cathie relating everything about their kidnapping and rescue. They didn't mention Elaya. That was for Chuck to tell, and if he was smart, he would tell Joy long before the news broke.

Stone made a quick call as he strolled down the still-bustling Riva Schiavoni. 'I presume you got the news,' he asked.

'Hell yeah,' Chuck replied. 'Vince called right after he took custody of your friend. And I've got some even better news. While you were enjoying a nice dinner cruise, the office got in touch with Ibrahim al Rahzi. He was kinda pissed at first, or so I'm told, but he came around quick enough. He was told his boy had already given up the connection to Smythe-Montgomery, so it would be better for him to cooperate. We're cross-checking his info with everything we already had. But by God, Stone, it's time to pull the trigger!'

'Tired of being in the doghouse, Chuck?'

'Darn straight I am! And are you ready to come home?'

'Yeah. Just one more thing—'

'Not to worry. I talked to the SecDef when I got the news. Told him we were ready to execute but I needed a little more support. There are four agents keeping an eye on Joy, Logan, and Cathie. But I'll tell you what, Stone, I think they'd be safe walking down main street in Tehran, now that al Rahzi knows we're not fuckin' around.'

'Better to be safe. We wouldn't want some Limey bastard taking a parting shot. Let's get those three home.'

'You'd better get home too. Pronto. We've got some planning to do.'

'You still at the house in Colorado with our guest?'

'Yeah.'

'I'll see you tomorrow. Sometime tomorrow. And not to put too fine a point on it, but hadn't you better tell Joy what's going on? I might have mentioned a couple of minor items to Cathie and Logan.'

Chuck grunted. 'OK, I figure we owe them after what they went through. Good decision.'

'I might have also mentioned a couple of things to Randy the day of his wedding.'

'Randy? Really? The day of his wedding? You're a fucking sieve, Stone, you know that? Is there anybody you didn't tell?'

Stone smiled. 'I didn't tell Joy. See you tomorrow, Johnson.'

Stephen Lance / Chuck Markussen

A wet, heavy spring snow was falling, lending a surreal background to what was already a fantastic scene ...

Chapter Thirty

Resurrection at Breckenridge

Barely a week had passed since Stone's return, and he and Chuck had been busy with their plans. A lengthy explanation and apology by Chuck to Joy had been grudgingly accepted, though promises of additional compensation involving expensive cuisine and carnal activities had also been required. She had reluctantly agreed to remain in California while Chuck, Stone, and Randy made preparations in Breckenridge. It was good to have Randy on board, fresh from his honeymoon. Though Gail had begged him to be careful, she knew this was the life he'd chosen, and she had married him with that understanding.

'Ten minutes,' said a tall woman in a business suit, the director from a local television station. A representative from the Associated Press was present as well as a small camera crew. They had recovered from their initial shock at seeing the 'dead' president of Iran walk calmly into the room, and were now attending to their duties. A media executive who had previously helped the agency by releasing or squelching information had discreetly contacted the necessary news people. Chuck had given strict guidance that they not be told the specifics of their unusual assignment in advance.

Elaya was standing in the family room of Stone's Breckenridge house, her back to the huge windows and the tree-studded slopes beyond. A wet, heavy spring snow was falling, lending a surreal background to what was already a fantastic scene: the resurrection of a 'dead' president. The camera crew made adjustments and did a light check, tested image quality, sound, and transmission from the satellite van parked outside. When all was to their liking, the cameraman nodded to the director. 'Good to go.'

'OK. Five minutes. Everyone take a deep breath.'

Elaya walked back to where Chuck and Stone were standing, near the fireplace. Logs crackled and threw off a pleasant warmth. She stared into the flames. 'It's time to make up for that horrible day,' she said, remembering the same harsh orange glow of her burning palace.

'You OK?' Stone asked.

'What? Yes, yes. It's just ... memories.' She drew a shuddering breath and stood up straight. Her eyes grew hard. 'Yes. And I will never be able to thank you enough, my friends.'

'Oh,' Chuck said lightly, 'I'll take a bottle Cab and a good word to my boss.'

Elaya laughed. 'Thank you. I must admit, I am rather tense.'

'You don't look it,' Stone said. And indeed, she did not. Dressed in a modest dark blue business suit, low heels, and a beige headscarf, she looked serious and presidential.

'Two minutes. Madam President, if you would,' the director said, motioning to the small podium draped with the Iranian flag.

Elaya smiled and walked back to her place near the windows.

'No translator?' Stone whispered to Chuck, as the director positioned Elaya and slipped back behind the camera.

'No. She said she'd be her own translator.' Chuck shrugged. 'More personal, I suppose. I kind of like it. Besides, the speech is short and sweet.'

The director turned to the two and scowled, putting a finger to her lips. Stone nodded, but Chuck couldn't resist sticking out his tongue. Undaunted, she smiled sweetly and flipped Chuck the bird.

'I like her,' he said, but very softly.

The director counted down the remaining seconds, then pointed at Elaya.

***

'My fellow citizens of Iran, and citizens of the world, I am President Elaya Andoori. I was not killed in the cowardly attack on my presidential palace, but I am alive and ready to return. I have remained in exile while evidence was gathered on the criminals responsible for the assassination attempt and the bloody coup that followed. Those who plotted against me, members of an evil alliance between the hardline usurpers and an insidious foreign element, have all been identified and will be exposed and brought to justice.

'My government, the true, duly elected government of Iran, is forming as we speak, and our exile is near an end.

'Have courage. Pray for the loyal fallen. Pray for our country. Justice is coming, swift and sure, and those who plotted to undermine our republic and dominate our affairs will suffer the most severe consequences. I will speak to you again in forty-eight hours, and all will be revealed. May Allah preserve us.'

***

Two heartbeats later, the director made a cutting motion, and everyone relaxed.

'The dung has hit the windmill now,' Stone said.

'You got that right, brudda.'

'How did I do?' Elaya asked.

'Very presidential, Madam President,' said Chuck.

'That should be hitting the worldwide feed in minutes,' the director said, joining the group and grinning.

'I reckon that pretty much made your career,' Chuck said.

'I should hope so! An exclusive with a dead president—pardon me, President Andoori.'

'I think a bottle of wine to celebrate,' Stone said. 'One resurrection and one gold-plated career! Not a bad day's work!'

***

Smythe-Montgomery stood, mouth gaping, as the BBC reported the incredible story of the reappearance of Elaya Andoori. 'The clever bitch!' He clicked the intercom. 'Ms. Lister, you and Mr. Colpoys in my office. Now!'

They entered nervously and Smythe-Montgomery eyed them coldly. 'I don't know what Andoori knows or thinks she knows, but she seems far too smug and secure. Mr. Colpoys, I want her *dead*! This time, you will put a bullet in her head. You will watch her breathe her last breath. Locate her! It was snowing, and the wires credited a local news station in Colorado. Take whatever resources you need. Use two of the Gulfstreams, if you need them. She plans to speak again in forty-eight hours …'

'She'll be dead in thirty-eight,' Colpoys said.

After he left, Smythe-Montgomery turned to Ms. Lister. 'Get me al Rahzi on the phone. I don't care what he's doing. I knew something wasn't right when he never got back to me about Cathie Fletcher. Blast him and his pack of fools. Also, check to see what cargo we have passing through Tehran over the next few days. We may need to reroute or cancel.'

Smythe-Montgomery paced back and forth in his office, struggling to find his composure. 'And Elaya's secret meeting at Crandall's country home! Diana Foster and Richard Crandall,' he muttered, 'just as I suspected. Have Colpoys—' He halted abruptly, realizing he had just sent Colpoys and many of his men to America. 'Richard Crandall,' he repeated.

'Richard Cranium,' Lister said softly.

'What's that?' Smythe-Montgomery snapped.

'Sorry, sir. It's just an American colloquialism. A rather elegant form of dickhead.'

'Appropriate, in his case. Still, he's no fool. Get in touch with Peters. Have him return from Ireland. We may need to call on Mr. Cranium.'

'Yes, sir.'

'Now get me al Rahzi.'

***

Yvette was staring at the TV, eyes on the verge of overflowing. Crandall came into the room. 'Yvette, tomorrow we should get busy on ... What the bloody hell?'

She turned to him, beaming. 'He didn't fail! It was all a ruse!'

Crandall's phone rang. It was Diana. Just before he answered, he turned back to Yvette. 'Forget about our plans for tomorrow. I believe we have some work to do that won't wait.'

***

Cathie and Logan watched the broadcast while drinking coffee on their back patio. The bright, sunny Tucson morning promised a seasonally hot day to come. Despite already knowing Elaya was alive, they were shocked.

'Chuck has a flare for the spectacular, doesn't he?' Logan said, with admiration.

'An amazing resurrection,' Cathie said. 'I wish I'd written it in one of my novels!'

***

'Umm, Becky,' Gary said, 'there's something on the news you really should see.'

The two were in the ARC Avionics offices discussing program schedules and staffing. Gary had just gone down the hall to get two fresh coffees.

'What now, Gary?' Becky asked, with feigned annoyance. She walked with him back to the breakroom and glanced at the television. Her jaw dropped in astonishment. 'What the hell?'

'Guess the president of Iran is alive after all,' he said, smiling broadly. He offered up his coffee cup to tap against Becky's in celebration.

Becky looked with disdain at the dark brown, caffeine-infused liquid in her cup, totally inappropriate for a toast, but shrugged and bumped his cup. 'To pleasant surprises!'

***

When the Defense Secretary told him the back story behind the news, the president's reaction was a confusion of delight and annoyance. His mind was already spinning with the new possibilities this resurrection presented, but his first words were, 'Did you really have to keep me in the dark, you SOB?'

'Mr. President,' the Secretary said evenly, 'the least secure holding ground for sensitive information is the White House … sir.'

There was silence on the phone for a long while, and then a hearty laugh. 'That's for sure!'

***

Stone had spent the afternoon of Elaya's announcement and most of the next day discussing the anticipated attack with Randy, Chuck, Luana, and Elaya. Accounting for planning, travel delays, and the timing of Elaya's next broadcast, it would certainly be tonight. They had reviewed their own strategies, but Stone had saved the best for last.

The sun burned an orange slash across the western sky, casting an eerie glow on a snowy landscape. More snow was falling steadily, adding to the base and delighting the skiers who were looking forward to some exceptional spring skiing. Chuck stood with Stone and Randy in the large family room of Stone's Breckenridge house, staring out the wall of glass. A fire crackled in the nearby fireplace, light and warmth spilling out. But Chuck fidgeted nervously. He had little interest in the ambience and none whatsoever in spring skiing. He checked his watch for the twentieth time.

'Settle down, will you, Johnson?' Stone said. 'You're upsetting Randy.'

'Hey, don't drag me into this!' Randy squawked.

Chuck ignored Stone's comment. 'When do you suppose our company will show?'

'About five minutes sooner than the last time you asked,' Stone said. He shook his head. 'Oh, not before 10:00, so maybe four hours or so.'

'Shouldn't we be getting out there? Setting up? Doing something?'

'You're right,' Stone said. 'We should be doing something. How about a game of pool?'

Without waiting for an answer, Stone walked into the hallway, opened a door, and descended a flight of steps. Randy and Chuck followed, Chuck muttering his disapproval.

Stone hit a switch at the bottom of the stairs and the room came alive. Recessed ceiling lights came on, and a large leaded-glass light above the pool table lit up, casting a diffuse, even light on the playing surface. Off to the side, a small wet bar was illuminated with hazy blue light that seemed to come from nowhere, but which sparkled off a granite countertop, four polished wood stools, an array of glasses suspended from a ceiling rack, and a collection of bottles containing an assortment of fine alcohol. At the end of the room, several padded chairs and a couch faced an enormous, wall-mounted television. A dartboard and a small poker table completed the scene.

'I don't think you guys have seen my game room.'

'Awesome!' Randy said. 'I think this room is bigger than my apartment!'

Chuck stood silently surveying the scene, but Randy walked over to the dartboard. 'The backstop is made of corks! Corks from really nice bottles of wine!'

The Reality of Chaos

Stone smiled. 'Logan Fletcher makes them for particular friends. Kind of a hobby after he retired. He even numbers 'em. See that little brass ID plate? Mine's number twenty-five. But right now, I'm kind of in the mood for a game of pool. Rack 'em up while I turn on the TV.'

'Stone,' Chuck began, his voice gravelly with irritation.

'Settle down, Johnson, and let me explain. Come and sit by the TV. I think it's time to explain something to you about woodpecker houses.'

'This day keeps getting weirder,' Chuck said, but he sat down.

Stone sat in another chair and reached for a remote. When the TV came on, it was neatly divided into six sub-screens, each one displaying a picture of an outdoor scene. Most had a somewhat grainy black-and-white image, but one showed a line of orange in the distance. Stone made a few adjustments, and the pictures began to slowly cycle—a new view appearing, holding steady for about thirty seconds, then switching back to the original scene.

'There are a dozen woodpecker houses out there. All of them have night-vision cameras and motion detectors. Nothing can get within two hundred yards of this house without being spotted, even a low-flying drone. A couple of the houses have a little something extra—a small C4 charge and some ball bearings.'

'Holy shit!' Chuck said, his eyes wide.

Randy had joined the two and was equally impressed. 'So not really for woodpeckers?'

'No self-respecting woodpecker would live in a house that I built.'

'I see Jason is finally letting you in on his little secret,' Luana said, as she entered the room. 'So dramatic!' Stone just smiled. 'Well, I'll let you gentlemen enjoy yourselves, but let me know when I should return.'

'Thanks, darling,' Stone said. To the questioning looks of Randy and Chuck, he added, 'She'll run the surveillance and keep us posted through these earbuds.' He held up three.

'And where will we be?' Randy asked.

'I plan to be outside intercepting these bastards as far from my house as possible, and I'm hoping you gentlemen will do likewise. As to where, that will depend on how they approach.' Stone switched the TV display to show an overhead map of the area. The house was at the center, and flashing green and red dots with numbers next to them indicated the location of the woodpecker houses.

'I suppose red is—' Randy began.

'Red is bad. Those are the special ones. Don't go downrange of those, but try to draw our visitors in.' Stone hit a control and cones appeared, each with its apex on a red dot. 'That's the kill zone. About forty-five degrees.' He hit the controls again and several blue-hashed areas appeared. 'Good cover from these locations.'

'Nice,' Chuck commented, nodding. But a moment later, he frowned. 'You said you can see out to roughly two hundred yards. If that's our first warning, it won't give us much time to get in position.'

'There are simple motion sensors located out beyond the wookpecker houses, more like four hundred yards, and there are additional cameras on the only access road to this property.'

'You've been busy,' Randy said, with admiration.

'You couldn't tell us this shit sooner?' Chuck asked, a sour look still on his face.

'What? And spoil my little surprise? C'mon, Johnson, let me have my fun! Speaking of fun, Randy, would you do the honors and break? I think we have time for a game or two before the real party starts.'

***

'Who are you?' Crandall asked. He had answered an urgent knocking, distracting him from his pleasant musing, and when he had opened the door, the man had simply bulled past him into the foyer of his modest home near London, kicking the door closed behind him.

'Ah, that's not important, is it,' the man said, with a smirk. 'What is important is that you've been meddling in the affairs of your betters.'

Crandall snorted derisively. 'Only Smythe-Montgomery would be so boorish as to send an arrogant lout like you to my home, and only he would be fool enough to consider himself better than anyone. The lowest worm in my garden has more nobility than he will ever possess.'

The man snatched Crandall's collar and forced him against the wall. 'Brave words, from a walking corpse. But first I think I'll have a few answers to my employer's questions. Are you alone here?'

As if in answer to his question, a young blond woman in a diaphanous pale-green nightgown entered the hallway, her hands clasped primly behind her back. The man eyed her in astonishment. 'Well, here's a pretty little bird. Perhaps when I'm done we'll get better acquainted, darling.'

Yvette raised her chin and stared daggers at the intruder. 'I think not,' she said coldly. 'Now, release Lord Crandall and be on your way. I won't tell you again.'

'Gawd! Now that's priceless!' The man continued to gawp. 'Well, this adds to the fun. Into the sitting room, both of you,' he said, his voice suddenly hard. He gave Crandall a shove, then turned his attention back to Yvette. 'I said move—' His bluster turned to confusion. The woman was now pointing a .45 caliber H&K directly at his heart.

'And I said I wouldn't tell you again.'

The man had barely begun to reach inside his sport coat before Yvette dropped the sights of her gun and squeezed the trigger. A sharp CRACK was followed by a shower of blood and bone fragments as the man's kneecap exploded. The man collapsed with a shriek of agony, then went completely limp and silent.

Yvette deftly flipped him onto his back and pulled the gun from his shoulder holster. 'Big baby,' she muttered. She stood and handed the weapon to Crandall.

'How …'

'Becky suggested lessons, and Mr. Stone has a few friends in London.' As Yvette spoke, her voice cracked and she began to tremble.

She fell into Crandall's arms and he held her tightly. 'What an extraordinary young woman you are. Heart of a lioness. I am so, so proud.'

***

Despite Chuck's nervous grumbling, Stone had obviously prepared thoroughly, and this included a discussion with Chuck on the merits of keeping Elaya at the Breckenridge house.

***

'It's a risk, Stone,' Chuck had said, shaking his head.

'This whole plan is risky. Keep the objective in mind, Johnson. It's not to keep Elaya safe, it's to lure Smythe-Montgomery into committing himself—and exposing himself—totally. If we move her to a safe house, like Cheyenne Mountain,' he joked, 'Smythe-

Montgomery backs off and we fail. If we bring in a dozen more agents, he backs off and we fail. She's the bait and we're the trap.' Stone thought about this for a while. *'Still, better have the cavalry standing by, just in case.'*

***

Randy sank the eight ball, winning the third game of their small tournament. Stone had won the first two, while Chuck had played abominably throughout.

'Time for a fourth?' Randy asked.

This time it was Stone who checked his watch, then shook his head. 'No, we'd better get ready. I'll pull up the map again and we can all get familiar with our primary and secondary plans. Then I'll call Luana down so she can take over monitoring.'

***

Luana had been upstairs with Elaya, discussing their own plans. If things didn't go as hoped, Elaya was to take a snowmobile—loaded with a radio, a weapon, and supplies—and head cross-country to the town of Pyrite, where help would be waiting.

As Luana prepared to move down to the game room, Elaya stopped her.

'It has occurred to me,' she began hesitantly, 'that you and Jason may have had something to do with interfering in the money transfer to your father long ago, when Hasim had purchased aircraft from him.'

This was a bland way of putting things. In fact, Luana and Stone had betrayed Luana's father, stealing the electronic payment of $50 million for two black-market fighter aircraft and framing Elaya's lover and co-conspirator, Ivor Vachenko. Elaya's husband, Hasim bin Wazari, had been forced to pay Wan Chu again—with a sizeable additional bonus—to partially placate his fury. Unfortunately, the second part of that appeasement process involved killing Ivor, who seemed to be the betrayer. Elaya had arrived too late to save her lover, but she had her vengeance on the husband she despised.

Luana stared impassively at Elaya, who continued. 'You should know that I hold no grudge against either you or Jason. In fact, I am so much in your debt that I could not repay you in my lifetime. I do miss Ivor tremendously. Especially during these dark times. But it was Hasim

The Reality of Chaos

who killed him at your father's wish, and ... it could have been prevented if I'd arrived a few minutes sooner. I share the blame. I wanted to make that clear, and to say thank you for all you have done and are doing for me now.' Luana's calm was nearly destroyed when Elaya stepped in close and hugged her.

They both turned to the sound of Stone's voice over the intercom. 'It's time, Luana.'

Elaya released her and smiled. 'Go. Allah be with us all.'

***

When Luana joined them, Randy and Chuck were donning grey parkas—parkas with an added layer of Kevlar—and checking their weapons. Stone was closing the shutters.

'Have they arrived?' Luana asked.

Stone pointed to the monitor and replayed a short video loop. Two large vans were seen coming up the highway towards their property entrance.

Luana frowned. They had estimated eight to ten visitors. The vans could easily carry twice that number.

'Yeah,' said Stone, as if reading her thoughts, 'that's the bad news. The good news is that those vehicles won't be able to operate on our property, not even on our rough, snow-covered entrance road. That is, even if they could get past the gate, which I doubt.'

The vans pulled off the road at the turnoff to Stone's property. A sturdy, tubular-steel gate blocked the entrance and a heavy chain held the two arms of the gate closed. The front-seat passengers of both vans were already out, evaluating the situation.

***

'Well, Colpoys, I doubt a bolt cutter will do any good on this,' his companion said, shaking the chain.

Colpoys grunted and looked to either side of the driveway. Just beyond the gate, a bridge crossed a deep ditch. Even if it hadn't been for the thick growth of brush and pines on either side of the gate, it would not have been possible for the vans to cross the ditch. 'Fine. On foot, then. You take the men from the second van, Teddy, I'll take these. Stay a hundred feet or so to the left of the road, I'll be on the right. On second thought,' he added a moment later, 'pick two men from your group, give 'em a radio, and have them go right down the road.'

'They're not going to like that.'

'Do I look like I give a fuck whether they like it or not? Just do it. They don't need to take the bloody house single-handed, unless they want to, but by God they'll take the road or I'll drop them here!'

Teddy walked to the open door of the second van, where men were listening intently. 'Dave. Checkers. Get out here.' He handed one a radio. 'You two take the road. Have a care, lads, and report regularly. Move as close to the house as you can, take cover, and wait for orders. The rest of you with me.'

Colpoys assembled his men, and the three groups headed cautiously out, plowing through thick snow and disappearing into the heavy dark of the surrounding woods.

***

Randy whistled as they counted the men. Two on the road, six on one side, eight on the other. 'Jeez, Stone, I mean, there're only sixteen of them. Are you sure you really need me and Chuck to help you with this?'

'I'm thinking about the cavalry,' Chuck said.

Stone shook his head. 'Not yet. Right now we've got them for trespassing and, presumably, carrying automatic weapons without a permit. Alert your people, but tell them *not* to move in yet. There's at least one guy left in each van, and you can bet they have radios.' He gave Chuck and Randy a wicked grin. 'What? Would you two have left your only escape vehicles unguarded? You need to take a remedial class in property invasion and assassination.'

Randy turned to Chuck with a crooked smile. 'I must have missed that class, boss.'

'OK, Stone,' Chuck said. 'What now?'

Stone pulled up the map of the house. 'You and Randy take position here, east of the road. I'll be here, west side. Luana will keep us posted on their movements.'

'You really want us together?' Chuck asked.

'They're moving in a pack. If they split, you'll have to split. Until then, stay together.'

'What's your play?'

The Reality of Chaos

'Ah. I get the fun part. I'll make a verbal challenge—here.' He pointed to an area just beyond his cover point. He turned to Luana. 'You know what to do?'

'Yes, Jason. We've discussed this.'

Randy laughed suddenly. The tone reminded him of conversations between Gail and him—simple domestic talks that usually involved groceries or laundry. The fact that this discussion would result in extreme violence and death was simply an artifact of the extraordinary couple who lived here.

Luana glanced at him with a smile. 'Be careful out there, Randy. You too, Chuck.' She turned to Stone. 'There really is no point in telling you, is there?'

In answer, Stone pulled her close and kissed her for so long that Chuck finally coughed nervously. 'We'll just head on out. C'mon Randy, we're not wanted here.'

Stephen Lance / Chuck Markussen

Gunfire resumed from the edge of the clearing, but Stone realized it wasn't intended to hit him.

Chapter Thirty-One

Going in for the Kill

A few minutes later, Randy and Chuck were settling in behind an outcrop of rock on a small hill thick with brush. Luana was communicating with them, confirming the path of the group moving towards them. If they maintained their path, they would pass within twenty-five yards of Randy and Chuck. Both propped scoped rifles on the edge of the rock and waited.

Stone was also in position, crouching behind a boulder. He had no illusions that this night would pass without extreme violence, but he and Chuck had determined that some attempt at communication with Smythe-Montgomery's men was necessary. Of course, that had been when their estimate of the number had been half of what it had turned out to be. To Stone, it simply meant more danger of being shot during this opening gambit.

Stone's hiding place was at the edge of a cluster of trees overlooking a relatively clear area: only a few small pines, boulders, and scrub. The snow had stopped, and the moon was peeking out between torn clouds. He looked up and over his shoulder and was just able to see a woodpecker house hanging from the side of a large pine. He smiled grimly.

'They're approaching,' Luana spoke through his earpiece. 'They should be at the edge of the clearing, roughly southeast of your position, in just a few minutes.'

'Got it,' he whispered into a small mike at his throat. 'Be ready. This will be fast.'

Soon after his reply, Stone caught movement in his night vision goggles. Near the edge of the clearing, fifty yards or so away. Men moving slowly and peering cautiously into the open area.

Stone took a deep breath. 'You men should turn around now. I have eyes on you and it will turn out badly if you don't leave immediately.' He was gratified to see the men halt and crouch down, but soon he could see orders were being given, and the men began to fan out along the edge of the clearing. *Shit. Can't have that*, he thought.

***

'I'm going to try to draw him out. You two, to the left. You three, there.' Colpoys pointed to a cluster of trees to his right. If anyone shows a nose, don't hesitate.' The men nodded and moved off.

'Teddy,' he spoke into his radio.

'Got you, Colpoys.'

'Things are about to light up. Keep moving parallel to the road. Your objective is the house. Coordinate with the two on the road.'

Now let's see how gullible this guy is, or how scared, he thought. 'You've got something we want,' he yelled. 'Just step out and drop your weapon. Then you walk out and we go in and get what we came for. How's that for a plan?'

'Sounds like something only a Limey with the IQ of a turnip could come up with. How about we stick to my plan. You turn around and go home.'

Colpoys hesitated. The voice sounded familiar. Where had he heard it before? He shook it off. It didn't matter. 'Last chance,' he bellowed. He looked to the left and right. His men were almost in position, and it would be strange if one group or the other didn't have a shot. The man calling down had to be behind one of the rocks up there.

A cloud passed over the moon, and the hard shadows faded for an instant, replaced by a diffuse grey. There was movement near the rocks and suddenly the night exploded in violent sound and flashes of lethal energy. At least seven automatic weapons were pouring fire towards the rocks. Bullets whined and ricocheted.

Stone returned fire with his favorite handgun, a .45 H&K similar to the one he'd recommended for Yvette. At this range and in this lighting it was unlikely he'd hit anything. He smiled. That wasn't his plan. But he knew the flash was seen by those at the edge of the clearing. He fired a few more shots, and automatic rounds filled the air in answer, whistling past like angry bees. He suddenly let out a yell of pain.

'Hold fire,' Colpoys called. In the near-dark a shape seemed to collapse behind a ridge just beyond the rocks. The men on Colpoys' flanks ran into the clearing and up the gentle slope in pursuit. The two men with him also moved forward, eager for the kill. Colpoys held back, a deep suspicion growing in his mind. He thought to call out, but the men were already nearing the middle of the clear space and converging on the rocks. He stepped out into the clearing just as a hellish orange blast lit the night and a stupendous BANG hammered his eardrums.

Stone had turned away and closed his eyes tightly just as Luana fired off the charge in the special woodpecker house. He whipped around, completely uninjured, and quickly scanned the clearing. Two men were down and were unlikely to get back up. As the moon reappeared, pools of blood, black in the frigid light, spread from beneath their bodies. Another man was alternately crying out in pain and struggling back to the cover of the trees. Stone ignored him and raised his rifle, targeting a man sprinting towards the edge of the clearing. A loud CRACK from Stone's .338 and the man dropped. Four others had made it back to cover.

***

Randy and Chuck turned in the direction of the gunfire, punctuated moments later by a blast and flash of light near Stone's position. After a few more heartbeats, a single shot, then silence.

'What do you think?' Randy whispered.

'Dunno. The last shot was a rifle, though, and I know Stone had at least one.'

'Should we move to his location? See what's up?'

As if in answer to his question, Luana spoke calmly in their earpieces. 'Jason is fine. Three dead, one injured, four regrouping. The other group is moving towards your location. Jason would like you to deal with them.'

'Guess that answers your question, Randy? Man, Stone is a cool customer.'

'So's Luana,' Randy replied. He slid back into position and scanned the approach with his rifle scope. 'Uh oh. Company.' Chuck joined him.

Warned by the gunfire and explosion, Teddy and his men approached with caution, darting from tree to tree as they advanced. All had weapons in hand.

'Do we challenge them, boss?' Randy whispered.

'Hell no! That hardware they're carrying isn't for squirrels. Besides, if they'd had a change of heart, they'd be moving the other way. I've got the lead man; you take whoever else is clear.'

Despite the tension, it was obvious that Chuck's mood was vastly improved at the thought of action. Randy picked a target just as Chuck said, 'Now.' Their two rifles barked out simultaneously and two men dropped, but before there was a chance to assess whether the men were dead or injured, the tree line below erupted in automatic weapons fire. Bullets and lethal rock chips flew in all directions, forcing the two to crouch below the rock ledge. Chuck could hear shouted orders from below, and though he couldn't make out the words, he knew exactly what was being said. A slightly diminished but steady fire peppered the rocks.

'We're not gonna get another shot from here, and men are moving to flank us.'

'How the hell do you know that?' Randy asked.

'Cause it's exactly what I would do.'

'So?'

'Back out. Sweep wider than their man, ambush 'em. You go left, I'll go right. Do it quiet.'

Randy moved to go, but Chuck grabbed his sleeve and stared intently into his eyes. 'Keep your head down, Grasshopper.'

'Got it, boss.' And though he really didn't need reminding, the use of his pet name sent a flash of Gail's sad smile into his memory. The look she'd given him when he left to do this job was an extraordinary motivation for him to keep his head down. He nodded tightly and moved off.

***

'What the fuck was that?' a man asked, gripping the sleeve of Colpoys' jacket.

'C4 charge. Son of a bitch did some planning. How many were hit?'

'Two down from the blast. George made it back to the tree line, but he may bleed out. Ken took a shot to the back and he won't be getting up. What do we do?'

Colpoys scanned the faces of the other men with him, experienced mercenaries who'd seen combat. Right now, they were dazed. They hadn't been expecting this type of resistance, and Colpoys realized they needed decisive direction or they'd begin to waiver. He pulled binoculars from his jacket and scanned the rock where the man—one man—had been hidden, and the ridge where he'd retreated. He cursed as the moon was briefly hidden by a passing cloud. But the wind soon swept it aside and the monochrome scene of silver light and inky shadow reappeared. He examined the trees all around, finally stopping at one. There was some sort of box partway up. He had to assume another nasty surprise waited there, but worse yet, their position would be compromised if they moved from cover. 'Fuck!' he muttered. He turned back to the men. 'Check the trees. He's got cameras and probably more explosives, which means someone else is watching.' Colpoys grabbed his radio. 'Teddy, report.'

'Two guys with rifles. Got 'em pinned behind some rocks. Two men moving to flank them.'

'Good. Keep those two busy, and check the trees. If you see a box up there, steer clear. Cameras and explosives. Let me know when you take care of those two, but keep them busy.'

'Affirmative.'

Colpoys switched channels on his radio. 'Checkers, you got me?'

'Got you.'

'We're gonna keep our friend here busy. Teddy's engaging two others. Get to the house. Someone is monitoring us from there. Watch out for boxes in trees, there could be more explosives. Get in the house, find the electronics. Kill whoever is operating them.'

'Got it. Out.'

Colpoys turned back to his men. 'You and you, left and right flank. Jack and I stay here and keep our friend busy.'

Gunfire resumed from the edge of the clearing, but Stone realized it wasn't intended to hit him. A few shots rang out to his right, followed by

Luana's voice. 'They've spotted the woodpecker houses. Station eight to your right just went dark.'

'Shit! All right, I'm moving to my left. What do you see?'

'One man moving to get behind the ridge.'

Stone continued to back towards the house, moving to shadow the man sweeping to his left. When he was some fifty yards from his previous location, he slung his rifle over his shoulder and climbed into the lower branches of a large pine.

***

Dave and Checkers moved along the side of the road, wading through the deep snow in the drainage. Soon they were nearing the house. Dave pointed to a shuttered room on the level below the huge porch. Checkers stared and allowed his eyes to adjust. Faint slivers of yellow light were spilling from around the shutters. There was a door to the left of the windows.

'Point of entry,' he said.

'I'm gonna cross the road and try to get to that stone retaining wall near the door,' Dave said, pointing.

Checkers nodded, and Dave crept up the embankment. He had made it about halfway across the road when Checkers caught a flash of moonlight reflected off glass from a boxy structure attached to a large pine tree at the edge of the porch. He swung his gun around, but his warning cry was drowned in a roar of automatic weapon fire. Cursing, he opened fire on the box, ripping it to pieces, and the weapon hidden within went silent. Too late. Dave was down in the middle of the road, splatters of blood dappling the blanket of new snow. There was no point in going to his aid; he was dead, nearly cut in half by the .50 caliber assault rifle Stone had hidden in this particular woodpecker house, intended to stop vehicles approaching on the road.

Checkers considered. If this was indeed a last line of defense, then the best approach now would be right up the road. He fired another burst into the remains of the woodpecker house and leapt onto the road.

Luana heard the automatic weapon fire and saw camera one go dark. An instant later she heard a crash on the door that opened to the outside. She glanced over to her handbag, resting on a chair near the door. Then Stone's voice whispered over the radio. 'Luana, are you all right?'

She hesitated, then abandoned the electronics and lunged for the chair. A second crash and the door flew open, snow, splinters, and a large man falling into the room. The man now blocked access to her purse and the handgun she had inside. In an instant she was on him, a kick to his face knocking him backwards. But he succeeded in grabbing her foot and twisting violently. Luana screamed and toppled to the floor.

Checkers leapt to his feet, scanning the room for other threats. He turned back to Luana just as a pool cue came whistling down on his wrist. Bone cracked and the cue split. His gun rattled to the floor. Luana moved to retrieve the weapon, but her weakened ankle failed her and she staggered. Checkers backhanded her with his left hand and she flew across the room, landing hard on her back. The world grew grey around the edges. She blinked her eyes and pain shot through her head, but the room gradually came into focus, the big man standing over her.

'Bitch!' he snarled. 'You've broke my wrist, curse you! Well, Colpoys said to kill whoever was at the controls, but he didn't specify how.' He reached clumsily to his belt and pulled out a long knife. 'Think I'll have you scream for a while. Might even distract the bastards out there.'

Luana moved her hand slightly and felt the smooth hardness of the pool cue just within reach. It had split along its length, and what was left was no more than a two-foot-long splinter ending in a jagged point. She held the man's gaze while she very slowly wrapped her fingers around it. The man smiled and dropped to his knees, straddling her. Luana stabbed upward with all her strength, piercing his belly just below the ribcage and shoving upward, nearly vertically, into his body. Checkers' eyes widened in surprise. 'Son of a bitch,' he whispered. Luana reached across with her left hand and gripped the cue, shoving with both hands until the broken end was buried in his chest. Blood ran from his mouth as he toppled to the side.

Luana lay there, her chest heaving, and then struggled to her feet. She limped across the room to the radio where Stone's voice had become more urgent.

'I'm fine,' she managed to say. 'The two men on the road are dealt with.' She glanced at the video display. 'Stop talking. Someone's approaching you.'

***

There was firing all around as Randy circled wide after leaving his cover point. So far, he had been unable to locate anyone. He was moving cautiously through snowy brush surrounded by pines and had just about concluded that he'd gone too wide and needed to move back towards his original starting point. He moved around three tightly clustered pines—and came face to face with the man who was hunting him.

Randy was in an awkward position, constrained to his right by the trees, but he struck out with his left hand, aiming for the man's windpipe. Cartilage crunched, and the man staggered back a step, raising his gun clumsily. Randy swept around him and brought his Ka-Bar to the man's throat, slicing deep. A warm spurt of blood hit Randy's face and hand as an artery opened. Randy lowered him quietly to the ground, and then stared in disbelief. He had never killed like this, close enough to smell the man's aftershave. His parka was washed in blood, and he turned away and wretched, the knife dropping from his hand.

***

Stone left his rifle slung over his shoulder and looked from side to side. Moon shadows danced across the ground as a light breeze nudged the branches of the pines, but he couldn't see anyone. His call to Luana had been ill-advised, but for him, necessary. He had installed only one automatic assault rifle, and that had been the one guarding the house. Its distinctive rattling fire told him that someone was far too close to Luana. She had said she was fine, but she sounded winded, shaken. And now? The man Luana had seen moving across the snowy landscape had probably heard him.

'He's stopped. Roughly twenty yards out to your east.'

Luana's voice, calm and firm again, was a great relief to Stone. He focused all his attention to the east, and he thought he saw the shadow of a man near a single tree and a cluster of rocks. Unfortunately, though his shadow was visible, the man was not. Stone waited. So did the man. There were shouts from the clearing—Colpoys. He was moving forward and would soon be at Stone's previous location. With a man on either side and two coming up the middle, Stone was running out of options, but there was one. He smiled grimly and sighted the rock cluster.

***

The Reality of Chaos

Chuck had also circled wider than he intended, or perhaps the man he was stalking had come in tighter. Chuck looked from side to side, but there was no sign of his quarry. He crouched down to dart between two trees and the shot intended for his heart clipped his shoulder, sending him spinning as the report echoed in the night.

'Fuck!' he snarled, feeling the blood flow through his probing fingers. He gingerly moved his arm and immediately concluded he had only been grazed. No bones broken, anyway. *Still hurts like a mother*, he thought.

A voice yelled out. 'I got him. He's down.'

'Check it out, then get back here.'

Chuck lay motionless on the ground, his hand moving to the Glock at his waist. He considered. The man who'd shot him was approaching with caution, gun pointed at him. *If I jump up and try to run, he'll drop me with automatic fire. OK, that's not a good option. But if the man is sensible, he'll stop about ten feet away and put a single shot into the back of my skull, just to be safe. Also not good. If he's careless, he'll assume I'm dead, come right up to me, and roll me over. Then I'll deliver a bullet to his grill. But what are the odds? I'm gonna rule out gross stupidity. So, my best chance: play dead until he's fifteen feet away. Hope to catch him napping. Gotta say, Johnson, that option sucks, but it sucks the least. I'm gettin' way too old for this shit!*

The rhythmic crunch of snow was a good indicator of distance, and as the pace slowed, Chuck realized that this man was not going to be careless. The footsteps stopped. Chuck gathered all his strength and rolled violently to the side in an explosion of snow. A confusion of sight and sound as weapon fire erupted. A round pierced Chuck's parka, thudding into his chest. He ignored the sudden flare of pain, paused for half a heartbeat flat on his back, sighted, and squeezed off one round. The automatic fire continued for a few moments, but now branches were being torn from trees and raining down as the man crumpled to the ground, a section of his skull torn off.

Chuck groaned in pain and collapsed. The world spun, and the cold began to seep into his bones. There was shouting and automatic gunfire close by. He waited for the burning pain of bullets entering his body, but there was only the cold. Then Randy's face was hovering over him.

'Chuck. C'mon man. You're OK. They're on the run. You're fine.'

'Well that's bullshit. But I'm not dead, at least.' He tried to sit up, but grimaced and flopped back. 'Jacket stopped the bullet, but there's at least one broken rib, near the sternum, and it fuckin' smarts.'

'Your shoulder?'

'Just a graze.'

'Not so sure about that, boss. There's a lot of blood. Better let me bandage it up before we move.'

'You say those guys were running?'

'Yeah. The two that are left.'

'Cavalry will pick them up. The automatic fire? I would have sworn …'

'That was me. Used this guy's piece when his friends poked their noses out.'

Chuck grunted. 'Better go help Stone.'

'I will. Soon as we get you patched up and back to our cover point.'

'Hey, Randy …'

'Yeah, boss?'

'Thanks.'

***

Stone fired three rapid shots at the rocks near the hidden man. They were mainly intended as a distraction, though a stone chip or a bullet fragment could do at least some damage if it hit. He was pleased when he heard a yelp of pain from the hidden man, but it was followed only moments later by a spray of gunfire that tore up the branches of the tree where he'd been sitting. *No serious damage, apparently*, he thought.

He was on the ground now, and took one more shot back towards his attacker before turning and heading west as fast as he could plow through the snow. Just as he thought he'd gotten clear, a stinging pain lanced through his calf. He stumbled and almost went down, but managed to keep moving. 'Luana, stand by with number five,' he said.

'But, James—'

'Just be ready!'

The man following him had ceased firing, and was yelling back to his friends. 'He's hit and on the run. We've got him!'

The Reality of Chaos

Colpoys and one other man joined him a minute later. 'Are you sure you hit him?'

The man who fired the shot just pointed to a series of bloody splotches in the snow that followed the path of churning footprints.

'Hmm. Hit, but still moving. Reckon we'd better finish him.' He whistled loudly, and the fourth man joined them as they followed Stone's tracks.

Stone's leg was still screaming pain and wasn't to be trusted. Twice it buckled, forcing him to scramble to his feet with difficulty. The sounds of pursuit were growing steadily nearer.

'This was a great plan until I got shot,' he muttered. 'This is gonna be way too close.'

As he came to a small clearing, he glanced to his right, and there was number five, another special woodpecker house. His plan had been to draw the men into the clearing before they realized the danger, dive into cover on the far side, and have Luana detonate the C4 charge. The only problem was that they were too close now. He could hear them, fanned out slightly and nearly close enough to open fire.

'Luana, when I give the word, detonate five.'

'James, you're too close!'

'Do it when I say or I'm dead.' He didn't bother adding that he'd be a lot closer soon. He waited for the count of three, then burst from cover, crossing the path of fire for the woodpecker house. He struggled to move quickly, but his leg wasn't cooperating. The sounds behind him changed, and he knew the men had entered the clearing. He also knew they could see him stumbling along and were raising weapons.

'Now,' he yelled into the radio, and dove to the ground. Before he landed, the night erupted in a blaze of orange light, and a sharp BANG knocked wet snow from branches. Stone felt a searing pain, as though someone had dragged a hot poker across his back. He lay still, waiting for the staccato sounds of automatic weapon fire, but there was nothing. As his hearing recovered from the blast, other sounds, quieter, more subtle, could be heard: the falling of branches, torn from trees, the growing wind through pine needles, a low moan. And then a voice.

'James, James, are you OK?'

With difficulty, Stone rolled to his side and keyed his radio. 'I'm OK. What do you see?'

'Two men are down near the edge of the clearing. The other two are gone.'

'Are you sure?'

'They've passed by station eleven heading towards their vehicles. They're gone.'

Stone lay quietly a while longer, then forced himself to his feet, grimacing with pain. He limped back to the edge of the clearing where two bodies lay. The man furthest from cover had multiple wounds: gut, leg, neck. It might have been him who had been moaning, but he was moaning no more. His eyes were dull. He was dead. Stone moved to the edge of the clearing, and there, lying on his back, was Colpoys, a red canyon gouged across his forehead, blood running sluggishly down the side of his face and ear. A cloud drifted across the moon, as though a curtain had been pulled over this scene of carnage. Stone delivered a kick to the body at his feet. Nothing. But the kick brought a wave of pain through his leg, and his sight nearly left him. He turned and, using his rifle as a crutch, began to head back along the shortest path to the house.

He was moving slowly, his leg and his back complaining bitterly with every step. Moon shadows sprang up and fled as the clouds scudded across the sky, and the rising wind was sighing in the trees. He was beginning to think he might need to take a rest, when the pain in his back blossomed into blinding agony, as though someone had stabbed him. He fell face forward into the snow with a groan. A heavy boot rolled him over, and there stood Colpoys, the butt of his weapon red with Stone's blood where he had clubbed him in his wounded back. Blood was streaming down Colpoys' face from the deep furrow cut by a nearly lethal ball bearing, and he was bleeding from several other wounds in his legs and chest. But Stone had been incorrect in assessing the head wound as fatal, and now the man reversed the gun and pointed it at Stone.

Colpoys paused for a moment, and a ghoulish smile lit his face. 'Well son of a bitch. If it isn't the bloke who ruined my suit in St. James's Park. When was that? A long time ago anyway. I've got a new suit since then, and a new Uzi.' He held the weapon out.

'I see,' Stone murmured. 'So you didn't swim for the old one?'

The Reality of Chaos

Colpoys stepped forward and brutally kicked Stone's injured leg. Stone cried out and took several gasping breaths. 'I'll take that as a no,' he whispered.

'You had a companion with you back then,' Colpoys said. 'A bit of a stunner. Is she in the house along with that bitch Andoori? I'll bet she is, isn't she? Well, that will just be a treat, won't it, killing both in one night. *And* you. I figure that will about settle the score between us.' He turned the gun back on Stone. 'Any last words, asshole?'

There was a sharp CRACK. Blood, bone, and tissue sprayed from the side of Colpoys' head as the .45 hollow point round exited in spectacular fashion and Colpoys collapsed in a heap.

'Just this,' Randy replied, as he lowered his weapon. 'In the immortal words of Tuco Ramirez from *The Good, the Bad, and the Ugly*, "When you have to shoot, shoot; don't talk."'

***

It took Randy the better part of an hour to help Stone and then Chuck get back to the house. When Stone arrived he was furious that Luana had been in such danger. But he also took a savage pride in the way she had disposed of her antagonist. As Randy had guessed, Chuck's shoulder wound was far more serious than a mere graze, and Chuck had lost a lot of blood. But neither he, Stone, or Luana would consent to a trip to a hospital. An EMT—part of Chuck's cavalry, called in when the shooting began—had attended to all of them, and the motley crew had assembled in the spacious family room another hour later, exchanging stories and enjoying the blazing fire.

'So the cavalry had a bit of a shootout at the vehicles?' Randy asked.

'Sure did,' Chuck replied, gulping at a drink in direct violation of medical advice. 'Apparently the two remaining guards didn't really want to become guests of the CIA.'

'Can't imagine why,' Stone quipped. 'And the rest?'

'Teddy and his companion were picked up, as were the last two who were chasing you, Stone. Every one of them is singing like a canary, and the songs all involve Smythe-Montgomery. Teddy was particularly forthcoming when he was shown Colpoys' corpse. He, at least, prefers CIA custody to being dead in the snow.'

Elaya shuddered. 'What you all have done is extraordinary. How can I ever repay you?'

'Well,' Chuck said, 'just a good word to our president the next time you two are hobnobbing it up at a formal state dinner would be a great start.'

Randy looked at his boss in shock, but Stone just chuckled. 'Madam President, my friend is somewhat overcome with drugs and alcohol. I wouldn't take him too seriously right now.'

'The hell you say,' Chuck muttered.

Luana brought them all back to reality. 'We aren't yet finished. It's safe to say that President Andoori is well on the way to returning to power in Iran, but we still have a British megalomaniac to deal with. He'll soon know the game is up, and he'll be dangerous and unpredictable.'

'What a buzzkill you are, darling,' Stone said dryly. 'Chuck, what say we return at least one of Smythe-Montgomery's G6s to him?'

'Say, that's not a bad idea. We could be to the airport and rollin' in a couple of hours.'

'Who could be rollin'?' Randy asked. 'You can't go anywhere, boss. A bullet through the muscle of your arm and two cracked ribs.'

'He's right, Chuck,' Stone said. 'Randy and I can manage.'

'You!' Chuck countered. 'You were shot through the leg, had a ball bearing skate across your back, and got knocked down and kicked a few times, if your story is true.'

'All true. But I've had far worse and managed well enough—out in the open, for days.'

'You were younger then, darling,' Luana said softly.

'Uh oh,' Randy said, 'domestic squabble. I've seen it before. Could get ugly.'

Everyone in the room enjoyed a short laugh. 'All right, Luana,' Stone offered, 'you call it. What should we do?'

It was a brilliant ploy, and Stone knew the outcome in advance.

'Elaya will be safe here?' she asked.

Chuck nodded. 'There's a small army guarding her now, and the threat is pretty much eliminated. The local reporter will be back here tomorrow—well, later today—and she'll have one hell of a tale to report.

The Reality of Chaos

I'm guessing the world community will be eager to have Elaya back in charge. But yes, safe.'

'Then we finish this,' Luana said. 'All of us. We'd better get packed. And I imagine you need to wake up the Secretary of Defense, Chuck. We wouldn't want an international incident after all this.'

Everyone but Randy was injured in some way. They were an unlikely group to be heading to England to deal with a cornered badger, but everyone was in agreement. As the room was clearing, Chuck spoke rapidly to the agent in charge, and Luana consulted with Elaya.

Randy was about to head for his room when a tap on the shoulder stopped him. 'That was some nice work out there,' Stone said. 'I can honestly say I was out of options when you showed up. Luana knows that too. Appreciate it.'

Randy shrugged, trying to hide his embarrassment. 'I wish I'd gotten there sooner.'

'Perfect timing,' Stone said, with a smile. 'And one hell of a nice shot.'

Randy laughed. 'Hey, I learned from a guy who never misses!'

'Pleasure working with you,' Stone said, holding out his hand.

Lister arrived at Smythe-Montgomery's aircraft hangar complex and immediately knew that something was wrong.

Chapter Thirty-Two

Cleaning Up the Mess

Bureaucracies never run smoothly or efficiently. Critical hours had passed, and the group was still waiting for official permission to seize Smythe-Montgomery's aircraft.

Chuck growled his frustration, pacing furiously in the executive lounge of the Denver Airport. 'Curse the morons at the agency! I've had to call the SecDef to try to spring the aircraft free. And we sit here on our butts. We're pissing away precious time!'

Stone considered this comment. 'Elaya goes back on the air later today. She doesn't dare postpone, not with her country's government sitting on a knife's edge. And once she goes live, Smythe-Montgomery will know Colpoys and his men failed.'

'So is this a wasted trip?' Randy asked.

'Maybe. But maybe not,' Stone said. 'The guy is a megalomaniac but not a moron. What would he do under the circumstances?'

'He could try to disavow everything. Say that Colpoys was working without instructions from him. That he welcomed the return of the rightful leader of Iran.' After saying this, Randy shrugged. 'Yeah, even I think that's bullshit.'

'So his nascent empire is crumbling,' Stone said thoughtfully. 'He'll have an exit strategy, but he's arrogant. He may believe he has a chance to salvage something. Maybe disappear for a while and start over again somewhere.'

'So he'll leave the country? But where to?'

'Follow the money!' Chuck said. 'Luana, can you track financial transactions based on Becky's intel?'

'Possibly. I'll make some calls.'

'Better give Crandall a call,' Stone said. 'Give him a heads-up and also see if he's been running any new predictions. Hell, I know he has.

Let's find out what they say about the likely next moves of one Conrad Smythe-Montgomery.'

'Why don't you call him, darling? I know a certain young lady who'll be delighted to speak with you. I believe she finds you fascinating—and irresistibly attractive.'

Stone chuckled and pulled his phone from a pocket.

***

Smythe-Montgomery was furious to the point of apoplexy and Ms. Lister was treading delicately. Elaya Andoori's second address had aired, confirming Colpoys' total failure, and she had denounced the ayatollahs, al Rahzi and his companions, and Smythe-Montgomery. Since then, he'd been in a volatile state between rationality and insanity. A small army of lawyers and spokespeople had been dispatched and were steadily refuting Andoori's claims of conspiracy. At the same time, they read statements from their employer pledging support to Andoori and her soon-to-be-restored government. With claims and counterclaims flying, no action had been taken against Smythe-Montgomery—yet. Lister checked her watch. Just past 8:00 p.m. She hoped that Conrad would soon be over the second stage of grief, *anger*, and proceed rapidly to the fifth stage, *acceptance*. But precious hours had slipped away and he was still livid and indecisive. She had been with him the entire time, letting him rave and nodding from time to time when he glanced her way. Now his ranting took an unexpected turn, and she listened with interest.

'Yes. Yes! Richard Crandall and that bitch Diana Foster! They're up to their greying eyebrows in this. No! They're *behind* it. Lurking in the shadows for years—decades. Planned it all. The crazy old man and his computers. Involved with Elaya Andoori! How is that a coincidence? No! It's not! Should have finished them long ago!' He turned on Lister. 'What news from Peters?'

Emma Lister licked her lips nervously. This was the third time he'd asked this. She'd explained it twice before. She opened her mouth to say as much, but a voice inside her said, *Don't be a fool. He's killing-angry. Lose your composure and die.*

'Sir Conrad, he's been arrested. Apparently he's also been shot ... while attempting to deal with Crandall. But he will recover, based on some very sketchy reports.'

'Recover! The damn fool failed! Shot by Crandall or Diana. Impossible! I'm better off without fools like that on my payroll. Get me Colpoys—' He halted abruptly. Colpoys wasn't here. His mission had been a failure. Yes. Smythe-Montgomery knew that.

The realization finally registered with both his mind and his heart, and his mood shifted to cold and venomous. The transition was frightening, and Lister feared his new state of mind far more than his irrational ranting. He sat down, his mind a calculating machine spinning at top speed.

'Have we heard back from al Rahzi?'

'No, sir. Still nothing. Though our staff in Tehran report arrests at the airport.'

'Of course. The coward. Taking steps to ingratiate himself to whomever comes out on top of the power struggle in Iran. We will see to him in good time. Perhaps a visit to that fine meat-packing facility. Yes. We'll arrange that. But for now?' He thought for only a brief while before turning back to Lister. 'Make all the necessary financial arrangements—transfers of funds, etc., to Site A. Contact our remaining security staff and order them to regroup there. Have the third G6 fueled and ready to fly. Contact our staff at the private terminal. No one—*no one*—from airport security is to approach. They are to take whatever steps are necessary. We will depart precisely at midnight.'

'But, Conrad, shouldn't we leave immediately?'

He turned on her with a snarl. 'Do not question my orders! Do as you're told!' A gun had suddenly appeared in his hand. She blanched. 'I have business to attend to—unfinished business that must be done before I leave.' He holstered his sidearm and she breathed again. 'Crandall and Foster!' He spit out the words. 'The aristocracy of a decayed empire. The detritus of British history. To think she had the gall to reject Father! But he taught her a harsh lesson, and so did I! Perhaps she needs another. And Crandall, an old, impotent pervert. Both unworthy of the empire to come. Scheming with Andoori. Scheming with Cathie Fletcher. Another peon whose time will come soon enough. Yes. Fletcher, Andoori, al Rahzi. Justice will come, swift and harsh. For today, Crandall and Foster. Have the car brought around. I have an appointment to keep.'

***

Yvette had rarely seen Crandall and Diana fight. Certainly there had been many squabbles peppered with verbal daggers, but this argument had a coldness to it that shocked her. Though the words were muffled, a fierce, visceral conflict was clearly taking place. Crandall finally turned away and stormed out of the study of his London home, yielding the field to Diana. She sighed and wheeled herself over to Yvette.

'You mustn't concern yourself. He'll come around.'

'But what were you arguing about? What did he want?' Yvette asked.

'Simply put, he wanted to run. Because of that,' she added, pointing to the computer monitor.

Over the last hour, Crandall had been running a series of scenarios based on Elaya's reappearance and the apparent collapse of Smythe-Montgomery's empire. Yvette had been uncomfortable with the work, since Crandall was attempting to use models best suited to large political and economic events—the geopolitics of countries over years of time—to determine the moves of one man, Smythe-Montgomery. It was poor science, but Richard had insisted. He had also insisted on running the simulations himself, harshly supplanting Yvette at the controls. He and Diana had sat hunched over the machine. When he was finished, he had blacked the screen and their argument had broken out.

'Go ahead,' Diana said. 'The old fool didn't actually erase anything. Refresh the display.'

Yvette did so, then stared in disbelief. Several actions were predicted for Smythe-Montgomery. Leaving England and moving his base of operations to a country with no extradition treaty was at the top of the list. Several locations were indicated, along with relative probabilities. At the bottom of the list was the one that had frozen Yvette in her seat. Assassinate Diana Foster and Richard Crandall: 97% probability.

'I won't run,' Diana said. 'In fact, it's high time my situation with Conrad Smythe-Montgomery was resolved. Permanently.'

Yvette waited, with a deep sense of foreboding.

Diana's eyes were troubled as she continued. 'Perhaps it's time you heard the final chapter of my story with that cursed family. It was Hubert, Conrad's father, who took my legs. Together, they took the man I loved. But it wasn't enough. Conrad, you see, is his father's son in every way. Shortly after the death of my love, Conrad came to my home and took something else.'

Yvette seemed not to understand at first. Then her puzzlement turned to pure horror. 'Lord, no!'

Diana swallowed painfully. 'Yes. Oh, please get me a drink, would you. And one for yourself.'

Yvette returned with two tumblers filled to the rim with Beefeaters. Both women drank incautiously for several minutes. At last, Diana reached for a hankie and wiped her eyes. 'Ah. Better.' She looked sternly into Yvette's eyes. 'I have never shared that information with anyone. Not even Richard. Had he known, he might have done something ... untoward. You must promise to keep it a secret. Richard thinks I'm being irrational, projecting Conrad's father onto Conrad, but as you now know, my grievance is far more personal. Now I've come to the end of the path, and I *will* kill him, or he will kill me. Will you help?'

Yvette's face grew stony, as it had been during her brief encounter with Peters. 'Tell me what to do.'

***

There had been a few more words—short and pointed—between Crandall and Diana, and then Diana was once again with Yvette. 'We'll go to my family estate.' She faced Yvette with embarrassment. 'Try not to be too disappointed. I'm afraid you've missed its glory days—by a century or so. But it does have a certain charm, and I'd rather be there than anywhere else.'

'And Richard?'

'He'll do just as he pleases, the stubborn old mule. But he has options. Places where he can go to be safe. I wouldn't want to see him hurt.'

Yvette glanced back as the two left Crandall's home. Seeing him standing in the doorway, confused and sorrowful, put a lump in her throat, but she continued on.

***

The limo turned onto a long gravel driveway bordered by ancient elm trees. All were long dead, victims of Dutch elm disease, though their stately skeletons still clung to an air of dignity. The nearby hedges and shrubs were untidy, nearly wild, and tangled weeds filled the drainage on either side of the raised roadway. Fields beyond the trees were filled with grasses, shrubs, and wildflowers. Diana sighed at this dismal introduction to her domicile, and she feared that Yvette's impression would only worsen.

The long straight drive ended in a large loop. On the right was an old carriage house, used in later times as a garage and now seemingly deserted. Then a few small cottages—possibly for servants, gamekeepers, and a stable master—also deserted and fallen into disrepair. At the center of the loop, a dry fountain was surrounded by what had once been a circular garden. Here, a few flowers made a bold attempt at survival, but clearly they received little help from humanity. Four walkways pierced the garden from the drive and ended at benches placed along a narrow path that circled the fountain.

Yvette was lost in the gloom of the surroundings. The car continued to swing around the drive until she finally had a clear view of Foster Manor. Her jaw dropped. Even in its decline, it was impressive in its size and dignity. The large main structure, three stories tall, was covered in ivy. Leaded-glass windows flanked a massive doorway at the top of a short flight of stairs. Above the doorway was a semicircular window of stained glass. As she stared, she could make out a stag standing proud against a field of green. Around the animal were other symbols, smaller in size: a key, crossed swords, and several others she couldn't quite make out.

The main house was flanked by extensive two-story wings, set at a slight angle that embraced the long looping drive. These wings were newer than the original structure, though not much, and they had been built in such a way that they complemented the older central section. Tall cedar trees, still quite healthy, were spaced evenly along the front of the manor between the windows and on either side of the stairs.

'It's gorgeous!' Yvette said, awestruck.

'Richard thinks I'm a fool for keeping it,' Diana commented. 'I haven't the money to maintain it properly. Neither had my parents. And much of it is shut up. I'm afraid only the western wing is habitable anymore.'

As if to emphasize the point, the driver continued on past the stately main entrance to a more humble opening halfway along the wing. 'I have

The Reality of Chaos

only Arthur to help me out now,' she said, nodding to the driver, 'and a few others who come around several times a week. And even Arthur doesn't remain in the evening.'

'You mean you live here alone?' Yvette asked, astonished.

'Mad, isn't it?' Diana replied, with a laugh. 'Richard is right, of course. I should sell it. I must admit that one very irrational reason I don't is that it's larger and of greater antiquity than Conrad's miserable dwelling. But mainly, it's because I grew up here, even as the old place was withering away. Well, let's get inside and I'll tell you my plan.'

***

'Oh, Diana, I don't like it at all!' A bold statement for Yvette, who had listened patiently while Diana explained her intentions.

'I should think not,' Diana said with a shake of her head. 'But it is what I wish. My life has been a prison for far too long. I will be free, and you know what that entails.'

Yvette considered Diana's words. She knew it was useless to argue, and there was a part of her, a part she almost feared, that not only understood but was eagerly, viciously supportive.

Diana saw the change in Yvette's face and knew she had won her point. 'I do regret having to involve you at all, but I need your help. Are you sure you don't mind the part you must play?'

Yvette smiled grimly. 'Not at all!'

***

When Smythe-Montgomery arrived at Diana's estate his mood was once again that of a spider: coldly calculating, patient, and lethal. He had ordered his driver to pull up at the main entrance. A few lights inside led from the entry hall into the eastern wing like a trail of bread crumbs. Had he been a more frequent visitor to Diana's home he would have realized that this was not normal.

'Stay with the car,' he said to the driver. 'I won't be long.' He checked his gun, a 9mm Glock, and walked boldly up the stairs. The front door opened with a dull creak, surprising him and casting a shadow of doubt for the first time this night. He scanned the entryway and his anxiety grew. A heavy layer of dust overlaid the marble floor, the dark wooden furniture, and the spiraling bannisters of the facing stairways. Vases on tables stood empty and the huge chandelier above him was dark. Small sconces on the walls provided the only light, giving the room the look of a haunted mansion. To his right, light trickled in from a hallway.

'She'll not frighten me with her absurd antics.' His words echoed in the cavernous room, an unnerving sound, but he turned and walked down the hallway. He glanced from side to side, noting the medieval decorations: crossed swords or battle-axes, shields emblazoned with the Foster coat of arms. Despite his dismissive attitude, he was forced to admit that the Foster family had been aristocracy for centuries. While the Crokers were still poaching deer from local barons, the Fosters had been lords and ladies all. To them, the Opium Wars would seem skirmishes of a modern era. Their sires had fought in the Wars of the Roses. Smythe-Montgomery snarled at the thought.

'Your days are over, your dignity gone along with your wealth and power. Do you hear me?' he yelled. His burst of anger stiffened his resolve and he plunged forward. In the feeble light he would occasionally catch glimpses into rooms, the white sheets covering furniture or draping chandeliers reminding him of dusty ghosts. He shook off his gloomy imaginings, and his long strides soon led him to a doorway on his left where pale light leaked out. Taking a last glance up and down the hallway, he entered what had been a large, formal dining hall. A bank of tall windows on the far side of the room looked out onto an interior courtyard, but all now was black. The few lights inside illuminated a long oak table surrounded by heavy carved wooden chairs upholstered in dark-green velvet. Candelabras with half-burned candles sat at intervals along the table, the dripping wax frozen in time.

He had entered the room at the foot of the table. More extravagant chairs were set at the far end. High on the stone wall above the head chair was a tapestry of the Foster coat of arms surrounded by other symbols of the family, the same symbols that had awed Yvette on the stained-glass window above the entryway. Directly across from him another dimly lit corridor opened.

'I'm growing tired of this, Diana,' Smythe-Montgomery snarled. He walked down the hallway, narrower than the grand hallway he'd followed from the entrance. At the end was a flight of stairs, going down. He guessed that at one time it had led to kitchens or a wine cellar. He

The Reality of Chaos

continued on with increasing irritation as well as a growing anxiety. *Perhaps I should have brought my driver,* he thought, but then banished the idea. *To dispose of one old cripple? Nonsense!*

At the foot of the stairs was another short hallway to a door—a modern steel door—thrown open, with bright light streaming out. He walked in and the door closed behind him, locking with a distinct *clatch.*

***

The driver of the limousine was startled when someone walked into the path of his headlights. A moment later he relaxed as he could see it was only an attractive woman in jeans and a loose-fitting T-shirt, smiling as she approached. She reached the driver's door and he rolled down his window.

'Now who are you and what are you doing wandering about all alone, love?'

'Oh, my name isn't important. But I'd appreciate it if you'd get out of the car and come with me.'

'Well, that's an offer I wouldn't normally refuse, but I'm on the job, darling. How 'bout you give me your number and I'll ring you up tomorrow?'

'I'm sorry,' Yvette said. 'Did I give the impression that I was asking?' Her eyes and voice grew hard. 'Get out of the car. Now.'

The driver's look of amusement faded, and he began to reach inside his jacket.

And there was a gun pointed at his face.

'As much as I'd regret shooting you …' Yvette paused, considering. 'You know, since you work for Smythe-Montgomery, I actually would enjoy shooting you very much. How refreshing. But I suppose I shouldn't. *If* you cooperate.'

The man wavered, and his hand hovered near the opening of his jacket.

'Do you happen to know a man named Peters?' she asked. 'He screamed like a little girl, and I only shot him in the kneecap.'

Blood drained from the man's face. 'You?'

Yvette smiled. 'Carla Jenkins, MI5. I'll show you my ID later. After you remove yourself from the vehicle, drop your weapon, and come with me.'

***

'What the hell?' Smythe-Montgomery growled, tugging at the door.

'Welcome,' said Diana's voice.

Smythe-Montgomery spun around and fired two shots in the direction of the sound.

'Tut,' the voice said. 'You might have hit the speaker.'

'Where are you, you bitch?'

'Nearby. I'll join you if you behave. Do you know where you are?'

'In your rotting old estate!'

'No, no. Specifically. Where are you?'

Smythe-Montgomery could barely control his confusion and anger, but he looked around the room. When he had calmed enough to take in his surroundings he was stunned. He was in a brilliantly lit room with high ceilings, no windows, and only one door. The floor was covered with rubberized matting and along one wall was a recess where a rack held numerous swords, some quite old. A photo of a group of women, mounted high on the wall, was the room's only decoration.

'I know what you're thinking,' Diana said, 'but as always you fail to see beyond the obvious. It's actually an ancient wine cellar converted to a training facility for swordsmanship. My driver is quite an expert.'

'Too bad he isn't here,' Smythe-Montgomery sneered. 'I might teach him a thing or two.'

'You fancy yourself as quite the swordsman, then? Excellent! So I have no fear that you will reject the offer I am about to make. There is a laundry shoot near the sword rack. You may deposit your weapon—and your backup weapon—and select any sword you like from the rack. You will then stand motionless and I'll join you, and we will settle our differences.'

'You? Fight me? With a sword?' He laughed hysterically. 'Like as not you'll come through the door with a gun.'

'Because that's what you would do?' She sighed. 'I give you my word, which, as we both know, is of some value. Or … you can simply stay locked in the wine cellar until the authorities arrive. Your next accommodations will be just as austere, and quite a bit smaller. If I'm telling the truth, and if you best me, then you walk out and our feud is at an end. If I win, our feud is still over. It seems an easy decision to me.'

The Reality of Chaos

'I accept!'

'Oh, lovely!'

A minute later, with Smythe-Montgomery still standing uncertainly near the sword rack, the door opened and Diana *walked* in.

Smythe-Montgomery gaped. 'You ... you ...'

Diana laughed. 'They're called prosthetics. Really! A man of the 21st century to be so shocked. I wear them often but, for obvious reasons, I rarely wear them in public. I would hate to have you think I was adjusting to my life when your father—and you—are so determined to see me suffer. And I could hardly fight you in a wheelchair, could I?'

Smythe-Montgomery said nothing, so Diana continued. 'Since my unfortunate encounter with a train over forty years ago, I've had to adapt, training as best I could. Nothing extreme. No more than two or three hours per day. It passes the time when I'm not engaged with my philanthropic work or visiting with Lord Crandall.'

Smythe-Montgomery snorted derisively.

'I've also become quite proficient on these.' She motioned to the unusual lower legs she now wore. 'I've often defeated my instructor, the man you were foolish enough to wish were here right now. Still, even if I still had my legs, I could never match my former skills. After all, I'm quite ancient,' she added, with a laugh.

As she spoke, Smythe-Montgomery could see her eyes wandering to the photo. He edged nearer and looked up. His eyes grew round as he studied the picture and the caption below it. A group of women, all in fencing gear, were kneeling under a banner boasting the Olympic logo. On the far right, smiling broadly, a dark-haired woman who couldn't have been twenty. A glance at the names below confirmed his growing suspicions. Lady Diana Foster.

Diana smiled. 'I was the youngest woman to ever make the team—as an alternate. I had high hopes for the next games. What's the matter, Conrad? Cat got your tongue? You were never much for intelligent conversation. And you haven't chosen a sword! What *are* we here for?'

Smythe-Montgomery gradually regained his composure. As he did so, he noticed for the first time the long rapier Diana held loosely in her hand. 'A beautiful weapon,' he said.

'Isn't it? And this,' she said, pulling a chain with a key out from between her breasts, 'is the door key. Kill me and it's yours.'

'A pleasure,' he said, with a smirk. He turned to the rack and selected a cavalry saber of his great-great-great-grandfather's era. He slashed the air several times, a whistling sound filling the room, then balanced the blade on his finger. 'Perfect. I shall enjoy killing you with this, Diana.'

'It's Lady Diana, you filthy peasant,' she replied.

In an instant he was across the room attacking. She defended with mesmerizing speed, her sword a blur, then feinted and stepped back to the wall, avoiding a heavy overhand slash. She took a quick half-step to her right and her sword darted in, Smythe-Montgomery's block coming a fraction too late. A red line appeared across his cheek, blood rippling down.

Smythe-Montgomery was an excellent swordsman, but fighting in anger did not suit him. Fighting while furious certainly did not. He plunged and hacked with far less skill than he possessed, and Diana, with great economy of motion and energy, deflected his strikes and stepped away, using the walls of the room to protect her flanks. She was surprisingly agile on her prosthetics, and years of practice had taught her how to gain the most, even with limitations on her mobility.

He continued his fruitless attacks for several minutes before finally mastering his blind anger. His motions became more precise and less frantic. They exchanged cuts and thrusts with blinding speed, but neither was able to penetrate the other's defense. Smythe-Montgomery finally stepped away, breathing heavily. 'Well, Diana, you have some skill with a sword. Far more than you ever had in bed.'

Diana's face contorted with fury and she attacked again. But she had fallen into the same trap as Smythe-Montgomery, fighting with emotion and not precision. That had indeed been his hope when he had baited her with the crude reminder of her rape. She moved forward—too quickly— and stumbled. His sword stabbed out. By a desperate twist of her torso she avoided being run through—pierced in the heart—but his blade cut a furrow across her ribs. She gave a gasp of pain and backed away, blood soaking her shirt. Smythe-Montgomery charged forward, once again driven by emotion and thoughts of victory. He attacked with a series of

The Reality of Chaos

overhead cuts, but on the third he pivoted slightly and turned the chop into a stabbing motion, aiming for the shoulder of her sword arm. But her arm wasn't there. She had twisted again and then slipped behind him as his momentum carried him past the point where she had been standing. She struck backhanded and sliced his left calf.

Smythe-Montgomery let out a piercing scream and nearly dropped to the ground. He swung wildly, but Diana was out of reach.

She stood waiting while he limped away, pain etched across his face. 'What's the matter, Conrad? Not quite so agile on one leg, are you? And I'll bet it hurts. In fact, I'm sure it does.'

'I'll have you yet, you decrepit old bitch!' he yelled.

'Tut. That's *Lady* Bitch.'

His anger overcame his pain and he attacked, but Diana was now in control. She lowered her guard, tempting him, and he took the bait, swinging with tremendous strength, trying to decapitate her. She took a half step back, and his blade whistled an inch from her neck. He yelled in pain again and nearly toppled forward as his injured leg twisted awkwardly. She slid past his left side, his sword blocked by his own body, and her blade streaked across the upper calf of his right leg. He howled and dropped to his knees. His face was twisted in pain and disbelief, and he scrambled back away from her until he was stopped by the wall adjacent to the door.

Diana stood contemplating him, blood covering half his face, his lower pant legs both soaked in blood—blood that had spoiled his expensive oxfords.

She suddenly cocked her head, listening. There were voices and a commotion in the hallway. Without warning, the door flew open and there was Richard Crandall, Yvette behind him, trying to hold him back.

'Diana!' Crandall cried, seeing only her and the blood soaking her shirt.

Before Diana could shout a warning, Crandall stepped into the room. Smythe-Montgomery stabbed upward, into Crandall's lower back. Yvette shrieked and pulled him back, blood pouring from his wound. Diana yelled an unintelligible cry of anger and despair. She punched the pommel of her sword into Smythe-Montgomery's face, feeling his nose crack, and violently knocked his sword away. With the speed of a striking snake she stabbed out—once, twice—piercing the muscle and tendon above each knee. He screamed.

'By God,' Diana growled, her chest heaving, her eyes flashing, 'how does it feel? The pain, Conrad, how does it feel? Imagine it going on and on and on! Day after day. Year after year! It's no less than you deserve. You should consider death a gift!' Smythe-Montgomery's was ashen and beaded with sweat. His look of manic delight as he had stabbed Crandall was replaced with one of agony and fear. Her sword tip dropped to his chest.

Diana glanced down the hallway and saw Yvette cradling Crandall's head in her lap, tears streaking her face. Yvette continued to stroke his head as she glanced up at Diana and from there to Smythe-Montgomery, kneeling in terror, blood pouring from his nose onto his chin and neck, and pulsing from his leg wounds to pool beneath his knees. Crandall moaned and Yvette's features grew hard, her eyes filling with hate. She tore her gaze away from the defeated man on the floor and stared at Diana, her eyes still blazing.

Diana turned back to Smythe-Montgomery and smiled.

***

Lister arrived at Smythe-Montgomery's aircraft hangar complex and immediately knew that something was wrong. Several black, unmarked SUVs were parked in a designated no-parking area and a few men were wandering around the entrances to the hangars and flight operations office.

She drove past slowly, assessing the situation and bypassing the entrance she had intended to use. None of Smythe-Montgomery's security personnel were present. As she drove past the buildings she caught a glimpse of the taxiway beyond a chain-link fence. She knew the aircraft she had ordered to be prepared would still be in the hangar, but out on the tarmac were not one but two G6s, lights streaming from inside their cabins, boarding stairs lowered. She slowed to a stop and watched as several individuals exited one of the aircraft: two men and a beautiful woman she didn't know, and one other man. During her belated investigation into Cathie and Logan Fletcher's friends and acquaintances she had obtained pictures of the key players. The third man, his arm in a sling, was Chuck Johnson, CIA. He was greeted at the bottom of the

The Reality of Chaos

stairs by individuals who could only be law enforcement or, worse yet, MI5. It was all she needed to see.

Lister continued driving until she reached a local park, where she pulled in and called Smythe-Montgomery. Inside his abandoned limousine a phone rang repeatedly, but the driver, who should have answered, was lying in a locked room at Diana's estate, arms and legs restrained with zip ties. In the other wing of the massive home, Smythe-Montgomery was on his knees, bleeding from multiple wounds and staring into Diana's stony eyes.

After a few frustrating minutes, Lister gave up. But she had not become Smythe-Montgomery's assistant by being a fool. She already had her own backup plans in case the unthinkable occurred, and a travel case was waiting for her in a locker at Heathrow as well as a one-way first-class ticket at the airline counter. She had already bought a small estate in Morocco. *Just one last thing to do,* she thought. The EMPR1 bank account held large, untraceable funds. She pulled out her tablet and typed in the commands that would transfer its entire balance to her Swiss bank account.

***

In Tucson, a warning beeped on Becky Amhurst's computer and an automatic algorithm provided by Luana efficiently redirected the funds. The software's development had been a joint effort. The final product incorporated an algorithm similar to the one Luana had used successfully against her own father. Yvette had extracted the encryption codes from the cache of data stolen from Smythe-Montgomery's computer. Becky checked the results at the conclusion of the transaction and smiled. 'Well, this will make Emma Lister very unhappy when she finds out. But it will make someone else *extremely* happy.'

***

'Well, hell,' Chuck said for the third time since his arrival at Diana's estate. He ran his hand over the stubble on his face then checked his watch. A little past 1:00 a.m. local time. He tried to calculate what that translated to in Oakland and failed. Every part of his body ached, his shoulder worst of all, despite the painkillers that had dulled his brain. He stood outside near the fountain at the main entrance and watched as local law enforcement took possession of Smythe-Montgomery's limo and drove away. The driver had long since been whisked away by MI5 for questioning. Richard Crandall had been treated by paramedics on site, then rushed to the closest trauma center. Yvette had insisted on accompanying him, but the prognosis was grim. Diana had been treated for her wound, bloody and painful but not serious, and had stayed. She was back in her own quarters now, talking with Stone and Luana. As for Smythe-Montgomery … Chuck cleared his throat and spat noisily onto the gravel of the driveway. *Well, the less said about him, the better*, he thought.

A minute later Randy emerged from the house carrying a bottle and two glasses. Chuck lowered himself carefully onto a stone bench. He had been craving a smoke, and he pulled out two cigars and a lighter as Randy arrived and sat down heavily beside him.

It wasn't until both were puffing companionably and sipping twenty-five-year-old cognac that Randy spoke. 'Well, we flew halfway around the world and didn't do shit!'

'Yeah. Ain't that a son-of-a-bitch! But you know, that's just how it works out sometimes. I called the SecDef and he's ready to skin my sorry ass, but at least he's helping to smooth things out. I guess we stepped on a few diplomatic toes along the way.' He grinned suddenly. 'It does help having the president of a sovereign nation pitchin' your case, though. I should've thought of that sooner. Save the leader of a country, then have her unfuck my fuckups, defend me to my boss, fix parkin' tickets. Shit like that.'

'Hell yeah, Chuck. That would've been real helpful to your illustrious career.'

'Too little, too late. Just like us showing up here.'

They returned to their drinks and private thoughts. The night air was chilly and damp, but off in the distance a nightingale sang, unperturbed. Chuck took a pull on his cigar and listened intently. He flashed Randy a weak smile. 'Well, hell.'

The Reality of Chaos

Stephen Lance / Chuck Markussen

It was a pleasant June evening, dry and not too hot now that the brilliant sun had slipped behind the hills near the Hollywood Bowl.

Chapter Thirty-Three

Back for Jazz at the Hollywood Bowl

Three couples sat drinking wine and waiting for the opening musicians at the Playboy Jazz Festival. It was a pleasant June evening, dry and not too hot now that the brilliant sun had slipped behind the hills near the Hollywood Bowl. To Chuck, it felt like an age since the damp early morning when he'd listened to nightingales with Randy. In a way it had been.

Cathie Fletcher sampled her wine and sighed with satisfaction. 'Well, you've kept us in suspense long enough, Chuck. What's this secret you promised to let us in on?'

Chuck reached up a hand to his chin, forgetting that Joy had insisted he shave before they left. There was only the slightest rasp of resistance.

Logan jumped in. 'Yeah, Johnson. I've asked Randy about it and he claims he knows nothing, but that's an obvious lie. No offense,' he said to Gail. 'Randy's only fault as a CIA agent is that he can't tell a convincing lie.'

'None taken,' she replied, squeezing Randy's arm gently. 'I'm pretty pleased with that failing.'

'And naturally Joy is mum as a mummy,' Cathie pressed, 'so how about it?'

'I'm retiring,' Chuck mumbled. 'Actually, my official last day was Thursday. Yep. Emptied my office out and everything. I am now unemployed.'

Randy squirmed uncomfortably but didn't say anything.

'Well, congratulations, you old coot,' Logan said, clinking glasses with his longtime friend. 'Maybe now we can take that trip to Philly, hit Dalessandro's for cheesesteaks, and can catch a 76ers game. My buddy Craig, the sports writer for the Tribune, can get us press box seats. It'll be awesome.'

'Yes, congrats,' Cathie echoed, 'though it isn't really much of a surprise. I mean, since you got back from London it seemed to be where you were headed. But sure, I'll drink to that.'

Logan smiled expectantly at Randy and asked, 'And would I be correct in guessing that one deserving Grasshopper will be taking over Chuck's duties?'

'No, you wouldn't,' Randy said flatly.

'What?' Cathie exclaimed. 'Why the hell not?'

'Two reasons, really,' Randy said. He looked to Chuck for help.

'We all know bureaucracies,' Chuck said. 'Despite his amazing record, Randy's too young and there are way too many experienced agents ahead of him. Most of them have bosses on good terms with the agency brass. One of those, a guy working for the chief in the Dallas office, got the job. I know him. He's a dick.'

Cathie scowled. 'That's not fair! Favoritism above achievement. Wasn't there anything you could do, Chuck?'

'It's OK, Cathie,' Randy interjected. 'Chuck tried, but it didn't really matter. I told you there were two reasons I wouldn't be getting Chuck's job. The second one is simpler. I left the agency.'

'What?' Logan yelled in turn. 'Why would you do that?'

Randy shrugged. 'I'm moving to Tucson. It's where we want to raise our family.'

A chaos of words now from Cathie, Logan, and Joy. At last, all was explained.

'We're not even positively sure yet,' Randy said sheepishly.

'I'm sure,' was Gail's quiet response.

'That explains why you're shunning this fine, fruity Chardonnay for that fizzy yuppie water,' Cathie said.

Gail nodded.

But after a few minutes, Logan realized that in the confusion and congratulations, Randy had dodged his question. He grew deeply suspicious. 'OK, Randy, we know *where* you're going to live, but not what you're going to be doing, new family on the way and all. So how about it?'

Randy squirmed a bit more and turned to Chuck again. 'Umm, well ...'

The Reality of Chaos

'Actually, Randy and I started a, well, sort of a consulting company,' Chuck said.

'What?' It was Joy this time.

'You mean you didn't tell her?' Randy asked, horrified. 'I told Gail right away.'

She squeezed his arm again. 'Your blessed failing.'

'It isn't just the two of us,' Chuck said defensively, looking into the furious eyes of his spouse. 'We have another partner.'

Joy continued to gape until understanding turned to shock. 'No. Oh, hell no! You don't mean to say …'

Chuck pulled a business card from his pocket and handed it to Joy. She stared at the logo: three words carved into a boulder. Stone Security Solutions.

'It was kind of his idea, and he had a cool name so …' Chuck faded to silence under the icy stare of his spouse.

The spell was broken as she burst into bubbling laughter. 'You wily old son-of-a-bitch. I *knew* you couldn't just walk away!' She handed the card to Cathie and Logan, who just stared at it blankly.

'All three of us are vice presidents,' Randy said proudly.

'And exactly how many employees are in your firm?' Cathie asked, her eyebrow raised.

'Three.'

***

When Becky received the offer to consult for Stone Security Solutions she eagerly accepted. True, ARC electronics had won the revised bid for aircraft avionics upgrades for the Pacific-Indo-Asia Airlines fleet of aircraft. But she had an extremely competent chief engineer in Gary Walkin, who enjoyed the overseas travel, though she guessed that the opportunity of working with his counterpart, Devi Idrial, had a lot to do with it.

Needless to say, Luana also consulted for Triple S, as they called it, as did Logan. An association with Stone promised to do away with any dull moments in his retirement. It also promised opportunities to be shot or kidnapped a bit more often than was really desirable. Logan smiled at the thought. Cathie would have plenty of fodder for future stories.

Stephen Lance / Chuck Markussen

A brass quartet, braving the elements, had just finished a beautiful arrangement of 'Carol of the Bells' ...

Chapter Thirty-Four

A Little Salvation

December, 2019

A gentle snow was falling, adding a lovely, seasonal frosting to the streets and buildings of London. It was Christmas Eve, and the short day was drawing to a close. Colored lights lit streets and shops everywhere, and in the distance, church bells tolled. A brass quartet, braving the elements, had just finished a beautiful arrangement of 'Carol of the Bells,' while a small group of last minute shoppers, drawn to pause and listen, applauded.

Several heavily bundled people walked over to The Salvation Army kettle and dropped in donations, to the thanks of the bell ringer and the four musicians. The last to come up was a young woman. The scarf wrapped around her head was tucked into a double-breasted coat. She stepped forward quietly and placed an envelope into the slot at the kettle's top. The five thanked her in turn, but as she glanced up at them, they could see tears in her eyes.

'Are you OK, miss?'

Am I OK? Yvette thought. *What a difficult question!* The events of the past year replayed in her head. Then years spun backward until she reached the pivot point in her life. She could hear his words clearly once again: 'Yvette, it looks like you could use a shower and a hot meal. Why don't you come with me?'

'Miss?' the bell ringer repeated.

An older gentleman wearing a suit and an overcoat came to her side, and she silently took his hand.

'I'm fine, actually,' she finally replied. 'Bless you for the work you do.'

The unlikely pair moved off as the band struck up another tune, 'Good King Wenceslas.'

After walking a block or two, Yvette turned to the man, tears still trickling down her cheeks. 'My name was Maggie,' she said, her chin quivering.

'Ah, so that's what you'd like on your business cards, my trusted ward and heir. Maggie Crandall, Vice President of the Predictive Chaos & Research Corporation.'

'Not at all, Richard. That *was* my name. My name is Yvette.'

Crandall smiled. 'Well then, Yvette, let's join Diana for that enormous Christmas feast!'

***

Late that evening, after a wonderful Christmas service, Major Rob Cox looked over the contents of the kettle from Oxford Circus. He was quite pleased to see the contributions. The brass quartet always drew a crowd. He yawned loudly and glanced at his watch. Perhaps he would count it tomorrow. But the white envelope caught his eye and he tore it open. Inside was a notarized bank check, a bit unusual. He examined the note written in the Memo space at the bottom. 'Please use to fight human trafficking.' He smiled. It was a mission that was often forgotten, but one of great importance to the Army. Then he looked at the donation amount. A shot of adrenaline drove away his evening stupor. He looked again. He turned on a bright desk light, rubbed his eyes, and looked a third time. Inside the envelope was a note from the bank confirming an anonymous donation for the amount shown: £121,454,524.55.

Naturally, Major Cox could have no way of knowing that, until recently, this had been the balance of an account identified as EMPR1. He collapsed into his chair, his heart pounding, as he realized the impact this would have around the world, and he said a quiet prayer of thanks.

Made in United States
Troutdale, OR
08/04/2024